"*Termination of Benefits* is a brilliant debut. I sat up until 2:30 reading the last hundred pages. It was impossible to put down. Good plotting is rare, and the final chapters brought me clever plot twists and surprises. I especially enjoyed the way Sloven blended her hero's legal background and her career as a therapist, as well as her Jewish community and the Portland, Maine setting. The episode on Mackworth Island was very visual for me. I felt I could almost smell the water.

—Steve Steinbock, mystery writer and reviewer, "The Jury Box," *Ellery Queen's Mystery Magazine*

"Hemingway wrote about becoming strong at our broken places. Sarah Green, the lawyer-turned-psychotherapist in Jane Sloven's stunning new mystery, *Termination of Benefits,* knows all about this. Still grieving the murder of her best friend, Sarah finds herself embroiled in a new murder investigation while discovering that she has inherited the family blessing/curse of clairvoyance. We feel Sarah's pain in our own broken parts and hold our breath as the danger mounts around her."

—Brendan Rielly, author of the award-winning Michael McKeon thriller series

"*Termination of Benefits* is a riveting, complex, psychological mystery/thriller. Sloven's writing grabs you by the throat and never lets go. Protagonist Sarah Green, an ex-lawyer turned clinical social worker with psychic powers, leads a cast of finely drawn characters who make the book come alive. Set in and around Portland, Maine, the book's issues are ripped from the headlines: friendship, blackmail, murder, drug addiction, health care financing, child sex abuse, mother–daughter relations, and old and new love. Sloven works them into a plot with more twists and turns than the coast of Maine. Warning: If you start reading *Termination of Benefits* after dinner, you're likely to stay up all night to reach the very satisfying conclusion."

—Michael Castleman, author, *Killer Weed, A Killing in Real Estate,* and other books.

Sarah Green is a lawyer-turned-therapist, honest about her own neuroses but wary of her psychic gifts. The murder of a well-known psychiatrist—a longstanding nemesis to Sarah and her best friend and colleague Louise Gold—envelops the pair in a swirling criminal plot with an undercurrent of mysticism that reaches back to an earlier murder that changed the course of Sarah's life. With its cast of memorable characters, *Termination of Benefits* is a fast-moving, often riotous tale that will be enjoyed by those who like a dash of humor with their dead bodies.

—Brenda Buchanan, author of the Joe Gale Mystery Series.

A smart, intuitive woman you wish was your best friend, a ghost who means only the best, a romantic dilemma with two attractive men, plus a strain of spirituality—what more would anyone want in a book? *Termination of Benefits* is an intelligent book that also manages to be a gripping, challenging mystery featuring a contemporary, insightful, compassionate heroine, an irresistible combination. I finished it in two nights and can't wait for the next installment.

—Michelle Cacho-Negrete, author, *Stealing: Life in America*

Termination
of Benefits

jane sloven

Termination of Benefits

© Copyright 2018, Jane Sloven

ISBN: 978-1-63381-130-0

Designed and Produced by
Maine Authors Publishing
12 High Street, Thomaston, Maine 04861
www.maineauthorspublishing.com

Printed in the United States of America

To Joe, the most remarkable man I've ever known.

Prologue

I stand on a dais looking out at a sea of purple and gold gowns, mortarboards with dangling tassels, and the exhausted but exuberant faces of law-school graduates. Sensing movement to my left, I glance over and startle at the sight of Miriam, who is standing beside me and smiling. Gaping at her, I barely have time to collect myself before the dean introduces me. I suck in a deep breath and step to the podium.

"Congratulations, graduates." My voice falters, but I pull myself together. "I'm honored to bestow the Miriam Moss Award upon a special student. The award is dedicated to the memory of my dear friend and study partner at this law school. Miriam's life ended too soon, but her unfaltering commitment to justice made a difference in the world. Please join me in applauding this year's recipient, a woman who shares that dedication—your classmate, Jessica Burns."

As the students stand and clap wildly, a fresh-faced young woman wends her way through the crowd. She runs up the steps to the podium and shakes my hand. I step back as she launches into a short acceptance speech. While listening to Jessica's words, an irresistible yearning prompts me to turn my head. Though Miriam's presence remains palpable, she's no longer visible.

Memories sweep me away. Freshman year, I dragged my suitcase into my college dorm room to be welcomed by my roommate, a young woman with long, straight, dark hair, almond-shaped eyes, and a wide smile. She wore dungarees and an Indian print blouse, and had already decorated the lower bunk with a purple bedspread and fringed gold pillows. The scent of jasmine wafted from a pot of tea, which sat beside a tin overflowing with homemade chocolate-chip cookies.

"Hi. I'm Miriam Moss. You must be Sarah Green!" She stood and flung her arms around me. "I know we're going to be the best of friends."

I had no reason to doubt that. Purple was my favorite color and chocolate-chip cookies my drug of choice. We bonded over politics, philosophy, and boyfriend debacles, remaining roommates all four undergraduate years. As seniors, we prepped together for the LSATs and chose our law school from the list of those that had accepted us both.

This law school was good to us. Boston was good to us—until Miriam was shot to death outside the law library by a criminal defense client who had originally been assigned to me. I'd insisted she come home with me to Brookline, but Miriam was as stubborn as a mule. If she had only listened to me, her implacable faith in the inherent goodness of people would still be gracing Boston's criminal courtrooms. If she hadn't been murdered, we'd have traded in the daily grind in the Public Defender's Office for our own legal practice. Ryan would still be my husband, and we'd be juggling a happy marriage with parenting and professions. But Miriam is dead, and I'm divorced, living in Maine, practicing psychotherapy, and pretending to be mentally healthier than my clients.

Applause brings me back to the present. I give the award winner a perfunctory hug and take pleasure in having brought Miriam back to life, if only in this way, if only for this moment.

Chapter 1

Something jostles me out of a deep sleep, and my eyes struggle open to see the cats, wide awake, fur ruffled, tails pointing to the ceiling. They howl, then leap off the bed and disappear. Looking up, I understand why. A luminous form hovers over my bed—and sends chills from the top of my crown to the tips of my toes. Given the anxiety that intermittently invades my waking state, I should be howling and leaping from the bed too, heart thudding right out of my chest. But the form crystallizes and looks like Miriam.

Instead of anxiety, what I feel is an intense mix of incredulity and grief.

"You're really here, aren't you?" I say, before breaking into tears.

A soft hand begins caressing the top of my head, and continues until used tissues are scattered all over my bed. Finally, I stop sobbing.

"I thought you'd be happy to see me." Miriam glides to the French provincial chair in the corner of my bedroom and tucks her legs beneath her, settling back against a tapestry of woven flowers. It seems an appropriate backdrop for a spirit emanating the fragrance of jasmine.

"I've missed you so much, and it's been so long," I say.

"I know. I'm sorry I couldn't visit sooner. Time is different on the other side, and they kept me busy until now. Are you okay?"

"In what sense? I think I'm talking with your disembodied spirit, but you feel so real."

"You are talking with me, and I am a disembodied spirit," she says. "But you can see me, right?"

I shift in bed and nod. "Actually, despite how weird it is, I am very happy to see you. But why are you here?"

Miriam deflects, a skill she possessed the day I met her but honed to absolute perfection in law school.

"How do you like my dress?" She gestures at a filmy mid-calf number.

"It's lovely, but I thought you hated wearing white."

She shrugs. "I did, but in my new locale, it's the chi-chi color."

I smile. "Did you come to talk about your wardrobe, or are you going to answer my question?"

"Gosh, you're still so bossy," she says. "Tell me how you are first."

"Honestly? Right this moment? I don't know." I lift my arm and gesture toward her. "It's rather shocking to be looking at you and talking with you. And a lot has happened in the past seven years. I fell apart after your death, completely apart, but…" I shrug. "I've reconstructed my life. Now, I'm happy, mostly." I shift in the bed, fluff the pillows up behind my back, and sit up straighter.

Miriam remains comfortably ensconced in the chair. A golden light surrounds her. "I know what happened to you. Now, back to my original question. Aren't you happy to see me?"

"Well…" I sigh. "In all this time, I've had an occasional sense of your presence and so much sadness. I've missed you so much. Then, suddenly on the dais, there you were. That wasn't funny, by the way. And now you're here like this, talking to me? I do have to wonder whether I'm losing it again, like I did after your murder."

"You aren't losing it, honey. This is real. You're just as clairvoyant as the rest of the women in your family." Miriam untucks her legs and crosses one over the other before settling back in the chair. "Remember those few times in college and law school when you let yourself be in touch? How helpful it was? It's long past time to recognize that your clairvoyance is a precious gift." She stares me down. "Sorry about startling you yesterday. I'm just learning to materialize," she laughs.

"I forgive you."

"Thank you. And I'm not here to give you a hard time, but this is important."

"Okay." I take a breath and begin to accept that I'm really seeing Miriam and having this conversation.

"I'm here to let you know that I'm available. It took me a while to adjust, but now you can call on me—anytime. And not to belabor the point, you've got to start trusting your intuition. You're going to need it." She smiles, blows me a kiss, and before I can say another word, dissolves.

The cats slink into view, sniff the room, and jump back on the bird's-eye maple sleigh bed, taking up posts on either side of me like sentries guarding a queen. Miriam's gone, it's the middle of the night, and what's a girl to do? I let myself feel soothed by the sound of the cats' purrs, close my eyes, and sink back to sleep.

At the ungodly hour of six in the morning, I jerk awake. The conversation with Miriam is my first thought. It's lovely to have actually talked to her again, to know that even though she's not embodied, she isn't completely gone. But now my heart is pounding. How will I come to terms with this reality? Is it reality? I'm not sure. I get out of bed, wrap myself in a soft robe, and hope this isn't going to be one of those days when it's difficult for me to put one foot in front of the other and walk out the door.

Chapter 2

Forty-five minutes after I awaken, the phone rings. I hear Louise talking before I can even get the receiver to my ear. "You're coming to court with me today, right?" The connection is clear, but since we live next door to each other, sometimes I think we should just open our windows and holler across the lawn.

"How about, 'Good morning?'" I tuck the phone between my neck and ear while bending down to set two bowls with fresh cat food on the oak floor of my kitchen.

"Who said it was good?" Louise gripes.

"Well, when you put it that way…" I pause. "I'm a tad sleep-deprived and in need of a hot shower. Call me back in thirty minutes."

I hold onto the railing while traipsing upstairs, then pad across the wide pine floorboards in my bedroom en route to the master bath. By the time Louise rings again, my hair is toweled dry, and I'm pawing through my closet.

"Any better?" she asks.

A peek in the mirror tells me the laugh lines that normally radiate from my hazel eyes look more like worry lines. "The shower helped," I lie.

"Nothing's helping me this morning," Louise says. "After testifying in countless custody cases, I shouldn't be anxious. But this one is just so ugly." Louise barely takes a breath before changing direction.

"You got home awfully late last night. What was up?"

"I was in Boston for the award ceremony."

"Geez, what an idiot I am. I've been so focused on court that I forgot all about that. How did it go? Do you want to come over for breakfast and fill me in?" I hear Louise putting her hand over the receiver and talking to her daughters. "I'm on the phone with Sarah. I'll ask if you can spend time with her later, but right now it's adult talking time. Yes, ask Daddy if he'll make the pancakes."

"Sorry," she says. "I'm back. Do you want to come over here or should I come to you?"

"Come here. I'll throw on my bathrobe and make tea."

"Be there in five."

Louise just has to cut through the bushes between our backyards, and she's knocking at the back door by the time I walk into the kitchen. I open the door and give her a hug. "Come sit."

She pulls out a chair at the round oak kitchen table as I fill the electric kettle with filtered water and set it to heat, looking fondly at my cheery yellow walls and painted white cabinets. Louise plunks down into her chair. "So tell me. How are you? Did you see Ryan?"

"Of course. He was there with Miriam's parents. And we all went to the cemetery together afterward."

"How was it to see him?"

"He was on his best behavior," I say, aware of the longing that colors my words. The first semester of law school, Ryan, Miriam, and I formed a study group that got us through all our exams, including law boards after graduation. And though Ryan took a job in civil litigation in the Attorney General's office after graduation, he was a steady support for Miriam and me as we slogged our way through one tawdry criminal-defense case after another. "It was a tough day in so many ways. I felt a huge sense of relief when I got home, but…" I pause, settling into the chair across from Louise, hesitating.

"Spill it," she says.

"I thought I saw Miriam standing next to me on the dais before I gave out the award, and then, at the cemetery, I had a flashback."

"What kind of flashback?" Louise sits up on alert.

"It felt as if I were in the morgue again, identifying Miriam's body." A shiver runs through me. "Ryan was great. He noticed that something was wrong and was right there beside me, talking me through it."

"Wow. What do you think about all that?"

"I'm pretty thrown. It wasn't only seeing Miriam on the dais, or the flashback, both of which would have been challenging enough, but Miriam showed up in my bedroom last night."

"Really? Did she talk to you?"

"Yes. She said I needed to trust my intuition, and to know she's available if I need her."

"That's kind of nice," Louise murmurs.

"It's nice for people who don't worry about their sanity." Years of therapy have helped me cope with much of the fallout from Miriam's death. After leaving law and doing my own therapy to heal from the trauma, I decided to go for a second career in social work. Now I'm a therapist helping others cope with trauma. But as Miriam pointed out, I'm still rejecting the psychic skills that run in my family.

Louise frowns, narrowing her eyes as she examines me. I know she gets impatient when I question my mental health, but now, after the Miriam revelations, perhaps she's taking a second look.

The kettle clicks off. I stand up to pour tea. "Rooibos okay?"

"Of course.

I hand her a teacup and saucer before setting a steaming teapot on a tea warmer in the center of the table beside a jar of honey.

We sip tea and talk about the ceremony, the flashback, Ryan, and Miriam's appearances.

Louise gets that squinty look again and announces, "You should call Janice," referring to my therapist. I've been doing so well that I haven't seen her in almost a year.

"I know. And I will. Not right now, though."

"Are you sure you're okay about coming to court with me?"

Since quitting the legal profession, I've avoided courtrooms, but Louise needs my support, so I'm going with her.

"Yeah. I'm okay."

"You sure?"

"Yes, Louise, I'm sure."

She sighs heavily. "Thanks."

"Friendships are mutual support systems, aren't they? And you're the one who needs support today. Testifying against Dr. Harold Henderson the Third is bound to be challenging. Remember, this isn't a jury trial."

"Henderson might sway the judge."

"Judges are tough to bamboozle, and it's hard to find anyone who respects a psychiatrist in bed with Constant Caring Managed Care."

"I hope you're right," Louise says.

I do, too. As the psychiatric consultant for Constant Caring, Maine's largest managed-care company, Henderson is widely respected by those who don't know him well and widely despised by those who do. Louise and I find him arrogant and sexist. We both reported him to his medical board after learning from his former clients about his approach—encouraging women to become more accommodating to their husbands and blaming them for their husbands' abuse.

"I'm actually more worried about George Tate," Louise adds, "since I'm testifying that his ex-wife should have full custody."

George Tate is the CEO of Constant Caring. The company approves psychotherapy treatment, oversees progress reports, and processes insurance claims. Lately, they've refused to reimburse Louise for sessions they'd agreed to cover. They also sent a notice of intent to audit her client files, highly unusual for psychotherapists. The company could demand repayment for sessions they deem poorly documented. Louise responded by suing them for harassment.

"If Tate and company don't pay me soon," Louise says, "I could be in financial trouble."

"You need clients with a different insurance company, honey."

"That's for sure," she says, pushing her chair back from the table. "But right now I've got to head home and get the girls ready for school. I'll call you as soon as they're off."

Normally, Fridays are my day for self care, and if absolutely necessary, overflow paperwork, billing, or emergencies. Trauma work is tough for therapists, and we have to nurture ourselves. I'm particularly careful because of all I've been through, and it's lovely to have time to prepare for Shabbat. Usually, I clean the house, make a tasty dinner, and attend synagogue on Friday evenings. This Friday is an exception since I'm going to court with Louise, then doing errands in the Old Port and baking in the afternoon so I can bring goodies to synagogue.

Louise calls me again, half an hour later. "The girls are off to school, I've showered, and am dressed in a conservative suit."

"Great, then you can help me decide what to wear."

I put the phone on speaker while holding up my favorite ankle-length gypsy skirt next to a long-sleeved black ballerina tee. "I'm torn between a skirt and tailored slacks."

"Wear the skirt. You're not a lawyer anymore."

"I'll always be a lawyer, even if I never practice another day in my life. But you're right. I don't have to dress like one! I'll wear the skirt with my favorite turquoise shawl."

"At least one of us will look smashing."

"You'll be doing all the important smashing from the witness stand. Besides, you'd look great in a paper bag."

Louise stands two inches taller than me. She's not classically beautiful, but with her long red hair, clear blue eyes, and a dancer's carriage, she causes more whiplash walking into a room than a string of rear-enders.

"You're so good for my ego." She laughs.

I've envied Louise's slender physique since we met at sleepaway camp as ten-year-olds. And I owe her big-time. Not only did she save me from a large hairy spider that first night at camp, she rescued me after Miriam's murder, when Ryan and I moved in with her, her husband Mark, and their older daughter, Naomi. Their youngest, Susie, hadn't been born yet.

I've made a point of steering clear of both Boston and courtrooms to prevent bad memories from arising, but some things cannot always be avoided. Just like I return each spring to hand out Miriam's award, today Louise needs me in court, so I'm bucking up.

Luckily, there's time to stuff my anxiety with a decadent breakfast. I take a bagel out of the freezer and when the phone rings, wonder what Louise forgot to tell me.

"Yes," I say, tucking the phone under my chin.

"That's the way you answer the phone?"

"Oh, hi, Mom. I thought you were Louise."

"This early?"

"Yes," I take a breath, "I'm going to court with her today. She's testifying for a client."

"Is that a good idea?" My mother's tone, often sharp, hides a big heart.

"It's fine."

"I worry about you. You need someone there for you, like your father is here for me. We all need that. Ryan still loves you, you know."

"I know, Mom. It was good to see him. But we're divorced, and we're staying divorced."

Her sigh travels the airways like a gust of wind. "You always had a mind of your own—not like your sisters who still listen to me. Come home soon for a visit. And take care of yourself in the meantime." Her voice softens. "I love you."

"I love you too, Mom. Say hi to Dad for me."

I pour hot water over a chai teabag in a tall white mug, add steamed milk and honey, and toss the bagel in the toaster. After piling cream cheese and smoked salmon on the bagel, I sit at the kitchen table, focusing on how far I've come.

I love living in Maine. Portland is a completely manageable city. In my new career as a social worker, Louise and I share a little cottage where we see our private-practice clients. My caseload consists of fairly ordinary people like me, struggling with difficult life situations: divorce, depression, anxiety, illness. The problem-solving fascinates me, and it's much less intense than practicing criminal law. I dealt with enough sociopaths in courtrooms. Now I don't want anyone in my office who could hurt me.

Chapter 3

Louise and I push open the double doors of the courthouse. It's 8:30 and my apprehension about being back in a courtroom has left my mouth so dry, I can barely swallow. Memories are jostling for space in my mind like commuters on a crowded subway.

"Ready?" I ask, speaking as much to myself as to Louise.

"Yes." Louise's pallor doesn't surprise me.

We hand our bags to the security guard, step through the metal screening section, and collect our things. In the elevator, I brace myself against a wall.

Louise notices. "What's going on?"

"Memories."

"Memories or flashbacks?" she asks.

"Hmm. I'm not sure."

"What are you seeing?"

"Law school. Legal practice." The images slide by so fast. Glimpsing Ryan the first day of school. Miriam, Ryan, and me studying, arguing, laughing. Ryan gripping my hand as we identify Miriam's body in the morgue. I look up. Louise is staring. "Sorry. Between Boston and Miriam's visits, I'm off my game." I force a smile. "Ignore me. I'm fine."

The elevator swishes open and there, standing at the edge of the door, is the smiling face of Billy Marshall.

"Billy!" Louise propels me out of the elevator and wraps her arms around the handsome detective. When she steps back, she smiles.

"Sarah, you know Billy Marshall, don't you?"

"Sure. You've introduced us, and we see each other at synagogue." Besides that, Billy's looks would be difficult to forget.

"What are you two doing here?" His teeth flash white against an early tan.

"I'm testifying in a custody case. Sarah came along for moral support." He steps into the elevator and locks eyes with Louise. "Call me. We're overdue for coffee." He waves goodbye as the doors slide shut.

"Now that's one sexy guy," I say.

Louise blushes. "He was just as sexy in high school when we had that little fling. You should let me fix you up. You have a lot in common. He left law too."

"I know that, Louise. But he's perfectly capable of asking me out if he has the inclination."

"Maybe he needs encouragement."

"You sound like my mother." Billy is a good distraction, but it's over too soon. I turn my attention to the crowded hallway as we wind our way through the mass of people. I follow Louise as she spies her client, Brooke Hart Tate. Brooke, wearing a tailored peach suit, is standing toe to toe with her soon-to-be ex-husband, George Tate, chief executive of Constant Caring Managed Care Company.

"Where is Brooke's attorney? George shouldn't be anywhere near her right now!"

"You're right. I've get to get over there." Louise strides through the crowd.

George is wearing a hand-tailored, navy pinstripe suit and is carrying a black leather briefcase. His chestnut-colored hair is perfectly coiffed, but he looks out of control, looming over Brooke, his cheeks flaming red, as he jabs his index finger in her face. She steps away from him and turns toward Louise. George turns too, to see what she's looking at. The condescension in his cold blue eyes is palpable. But then he straightens his posture, adjusts his tie, and nods at Louise before walking away.

As Brooke and Louise confer, I square my shoulders and cross the threshold of the courtroom. My friend, and Louise's and my attorney, Kate Lincoln, waves me over to the seats she's saved. She's wearing a tailored black suit, black pumps, and a cream-colored silk blouse. A strand of pearls glistens at her neck, and a tapestry briefcase sits at her feet. "I just won a motion hearing down the hall," she says. "It gave me time to grab us good seats."

I settle in beside her, notice her raised eyebrows, and follow her gaze.

Dr. Harold Henderson strides down the aisle, smiling as if he's running for office. Tufts of gray hair crown the back of his shiny head. Chameleon-like, Henderson portrays himself as the epitome of a Boston Brahmin, but I've seen him acting down-home at the Yarmouth Clam Festival and the Kennebunkport Dump Parade, wearing a Red Sox cap, jeans, and a T-shirt—and chowing down on lobster rolls. "He looks like a million bucks, doesn't he?" Kate comments.

"Sure does. I just don't get how he's able to fill his practice with wealthy women when his orientation is so infused with contempt." I mimic his voice. "'Women have only themselves to blame when their husbands stray. Have they let their figures go? Are they guilty of nagging? Have they neglected their role as robust sexual partners?'"

Kate sniggers, but we're immediately distracted by George Tate's entrance. Like Henderson, he looks every inch the part he plays, the respectable executive—not hard with his head start in life. Tate's family arrived on the Mayflower, and people say he has so much inherited wealth that he could purchase all the beachfront property from Ogunquit to Kennebunk and still have enough left over to acquire all of Cape Elizabeth, too.

"My cousin went to prep school with Tate," Kate whispers. "None of his classmates understand why he gave up collecting cars and breeding racehorses to take on the hassle of a managed-care company."

It's a good question. "If I had all that money, I certainly wouldn't focus on finding ways to deny people the insurance benefits they've paid for," I reply.

Louise slides in beside me and smiles at Kate. "Thanks for coming," she says.

Kate reaches over to pat Louise's shoulder. "I want to be here. It might give us more fodder for our lawsuit against Constant Caring."

"Did you guys see the story in yesterday's paper?" Louise asks. "The one where Henderson was quoted about anaphylactic reactions to bee stings?"

Kate smirks. "The article was hard to miss. It's odd to think of such a big man being brought to his knees by a bee."

"Well, if Henderson really has an anaphylactic allergy to bees, I bet the EpiPen he carries to counteract a fatal reaction is inscribed with his initials and embossed in gold."

I shake off a gruesome image of a ghoulish Henderson wandering aimlessly around a cemetery and wonder if it's simply a product of my weird imagination or another psychic phenomenon. I've repressed these things successfully for many years, but it's clear that something new is happening.

The clerk stands up and calls everyone to attention. The judge enters, and court is in session. Soon, Louise is called to the stand, and after preliminary questions about her training and experience, Brooke's attorney gets right to the issues. "Could you describe the focus of your treatment with Mrs. Tate?"

"Certainly," Louise replies. "Many of our sessions focused on Mrs. Tate's concerns about her husband, George Tate, and his drinking."

"Could you enumerate those concerns for the court?"

"May I refer to my notes?" Louise asks.

"The witness refers to exhibit number twenty-three, psychotherapy notes entered into evidence during deposition," says the attorney. The judge nods assent. "Please continue, Ms. Gold."

Louise reads from her notes. "Brooke appears this morning tearful and shaky. She relates these events. Her husband, George, arrived at home last night at one a.m. and was unable to unlock the back door to the house. His yelling awakened and frightened the children. Brooke says she ran downstairs and unlocked the door. Her husband reeked of alcohol. When she asked if he'd been drinking, he lashed out with his fist, hitting the left side of her face. Bruises are apparent on her left cheek. I advised her to contact the police and file a report. We discussed her desire for a marital separation and the importance of consulting with her attorney and filing for a Protection from Abuse order." Louise finishes reading from her notes and adds, "Brooke did contact the police and obtained a protection order."

Brooke's attorney leads Louise from date to date and entry to entry, describing George Tate's drinking and abuse. On cross-examination, George's attorney attempts to discredit Louise, but Louise's notes concerning Brooke's sessions are highly incriminating.

As Louise's testimony continues, George looks less and less like a respectable executive. He fidgets, passes notes to his attorney, and turns beet red when incriminating details are highlighted by his wife's attorney. After Louise returns to sit beside me, he turns to glare at her, and his rage is so palpable that I start to sweat.

Harold Henderson takes the stand. After George Tate's attorney establishes Dr. Henderson's treatment of the Tates in marital sessions, as well as Brooke Hart Tate's participation in one of Dr. Henderson's women's groups, the attorney asks Henderson, "Could you comment on Mrs. Tate's allegations regarding her husband's drinking?"

"I believe Mrs. Tate's accusations of her husband's alleged alcohol and physical abuse are gross exaggerations."

"On what do you base this belief?"

"Mrs. Tate is similar to the other women in my Wonderful Wives groups. Their unconscious desires lead them to engage in behaviors that provoke their spouses. If they have the capacity to explore those unconscious motivations, they repair their marriages and stop blaming their husbands for their despair. Some of my clients, such as Mrs. Tate, are unable to do the in-depth work called for in my model of treatment and they leave my practice for easier orientations."

"And you think this is why Mrs. Tate terminated her work with you?"

"Yes. She was unable to face her unconscious conflicts. She insists on blaming her husband. She refuses to accept any of the responsibility for the failure of their marriage, which is, of course, a two-way street."

"Dr. Henderson, what do you make of the fact that your colleague, Louise Gold, presents an opposite opinion?"

"First, I don't consider Ms. Gold a 'colleague.' She and I have very different educational backgrounds. I'm a medical doctor with a specialty in psychiatry," Henderson stresses. "Ms. Gold is a social worker. Our training is vastly different in terms of the number of years we have studied and practiced under supervision, and in the depth of our understanding of psychiatric disorders."

"So, the different orientations lead to different conclusions?"

"Absolutely," Henderson says. He sips from the glass of water beside him. "And as therapists, we have our own struggles in life, struggles that are not dissimilar to our clients' problems." He smiles at Louise. "For example, we may wrestle with spousal addictions and infidelity. If therapists aren't careful, our own issues can become entangled with those of our clients." Henderson pauses. "I've found Ms. Gold to be rather naively supportive of her female clients' anger and their outlandish accusations against their spouses." He pauses again, as if considering his next words, and adds, "I have also experienced her as generally hostile to men."

I cringe at Henderson's testimony. It brings up unpleasant recollections of my days practicing law. Back then, the bar was a fairly exclusive men's club, and I used to say the rules had been conceived by sociopaths: intimidate your opponent and their clients, delay and obfuscate, encourage anger and retaliation. Despite the fact that many more women practice law these days, the performance I'm watching indicates that the rules haven't changed much.

I can tell that Henderson is really riling Louise, but she's collected herself by the time she's called back to the stand, and she lets Henderson have it.

"What is your opinion of Dr. Henderson's treatment approach?" Brooke's attorney asks.

"Clients who have entered treatment with me after leaving Dr. Henderson uniformly report his tendency to accuse them of provoking their spouses' anger. They also routinely decry his minimization of abuse. No one should tolerate abuse." Louise stares at Henderson. "Not from their spouse, and certainly not from their therapist."

Henderson sits stone-faced, though when Louise describes the ethics complaint Brooke Tate filed against him, he actually smiles slightly.

"Dr. Henderson's testimony may be influenced by the fact that he's employed as the psychiatric consultant for Constant Caring Managed Care Company. His client, George Tate, is the CEO of Constant Caring. Some might consider the fact that he treated both George Tate and Brooke Hart Tate a conflict of interest, as well as a violation of the medical ethics governing 'dual relationships.'"

A few other people testify, and the judge concludes the case, saying she will take some time to consider all the testimony before rendering a final opinion. Louise pulls at my sleeve, and whispers, "Come with me to the ladies' room."

"Wait!" Kate fishes in her purse and hands Louise a key. "The public restrooms will be jammed. My friend in the DA's office lent me her key to the private bathroom. Go out the door, turn right, and

walk halfway down the corridor. It says Staff on the door and there's
a large W."

"You did great," I murmur as we walk out of the courtroom. "I
wouldn't have done nearly so well. Henderson sure took a beating from
your testimony." We turn the corner and see Henderson ensconced in
an alcove. He motions to Louise and she walks over to him. Their conversation doesn't last long. Within two minutes, she grabs my arm and
drags me down the hall to the ladies' room.

"What the hell was that about?" I ask, taking the key from her shaking hand to unlock the door and usher her inside.

"I threatened him and he threatened me."

"How?" I lean against the bathroom wall with my arms crossed over
my chest.

Louise looks in the mirror and rubs her hands across her face,
stretching the skin so taut that she looks like a skeleton. "I'll tell you
later. What I don't understand is why the board hasn't revoked his
license." She sighs. "I'm so looking forward to suing him."

"That's the only thing that makes me wish I was still practicing law,"
I say. "Shredding him while he's on the stand." I picture Henderson, the
preening rooster, being peppered with hostile questions. I know, however, that Kate is more than capable of grinding him to dust.

"We should have known what to expect from him the minute we
heard about his Wonderful Wives groups. What kind of a man does a
women's group with a name like that?"

"A misogynist," I say. "And he'll eventually get what he deserves,
from the board or someone else. But what did he say to you in the hall?
You're still shaking."

"I can't tell you. Not right now."

"Could he know about Mark's drinking, or your marital history?"

She leans against the sink and shrugs. "Mark's been in recovery a
long time. Portland is a small town, and though AA is wonderful, things
said there don't always stay there. I wouldn't put it past Henderson to
misuse information he hears in sessions." She sighs. "If there's any justice in this world, he'll get swarmed by bees."

I shake off another gruesome image of Henderson's ghost hovering
over a cemetery.

Half a second later, the toilet flushes. We spin around to stare at the district attorney stepping out from a stall. She stands there, silently looking us up and down, before washing her hands at the sink with slow deliberation. She dries her hands, tosses the paper towel in the trash, and turns to Louise. "This is a private restroom for my staff." She holds out her hand like an elementary school teacher. "I won't ask who gave you the key, but I want it back."

Louise, speechless, simply stares. I break the standoff by retrieving the key from my pocket and placing it in the DA's outstretched hand. She walks out without another word.

"Whew!" I say as I walk into a stall.

"How did we not notice her?" Louise asks.

The DA and Louise have a tenuous relationship, developed years earlier, when Louise unsuccessfully pleaded for the prosecution of the husband of one of her clients for domestic abuse. After the batterer beat his wife so severely she was hospitalized for months, Louise gave the press the gory history, including the DA's failure to pursue the earlier assault. Our DA tends to hold a grudge, and I know from my former legal practice just how dangerous grudge-holders can be.

Chapter 4

I dry my hands and look in the mirror to see Louise's pale face behind mine. "We have to lighten up," I say, scrambling in my purse in search of lipstick. "Hmm." After applying my favorite color—Ruby Red—to my lips, I add, "Just imagine the DA striding confidently into the courtroom, failing to notice"—I pause dramatically and hold up my hand for effect—"that the back hem of her skirt is tucked into the waist of her pantyhose."

When we finally stop laughing, I urge Louise to come shopping with me. "It's only eleven. We thought court might last a lot longer. We can lust after material objects and pick up the shawl I'm wearing to synagogue tonight."

"Sorry," Louise answers. "I need to get home."

I can't persuade her. En route home, I call into voicemail to make sure no clients have called with emergencies. I'm thankful to be in private practice, able to arrange my schedule to meet my own needs as well as my clients'. Luckily, my present caseload mostly consists of very stable clients. There are no messages. At home, I check on the cats and change into a pair of jeans before driving back to the Old Port.

Maneuvering the car down lower Exchange Street proves challenging. Locals and tourists mob the sidewalks, some edging into the streets, oblivious to the cars, apparently mesmerized by the trendy shops and coffee bars. It took only a year of living in Maine to learn that crowds are a spring, summer, and fall phenomenon. During our bitterly cold winters, the sidewalks can become icy and treacherous. Visitors remain in more southerly climes, and the local population hibernates. We all reappear en masse after the March thaw. On this warm mid-May day, flowers are blooming, the sun is out in an enormous blue sky, and both locals and tourists are happy.

Angelic intervention is a necessity when seeking a parking meter in Portland, and my angels help me score a spot directly across from The Exchange, our quirky version of a mini-mall. I lock the car and scan the storefronts across the street—a funky clothing store and the linchpin, D. Cole, a locally owned treasure trove of beautiful jewelry. I look up to the floor above, home to a discreet sex boutique and a few offices. One, with three large windows overlooking Exchange Street, is the office of Dr. Harold Henderson.

D. Cole's dazzling display of gems lures me across the street, where precious and semiprecious stones sparkle temptingly from the windows, but time is short. I push my way through the crowd to a snazzy boutique with beautiful clothing, cool jewelry, and unobtrusive clerks. The owner had called to say the shawl I'd ordered had arrived. After making my purchase, I follow an irresistible aroma to a local coffeehouse where a chai latte topped with whipped cream and chocolate slivers offers refreshment. Soon, I'm threading my way through the Exchange Street crowd. The screeches and squeals of seagulls draw my attention upward, and my eyes lock onto the windows of Dr. Henderson's office. He stands with his back to the center window, partially blocking the silhouette of a woman who looks remarkably like Louise.

I stop short, wondering why Louise would be in Henderson's office. As I step into the street, gaping at the two figures in the window, a colorfully tattooed adolescent on a skateboard slams into me, knocking the chai out of my hands. The collision apparently cracks his iPod-induced trance, since he steps off the skateboard, bends to retrieve my drink, and offers a sheepish apology. When I glance back up at Henderson's window, it's empty.

My mind sweeps through possible reasons for Louise's presence in Henderson's office. None of them are good. Without inhaling a shred of self-control, I dart across the street and race up the staircase of The Exchange.

I burst into Henderson's waiting room, to find women attired in Talbot's spring line. No mysteries here—they have to be waiting for one of Henderson's Wonderful Wives groups, where he'll preach a return-to-fifties-style passivity and servitude. I stop short for a moment, noting the contrast between their preppy WASP style and the jeans I'm wearing over a black leotard, my high leather boots, and silver hoop earrings that are probably snagged in my unruly curls.

I pull it together and focus. "Umm, excuse me," I gasp, short of breath from the sprint and from my concern that Louise might have actually run into Henderson's office to have it out with him. "Do you know if Dr. Henderson is in session?"

Heads turn side to side in unison. "I doubt it," says a bobbed brunette wearing a pink suit topped with pearls. "I came out of an individual session with him fifteen minutes ago, and our group is starting in five minutes."

An older woman clears her throat. She's dressed in lime-green pants and a matching jacket in a color that reminds me of Popsicles and makes me look like a dead chicken. It doesn't make her look much better, but Mrs. Popsicle's smile is kind. "I watched the doctor come out of his office and return with his lunch. I think he's eating now. He usually does that before group begins."

Just as my head swivels to look at Henderson's door, it opens. His eyes widen in surprise before narrowing in apparent indignation as he notices me. "What are you doing here, Ms. Green, attempting to poach my clients like some ambulance-chasing attorney? Oh, excuse me," he says, waving his right hand through the air. "You *were* an ambulance-chasing attorney, weren't you?"

Flushing with anger and embarrassment, I stand up, mustering every ounce of self-restraint in my repertoire. "I just need two minutes of your time, Harold, and I wouldn't be here unless it was extremely important."

"Oh, all right." He sounds exasperated, but waves me into the inner sanctum while making a pained announcement that group will be briefly delayed.

"I'm looking for Louise," I say. "Where is she?"

"Excuse me?" He raises one eyebrow in an attempt to intimidate me, but it fails to work. My law professors tried that too. "I thought I saw Louise in the window just a few minutes ago."

Henderson harrumphs. "As much as I relish the thought of treating your colleague, and as certain as I am that she needs professional help, I doubt I will have that opportunity. And as you should know, there is such a thing as confidentiality. Are we done yet?"

I notice the remains of his lunch in the trash: fries and a sub, congealing unappetizingly in a Styrofoam container. He reaches for the door.

"I don't normally act like this," I say, "but after your hostile interaction with Louise in court this morning, I want to make sure you aren't continuing that fight here. I thought…"

"I can guess what you thought, Ms. Green, but your colleague is not here. And, despite my fantasies, there is no bullet-ridden body on the floor."

Gripped by a gruesome image of Miriam's body in the morgue, I grab the back of a tawny leather club chair. The room spins.

"Ms. Green? Are you okay?" Probably fearing I'll faint, Henderson sighs, settles me in the chair, and pours me a glass of water. He throws some papers in the trash on top of the remains of his lunch while I drain the glass and collect myself.

"I'm sure your colleague is safe and sound at home. Ready to go now?" Henderson directs me to the door. On my way out, I notice the soft smile tendered by Ms. Popsicle.

At the bottom of the steps, I speed dial Louise. She answers on the second ring.

"Did you come back into town and go to Henderson's office?"

I count to ten waiting for Louise to respond. "Are you okay?" She speaks slowly, in the carefully modulated voice I've heard her use with clients in crisis.

"Just answer the question."

"Am I back on the stand?"

"No. I'm asking you a simple question."

"Yes. I was in Henderson's office."

"What were you thinking?" I shout. "You're suing him!"

Louise laughs, but it's a sad laugh. "I'd have preferred not to ever speak to him again, but we had something personal to discuss."

"That's interesting. Why do think he refused to say whether or not you'd been there?"

"What?"

"I just ran up there and pushed my way into his office. He wouldn't tell me whether or not you'd been there. What could you and Henderson have to talk about, especially after this morning's testimony? And why would he cover for you?"

"I can't believe you went into his office," Louise says. "What is going on with you?"

"I was worried about you! And the more germane question is, what's going on with you?"

"I'd like to tell you, Sarah. And I'm going to tell you. But I can't tell you right now."

"What? You normally tell me everything."

"Trust me here. Sometimes things aren't what they seem."

"What *are* they, then?"

Louise sighs before she answers. "Complicated. Things are too damn complicated, especially right now. And I've got to go."

"You're just going to avoid answering me?"

"Yes. I need to think about what I can tell you, and the girls just walked in, and they're arguing. Why don't you come by when you get home?"

"I have baking to finish. I'm making the desserts to serve after Shabbat services this evening. I'll come by if I have time." I step out on the sidewalk and notice that traffic has been gridlocked by a rear-end collision at the corner of Exchange and Fore Streets. Disappointed by my inability to drive right home, I console myself with a late lunch at a nearby restaurant. The lunch crowd is unusually thin, and the hostess seats me at a table in the front window. I fortify myself with a big bowl of fish chowder and a small salad, and look up at Henderson's office windows as I finish eating. He's drawn the blinds.

Once home, I get right to baking, cracking eggs, spilling chocolate chips into a sticky batter, and sliding baking sheets into the oven. I wonder why Louise was in Henderson's office. Then I fantasize about romance and rue the lack of it. As the cookies bake, I open my computer to check email, freezing at the sight of a message from Ryan.

Dearest Sarah, How can it be so difficult to begin a personal note? Perhaps I should take that up in my next session. Yes, I'm in therapy, if you can imagine that, and it's really helping. Being with you and Miriam's parents last weekend brought back a lot of pain. How are you doing? I know it was rough at the cemetery. I'm here if it would help you to talk.

I'm writing not only to check in on you, but because I want you to know that I'm finally understanding how Miriam's murder created havoc in our marriage. It would be really helpful for me to see you to talk through some things. Please call me when you feel up to doing that.

I don't want to call Ryan despite how incredibly kind he was to me in Boston, but his email is so full of vulnerability that I can't ignore it for long. Louise and I are scheduled to attend a conference in Boston soon. I decide to call him then, and save his email while imagining meeting someone new who inspires the kind of passion in me that Ryan did.

Between the award ceremony for Miriam, my flashbacks, Miriam's ghostly visitation, Ryan's email, the morning in court, and Louise in Henderson's office, I figure Shabbat services can only bring relief. Seeking help from above seems like a good idea.

When the final baking sheet comes out of the oven, I call Louise. "Ready to chat? I can bring over some freshly baked cookies."

"Sure. I'll set out some iced tea."

A handsome red cardinal perching in the lilacs separating Louise's yard from mine, takes off as I duck through.

Louise sets down a watering can and waves me over. "The iced tea is on the deck."

I pour two glasses and hand her one, along with a warm cookie, which she immediately demolishes.

Despite the green-and-white-striped cushions beckoning from the patio chairs, Louise sinks down onto the deck, sitting cross-legged with her back against the railing. She nibbles on her nails, the only sign of agitation I see, and I'm expecting to see agitation.

I sit across from her, doing the same yoga pose, albeit far less gracefully, wishing for the millionth time that my mother had let me continue with dance classes. I'd been a clumsy but blissful ballerina until age ten, when Mom assessed the possibilities and insisted I focus on academics, dashing my dreams of becoming a Radio City Hall Rockette.

"Are you ready to talk about Henderson? I notice you're biting your nails."

Louise stops, reaches for her iced tea, sips it. "No. Don't ask me anymore. I will tell you what I can, when I can."

Her voice is harsh and I'm shocked. I've never heard that tone from Louise, certainly never heard it directed at me. I feel myself pulling back. As if sensing my need for comfort, Louise's cat, Emma, curls up in my lap.

"Sorry about that," Louise says. "I'm really upset right now. There's a lot going on. Normally I confide in you, but I can't talk about this yet, not even with you."

I give a halfhearted nod. "Okay. I get it. Sort of. It's been a long day."

"Yes. We've both been better. I've certainly been better. But at least I'm not being visited by ghosts."

"Good point. I'm still thinking about how it didn't scare me. I've got to ask someone about that. It's not what I expected."

"You're probably more used to it than you let on, especially since you had experiences like that earlier in your life. I know you repressed them, but you've also spent years listening to your Aunt Zelda talk about her many conversations with the dearly departed."

The clairvoyant legacy that runs through my family tree affects its recipients in different ways. The Bergs, on my mother's side, experience a jolt of dread with their premonitions, which produces women with a some-what paranoid orientation to life and an understandable reluctance to embrace "the gift." The Greens, on my father's side, feel enveloped by love and peace when in contact with the other side. Many of them enjoy all sorts of psychic phenomena, but my Aunt Zelda is the most masterful, occasion-ally offering private consultations to indulge her favorite pastime, com-muning with the dead. Louise and my aunt hit it off famously the first time they met, when Zelda accompanied my parents to my summer camp for family day, and Louise and her parents joined us at the dinner table.

"I bet your aunt would tell you to embrace Miriam's appearances and delve deeper into conversation with her," Louise says. "You should call Zelda."

"I left her a message." I rub my palms against my eyes, reluctant to fully embrace what's becoming all too clear: that the ability to talk to the dead has definitely been passed on to me. I wonder whether I can control it or whether I'll be inundated with spirits clamoring for atten-tion. I've read that some people become overwhelmed when psychic abilities break through. I don't want that. I'm already overwhelmed. I want to be normal, and normal folks aren't psychic.

"I know you've worked on this with Janice, but maybe you could have a chat about this with Jim Barr," Louise suggests. "Are you seeing him for supervision anytime soon?"

"Nothing's scheduled, but I can always call him." Jim, a local psychiatrist who taught me clinical hypnosis and dream analysis, remains my mentor. "We've talked about this in the past, but I don't know if I want to bring too much of this stuff into my clinical supervision sessions."

Louise laughs. "How can you avoid it? Your intuition is often spot-on about your clients. Where do you think that comes from? At the very least, discussing it with Zelda will help you get more comfortable with Miriam's spirit."

"You know how I feel about communicating with the dead. It's difficult enough to communicate with the living."

"I don't think you have a choice, honey." Louise holds my gaze with magnet-like force. "They're communicating with you."

As a child, I'd been reassured by my aunts' abilities to speak with those who'd passed. If Aunt Zelda could talk to Uncle Morty, that shovelful of dirt she'd tossed on his coffin was far less final than it first appeared. I had experiences as a child with spirits, and was becoming conversant with other realms. However, as my teenage years descended, all I wanted was to fit in with my friends, and I shut that channel right down—becoming distrustful of my intuition and wary of dalliances with spirits. Unwilling to cross the thin line that separated so-called normal folks from those society considered weird, I politely deferred the tutelage of my aunts and chose therapy to help me cope, holding tight to my counselor's assurance that I wasn't nuts. This afternoon, it seems clear I've crossed the line.

I don't want to talk about Miriam right now, so I can't insist Louise talk about Henderson. Some things just have to wait until the time is right.

Louise scoots over to sit beside me just as Emma creeps out of my lap, intent on stalking a bug. Louise intercepts, picking up the cat for a snuggle.

"Wise One," she murmurs in the cat's ear, "how can I cope with horrible Henderson and the other annoying employees at Constant Caring?"

Emma leaps out of Louise's lap with a howl and pounces on a gigantic beetle. We watch as she decapitates it with her teeth before settling on the sunny lawn to devour it.

"Hmm…" Louise smiles. "That's one way to go."

Chapter 5

"How did it go today—with you and Louise in court?"

"Mom," I say, invoking all my therapy training and personal work to keep my voice modulated, "please don't hover. It went well. Louise testified, she did a great job, and I'm getting ready to go to temple. I can't talk now."

"What?" she says. "It's a crime to call my daughter to say Good Shabbos?"

"Mom, you called me this morning. I know what you're doing. Stop. I'm okay. I promise, the minute I begin to fall apart, I'll pick up the phone and let you know."

"Don't open a mouth to me. It's my prerogative as your mother to worry about you, and I intend to indulge. But I'll let you go now. Have a sweet and restful Shabbos." My mother can pivot faster than an Olympic skater from suffocating over-involvement to pure kindness.

"Thanks, Mom. You have a good Shabbos too. And stop calling me so much. I love you."

I shower and dress, eat a light meal, and transport the goodies. Once I've unloaded everything and settled into my usual chair at the back of the sanctuary, the melodies sweep me into a meditative state, which lasts until I sense someone taking the seat beside me. Detective Billy Marshall's smile radiates warmth. "Good Shabbos," he says.

"Same to you." I return his smile and try unsuccessfully to refocus on the prayers, all too aware that Billy's intermittent appearances at services add a special kick to my spiritual experience. Billy closes his eyes during the meditation and seems to go deep fast. I go deep too, meditating on how the streaks of silver in his curly black hair glimmer in the light and his long legs extend under the chair in front of him. His tan complexion, straight nose, and long black eyelashes are compelling, and in no time I find myself on a perfect path to impure thoughts.

Billy's arm is resting on the back of my chair as the service concludes. The rabbi chants the priestly benediction. "May God's presence be with you, may God's countenance be lifted up upon you, and may God grant you the precious gift of peace."

"I've loved that prayer since childhood," I whisper to Billy. "Whenever I hear it, I have the sensation of being wrapped up in holiness."

He walks beside me to the social hall, and I shamelessly point out everything I baked. He gazes admiringly at the spread and after demolishing two brownies, says, "If the road to a man's heart is truly through his stomach, you must have left a long trail of broken hearts behind you."

As folks begin drifting out of the social hall, Billy helps me clean up and accompanies me to my car. I reward his attention by fortifying him with leftovers.

On the drive home, I think about the close Jewish community in Portland, the shared prayer and traditions. I like lighting candles and chanting blessings over wine and braided challah on Shabbat. The Judaic tenet that God is present at every moment, in every experience, provided great comfort to me after Miriam's murder. I wanted Ryan to attend services with me on Friday evenings, but it wasn't his tradition and he wasn't interested.

Shaking off useless regrets, I walk into the house, suddenly aware of my exhaustion. In no time, I'm snuggling in bed with my cats and drifting to sleep.

The ringing phone startles me out of slumber. Louise's anxious voice only increases my fear. "Turn on the news. Right now. Channel six."

"What's wrong?" I mumble, peering at the clock and fumbling for the remote. It's five minutes after eleven; I'd only been asleep for a half hour. I grab the remote, and the sound echoes through the telephone from both our TVs. A photo of Henderson fills the screen.

"What's he done now?"

"Dropped dead."

"No!"

"Yes."

"Where?"

"In his office."

"I'll be right over." I throw on clothes, grab a flashlight, flip on the outside lights, and run across my yard.

Louise is waiting on the deck beside her back door.

"Seriously? He died in his office?" I step inside.

"That's what they're saying on the news."

"Nothing more?"

"Nope."

Louise takes my hand and leads me through her recently remodeled kitchen, past top-of-the-line granite countertops and glass-fronted white cabinets into the kitchen–lounging area, with its cushy blue-and-white-striped sofa and flat-screen television. We sink side by side into the couch.

I'm taken by the beauty of her silk kimono-style robe. It's cream-colored and looks like a painting of cherry blossoms. "Wow, that's absolutely gorgeous. Can I touch the fabric?" My fingers are already brushing the sleeve.

"Don't go getting distracted," she warns. Louise's house and clothing often meet my definition of perfect, but I check *her* more closely and notice she looks anything but. Her face is pale, and her eyes are pink and puffy.

"You weren't crying over Henderson, were you?"

"Of course not." Louise scowls. "Mark and I had another argument. I need to tell you what's going on with Mark, with us, but…" She hesitates.

"But what?"

"I'll fill you in after the news. I want to hear everything they report about Henderson."

"Looks like they've moved on." I eye the TV screen. "So what's up with you and Mark?"

Louise sighs. "He's been impossible. Really critical and snarly. Sharp with the girls, nasty to me, and after months of this, I finally know why." She pauses. "I'm hurt, and very angry." She bites her lip, looks at the television. "Take this, will you?" She hands me the remote and stands up. "I put up tea and am about to dive into my second piece of chocolate cake."

I spy an extravagantly frosted cake on the countertop. "Is this one of Kitty's?"

"Of course. I couldn't concoct something so exquisite."

I love Louise's mom, Kitty. She's like a second mom to me—one much less complicated than my mother, though they compete for the title of most talented baker. "Can I have a sliver?"

"Of course." Louise slides pieces of cake onto floral porcelain plates before continuing. "I cannot believe Henderson died in his office, during a group."

I shiver, thinking back to my image of Henderson hovering over a cemetery. "Do you think he had a heart attack? Wait, he does a group on Friday nights? The guy has no social life?"

Louise whips her head around. "It happened early this evening, and the guy is dead! Who cares about his social life?"

"Well, he's lost his chance for one now."

"Jeez, Sarah."

"You're awfully touchy, Louise."

"His death is throwing me in some weird way." She glances at the television. "Turn the sound back up if they show his photo again, okay?"

I nod, watching Louise pour steaming water into footed glass mugs. "So, where's Mark?"

"The guest room."

"What's going on here? I depend on the two of you to model the perfect marriage."

"You're out of luck on that one, honey."

"Did he relapse?" Mark's problems with alcohol ended the day Naomi was born. As far as I know, he's been a faithful member of AA ever since.

Louise, dunking tea bags in the mugs, doesn't answer.

"Louise?"

"Later." She waves me off. "News first."

I yawn and stretch my legs, as Louise picks up the plates and heads my way.

"I just saw Henderson, both this morning and again this afternoon in his office," I murmur. "I should feel sad that he's dead, but I don't.

That isn't a nice part of me. Every human being's death should be sad, except for awful people, like Hitler. His death wasn't sad, unless you were his mistress, or his mother."

"You're getting stranger by the day." Louise sets my plate on a white-painted coffee table, one we'd snagged at a yard sale. "But I feel relieved," she says, "and a tad guilty."

"For what?"

"For feeling relieved, of course."

I sit up as she walks back and forth, retrieving our tea, fishing napkins from a drawer, forgetting the silverware, going back for it. When she finally sits beside me, I lay my hand on top of hers. "He was a real schmuck, Louise, especially to you. We all wished he'd disappear. Besides, now you might get some checks from Constant Caring." I stab a piece of cake.

"Isn't it creepy to think of him getting sick and dying during a group, in front of his clients?" I wrinkle my nose at that thought, even as I savor a lick of chocolate icing from the tines of my fork. "I've felt sick in the midst of a session. You don't want to cancel precipitously, but you don't want to throw up in front of your clients either."

Louise shivers. "Talk about trauma. I bet we'll end up with at least some his clients in our office. We get a disproportionate number of them anyway. Do you ever wonder why? When one of us sees a refugee from his practice, the word must go out to others so they come to us too. There's probably a network of his former clients who put us at the top of the list for therapists."

Another long line of advertisements begins and ends before the news anchor reappears. I click the sound back on. "The coroner's van has arrived at Dr. Henderson's office," the reporter says somberly. The camera moves to a State Police evidence van.

"That evidence van means there's a question about his death," I say. "I remember that much from my law practice."

"Shh."

"We will keep you posted as details become available," the reporter intones. "Check our website for updates."

"Well, I'm afraid we'll have to wait for the gory details like everyone else." As the credits roll, I shift position to see Louise better. "Talk to me. What's going on with you and Mark?"

She whispers, "I haven't been able to tell you about it, but now I need to."

She clamps her mouth shut as Mark strides into the kitchen. He's wearing blue plaid pajamas and a flannel robe. A former football player, Mark remains broad-shouldered and tall, but his hair is prematurely gray and he looks like he's aged five years in the last two. Deep horizontal lines etch the sides of his mouth. He looks tired, and I'm worried. I love him like a brother.

Mark acknowledges me by squeezing out a wan smile before propping his hands on the kitchen counter. He treats me like a member of the family, but at this moment, his ice-blue eyes are fixed on Louise. She pushes herself off the couch and walks over to meet him. I wonder if he's overheard our conversation.

"You woke me up. Thankfully, the girls are still asleep."

"Henderson died. We were watching the news."

"Henderson? How?"

"Keeled over in the middle of a therapy group."

"Why didn't you wake me?" he snarls.

Louise bristles. "I didn't want you to bite my head off for disturbing you."

"Don't be ridiculous. Of course I'd want to know if Henderson is no longer in the picture!"

Louise takes a deep breath and I notice how hard she seems to be trying to control herself. When she speaks, her tone is even, but frosty. "I'm sorry, then, for not letting you know. Now you do, so perhaps you could just go back upstairs, close your door, and let me talk to Sarah. If your light's on when I come up, I'll come in and talk with you." She turns away.

Mark reaches out and grips her arm. "We have an agreement!"

I stand, stunned. I've never seen Mark grab Louise, not ever. Louise, a black belt in karate, twists his wrist so fast he has no time to respond. I know she could easily snap his arm in half.

"Let go, Louise!" he demands.

She releases him, slapping her hand over her mouth as if shocked by her own behavior. They step away from each other. He encircles his wrist with his other hand, grimacing.

"Mark, I'm sorry, but you should know not to grab me, especially now. I just…"

"Never mind." He cuts her off, looking at me. "I'm sorry you had to see this, Sarah. Neither one of us is on our best behavior these days."

Shock doesn't come close to describing the emotions coursing through me. What the heck is happening with these people I love and know so well? We've spent so much time together, as a foursome when Ryan and I were married, and even more since. I really care about Mark, and he cares about me, but Louise is my best friend.

"I'll wait up." He pulls an ice pack from the freezer and stares at Louise, his eyes sizzling the space between them. "Keep it down, okay? The girls need to sleep through the night."

As we listen to his departing footsteps, I stare into the flames of the gas-fired stove. I'm chilled, and not from the temperature outside—although in Maine we sometimes light fires even in July. I wonder if Louise and Mark will divorce, and if so, whether they'll have to sell the house. We're braided together as an extended family. If they unravel, I fear I will, too.

Louise sinks into the couch beside me, her face bright red, her head in her hands. "I'm so embarrassed. As a therapist specializing in domestic violence, how could I get to the point where I almost broke Mark's wrist? Things are so out of control here. If something doesn't shift, Mark will have to move out."

Before I can respond, the telephone offers another annoying interruption. Louise grabs it.

"Oh, hi, Kate. Uh-huh. Yeah. Just saw it on TV. Sarah's here. No. Why not? Oh, okay. Listen, someone is trying to call on the other line. I'll phone you tomorrow."

I listen to her take another call and she scribbles something on a pad of paper. "Answering service." She rolls her eyes as she hangs up. "I've got a client to call, someone who used to be in treatment with Henderson. We'd both better be prepared for this. I'm sure your caseload has as many former Henderson clients as mine."

"I'll wait. What did Kate want?"

Louise looks out into the yard. "She wants me to keep my big mouth shut, especially if anyone from the news asks me about Henderson." Louise sighs. "I don't think you should wait. This client is a talker. Let's get together tomorrow."

"You sure?" I yawn.

"Yes. Once I get off the phone, I'll need to make nice with Mark."

"Yeah, right, Louise. Making nice is not your strong suit."

"Don't give me a hard time, Sarah. I'm always nice to you."

"Yes, you are." I stand up and hug her. "You still come over to kill spiders. What more could I want in a best friend?"

Louise opens the back door while she dials the phone. "I'll watch you out the window. Flash your outside lights when you get home, so I know you're okay." As kids in camp, we'd signaled with flashlights; not much has changed.

I run home through the wet grass, wondering how many emergency calls I'll be fielding.

My sleep isn't interrupted by clients, but it is, twice, by nightmares—old ones featuring Miriam's murder. As soon as I awake in the morning, I call Louise. "Want to talk over tea?"

"I can't. Things here are pretty tense."

I know Louise won't talk until she's good and ready. But we don't have that conversation the next day either. Over the next few weeks, a lot of our clients go into crisis, including a few new referrals who'd been seeing the late great Harold Henderson. He's dead and buried, but we still can't get rid of him.

Chapter 6

A guitarist stands on the makeshift stage in the middle of Tommy's Park, strumming a familiar folk melody. His sultry-voiced fellow performer belts out the words to an appreciative, oddly mixed audience, typical of those drawn by Portland's art programs. Suited-up executives scarf up spots on park benches beside kids in dreadlocks—all right there on Exchange Street.

It's early yet, but the steady line of cars parts at the crosswalk, allowing me to cross Middle Street. A salty sea breeze wafts in from the harbor, and I pause to collect myself. This will be my first therapy session in a year. Workers polishing the brass fittings on the office entrance step aside as I approach the door, which shines like a beacon.

During the drawn-out disintegration of my marriage, Janice served as a steady support, and my body relaxes as she welcomes me. She hasn't changed much. I'm struck by her graceful bearing and notice a little more silver in her hair. The office looks the same too, white walls bedecked with paintings of doorways, mysterious inviting entrances to the unknown. I sink into one of the cream-colored couches as Janice settles on its twin across from me. Large windows offer a view of Casco Bay. From this vantage point, ferries look like toy ships, sailboats mere specks on a blue sea.

"Thank you so much for squeezing me in this morning. I really appreciate it."

"Of course. I'm happy I had the opening. It's been awhile, Sarah." I feel as if her thoughtful brown eyes take all of me in.

"It has. I've been mostly good, but as you heard during our short call yesterday, I'm starting not to be so good."

"Uh-huh."

"Things are just piling up. I went to court with Louise when she testified against Henderson, then Henderson died. And even before that, I knew I needed to come back in because I've had these sort of... visitations." I pause. "Miriam's shown up. At first I thought I was dreaming, but that's not what's happening. She's really there, and we're having conversations."

"About what?"

"She says she's watching out for me. It's kind of nice, but also rather disconcerting."

"Hmm," Janice responds with the quintessential therapist's murmur.

"After the award ceremony at my alma mater, Miriam's parents drove Ryan and me to the cemetery. We put flowers on Miriam's grave, and each took time alone there. When it was my turn, I suddenly found myself in the middle of a flashback. It was as if I were standing in the middle of that cold sterile morgue again, identifying her body. Ryan noticed that something was wrong and came over. He talked me through it." I look up at Janice and breathe deeply. "I was embarrassed. I thought I had worked through all the effects of this trauma, that I'd done the work I needed to do. But now it's up again." I swallow hard. "I feel as if this is never going to end. Will I ever have a normal life? Will I ever stop feeling as if I should have been able to prevent Miriam's murder?"

"This will change, Sarah," she says. "And you do have a normal life. You are already a gifted therapist yourself. You know the wounds we carry deepen our empathy for our clients, and often allow us to help them find the most effective paths to healing. Don't be so hard on yourself. You've just described a number of reasons why you might have had a flashback. You were in Boston, where Miriam was murdered. You were with Ryan, your ex, and Miriam's dear friend. You gave out an award at the law school from which the three of you graduated. Then you went to court with Louise, and then Henderson died. That's a lot of pressure."

"What about Miriam's visitations?"

"We've talked about your family's psychic skills, and how long you have pushed them aside. Perhaps under these circumstances, they're breaking through. However, let's focus on the things I can help you with, since psychic phenomena are not my bailiwick. We can find other resources to help you with those issues. I am thinking that for now, it would be best to start with the flashback at Miriam's grave. Do you agree?"

"Yes." I reposition myself on the sofa, settling back into the cushions, and begin to acknowledge things to Janice that I haven't been even willing to admit to myself.

"When it happened, my body got very cold. There was a chemical smell, like formaldehyde, or cleaning solutions mixed with something rotten. My heart started to pound and I got dizzy and sweaty, but also numb." I close my eyes. "It's as if I'm really there."

"You know these are symptoms of post-traumatic stress syndrome, right?" Janice's voice is gentle. "Classic flashbacks, yes?"

"I know. And I know what it means. I have to go back into the memories and work them through."

She nods. "Anything else?"

I squirm, uncomfortable to be sharing these doubts about myself, but I push on. "It's pretty clear my conversations with Miriam are psychic phenomena. But I don't want them to be. I don't *want* to be clairvoyant. Honestly, it's enough to have my Aunt Zelda as the family seer."

Janice looks at me thoughtfully. "These may be psychic phenomena. I think it would be good for you to talk with your aunt. But you don't have to focus on all that right now, because there are still trauma issues here to resolve, yes? What do you think about using EMDR?" Janice is referring to a specific type of treatment known as Eye Movement Desensitization and Reprocessing.

Again, I hesitate. Though I use EMDR with my own clients and have no doubts about its effectiveness, I don't really believe anything can help me recover from Miriam's murder. On the other hand, I trust Janice.

"I know you use this protocol in your own practice," she continues. "But here, you're the client, and I'll go through the process with you just the way I would with anyone else."

Relieved, I sink back into the sofa, close my eyes, and listen to Janice's familiar voice.

"Sometimes when we experience a trauma, the shock prevents our brain from engaging in the normal processing of experiences. And the trauma remains unresolved, leaving images, sensations, and feelings too accessible, too easily reignited when our current life mirrors some aspect of what happened in the past. We can become anxious or depressed as a consequence."

I nod.

"So we will reengage the images and the sensory matter, along with the emotional charge held in your right brain, and get that moving to the left side of your brain where language and meaning can be attached to the experience," she says. "We can use light, sound, or the hand tappers to move the material between the two hemispheres of the brain."

"Let's use the light bar." I opt for a marquee-like machine that flashes lights from right to left and back again. "What should I focus on?"

"A distressing scene from the day of Miriam's death."

"Okay." I shift in a futile attempt to get comfortable. "Let's see…" I sigh. "We met for breakfast, near Miriam's Beacon Street apartment, and talked for almost two hours. At first, I groused about the tedium of legal practice. Then Miriam mentioned she'd been having dreams about a troublesome client. The one who was originally assigned to me. She said that in her dreams she was running for her life. She said she was afraid, really afraid."

"What's the worst part of that memory?" Janice asks.

"My feeling that I should have done something to prevent Miriam's murder."

Janice asks a few more questions. I identify my feelings: shame, guilt, and anger.

"Okay, let's go with that," she says, and I begin, allowing my eyes to follow the changing lights, right to left and back again.

Time tilts. Though I know I'm in Janice's office in Portland, I feel as if I'm back in Boston having breakfast with Miriam. "I'd been having dreams too—bad dreams, about Miriam. I kept dreaming of seeing her body on a table in a morgue." I pause, chewing my lip for a moment until I can continue. "And then she really was lying on a table in a morgue."

I reach for my water bottle, but my hand trembles too much to pick it up. "You know, in my flashbacks, she looks exactly the way she did when I had to identify her. But I never told her about the dreams. I didn't have a clue what they meant and didn't want to frighten Miriam."

"Go with that," Janice says, and I return to watching the lights move back and forth.

"What do you get now?" she says.

"I asked Miriam whether she thought the client was stalking her. She said she wasn't sure, but she suspected he was; she'd seen him near her apartment a few times. I suggested she take out a restraining order."

And as I sit in Janice's office, time dissolves, and I'm telling the story from the inside of it, as if it's happening all over again.

"I don't know. I don't want to do that," Miriam says. "There's nothing he's doing that is threatening to me, even though I get the sense he's nearby frequently." She looks around the restaurant and pulls her cardigan more tightly around her. "It sounds paranoid. There isn't anything creepy about him, and there isn't enough for a restraining order. How would I do that anyway? He's my client."

"You can drop him."

"I'm not ready to give up on him." She pauses. "And there's something else that I don't think has anything to do with him."

"What's that?" I ask.

"I'm getting phone calls again."

"Didn't you change your phone number two weeks ago?"

"Yeah. And the calls stopped for two whole days. They're always at night. I hear someone breathing on the other end of the phone, but they don't speak." Miriam's eyes tear up. "It's such an adolescent, high-school-prank kind of thing, but I'm scared."

"We'll figure something out." I reach across the table to take her hand and knock over my teacup. We both watch as a dark stain spreads across the table. "What does Peter suggest?" I ask, referring to the psychiatrist she's dating.

"He wants me to move in with him. He thinks I'll be safer that way, but his hours are awful." Miriam shrugs. "And he's a little quirky. I don't want to rush the relationship just because I'm afraid...of a client."

"Then move in with us. You already have a key to our place. The guest bedroom will become your bedroom."

"I was hoping you'd offer." Miriam smiles.

"Great. That's settled. I'll go call us a cab. Ryan can move your things later." I motion to the waitress for our check. "What about dumping the case?"

Miriam shakes her head. "I can't yet. I don't have a justifiable reason until I know for sure it's this client. Peter helped me arrange a psychiatric evaluation for the guy. I'll know more after that." She pauses, stares at the floor. "I like this client. That's what's so odd. But he may be mentally unstable. Maybe he's obsessed with me, maybe not. His history is strange, and the criminal case is all about a break-in at the research lab where he used to work. You remember, don't you, that he was also charged with assault—when he went back to confront his supervisor after he'd been fired?"

I bite my bottom lip. "I remember. I think you should dump him as a client."

"If the psychiatrist says there's a problem, I'll do it."

We stand up. I pay the check. "Let's go back to my place."

"Not just yet," Miriam protests. "I have research to do at the law library for a trial tomorrow."

"Are you crazy?" I shriek. "If you really have to do research, Ryan and I will take you to the law library later. There's safety in numbers."

"Let's not exaggerate the risk or make this more problematic than it has to be," Miriam says. "I can go to the library now and take a cab to your apartment after I'm done."

"Miriam, I listened to what you just told me. Carefully. This guy is already facing an assault charge. The whole thing's giving me the creeps. Why risk it? Just come home with me now and do the research later."

"I'm the one who is supposed to be anxious." Miriam pokes me. "And I think the law library's safe enough. I'll need to stop at my apartment for my briefcase, though."

"There's no way you're going anywhere without me glued to your side."

"Fine. Come with me to the apartment. I'll pack and you can take my suitcase to Brookline while I go to the library."

"No. I'll help you pack and we'll both go to the law library."

She looks at my narrowed eyes. "You are being ridiculous. I have no idea how long I'll have to be there. Just help me pack and take my clothes to your house. I'll take a cab to the library. You can even wait and watch me get into it. When I finish my research, I'll take another cab right to your house. Now back off!"

"Okay," I say reluctantly. We march down the brick sidewalks to Beacon Street. I scan every passerby. At her apartment, we fill two suitcases and argue again about the afternoon's itinerary. She wins. We call for cabs. She takes one to the library, and I take the other home to Brookline. An accident snarls traffic into a nightmarish gridlock and my ride takes an hour instead of twenty minutes. Ryan meets me at the curb, his face ashen.

"What's wrong? Did something happen to Miriam?"

He wraps his arms around me and we sink onto the front steps.

"What happened? Where is she?" I can barely get the words out.

"Someone shot her in front of the law library. The police phoned half an hour ago. Our number was in her wallet."

"What hospital is she in? Let's go there right now."

"Sarah"—Ryan's voice breaks—"She's not at a hospital."

"What do you mean?" I pull away from Ryan and stand up.

"Miriam is dead. The police are waiting for us at the morgue."

My body begins to tremble.

I couldn't control the shaking in my arms and legs, not then with Ryan, and not now in Janice's office. I knew the truth; I'd seen it before it happened. I'd seen it in my dreams.

"Sarah?" Janice's voice pulls me back to the present. "What's happening now?"

"Janice, I know I did what everyone does when tragedy happens. I reviewed it incessantly. I kept wondering, what could I have done differently? If only I'd told her about my dreams, maybe she'd have come back to Brookline with me, and she'd still be alive. Each time I imagined a different action, I also imagined Miriam still alive."

"Go with that," she says and refocuses me on the light bar.

Reality has never changed. Miriam is dead. In the years since, I've cycled through the stages of grief, and cycled through them again, but I've never gotten over the loss. I see that clearly now, as the movie plays in my mind and I remember more details. My level of agitation lessens, as does my guilt, but now I'm angry at Miriam for being so damn stubborn.

We end the session with clinical hypnosis, a way of accessing deep states of relaxation that can enhance therapy. Today, the focus is on dissipating any residual distress by anchoring deep relaxation in my body. Janice suggests imagining a place of serenity. I describe my favorite beach in Florida. The sand is white and soft, the sky is a beautiful blue, seagulls wheel overhead, and playful dolphins break the surface of the warm water. She repeats the descriptions back to me. My breath becomes more even, and I'm calmer. Janice brings me back to the present, and we schedule another session for early the following week.

"Don't hesitate to call me if you need to come in sooner," she says.

I leave more hopeful and determined, but cautious. It took courage to wade through these memories, but I'm well aware that there's a lot more work for me to do before the guilt, grief, and horror can be siphoned out of my cells.

Sunlight shimmers on Casco Bay as I walk along the waterfront. Fishermen are hauling in traps. People are walking dogs, riding bikes, living their lives. The relaxation Janice and I did before I left her office is enhanced by my focus on being here, now, in the present—alive, aware, and grounded. With that, I can step back into my own role as a psychotherapist.

The whole week is intense, with new clients to get to know, and regular clients deep in their own work. I love this profession. As a social worker in private practice, I appreciate the way people trust me with their feelings and long-held secrets, their fears and insecurities. I love holding an image of how they will be when we have completed our work—healthier, happier, more settled in themselves. Those images buoy me on the days we walk in darkness. I trust that together we will craft a path through it.

Thursday night Miriam appears again, floating into the room, sitting in the chair, and humming before she finally speaks. "I just want you to get used to seeing me. I'm here as your guardian. I didn't tell you that last time, but things are going to be happening that challenge you to grow into your fullest self. You can do it, and I'll be here to help you."

"I'm glad to hear that, Miriam, but we have past history to deal with. Do you know how guilty I feel about your death? Do you know responsible I feel for not making sure you came home with me to Brookline?"

Miriam's gaze is magnetizing. "It wasn't your fault," she says. "You tried your hardest to get me to go home with you. You offered to come with me to the library. I insisted on going to the law library by myself. You could not have done anything more. It was my fate to die that day and in that way, and you are not responsible for my death."

It's good to hear that from her, and I wonder if receiving absolution from Miriam will allow me to move on. Yet I don't feel completely reassured, because I am clearly talking with her ghost, and she evaporates as I watch. I take what might be the slowest, longest, and deepest breath of my life.

Chapter 7

An untouted benefit of the psychotherapy profession is the opportunity to submerge oneself in other people's problems and entirely avoid one's own. The opposite is also true. Sometimes our clients' issues are all too reminiscent of our own.

On Monday morning, while I am fumbling with the keys to my cottage-style office, a taxi squeals into the driveway. The first thing I see as the back door of the cab opens is a pair of six-inch, periwinkle, stiletto heels.

The shoes adorn the long legs of Louise's client, Harriet Connors. I can't help thinking Harriet's willowy frame is a perfect advertisement for Levi's. I should look that good in a pair of jeans. A sky-blue cashmere cardigan and glittering gold hoop earrings top off Harriet's outfit. Absorbing every detail, I hope to snag some tips from the internationally known model, though I can't even stand, much less walk, in a pair of high heels.

"Hi, Sarah. I saw you on the steps and wanted to, um, drop this off for Louise." She hastily scribbles a check and tears it from her ledger.

"Are you okay?" Distress radiates from her dark eyes. I wonder when Harriet last saw her psychiatrist, my mentor, Jim Barr. Although I'm sure Harriet and Louise are doing good work in therapy, Jim manages Harriet's medications and does her clinical hypnosis.

"I'm fine," Harriet says. As she nods, the highlights in her auburn hair gleam in the sun. "I just had to cancel my appointment with Louise.

I'm on my way to the airport, but I saw you here, and, well, that gives me a chance to drop off this check." She bends over, enfolding me in a hug and the ambience of Chanel No. 5. "Say goodbye for me, will you?"

"Where are you headed?"

"The Adriatic coast. Last-minute assignment."

I wave goodbye and walk into the cottage, simultaneously envious and aware that a glamorous life can't erase the pain of past trauma. Louise had referred Harriet to me for clinical hypnosis, but her situation was so complex that I recommended she see Jim. He has much more expertise.

While plumping the pillows on the tweedy gray sofa in the waiting room, I think about the war between Harriet's therapists, Louise and Jim and Henderson. Intense hostility arose after Constant Caring refused to pay for Harriet's hospital stay, one recommended jointly by Louise and Jim. They appealed the company's denial. Then Henderson retaliated. He slowed down payments to Louise and removed Jim from the "approved provider" list. That meant Jim's clients had to pay him directly and submit their receipts to the insurance company. Since services by non-approved providers are reimbursed, if at all, at a lesser rate, some of Jim's clients left his practice for in-network psychiatrists. Jim's lawsuit against Constant Caring is still pending. I wonder how Henderson's death will impact that lawsuit.

I step into Louise's spacious, light-filled office, the former living room of the house, scribble a note, and set it down on her desk with Harriet's check, before climbing upstairs to my office, a former bedroom perched amid the treetops. The room is filled with green plants in cheery Italian pots. When I work nights, the wide windows offer a view of the sunset splashing pink and orange across the sky. Today, a birdsong serenade greets me. I soak in the mid-May sunlight bouncing off the creamy yellow walls and sit in my comfy chintz armchair to do a short meditation.

The timeout is replenishing, and my first client session flows smoothly. A woman who began having panic attacks after the death of her father has begun to respond well to our sessions. She reports on the changes in her life since she began incorporating mindfulness meditation at home. Her relief is palpable. So is mine.

My second session is a different story. The couple I'm counseling,

Todd and Elena Owens, present many challenges, partly because Portland is such a small city. Todd Owens is George Tate's first cousin, and Elena Owens and Brooke Hart Tate became close friends as cousins-in-law. Sometimes figuring out the boundaries in such situations is as difficult as working on the clients' issues. And of course, the ubiquitous managed-care company, Constant Caring, is involved, as Todd, a lawyer, is a major shareholder and board member. Todd and Elena arrive ten minutes late.

Elena stomps into the office. "I can't stand when you do that!"

"Could you please control yourself?" Todd spits through a clenched jaw.

"You're completely inconsiderate. It's all about you, all the time." Elena takes a seat on the peach striped couch. "We're late because Todd had to stop at Starbucks for his coffee. He couldn't get ready a few minutes early or wait to have it after the session. No, not Todd. Todd wants something, Todd gets it, no matter who's inconvenienced."

Todd glares at Elena. "You just don't stop, do you? Complain, complain, complain. Is there anything I do right?"

Contempt suffuses his tone, and I feel myself reacting with a wave of intense dislike. I remind myself that his contempt might be a symptom of the problems in the marriage and that the issues are between Todd and Elena, not Todd and me. "Perhaps you could describe the sequence of events this morning, the ones that got you both so angry?"

"Sure." Elena's nostrils flare. "I woke early, as usual, threw on my exercise clothes, race-walked with a friend, returned home in time to feed the kids, got them dressed, drove them to school, and drove back to the house to shower and dress. Todd here—" she flips her hand toward him dismissively, "took his sweet time shaving, showering, and putting on his three-piece suit. Then he sat at the dining room table with *The New York Times* and an English muffin. The days we see you at ten o'clock, the routine is changed, because he's normally at the office by eight or nine, but no matter what is on the schedule, while I'm getting the kids ready, Todd reads the *Times* and starts on *The Wall Street Journal*. He usually finishes the *Journal* at the office, except on the mornings we're scheduled to see you. On these days, he makes a point of not leaving the house until he finishes both papers, as if to indicate how unimportant marriage counseling is to him. Today, we only have one car, so I'm dropping him at the office after the session. Of course, this morning, he insisted on stopping at Starbucks, which made us late."

"So we're ten minutes late for the session. What's the big deal?" Todd lifts his chin and stares at me. "She doesn't care as long as we pay her fee."

"In fact, Todd, I do care." The words fall from my mouth before I can catch myself—his arrogant tone and contemptuous attitude are too hard to ignore. "When you show up for sessions late, it can be symbolic—an indication that you don't take the process seriously or that you're avoiding the work. It demonstrates your level of commitment or lack of it—to therapy, to your relationship, and to yourself."

"It's my commitment to my marriage that's the issue, not my commitment to you." Todd says, his voice imbued with disdain. I scan his lawyerly face, noting how it's permeated with carefully cultivated intimidation.

He doesn't scare me. I simply take a breath, so my response will be more therapeutic than lawyerly. "Well, Todd, Elena seems to be upset by what she describes as the sense of entitlement she experiences from you, along with a disregard for her needs. What do you think about that?"

"I think Elena has an idea in her head of how people should behave, and I don't always fit her tidy little model."

"What does that mean?" Despite all my training and my awareness that the conflicts between couples usually have deep roots, I'm snagged so hard I revert to lawyer mode. I want to take Todd on, as if we're arguing a point of law before a judge and jury.

"Ask Elena." He sips the last of his coffee and sets the cup on the end table beside his chair. I watch coffee seep from the bottom of the cup and form a puddle on the maple tabletop. Could he possibly be more insolent?

"Why don't *you* ask Elena?" I say. "And while you're at it, please deal with the puddle under your coffee cup."

Todd directs an icy stare at me before slowly lifting a tissue from the box beside him and setting it on the table. He lays another tissue on top of the first, watches as they soak up the puddle, crushes them in his hand, and pushes them down into the cup. Instead of dropping everything into the small wicker trash pail next to his chair, he tosses the cup and its contents across the room into a larger trashcan next to my desk. I wait to see if he makes the basket. Lucky for us both, he does.

The session continues to careen downhill. Elena accuses Todd of spending too much time on his board work for Constant Caring and neglecting the family to help his cousin, George Tate. Todd's face turns to stone when she refers to the company's lack of ethics. Meanwhile, my response to Todd's defensiveness makes me question my aptitude for social work. Okay, he doesn't seem the least bit interested in his wife or therapy, but he's here, so it's my job to help his marriage, not to react to provocation or fire off questions as if my clients are hostile witnesses under cross-examination. Psychotherapy training encompasses diverse approaches, but rapid-fire interrogation is not in the recommended repertoire.

The session ends on the dot of eleven. I feel awash in feelings of incompetence, but push on. My next client is a thirty-eight-year-old woman whose mother is dying of cancer. We talk through a variety of ways she can support her mother, a proud and independent woman who doesn't wish to discuss her illness. We sort through resources in the community that can support them both, and my client leaves the session more accepting of her mother's coping style, and more aware of her own.

I break for lunch and start again at one o'clock. This session is with a young father who recently recovered memories of childhood sexual abuse. His son just reached the age of six, which was the age he was when his abuser began targeting him. The session is painful for both of us, but we settle on trauma treatment modalities that will help him reprocess the experiences and eventually move on in his life. It is difficult to see clients with trauma histories and not take in the pain of their experiences. Often it's not just difficult, but impossible. Making sure I schedule days off, meditating, doing yoga, and letting myself have plenty of time to focus on other things are all strategies that help me and other therapists avoid feeling inundated by the pain we witness. Though I think about my clients when I am not in session, I also make sure to compartmentalize. My commitment to working with trauma survivors requires building time-outs in my life so I don't burn out. My next client isn't until three, so I head downstairs to see if Louise is free. Her door is wide open.

"Hi," she says. "How's your day going? My phone hasn't stopped ringing."

"Any good news?" I ask.

"Yes. Brooke got full custody. George will only see the kids with supervised visits right now."

"That's great," I say. "Congratulations."

"On another note," Louise sighs, "I've had a number of calls from past and present clients who saw Henderson before coming to me, and even more calls from trauma clients who've read about his death. Clients with early life losses. Reading these newspaper articles about Henderson's death is setting them off. They're worried that I will die, like their father or mother—and Henderson. Abandonment issues are up in many of my sessions too. Are you seeing that?"

"I am," I say. "But I hadn't connected the dots yet. Thanks for clarifying the precipitants."

"Quite a few of my clients today have wanted to discuss Henderson's death. I fear my relief at his departure from the planet is impairing my ability to dredge up an appropriate amount of empathy," Louise says.

"My day hasn't been so good either," I laugh, leaning against the doorjamb, watching Louise paw through paper clips, note pads, and the odd assortment of pens and pencils in her desk drawer. She turns to look at me, and a shaft of sunlight illuminates her long red hair.

"Come in and have a cup of tea." Louise points to a floral teapot. Her blue eyes scan my face before she resumes riffling through her desk.

"Are things any better between you and Mark?"

"We had another fight this morning, so I'd have to say no." Her freckles look dark against her unusually pale face.

It's a shock to see her marriage under such serious strain. It was seven years ago when Ryan and I moved in with Mark and Louise and their daughter, Naomi, a few months after Miriam's death, when I couldn't stand living in Boston anymore. We remained in Portland after Ryan found a plum position at a local firm. When the hip roof colonial right next door to Louise and Mark went on the market, Ryan and I snatched it up before the For Sale sign made it onto the lawn.

The four of us spent a good deal of time together. Then, during my divorce, Louise and Mark held me together. After Ryan moved back to Boston, I settled in as part of their family. Mark helps me with routine household maintenance. Their two daughters, Naomi, now an adolescent, and Susie, now six, sleep at my house once a month, and I frequently have Shabbos dinner with Louise's mother Kitty, a retired history professor. The confidences Louise and I have shared over the years have kept us both relatively sane, so her silence now confounds me.

"Does any of your trouble with Mark have to do with Henderson?"

"Why do you say that?" Louise snaps her head around and stares at me.

"Take it easy. I'm only asking because Mark's reaction to Henderson's death surprised me."

"Why should it surprise you? Henderson was harassing me. Of course, Mark would want to know."

"Okay." I take a breath and try another tack. "Do you want to tell me what's really going on with you and Mark and your marriage?"

"I do and I don't." Louise stares out the window. "I have clients to see, and if I focus on my own distress, it'll get in the way of my ability to be present for them. That reminds me. How did Harriet seem to you? I'm perplexed about her departure. In her last few sessions, she insisted she wanted to stay put, here in town, in her own house, for at least a few months."

"She seemed stressed, but she also said this was a last-minute assignment."

"Well, I'll call her, make sure she's okay." Louise turns toward me. "How did your sessions go this morning?"

"I'm afraid I mangled one."

Louise smiles as she finally finds what she's looking for and extricates a bag of trail mix from her drawer. She spins around in her chair, swings her legs onto an ottoman, and gestures to the couch off to her left. "Sit already."

Slipping off my shoes and padding across Louise's Oriental rug always leaves me marveling at her ability to snag bargains at Home Goods. "I totally blew this couple's session," I say, feeling my face flush with embarrassment. "They wrote me a check, but I'm not sure I was entitled to it."

Louise waves her hand dismissively. "That's an exaggeration. Your work with couples is stellar."

"Not today." I sink into the green-leather sofa and begin combing my hands through my unruly curls, piling my hair on top of my head and pinning it up before taking it all down. I developed that anxious habit back when I was practicing law. I'd been oblivious, until a colleague disclosed the betting pool he ran on the number of times I'd fiddle with my hair before it was my turn to cross-examine. Another reason I left that field. Who wanted to work with colleagues like that?

"Earth to Sarah." Louise slices through my distraction. "What happened in the session?"

"I'm not sure." I sip tea and watch Louise paw through the bag of trail mix and pop a handful into her mouth. She dangles it invitingly in my direction.

Even from a distance, it's clear that trail mix has been in her drawer for some time. Nevertheless, I'm tempted. I'm always tempted. The brightly colored M&Ms nestled among nuts and raisins call out to me, but for the moment, I resist. My weight hovers at the tip-top of the height and weight chart. I'm five-four, and an extra fifteen pounds adorns my breasts and hips; it's a struggle to accept the fact that my body will always be curvy, never model-thin. Restraining myself rarely works, since my resolve disintegrates almost as soon as I start a diet. "No, thanks. Can I talk about this case?"

"Of course."

"In a funny way, a very small way, the guy reminds me of Ryan." I pause thoughtfully. "They're both corporate lawyers. This client likes the status and money and power, and sometimes, you know, I wonder if Ryan doesn't also enjoy all of that."

"Why shouldn't he?"

"Because I wanted him to stick with public-service law, that's why!"

"Oh, Sarah," Louise says. "The corporate law thing always gets you, doesn't it? You can't imagine that anyone working for the big bad corporations can be ethical. But Ryan is ethical and always has been. Maybe this guy isn't, but be careful about comparisons."

"You're right, of course, but this guy seems to trigger me. He doesn't want to be in therapy."

"Nothing new about that. Most men who come to couples therapy don't want to be here."

"True. But there's more. There's something really hard and contemptuous about him. The contempt makes me think he's narcissistic— he might actually have a narcissistic personality disorder. I wonder, occasionally, if there's something else, like if he's a little crazy." I look up and smile. "Very astute clinical observation, wouldn't you say?"

Louise laughs. She knows I prefer to work with clients who struggle with the normal challenges of living. Clients with personality disorders are much more difficult for me. Their flaws are so deeply embedded that change is difficult if not impossible. Often, they don't want to change. They don't think they need to. Todd certainly doesn't think he needs to, and like Todd, those with such disorders frequently only enter therapy at the insistence of family members.

"Ryan certainly isn't narcissistic," Louise says. "And the only crazy thing about him is how crazy he is about you."

She's right. For years that love was mutual. During the first week of law school, Miriam caught me staring at Ryan O'Malley, a tall, reddish-blond, Robert Redford lookalike. She scribbled in ink across my legal procedures textbook, "You're going to marry this guy." I laughed, earning the enmity of our pompous professor for the rest of the semester. I had mixed feelings about my first year law classes. I loved some classes, felt incredibly challenged by others, and totally bored by one or two. I dealt with boredom by writing notes to Miriam and lusting after Ryan.

Louise stands up, stretches her arms overhead, and bends down to touch her toes. I slide down the couch into the yoga corpse position, flat on my back, legs straight out, arms at my sides, and cover myself with a purple throw. I watch Louise straighten up, wishing I had her lithe body. She began dance at age six and still takes classes. Taller and twenty pounds thinner than me, she inhabits her almost boyish body in a fluid, seamless way. She envies my larger breasts, and I envy the way her weight never fluctuates, despite the fact that she always eats twice as much as me.

"Anything about this guy's appearance that reminds you of Ryan?"

"No, not at all, except they're both tall." I pause, comparing them in my mind. "Ryan's got that classic Boston-Irish, slightly freckled sexiness, while this guy is polished. He's blond, with green eyes, New England been-here-since-the-landing-at-Plymouth-Rock. He's condescending—you know, in the way attorneys in Armani suits working for big firms can be." I hesitate. "In sessions, he's antagonistic, both to his wife and me. He annoys me—well, today he infuriated me. I often can't stop myself from arguing with him, as if I am taking his wife's place in the tussle."

"I'm sure it was worse for you than for him." Louise laughs.

"That'll be clear if they cancel the next session." I squirm, then start thinking about Ryan, and soon I'm extending my hand to Louise. "Can I have the trail mix?"

Louise tosses me the bag. I pick through for the perfect combination—a peanut, a raisin, and an M&M—as memories float up from storage. Ryan came so close to what my mother wanted for me, except he wasn't Jewish and wouldn't convert. The fact that these issues were a thorn in my mother's side made Ryan even more attractive to me. During our marriage, Ryan completely charmed my mother, and they've stayed in touch despite our divorce.

"Sarah." Louise again breaks through my reverie, waving her hand in my field of vision.

Thank God for Louise. I've relied on her since that first day at camp. She emanates wisdom and strength, and her tender caretaking helped me survive both Miriam's murder and my divorce.

"Close your eyes and picture your clients," she suggests. "What do you feel in your body?"

"Tension. I've absorbed their anger. They're arguing about her dislike for his cousin and his refusal to curtail both the relationship and his role on the corporate board." I pause, recognizing the convoluted conversation I've just stepped into without having thought it through. There's no way to avoid discussing Constant Caring.

Of course, I won't mention the name of the board in question, which would violate client confidentiality, but I believe I can discuss this with Louise if I tread carefully. Therapists can discuss clients with colleagues, as long as we don't identify them. And we still have to remain aware of conflicts of interest. In this case, Louise's lawsuit against Constant Caring hasn't been eliminated by Henderson's death. She'll undoubtedly notice Todd and Elena in the waiting room, if she hasn't already, and know who they are soon enough. It won't take much for her to connect Todd with the insurance company. I clear my throat and buy a few seconds of time to shift the focus. "His wife wants him to resign from the board."

Louise frowns. "When Ryan went from fighting big insurers to defending them, it strained your marriage, so I can see how this guy's corporate affiliations would bring up uncomfortable associations. But there's got to be more to this."

I nod. When Ryan switched allegiances, I said he was choosing the dark side. He said I was being sanctimonious. "This guy's defensive and challenging and hard. He's got a Clint Eastwood kind of attitude, and in the session today, I was thinking he's incapable of change, he's a complete jerk, and his wife should divorce him. Thankfully, I caught myself." I sigh. My eyes communicate way too clearly what I'm thinking, and I've been told when I'm angry the color shifts, with shades of copper infusing the hazel.

"What else?" Louise rolls her hand, indicating I should continue.

"I felt as if he was challenging me, and I took it personally."

"Uh-huh. I think this is indicative of the depth of your client's problem, that you got riled up in some way. That happens, as you know, when the level of disturbance is so deep. When the client has a personality disorder."

I know she's right. And, as therapists, we have to be on our toes, doing our own work, or our personal issues can get triggered by our clients' problems. Clearly, a lot is going on with Todd and Elena Owens, but the ghost in the therapy room that really needs exorcising is the failure of my own marriage.

After Miriam's murder, I was too traumatized to practice law or stay in Boston. Ryan accommodated my need to start our lives over elsewhere by taking the corporate law job in Portland, which meant leaving public service.

A memory of a formal dinner at the firm's favorite country club floats up. Too much alcohol impaired my ability to contain my disdain for his clients' crowing over the latest corporate acquisition. On the uncomfortable drive home, Ryan highlighted the deterioration in our marriage, the lack of respect we'd begun evidencing for each other's life choices. We went to couples therapy, where I accused him of being rigid and defensive. He said I was critical and self-righteous. We were both right.

I reach into my purse, blindly searching for my Ruby Red lipstick—fingering pens, pencils, lifesavers, and a variety of unidentifiable objects before locating it. Since childhood, I've been seduced by lipstick's transformative power. It's like a totem, providing an irrationally dependable, instantaneous boost of self-esteem. Standing in front of a mirror on Louise's wall, I spread Ruby Red on my lips. Ah, immediate relief.

"I have to be on my toes. Couples work is difficult enough for happily married therapists, but especially for those of us who are divorced. I'm vulnerable after just being with Ryan. He also sent me an email, which I didn't even get a chance to tell you about." I lean against the wall and stare out the window. "Quite a bit of my emotional energy remains tied up with Ryan, and I've got to clean up my own issues before they slide into more of my sessions."

"Don't beat yourself up. We all get hooked. There also may be something else going on with this couple, something that has nothing to do with what it looks like on the surface. As a therapist, you don't have to be psychic to unconsciously pick up on things you don't or can't understand until later."

I think about that until my three o'clock client arrives. The session flows smoothly, and I finish my day making sure my notes are complete, my billing up to date, and the calls that came in during sessions are answered. At 5:30, ready to head home, I am suddenly aware of how much Louise's earlier comment unsettled me. I wish I weren't psychic. I don't want Miriam showing up in my bedroom again, as much as I miss her. I don't want to be that person who can talk to the dead. I love the insights about clients that spontaneously come to me, but how can I know whether my clinical judgment is based on knowledge and experience or psychic intuition? It's clearly time to talk to my aunt, to delve into these questions more deeply in my own therapist's office, and to schedule a consult with Jim Barr. I may not want to accept reality, but I have no choice.

Chapter 8

Our work is intense, with clients struggling through all the challenges life presents—death, divorce, illness, job losses, memories of abuse and trauma. Tuesday night, after a very long day, I look out the window and see Louise on her front porch. I grab an iced tea from my fridge and walk out the door. It's a flawless evening, the air is warm, and a light breeze ruffles my hair as I walk over. "I'm beat but not ready to sleep yet," I say.

"Me too. The girls went to bed hours ago, and I just want to sit here on the porch and rock a bit," Louise says.

"Not that I want to make it more difficult for you to get to sleep tonight, but I have a question," I say. "Are any of your clients being interviewed by the police? Some of mine, former clients of Henderson's, are scheduled for interviews."

"Mine too. I'm not sure what's going on, and Kate hasn't said much. Maybe someone did kill him." She shivers. "I don't want to talk about him."

"We're going to have to at some point. You had that altercation in the courthouse, you visited him in his office, and I charged into his office to see if you were really there. We might have to talk about that with the police because he died just a few hours later."

Louise jumps up and paces the porch, running her hands through her hair. "I know, I know," she says. But I can't go there now. Can we drop it until we have to deal with it?"

"It's not like you to avoid things like this," I say. "And you can't avoid it forever."

"I am not talking about forever. Geez! And you don't know everything about me. There were times in my life when I was a champion avoider. Sometimes that skill makes a comeback, like right now."

"Okay, okay, I'll move on," I say, sipping my tea through a red-and-white-striped straw. I cross my legs beneath me on the porch swing. Louise, mollified, sits down, picks up her knitting, and rocks back and forth in a white painted rocker, almost in time with the clicking of her knitting needles.

"I've packed all my clients sessions into Monday, Tuesday and Wednesday this week like you have. Those will be long days, but my Thursday clients were really accommodating about switching their times. They know anything I learn at the Thursday workshops at the Boston conference will just deepen our work. I can't do this too often, because some clients really prefer the early morning or late evening appointments, but those are tougher times for me. What about you?" I ask.

"Same thing. If we scheduled according to our clients preferences, we'd be working until eight every night and all day Saturday. We have to be careful to make our private practices work for ourselves too, especially given how much trauma treatment we both do."

"In terms of the conference, what do you think about leaving here at six thirty a.m. Thursday? I think I can do it, and that way we can arrive in time for the first workshops. Can you do it?"

"Yes."

"The schedule looks good for Thursday, plenty of solid workshops on trauma treatment. Friday has other workshops that interest me, but I'm not compelled by the offerings on Saturday."

"I'm fine with the workshops Thursday and Friday. I think trying to stay for Saturday will over-saturate me. I'd rather play in Boston Saturday morning and drive home in the afternoon."

"Great," I say. "I'll be on call for my clients, but I'm not expecting any emergencies."

I stand and crane my neck to get a better view of the stars. "Look at how gorgeous this sky is."

Louise stands beside me and we watch a falling star. "It's such a beautiful night," she says.

"We're lucky to live here. Speaking of living here, I need your advice. Do you think I should call Ryan now or wait until we get to the conference? I didn't respond to his note because I'm feeling so vulnerable. And you know I'm still so sexually attracted to him."

"I know that." Louise smiles. "And he's finally doing the work in therapy you always wanted him to do."

"Exactly. It's easy to be seduced into thinking we can make it work."

"How many times have you tried that?"

"Too many to count." I look away. "The only reason I haven't cancelled on the conference is because you're coming with me. Your presence will curtail the temptation."

Louise snorts. "I'm not going to be your buffer."

The next night, Louise walks into my house, plops down on the lavender sofa in my living room, and dispels any hope I have that she's reconsidering that pronouncement. "I'm sorry, Sarah, but I can't go to the conference. I've been so busy with clients that I didn't notice Susie was a bit off. She came down with a bug tonight. Mark took care of her until I got home but she's still rather ill. My mom is unavailable this weekend, and Mark is scheduled for a business meeting in Massachusetts Friday that he can't cancel."

"What's wrong with Susie?"

"She's got a stomach bug. I can't leave her with a sitter when she's throwing up."

"Of course not." I unpin my hair and comb my fingers through the curls. "Mark won't change his plans?"

"He insists he can't."

"I'm sorry," I say. "For Susie, for you, and for me! Damn, another trip to Boston by myself. This is really challenging for me, but I can do it. My only real concern is whether I can connect with Ryan and still keep an appropriate distance if you're not there."

"I never said I'd be your stand-in for self-control. You need to see him, but don't sleep with him, or you'll make yourself and me totally crazy! Neither of us needs that right now."

She gives me a quick hug before leaving, and I rearrange my plans to travel solo, ditching the train reservations and driving to Boston by myself early the next morning. That's my insurance—that the car will provide an immediate escape should one be needed. It's like choosing the seats in a room where you can see all the exits—war veterans aren't the only people who scope out those spots.

The Thursday workshops on trauma are packed with compelling information and new details about the effectiveness of treatment. I am glad I came to the conference. Despite the painful case examples, new therapy techniques are dramatically shifting the capacity of clients to heal, and shortening the length of time needed for effective therapy. That night, while curled up under a soft comforter in the hotel's air-conditioned room, and listening to a relaxation CD, sleep comes easily.

Something awakens me, and I open my eyes to see Miriam sitting at the foot of my bed. "Hey, what are you doing here? Do I need protection?"

"We haven't been in Boston together since I was alive. I know you've had trouble coming down here since my death, and I wanted to make sure you're okay."

I sigh. "I do avoid this city, and right now I'm a bit challenged about when to call Ryan. He was wonderful when I had that flashback about you, you know the one I had at your grave?"

"I do know," Miriam says. "I was aware of what was happening to you at the time, but it wasn't the right place for me to make an appearance."

"Ryan also wrote me a sweet note that I've yet to answer. I want to see him, and I'm going to call him, but I'm afraid of getting involved again."

"Trust yourself. You'll make the right decision."

"Really?"

"Really. It's Ryan, honey. It's only about love, not death. Clear things up with him. It's way past time for you to figure out whether you can move forward or finally let go. Just do it." Miriam blows me a kiss and floats up before disappearing.

The clock reads three in the morning, but it's the end of sleep for me. This visit with Miriam unsettles me for many reasons. Is she going to be making regular appearances? If so, how many friends can I share that new reality with? Maine is a small state. News gets around. Is this going to mean I can't be real with everyone I know? Will colleagues think I'm weird and stop referring clients? Miriam was pretty definite when she said I should call Ryan and clear things up. Am I ready? I mull the questions for an hour before pulling a novel from my suitcase and reading until daybreak. Before I leave the room for my first morning workshop, I dial Aunt Zelda and leave another message, saying I really need to talk. I wonder why I haven't heard back from her.

The first workshop Friday morning focuses on mother–daughter relationships, and is so dead-on in its discussion of typical conflicts that it sends my mind tripping over my relationship with my own mother. Despite my personal work in therapy, along with my awareness that my mother truly loves me, a few choice words from her can still eviscerate my self-esteem. My life choices have never pleased her, including my move to Maine. She's an intelligent, well-traveled woman who believes civilization is centered in Manhattan and ends in northern Connecticut. She was less than thrilled when I moved to Boston, but Maine—a state she believes is primarily populated by forest rangers and wild animals—is entirely off the map. In my mom's cosmology, no sane Jew whose forbearers escaped Siberia would choose to cohabitate with bears in vast stretches of frozen landscape.

The next workshop is a panel discussion on divorce, which, predictably, triggers my own unresolved issues instead of illuminating any understanding of my clients' dilemmas. My marriage dissolved after Ryan's ultimatum: either I was in or out. He'd been headhunted by a prestigious Boston firm offering a partnership track, and he wanted it.

I loved him, but I couldn't move back to Boston, especially not to be the wife of a corporate lawyer. He loved me, but he wasn't willing to be limited by my fears or judgments. We separated and reconciled like yo-yos for two years, until we were burnt out enough to divorce. Like most couples, after the court severed our legal ties, the emotional ones remained. We continued to try to get back together, then cut off contact, then reengaged. We'd been out of touch for six months before Miriam's award and gravesite visit.

I dial Ryan's number and his secretary puts me right through.

"Hey there." I try to keep my voice light and breezy. "I'm in town for a conference, and I thought I'd call and say hi, and let you know I got your email."

"What a pleasant surprise, Sarah, and great timing. I finished up a trial unexpectedly early yesterday. I'm signing a few papers right now and planning to start the weekend early. I'd love to see you."

Hearing his voice dissolves my hesitation. "I'd like to see you, too."

"How about lunch at the Boston Harbor Hotel?"

"Sounds good."

"Shall I pick you up or would you rather meet there?"

I choose the latter and pack, figuring I'll ditch the afternoon work-shops and drive back to Maine…well…when I'm ready.

En route to the Boston Harbor Hotel, I wonder how much of my yearning for Ryan is influenced by the fear that no one else will ever love me. After handing my keys to the valet, walking into the lobby, and tak-ing one look at Ryan, I know my attraction has nothing to do with fear.

A weathered leather jacket is slung over his shoulder. His face is tanned and freckled, his hair more blond now than red. He looks so sexy that at first I can't catch my breath, but when his arms wrap around me, I begin to relax.

"I'm happy you called," he says, his breath tickling my ear. "I've been thinking about you since the award ceremony, and it's been mak-ing me crazy."

"Isn't that my job in life?"

He smiles. "I take it you weren't sure you were going to call me?"

"No, I was—"

"Sure? Yeah, uh-huh." He tucks a curl behind my ear.

"I just hadn't—"

"Gotten to it yet?" Ryan's eyebrows rise. "Never mind. You're here now." He clasps my hand and motions to the hostess. She seats us at a round table covered by a white tablecloth and topped by a vase of fresh flowers.

Ryan asks how I've been doing since the flashback. I tell him about going back to therapy, and then fill him in on Louise's court experience and, with the distance, laugh about my dread. I describe Louise and Henderson's fireworks in the testimony, the scene in the ladies' room with the DA, and Henderson's subsequent death. We puzzle over the circumstances, I add my concern about Louise and Mark's marriage, and then we move on. Ryan entertains me with stories about mutual friends from our law-school days. He talks about his work—selectively, I assume, choosing cases that won't provoke a recoil from me.

The sexual yearning evoked by his presence wallops me, and I'm high from the scones, the many pots of black tea laden with cream and sugar…and Ryan's nearness.

The atmosphere changes, however, when he says, "It's so great to laugh with you, but I want to get serious too, and talk to you about my work in therapy."

"And I want to hear all about that."

He takes a moment, holds my gaze, then speaks. "Therapy has changed me. I know much more about myself, about my behavior, and the possible motivations for other people's."

I nod.

"I see now how completely shattered we both were by Miriam's murder. After her death, I was so focused on you that I didn't do my own grieving." He stares out the window, then back at me. "She died five weeks before our wedding anniversary. We were never able to mark our anniversary, to celebrate our marriage after her death."

"I hadn't thought of that," I say, and we sink into silence for a bit before I speak. "It sounds as though you've been doing serious work."

"Yes, and I've wanted to talk to you about it, but I didn't know whether to call you. It's hard to know how you'll be."

"I'm sorry about that, Ryan," I say. "I want you to be able to talk to me, especially about this, and I know I'm unpredictable. You've been in my thoughts often, too."

"That's nice to know."

"I have something else to tell you." I look around, not wanting to be overheard.

"What?" Concern fills Ryan's face.

"It's a psychic kind of thing." I watch him relax into his chair.

"Tell me."

"Miriam's visiting me."

Ryan smiles. "Really?"

"Really." I'm not smiling. "I haven't exactly invited her, but she's been showing up, mostly when I'm sleeping, but it's not like I'm dreaming. She wakes me up. She's always wearing white, but she looks the same otherwise, and she talks to me. I told her how guilty I felt about her death, and she said there was nothing I could have done to alter her fate. But the fact that I am discussing things with her ghost makes me feel a bit crazy."

"You've never been crazy, Sarah. I don't understand why this scares you so much. You're just psychic like your family. Miriam and I both knew that."

"Yeah, well, it's difficult for me to come to terms with this as a reality and not some sign of a psychotic break, especially given how I fell apart after Miriam's death."

"Nobody copes well with the murder of a loved one. Stop pathologizing yourself for your grief."

"Stop pathologizing myself? You've clearly been in therapy!" I say.

"It doesn't take much insight to see how hard you've always been on yourself." He reaches across the table for my hand. "What does Miriam want?"

"Mostly, it seems, she wants me to know that she's available to help if I need her and she's pushing me to accept the clairvoyance."

"That sounds reassuring." He shrugs. "Can you do that? Can you work on accepting your gifts and begin appreciating the experience of having a guardian angel?"

"I suppose I can try."

"Okay, now that that's settled." Ryan drops my hand, sits back, and looks me over. "Dating?"

"No." I'm suddenly self-conscious. "That was a quick lawyerly pivot," I say. "I loved you and I still do. If we couldn't make it work, I'm not sure what to expect with somebody else."

He leans forward and takes my hand again. Suddenly, all my reasons for leaving the marriage strike me as irrelevant. I drift off, wondering how we get the lives we end up with. When I was a kid, my dad and I used to take long walks through the neighborhood after dinner. We'd peer into the lighted windows of houses we passed and imagine the lives of their inhabitants.

"He's a fireman," I'd say.

"She's a Broadway actress," he'd say.

"And they have two cats and three dogs," I'd add.

We'd laugh, giving them names and backgrounds, constructing their stories as we continued our walk.

When Ryan and I were married, we had our own version of that game, imagining the lives of people in the towns we visited on vacations, speculating on what it would be like to live in those towns ourselves.

Looking up at Ryan's face, nostalgia and desire consume me. "What about you? Are you seeing someone?"

He doesn't respond until the waitress clears the table and departs.

"I have met someone." He speaks casually, but his face is anything but casual and his words almost knock me from my chair. "She's the first serious contender. That's why I wanted to see you. I'm not sure. I don't want to foreclose on us if you haven't. Because I still love you, Sarah. You just have to say the word." He takes a deep breath before continuing. "Any possibility you're having second thoughts?"

"Right now?" I laugh. "Of course. I just want you to hold me." I reclaim my hand and comb my fingers through my curls. "What *is* it with the two of us?"

He shrugs. "Maybe fate's at work and you're supposed to move back to Boston." He tips his head sideways. "Why don't you come over to see my condo?"

"What, you're going to show me your etchings?"

"I'm going to show you a lot more than that." Ryan places a hundred dollar bill on the table. We walk out the door, get into my car, and a few minutes later, we're parked at the entrance to his waterfront condo. As we step into the elevator and its brass doors slide shut, a short-lived skirmish scrambles my brain, but my reservations are overtaken by longing—and the sensual pleasure of Ryan's mouth on mine. The doors open with a *whoosh* on the eighth floor, and we walk into a sleekly furnished condo, dark leather sofas, large modern oil paintings punctuating the high ceilinged walls, a stunning view of both the skyline and the harbor through enormous glass windows.

I kick off my shoes. Ryan pulls off his leather boots. He gently pushes my back to the wall and leans in, his hands meandering down the curves and valleys of my body. He unbuttons my blouse. I pull his sweater over his head. We leave a trail of clothing across the polished wood floors en route to the black-lacquered platform bed. Our bodies move in an undulating rhythm, exploring anew and remembering, rubbing and rocking, until we crest a tidal wave of pleasure. I drop off into a deep, satisfied sleep.

Ryan nudges me awake. "Will you stay the night?"

"Yes," I murmur, stretching contentedly.

"Dinner in the North End?"

"Definitely."

He makes a nine o'clock reservation at a restaurant Mark and Louise also love. The four of us used to indulge in occasional weekend splurges, driving to Boston for shows and special dinners before heading home to Maine. I think back to those days, consider all the changes, then push those thoughts aside to sink into Ryan's embrace.

A luscious soak in Ryan's Jacuzzi is followed by the tantalizing exercise of dressing each other. We walk hand in hand through familiar streets to the North End, where we eat an intimate candlelit dinner.

I'm so enveloped in lust and possibility that serious conversation is out of the question. Ryan obligingly keeps it light. I wonder what craziness led me to divorce him. Who cares that he isn't Jewish? What difference does it make that he opted for corporate law? He's a kind, loving, intelligent, humorous, talented man—and a fabulous lover. What more could I possibly need—or want?

As the waiter clears the dishes, I walk dreamily to the bathroom, but I'm wrenched from reverie when the occupants of a corner table come into view. I do a double-take when I see Mark speaking earnestly to an attractive woman with short dark hair and a swanlike neck. Her long, delicate fingers curl around a wad of tissues as she dabs at tears. He must sense my eyes on him, because he looks up just as I bolt into the bathroom. Not long after my return to the table, Mark walks over.

Ryan stands to give him a hug; they slap each other on the back. "What a coincidence. Where's Louise?"

"Home. I'm here for a business meeting."

"Here?" Ryan's eyebrows rise. "On a Friday night?"

Mark rests his hand on Ryan's shoulder and looks me in the eye. "Yes. Here."

I hold his stare, questioning him silently. He doesn't look away.

Ryan attempts to alleviate the awkwardness. "I'm trying to woo Sarah back."

It's Mark's turn to stare appraisingly at me. Then he focuses on Ryan. "Come up for a weekend. I'd sure love to go golfing with you again."

I remain silent until they finish chatting and Mark departs.

"That's no business dinner. I told you about the tension between Louise and Mark. And now he's here, at this romantic restaurant, with a beautiful woman who's crying?"

"Seriously?"

"Yes, and I have no idea what to tell Louise."

"Maybe you don't need to tell her anything. If something's going on, she'll find out soon enough."

"I can't keep this a secret. It will hurt her terribly, but I'd want her to tell me if our positions were reversed."

"Okay," Ryan says, "but is there another problem here? Are you worried about her reaction to the news that you've spent the weekend with me?"

"Yes," I acknowledge reluctantly.

"That might change, though, honey, once we make some decisions about our future. When do you think we can we talk seriously?"

"I don't know, but not here—and not now. What's important at this moment," I say, peering at the menu, "is tiramisu."

Chapter 9

My time with Ryan settles nothing, just stirs things up with a long weekend of languid lovemaking and visits to all the places in Boston I've missed—museums, cafes, shops, and restaurants. I tear myself away after a sumptuous Sunday brunch.

"I'm not waiting six months to see you again," Ryan admonishes. "So don't get funny on me once you're back in Portland."

I grin. "I won't get funny on you. I enjoy being treated like a queen."

"In that case, why don't I arrange a long weekend in Manhattan? We could go to the opera." He draws me back into his arms. "We could indulge in New York pleasures and plan our future."

Sensations of wellbeing and sated sensuality infuse me until I cross the bridge over the Piscataqua River separating New Hampshire from Maine. Then the stresses flood back. In the past two weeks, so much has happened: Miriam's visitations, Henderson's death, Louise's and Mark's marital difficulties, my struggles with the couple I'm counseling, reconnecting with Ryan. For once, reconciling seems like an option that could provide relief.

I walk through my front door, immersed in imaginings, to find Louise on the living room sofa, petting my cats. Dark circles sit underneath her eyes. Her hair is pulled back into a ragged ponytail.

"I'm glad you're back." She gets up to hug me. "It's been a rough few days."

"I can see that. What's been going on?"

"I haven't slept. Both kids were sick, and fighting. I hate my husband, and I can't listen to another client talk about Henderson's death. Your cats, however, Velcroed themselves to my lap and loved me up—and gave me a break from Mark, before he took off for his meeting in Boston."

Some meeting. "Let me bring my suitcase upstairs and I'll tell you about the conference. You didn't miss much."

Solitude is calling, but Louise looks like a train wreck. My mood is plunging along with the outside temperature, so I pluck a sweater from a hook in the hall and say, "How about some hot cocoa?"

"Sure." Louise pulls a chair out from under the kitchen table.

I fill a new tea kettle, set it on the burner. "So, what's happening?"

Her shoulders slump.

"Hey, you don't have to talk about it." I reach into an overhead cabinet for the cocoa powder, spoon it into glass-footed mugs, and pour in the hot water.

We move to the living room, snuggling up against opposite arms of the couch with our feet pulled in beneath us. I babble on about the conference, wondering what to tell her about Mark.

"Spill it already," Louise says, and my face flushes. "You're oozing pheromones. You must have seen Ryan. I bet you slept with him, didn't you?"

A grin spreads across my face. "Yes, and yes."

"What's next—remorse and regret?"

"Well, not so far. Ryan's in therapy, doing his work. It was wonderful to be with him." I pause. "And I'm already back in therapy."

"Good thing you're seeing Janice. When it comes to Ryan and relationships, you've got a lot to sort through." She elbows me in the ribs. "Personally, I don't think you'll move on until you've had fabulous sex with someone else."

Irritation rises in my chest. "Why don't you arrange that for me? Call your friend Billy Marshall and see what's on his social schedule, and while you're at it, make sure he's been cleared for STDs."

Louise untucks her feet and kicks me. "Aren't you touchy since getting home?"

I suck in a breath. "I guess you're right." Then I plunge forward. "It's probably because I have something to tell you."

"I'm all ears."

"Ryan and I had dinner in the North End Saturday night."

"At our restaurant?"

I nod. "And Mark was there."

She sits up, bewilderment flooding her face.

"Here's the thing." I hesitate.

"What?"

"He was with a woman. A very attractive woman. She was crying."

"You sure took your sweet time telling me." Louise unfolds her legs, stands up, and walks over to lean against the white painted fireplace, looking as if she's struggling for control.

"I wasn't going to blurt it out the moment I walked through the door. You already looked like you'd been flattened by a steamroller." I pause. "Mark told me it was a business meeting."

"You talked to him?"

"He cornered me." I hold my hands up and out in front of my chest. "I'm only the messenger, so don't shoot me."

"Damn him," she says, staring out the back windows. "I'm well aware that we all have secrets—even you and me. But he better not be having an affair. He said he had to be in Boston for twelve-step work."

"Seriously?"

She shoots me a look so fierce I close my mouth. "Yeah." Her head bobs up and down. "He's relapsed, after all this time. He's been acting like an ass because he's been one. He spent the past year snorting cocaine. Our home-equity loan has been going right up his nose."

"You're kidding." I'm shocked that Mark would lie, and I can't believe he put their financial security at risk. But, I remind myself, that's the nature of addiction. I stand up, walk to the mantel, and wrap my arms around Louise. "I'm so sorry."

She rests her head against mine. "Me too," she says.

I step back, and voice a thought that even I consider slightly paranoid. "Louise, do you think Henderson knew about Mark's relapse? Do you think he might have used his position at Constant Caring to look at Mark's psychotherapy records? Is that what he was referring to in his testimony during the Tate custody hearing?"

Louise holds my gaze. "I thought so at the time, but it doesn't matter now. Henderson's dead. What's important is that Mark is committed to ninety meetings in ninety days, and he'd damn well better do it." She scratches her head. "You know, Mark said he needed to see a friend in Boston to let this friend know he was choosing sobriety, and to suggest they do the same. I was okay with that, because I assumed it was a male friend. He never said it was a beautiful woman or that he'd be taking her to our restaurant." Louise bites her lip. "I'm so tired of drama. I don't know how much more I can take."

I look at her, think about the interaction I witnessed between Louise and Mark the night of Henderson's death, picture Mark's dinner companion in Boston, and wonder what secrets she's keeping from me, which ones he's keeping from her. I also wonder how much more Louise can take.

Chapter 10

I see Janice again first thing Monday morning. We talk about my time with Ryan and my conversation with Miriam about her death and my guilt. I fill her in on my concerns about Louise and Mark. Then we focus on the trauma work around Miriam's death. EMDR takes me further into the memories, but this time I'm more grounded in the present, which helps me as I dip back into the past. My sense of responsibility for Miriam's death is dissipating, along with my guilt.

I start with my own clients at 10:30 that day. With a bit of time before I need to get to the office, I stop to check in with my friend Kate, whose law office is right down the block. After hiking three flights of stairs, I fling open the door to her suite. Large windows framed by white-painted woodwork punctuate refurbished brick walls above gleaming oak floors. The receptionist smiles as she buzzes Kate, and I catch my breath.

Kate steps out of her conference room, stunning in an unstructured linen suit. She moved to Maine from California to take a temporary teaching post at the law school, and loved Portland so much she settled here—though she never relinquished her West Coast chic for LL Bean's down-home fashion practicality. "Good timing," she says. "I just finished a long conference call, and I'm ready for a break." She ushers me into her private office.

"How are things?" I settle onto an elegant mid-century modern dark purple couch.

Kate perches on the edge of her enormous oak desk. I glance out the window, distracted momentarily by noisy pigeons nesting on the roof of the federal courthouse.

"You tell me first. You look kind of washed out." Kate kicks off her heels.

I tell her about my therapy session.

"It's hard to get over those things, isn't it? Sometimes I think about how violence charted my own career path. Did I ever tell you that my nanny was physically abused by her boyfriend?"

"No, you didn't." I raise my eyebrows. "This is news to me."

"Growing up, my sisters and I were taken care of by Juanita, a phenomenal cook and the most loving woman I've ever known. I've told you that my parents both worked for the Hollywood studios, and their hours were crazy. Juanita was there twenty-four seven for the first twelve years of my life. Then she fell in love with a man she'd just met and began to take more time off. One day, only a few months later, she called my parents crying. Her boyfriend had beaten her so badly she'd been taken to the emergency room of a local hospital. She was admitted and kept there for a few weeks, then sent to rehab for two months. My parents paid for everything. When she came out, she just wanted to go back to Mexico to her own parents. We kept in touch for years, writing letters back and forth, until one day when my letters began to come back marked 'return to sender.'" Kate tears up. "I never found out what happened to her, but if it weren't for Juanita, I probably wouldn't be as committed to this work."

"I'm so sorry, Kate."

She nods, and we sit in silence for a few minutes.

Speaking of relationship troubles," I say, "I'm worried about Louise and Mark. I saw Mark grab her arm, then watched while she almost broke his wrist. She and Mark…" I trail off.

"I probably know all there is to know about that situation, and I think they'll be okay. Louise just has a lot on her plate right now."

"You sure?"

"Yup."

"In that case, there's something else I want to ask you. Was Henderson murdered?"

Kate stands up and steps back into her shoes. It's hard not to notice the muscles in her calves. She was a competitive tennis player in high school and college and hasn't lost the capacity to slam balls over the net, even if these days the lobs are more often verbal and taking place in a criminal court. "Why do you ask? Just curious?"

"A few of my clients used to see Henderson, and they've been asked to appear at the police station for interviews. I'm wondering if they'll call me in."

"Why?"

"I don't know. Just wondering how thorough their investigation is going to be. Many therapists had contact with Henderson because of his position as a psychiatric consultant for Constant Caring."

"All I can tell you is that information is tight, but his death has been classified as suspicious."

"I figured that, but do they have any evidence of murder?"

"The autopsy results haven't been released yet."

"Then there's something else I need to ask you."

"What?" Kate's voice fills with concern.

"Did you know Louise was in Henderson's office the day he died?"

"Did she tell you that?"

"I saw her. She was standing in his window. When I asked her if she'd been there, she didn't deny it, but she wouldn't tell me why she was there. She still hasn't told me."

"I know she was there," Kate says, "but I'm not thrilled that you know about it. Any contact between Louise and Henderson will raise a red flag. She's already on the radar because of the hostility between them, the lawsuit we filed against him and Constant Caring, and the courtroom fireworks the day he died."

"Well, if the police call me in, what do I say?"

"You'll have to tell them what you thought you saw and what you know—if you're asked a direct question."

Turmoil rises inside me. I failed Miriam. I cannot fail Louise.

"What?" Kate says, and I assume she's watching the struggle play out on my face.

"I hope Louise and Mark can work things out."

"Me too," she says. "But if they split, he's going to be eating dirt for dinner for a long time. I'm her attorney, and nobody fucks with my friends."

I'm so startled by her language that I laugh. Kate does too.

I look around the office, noting the many folders on her desk, papers stacked atop a file cabinet, notes tacked to a board. "How are you doing?"

She tips her head. "Honestly, I'm a bit over the top with all these domestic-violence cases, so I'm hiring an associate and planning to cut my hours back for the summer."

"That sounds sensible." Kate may be as smart as they come, and incredibly skilled as an attorney, but she also has adult attention deficit disorder, or ADD. It shows up in the piles of paper under which, on occasion, she locates her bills. She has a temper, doesn't deal well with frustration, and gets irritable easily. Luckily, she's kept tightly organized by her legal secretary and religiously checks her iPhone. She's also capable of amazing hyper-focus, which, when added to a near-genius IQ, helps her sort through the myriad complications in the cases she takes. "What does Alex think?" Kate's partner, Alexandra Pappas, runs a successful private-investigation practice. She and Kate often collaborate. Both Alex and I have pushed Kate to get a more thorough evaluation, work with a coach, and start medication, but she puts us both off.

"Alex wants me to cut back my hours. She's also way too busy herself."

"I'm not surprised. Say hi for me." I extricate myself from the couch and pick up my purse.

Kate walks over to hug me. "Everything will work out, one way or another."

"I sure hope so," I murmur. It's been a hell of a start to the day. I grab a chocolate chip muffin from a local bakery before driving back to the office. No matter what the *tsuris*, I can count on chocolate to help.

Late morning sun filters through the branches of the graceful willow outside my office, creating intriguing silhouettes, a welcome counterpoint to the argument unfolding inside. The shadowed leaves gently swaying on the wall behind Elena and Todd Owens allow me to distance myself from their anger and hone in on the emotions underneath. A few hours ago I sat in the client's seat, now I'm in the therapist's chair. As a therapist, there's no way around facing your own issues. If you don't, you can't help your clients face theirs.

"You're doing it again," Elena sniffs.

"What?" Todd's stunning suit probably came straight from one of

Portland's high-priced men's clothiers, Joseph's or David Wood. I note that, along with the annoyance permeating his tone. "Raising my eyebrows?" His sarcasm stings, even though it isn't aimed at me.

"Todd, try not to be so patronizing. Please? You know what I'm talking about. You did it just now, not only raising your eyebrows, but also curling your lip into a sneer."

"So what?"

"What kind of way is that to relate to me? I'm your wife." Though they sit on the same sofa, Elena has positioned herself as far from Todd as possible, which also leaves plenty of room for her to fling out her arms to punctuate her point. "I'm not a complete idiot, despite your thoughts to the contrary. Do you think I could possibly miss the ridicule you're directing at me?"

"You've got a million explanations for my facial expressions, and they often have very little to do with me. Did you ever consider the possibility that you're imagining things, imputing motive where none exists?"

"I'm losing patience." Elena looks at me before returning her gaze to Todd. "What's so difficult about acknowledging that you're angry? Why can't you be honest for a change? Remember what I said about being passive-aggressive?"

Todd looks at her blankly.

"When you don't take responsibility for your anger, you act it out, and the way you do that is calculated to piss me off. Then I carry all the irritation and resentment from both of us and you get to act like I'm overly emotional. Well, I'm done playing that game. It might get you somewhere, but it does absolutely nothing for me." Elena swings her hand out as if swatting away a bug. "What's happened to you?"

Todd jingles the coins in his pocket. "This is ridiculous. We're wasting our time. We do this often enough at home, where we don't have to pay someone to watch us."

"It sounds frustrating. Is this the tone of most of your interactions?" I ask.

"Yes," Todd says scornfully. "It's becoming intolerable."

"What have you done to change it?"

"Not much." Elena looks at me as she speaks, but directs her next comment at Todd. "It's your attitude that's intolerable."

"Okay, stop," I interrupt. "While it's important for me to get a sense of how you manage disagreements, I think I've heard enough. How you speak to each other is at the top of the list of things to work on. You're right, Todd. Verbally jousting with each other isn't useful, whether it takes place at home or this office. Let's see if you can both readjust your perspectives, perhaps consider that neither of you is the enemy, hmm? You chose to marry each other and I know, given our earlier conversations, that choice was made out of love and affection. Perhaps you can each take a few breaths and bring that affection back to mind before returning to this conversation."

Elena's face softens, as does her voice. "You know, Todd, if we don't tell Sarah what's really going on, she can't help us."

"You seem to know everything, Elena. Why don't you tell her?" He closes his eyes and takes a deep breath.

For the tenth time, I wonder about him. Does he just have tendencies that are narcissistic, like any number of people? Or does he have a narcissistic personality disorder? It makes a big difference in terms of his ability to alter his behavior. Tendencies can be worked with, but a personality disorder—that's not so amenable to change. The difficulty I feel connecting with Todd troubles me. It's my job to find a way to empathize with all my clients, and that's especially true in couple's therapy, but Todd's lack of empathy for his wife makes it difficult for me to feel any empathy toward him. That's a problem I know I'll have to wrestle with.

Elena watches Todd for a few moments before turning toward me. "He's been incredibly stressed. Between his job at the law firm and the board he serves on, he hasn't had any time for me or the kids, or even himself. Isn't that right?"

"That's certainly your version of reality."

A memory of something called a "yes-set" pops to the surface: If one can phrase a variety of questions in such a way that the answers are all yes, even intractable hostility can be reversed. If Elena's next comments don't shift their interaction, I'll intervene.

"George Tate and Todd are first cousins," Elena continues. "George manages the Constant Caring Managed Care Company."

I watch Todd watch me and wonder how much he knows. Is he aware of the details of Louise's battles with Henderson and Constant Caring, the audit, the struggles over reimbursement, the lawsuits?

Elena continues, "We've already mentioned that Todd isn't happy about the state of affairs at the company. Right, Todd?"

"Yes," he agrees, albeit warily. My hopes are still on Elena to get the "yes-set" rolling.

"But George is Todd's cousin and Todd feels responsible for him."

Todd turns toward Elena and stares. He looks as if he's gearing up for another battle, but his words surprise me.

"That's not the problem. Just because you and Brooke are best friends, you can't take everything she says as the gospel truth." Todd shifts his attention to me. "George is my first cousin. I'm forty-four. He's a year and a half younger and it makes no difference now that we're this age, but we grew up together and as kids I kind of looked out for him. He's like my little brother. Until this nasty divorce, Elena and I spent a good deal of time with George and Brooke and the kids. I can't cut him off like his wife did. We're family. I'm sure you know all about this stuff. Anyone who reads the local paper can't avoid the gory details, and your colleague is Brooke's therapist," Todd says. "We saw you in the courthouse during the last hearing."

"Oh," I say, taken aback. I hadn't noticed them.

"She can't acknowledge the fact that Brooke sees her colleague," Elena interjects. "It's confidential."

"You must get an awful lot of pleasure from correcting me." Todd's face is so hostile it kind of scares me, and then he turns toward me as if seeking an ally.

A creepy sensation slithers up my spine and I return his gaze without indicating any alliance. "Perhaps, Todd, if you assumed a more positive intention on Elena's part, you might hear what she says differently. What's turned you into enemies?"

Todd turns to face Elena. "I apologize and defer to your greater knowledge of therapeutic proprieties."

His sarcasm annoys me. As does the deliberate manner in which he adjusts the cuffs of his shirt sleeves. I realize that anything he does will annoy me now unless I get my own reactivity to his provocations under control. I wonder again what I'm picking up about his personality.

"In answer to your question, Sarah," he says, "and as I was saying before I was so rudely interrupted..."

"Stop the jabs," I say. "If you can't put the knife away, your work in here will have no chance of improving your marriage. If your goal is to win, you might as well marry your law firm."

"Point well taken," he says, surprising me. "But you need to understand the issues. Our marriage has been rocky ever since George and Brooke split up. Elena took Brooke's side and all men have become evil." His nostrils flare. "That includes me, because I refuse to abandon George, even if he has been acting strangely."

"It's about time you acknowledged that," Elena says.

"Yes, George is over the edge, but he's family, he's in trouble, and I'm not deserting him."

I wonder what kind of edge, what kind of trouble. Is there something more than his bitter divorce?

"What about the position he put you in with the company?"

"I have no intention of discussing that here." Todd glares at Elena. "Have some confidence in me. I'm dealing with it."

"Stop. Both of you. Take a breath and when you respond, pay attention to what you're saying and how you're saying it."

Elena looks at Todd, then at the floor. "It's not that I don't trust you."

"No? It certainly looks that way. Feels that way," Todd mutters.

"I'm worried about you, Todd. It's George I don't trust!"

"Well, you aren't alone in that. No one trusts George at the moment. I'm doing what I can to help him, and that's all I'm going to say."

"Has he inveigled you into something?"

"Elena, she does not need to know these things!"

"I think she does. Be honest. You only agreed to see Sarah because she's not just a therapist, she's also a lawyer. You obviously wanted that expertise." Elena pauses. "We have to talk about George."

My thoughts wander, imagining the problems at Constant Caring, the differences between George and Todd, and Henderson's part in all of it. When Todd shifts his weight on the sofa, my attention returns to him. I remind myself that my job is to work with this couple, not to use the troubles in their marriage as a way of discovering more information about Constant Caring. Refocusing, I notice that George's anger seems somewhat deflated.

"We're here to talk about us, not Constant Caring," he says.

Elena doesn't snap back, but disagrees respectfully this time. "Todd, this *is* about us. George is a big part of our problem."

Todd puts his hands up in mock surrender. "Okay, I'll grant you that."

"In the meantime, please don't take it out on me. I'm your wife, not a hostile witness." Elena's retort could begin the cycle of anger all over again, but it doesn't, because she holds up her hands too. "Sorry, I didn't mean to sound so angry."

Todd's response surprises me. "It's okay. You're right. I have been under a significant amount of stress." He reaches for her hand. "And I have taken it out on you. I'm sorry too."

Elena clasps his hand and shifts her body close to his. He readjusts to meet her and slides his arm around her shoulder.

I'm not sure whose relief I'm sensing—theirs or mine.

Todd checks his watch. "Our time's almost up. Just how much of what we say in here is confidential?"

"Most of it, except what your insurance company wants to know in order to cover your sessions, and there are exceptions to that confidentiality."

"Right," Todd says. "If one of us is suicidal, homicidal, or abusive."

"Yes, and if I'm subpoenaed. It's delineated in the treatment contract you both signed. Would you like another copy?"

"Yes. Please."

I write out a receipt and hand a copy of the contract to Todd as he rises to leave. "I've written the title of a book I recommend on your receipt. If you both can read the first two chapters before our next meeting, it will help you become more aware of the way you talk to each other, and we can focus on that in our next session. Okay?"

"Yes," they respond in unison. Todd shakes my hand. Elena smiles gratefully.

My next client is a pediatrician struggling with grief over the unexpected death of a young patient. That session breaks my heart, but it's followed by good news from a young couple whose infertility has been the subject of many sessions. They've just learned that a birthmother has chosen them as her baby's adoptive parents. The baby is due in a month and their excitement is contagious. I take a short break for a late lunch, traipse down the stairs and peek in through Louise's open door. She holds the phone to her ear with one hand and waves me in with the other.

"Teresa, it's only one hour. You can manage that, can't you?" Louise scribbles notes and murmurs reassurances before hanging up. She turns the ringer off and pours herself a cup of tea from a floral carafe as I sink into her couch.

"You okay?" I ask.

"Sort of. That was the very fractured trauma client I've spoken about with you."

"Problems?"

"She is the most dissociative client I've ever treated, and that's saying something. Multiple abusers, parents' rights terminated when she was six, a slew of foster homes. And she talks about a husband, but he's in and out of prison. She's been deteriorating steadily and I don't know why. I might have to hospitalize her."

Clients with dissociative identity disorder, a condition that used to be called multiple personality disorder, require a level of stamina and equanimity out of my reach—but Louise dives right in without a shred of hesitation.

"I've watched this client's voice and appearance change with a shake of the head or a blink of the eyes."

"It's such hard work. Are you at least getting paid?"

"Yes, for this client, for some strange reason, there's never been a problem with Constant Caring. Even when Henderson was alive, I got anything I asked for. He did the psychiatric consultation and approved the referral. Henderson must have known how horribly wrong things could go if she wasn't in the right hands."

"I'm surprised. It seemed sometimes that he couldn't care less about clients. It was all about the bottom line. And how are things going with Constant Caring? Are they paying you for your other sessions now that Henderson's dead?"

"Yes. They also cancelled the audit. I forgot to tell you. The letter came last week. Interesting, huh?" She rubs her eyes. "That allows me to focus on my clients' needs without distraction, and I sure have to focus with this client. She's much more splintered than I originally suspected, and I thought she was seriously fractured when we first began. So far, she's demonstrated at least three different alters—alternative personalities—and I'm sure there are more."

My fingers fiddle with my hair while Louise speaks.

"I see you're getting anxious," Louise says. "I don't understand why this kind of pathology scares you. Okay, yes, most of us aren't so splintered that the different parts of our personalities are oblivious to one another, but we all dissociate. We slip away into another place when we listen to music, read a fabulous novel, watch a movie. You're completely comfortable using hypnosis and meditation to create trance, and you know that's a form of dissociation."

"Yes, but those aren't exactly the same thing."

"True. But we all have different parts to our personalities. We struggle with smoking and eating and addictions." Louise pauses. "We argue with ourselves about many things. What's so different about this?"

I raise my eyebrows to indicate disbelief. "Come on, Louise, your client's level of dissociation is qualitatively different. It's a serious mental disorder, not a state of relaxation or disagreements among parts that are in communication with one another." I close my eyes. "I'm squirmy because it reminds me of visiting my grandfather at the nursing home. Sometimes he'd hug me. Other times he'd confuse me with a Cossack about to burn down his village. It freaked me out when he'd start screaming at me in Yiddish. Now, even with my training and experience, some issues push my own buttons. And sorting through the reasons this disorder bothers me is not a high priority right now."

"Okay. Forget it. Just because I love these cases doesn't mean you have to."

We hear our front door open. Another client arriving for a session. Louise checks her watch. "I had two cancellations for the end of the day today. How late are you working?

I push off the comfortable couch. "It's weird how these things are synchronous sometimes, isn't it? I have two more hours and then I'm done at four. My last client cancelled."

I stand up and stretch. "Honestly, it will be good to stop early." I think about my next client, a woman with whom I'm doing clinical hypnosis. She was left with chronic pain after a car accident. Hypnosis not only relaxes my clients, it relaxes me. That will be good, as my last client for the day is a former client of Henderson's, a woman who is just beginning to recover from the damage he did to her self-esteem.

Louise stands up to stretch herself. "Come over after work then. The girls are going home with friends after school. Their mom will drop them off by dinner time, and Mark is working late, so I'll have the house to myself."

"Terrific. We can have a few hours of down time together." With Henderson's death, Louise and Mark's difficulties, my continuing ambivalence about Ryan, and the pressures of our clinical practices, it's gotten harder for the two of us to simply relax together. I can't imagine that life might get any more challenging. But I do know it's a distinct possibility.

Chapter 11

It's still rather warm at 4:30, unusual for the first week of June, but I'm not complaining. I walk over to Louise's, where I find her front porch strewn with magazines and two newly whipped fruit frappes. We sip and chat about nothing important until a car turns into the drive. Seeing Billy Marshall step out of an unmarked cruiser gives us both reason to smile.

"He's looking rather handsome in those khakis and a sports coat."

"Time to make your move." Louise winks.

Billy strides up the steps, and though his smile is brief, it provokes a disconcerting shiver of anticipation. I've just been with Ryan— why am I so attracted to Billy? My musings are cut short, however, by Billy's words.

"I'm sorry to interrupt," he says, "but I'm here on police business related to Henderson."

Louise sits up warily. "What about Henderson?"

"Gene Pomerleau, the lead detective on the investigation, wants to interview you."

"I can't share client information without a subpoena," Louise says. "And I haven't received one."

"This isn't about your clients." Billy's face flushes beneath his tan. "It's about you."

"Me?" Louise jumps out of the rocking chair so fast, she loses her balance. Billy catches her. She leans into him. Something about the way they look at each other makes me wonder if their high-school "fling" involved more than a brief attraction. "Now?" I hear the panic in Louise's voice.

"Yes." Billy's hand rests on her shoulder.

"Why?"

"I'm not privy to that information."

Louise looks down at her jeans. "I'll have to change my clothes."

"I'll wait." Billy steps back.

"It's kind of late for this, isn't it?" Louise asks.

"Later than usual, but nothing is operating the way it normally does." He shrugs his shoulders. "I'm not in charge."

"I've got to call Kate and ask her to meet me." Louise yanks the screen door open and disappears inside.

Billy sits beside me on the porch swing, smiles, and rests his arm behind my shoulders. We swing companionably until another car peels into the driveway.

Mark slams his car door shut before trotting up the steps with a worried expression on his face. "Louise just called. What's up with this interview?"

Billy shrugs again. "Like I told Louise, I'm just delivering a message. They know we're friends."

Louise flings open the upstairs window and pokes her head out. "Sarah, would you call Kate for me? Her line's been busy. Mark, will you come upstairs, please?"

Mark holds the door as I extricate myself from Billy's orbit. Grabbing my cell phone, I walk into the kitchen where I'll have privacy. Kate answers on the first ring.

"I'm so glad you're there," I say.

"What's up?"

"Billy Marshall is here at Louise's asking her to go her downtown for an interview with Pomerleau. She wants you to meet her there. Do you have a clue about what's going on?"

"They must have the autopsy results back on Henderson. I suppose that means they've also completed the protocol for suspicious deaths."

I perch on a stool. "And?"

She hesitates, "I was just thinking out loud. I don't have time to go into it. Just tell Louise I'll meet her at the station."

Footsteps sound from the stairs and I walk into the front hall. Louise looks chic in white linen pants, a black silk tank, and a white linen jacket. After passing along Kate's message, I give her a hug and follow her and Mark out the front door.

Billy is leaning against the porch railing. He rests a reassuring hand on my shoulder for a few moments before he trails Mark and Louise to their car. The heat from his hand lingers long after he's left.

The rest of my body is buzzing with agitation, which I try to manage by flipping through the pages of Louise's decorating magazines, focusing on the warm and welcoming images of cottage homes. The ringing of my home phone pierces the silence and I race across the lawn, missing the call, but hearing the message from Aunt Zelda. I ring her right back.

"Hello, darling," she says. "Your sweet face kept coming to me while I was on the cruise, but there was a cloud around you. Did you get my note?"

"No. You sent me one?" My heart warms as I picture my loving aunt.

"Oh, let me see." In the lengthy pause, I envision her closing her clear blue eyes and pressing a hand to her forehead, fingernails adorned in bright red polish. "That postcard was held up in a small post office. You'll get it in two days. Now, dear, tell me everything."

"Miriam keeps showing up in the middle of the night," I say. "She floats into my bedroom and talks to me."

"How lovely," my aunt says.

"For you, perhaps. It's not entirely comfortable for me."

"You must remember, dear," she says, "that things only come to us when we're ready to deal with them. Perhaps you're finally there."

"I don't think so. It still freaks me out." It's difficult trying to talk over the lump in my throat.

"What's to be afraid of? These kinds of communication are simply a form of assistance from spirits who care deeply about your welfare. You're blessed to have this gift." The warmth in my aunt's voice enfolds me like an embrace. I imagine her reclining on the chintz chaise in her living room, where landscape paintings adorn the walls, plants bask in sunlight, and cats purr on windowsills.

"Then why *am* I so scared?"

"You know what I'm about to say."

"Yes, but please say it anyway."

"Psychic awareness is something our society demonizes. Children, like you, my dear, are born with these skills, but learn to repress them. We're taught to dread death and see communication from the other side as something fearful. It takes courage to embrace psychic skills and to accept that they're real. But as you know, and are currently experiencing directly, there's only a thin veil between the living and the dead. Those who love us send messages in a variety of ways. They safeguard our wellbeing as best they can."

"Why is Miriam showing up now?"

"Let me see what I can find out." After a minute of silence, she continues. "You're about to face some unique challenges. Miriam can help you in a way no one else can. At least that's what I can get at the moment."

"Miriam mentioned that," I say.

After another silence, Aunt Zelda says, "Do your best to stop being so reticent. The dead are all around us. The ability to talk with them is a gift, dear, and it's far past time for you to accept it and use it to help yourself and others."

"I'm not there yet, Aunt Zelda."

"Talk with Miriam about it. And call me anytime. I have to go now, but remember that you are so dearly loved." Her caring and concern pulsate through the wires. "By me and many others, in and out of physical form. And," she adds, "by your mother, who is about to phone you right now."

I hang up the phone and it rings again. Aunt Zelda nailed it. "Hi, Mom. How are you?"

"I'm fine. How come you didn't tell me you spent the weekend with Ryan?"

"How do you know?"

"I called him about a little legal matter for a friend."

"You're kidding? How did you get him to tell you I'd seen him?"

"Why do you always suspect wicked motives, Sarah? We chatted. I asked if the two of you had been in touch. He told me you'd been in Boston and you'd spent some time together. Isn't it a mother's prerogative to hope her daughter will be happy with a Prince Charming? Any thoughts of getting back together?"

"You'll be the very first to know, Mom. The very first," I say through clenched teeth.

"So what's going on up there? I get worried whenever I think about you. Is everything okay?"

I don't want to tell her about Louise or Miriam or anything else at this moment, since she seems to have too clear a beam into the realities of my life. So we chat about nothing for five minutes until I can hang up and walk back to Louise's house. I put the kettle on the burner and begin to straighten up the house, composing a story for the kids about their parents' whereabouts.

A knock on the door catches my attention and I open it to find a forty-something woman in jeans and a pink T-shirt ushering Susie and Naomi into the house. "Hi," she says. "I've had the kids for the past few hours. Susie plays with my youngest, and Naomi and my daughter were working on a homework project together. Where are Mark and Louise?"

Before I can answer, Susie flings herself into my arms. "Auntie Sarah!"

"Louise and Mark had an unexpected meeting in town. I'm the next-door neighbor, Sarah Greene."

"It's not a problem, Mrs. Peters," Naomi says. "Sarah is our honorary aunt."

"Okay," Mrs. Peters says, "Give my best to your parents."

I set Susie down, ruffling her tousled red curls.

"Where's Mommy?" she lisps through the gap that's recently replaced her two front teeth.

"At a meeting. She'll be home soon."

Susie and I sit together in the rocking chair. Naomi does her homework at the counter.

As the clock hits six I suggest we go out for pizza, which gets an enthusiastic response. I leave a note for Louise and Mark before we pile into the car and drive to Ricetta's in Falmouth. It's busy, and everyone's conversation seems to bounce off the walls, but we fill ourselves with pizza, chatter away, and head home happily stuffed. By the time we pull into the driveway bearing a pizza for Mark and Louise, they've returned. Louise looks bedraggled, lying on the kitchen couch. The kids swarm around her before Mark corrals Susie for a bath and suggests Naomi focus on finishing her homework in her room.

As they depart, silence descends. I wait a minute or two, but Louise doesn't say a word.

"You look completely wiped out."

She slips off her shoes. "I am."

"What happened?"

"I was grilled mercilessly, and honestly, I'm frightened. They're honing in on my history with Henderson, my lawsuit against him and Constant Caring, the hostile exchanges in the courthouse, and my visit to his office. I think they want me to set me up as the primary suspect in his murder. Can you believe that?" Louise drops her head into her hands. "How did everything spiral so far out of control?"

"I don't know, honey, but I'm not in possession of all the facts. You still haven't told me what provoked you to go to Henderson's office, or what's going on with Mark."

"I'll tell you tomorrow." Louise gives me a wan smile. "I promise."

I could say ignorance is bliss, but in this case, I have the sense it's not going to work out that way.

Chapter 12

"So, will you meet me in New York City for the weekend? You never did give me an answer." Ryan's face smiles at me from my laptop as we Skype.

I'm lying on my stomach on the king-size sleigh bed that Ryan and I used to share, propped up on my elbows, swinging my legs back and forth. "Only if you promise not to tell my mother."

"Ah, you talked to her."

"I sure did. Would you mind keeping our time together just between us? The last thing I need is Shirley planning our second wedding."

"Would that be so bad?"

"You're moving really fast," I say.

"I beg to differ. I never wanted the divorce."

"I'm sorry for hesitating, and I don't want you to think that I've set you up like the last time. But we both know the issues that drove us apart, and despite how much we love each other, I'm not sure those things have changed."

"You didn't seem to have any issues in Boston."

"That's undeniable."

"Besides, we've both grown. Why can't it be different this time?"

"Maybe it can. I hope it can. I'm just more cautious than you."

"You weren't cautious in bed."

Heat suffuses my face and I laugh. "We're really good at that part. It's the long-term commitment that trips us up."

"If you'd simply accept that I'm no longer working for peanuts in the public sector, you might enjoy the perks of a corporate life. It doesn't have to impede your commitment to social justice. I still have mine."

I smirk into the screen. "You work with the enemy, honey."

"What do you want, Sarah?" The vulnerability in his voice tugs at my heart. "You want me to jettison my career? Is that what it'll take?"

I cringe, remembering our heated arguments once Ryan made the career switch. He left public service in Boston for the corporate world in Maine, the only positions available, when I could no longer stay in Boston, when I needed to be someplace safe—preferably near Louise. Despite the fact that Ryan made the big change for me, I had an attitude. Then he came to like his job, and I gave him a hard time about it. I still do.

Ryan, intently focused on the calendar, misses my expression, and by the time he looks up, I've stuffed the memories. "So, can you meet me in New York this weekend?" he says.

"Yes, but isn't Wednesday kind of late to be making arrangements?"

"Not for me. I've got meetings scheduled in Manhattan all week. I'm flying down in a few hours. I can just extend my reservation for the weekend, book your flight, and get tickets for the theatre. I'll call you tomorrow with details. Can you clear your schedule to meet me Friday afternoon?"

"Sure, as long as you promise never to tell my mother that we were in New York City and I didn't call her."

Ryan laughs. "I promise. And Sarah," he adds before disconnecting, "you'll be glad you came. Bye, honey."

"Bye," I say, and roll onto my back so I can stare at the ceiling. A breeze blows in from the window, bringing along a raft of doubts. Is this sheer stupidity, trying to make something work that's already failed, painfully and repeatedly?

I traipse downstairs and pull an old photo album from under the couch. Munching on cookies, I flip through the pages. There's a nine-by-twelve of Ryan, smiling and standing in front of our law school, his hair shining in the sun. A smaller shot of Miriam, her arm tucked into Ryan's, sitting on the front stoop of our first apartment. My favorite photo of Ryan and me looks a bit tattered. It was taken in the kitchen of our old house; my arms are wrapped around his neck as I stand on tiptoe to kiss him. Finally, I look at one of Miriam and me, swathed in graduation gowns, expressions of victory on our faces, an encapsulated history of our lives before her murder. Before I fell apart. Before everything fell apart.

I reach for another cookie and realize I've already emptied the entire box. Great, I've just added a few more pounds to the hips. My mind whirs. Going to New York will mean great sex, fabulous theatre, elegant dinners, a fancy hotel—all sorts of enticements to reconciliation. I want love, companionship, and commitment. I want Ryan, his warmth, his loyalty, his charm. We also have so much history. Yet I still haven't figured out how to be with Ryan since Miriam's murder. The shock of it ripped as big a hole in the fabric of our relationship as it did in our hearts.

The cats clamor for attention. A familiar sensation corkscrews through my belly as I scoop out their food. I can see Ryan wining and dining me. I can see us reconnecting in the most intimate of ways. And I can see myself closing up, fearful of loss, getting protective. After that, despite my fantasies of remarriage, despite spending every weekend together—one day it will fall apart. Again. Shaking off my negativity, I tell myself we can make it work this time. I can make it work.

When Ryan phones the next evening, I'm more hopeful.

"I've been swamped with work here, but I've booked your ticket."

I put down my book and stretch my legs out on the couch, imagining his arms around me, wishing he were lying beside me.

"We're going to have a fabulous weekend," he says. "Louise will watch the cats, right?"

"Yes. I talked to her this afternoon." I don't tell Ryan about my annoyance when Louise started lecturing me. She seemed dead set against another fling with Ryan, and I didn't want to hear it.

"So we're set," Ryan says. "You'll fly out of Portland at noon tomorrow and arrive in New York by one thirty. The boarding pass was emailed to you ten minutes ago. I've booked you an appointment at the spa at three. We have dinner reservations at six and theatre tickets at eight."

"What are we seeing?"

"It's a surprise, but you'll love it."

"What hotel?" An expansive view of the city skyline floats through my mind.

"The Carlyle. A top-floor suite."

A decent massage, a passionate weekend, and as usual, Ryan is way ahead of me. "I'll start packing." Excitement erases any second thoughts. Then call waiting beeps.

"Hold on." I click to the other line.

Louise's voice is barely recognizable. "We're in big trouble over here."

"Hang on." I click back to Ryan. "Something's wrong at Louise's. I've got to go."

"Call me later and let me know what's happening." Ryan's voice is filled with concern. "But please, Sarah, unless there's a major crisis that requires your presence, remember our priorities. This is our opportunity to reimagine our future."

I want that chance, and I'm afraid of it. Louise was right when she said we all have different parts to our personalities. One part of me can't wait to spend the weekend with Ryan. Another part is wary. At least I won't have to wait too long to see which part prevails.

Chapter 13

I click back to Louise. Blue lights on police cars flash from the street. "What's going on over there?"

"Four detectives just showed up with a search warrant. They're tearing my kitchen apart." Her voice breaks.

"What can I do?"

"Take the girls for the night."

"Of course." I switch on the backyard lights. "I'm at the door waiting for them." I watch the girls squeeze through the lilacs. Naomi, fifteen, carries a cloth grocery bag with pajamas spilling out of the top. The hem of her jeans snags on a twig and she yanks it free, snapping the twig right off the bush.

Six-year-old Susie trails behind, clasping Naomi's other hand. The cuffs of her overalls are tucked into yellow rain boots and she holds tight to the arm of her raggedy Teddy, snuggled in the bib of her overalls. "Auntie Sarah," Susie lisps as I meet them on the back porch. "Policemen."

"I heard, honey. They're noisy. I'm glad you're sleeping at my house."

Naomi looks back toward home before meeting my eyes. "Mom said she and my dad would be up late and we'd be better off here."

"Yup." I usher them into the house. "And you know my cats are going to be all over you the minute they realize you're here." Lola and Tillie appear on cue, meowing and winding their way through Susie's legs.

Naomi dumps the bag of clothes on my kitchen table and nibbles a fingernail. "Can I call my boyfriend?" Though she turned fifteen only three months ago, the switch from innocent to adolescent has been swift. Smudges of liner shadow her eyelids and the hue of lipstick clings to her mouth.

"Sure. Use the phone in the living room, unless you want more privacy. If so, you can use my study." I herd Susie and the cats upstairs. "I'll be down once Susie's settled in bed."

"Can I have a bath?" Susie asks hopefully.

"Of course you can." I know a warm bath will soothe her. While she plays in the claw-foot tub with the rubber ducks I keep just for her, I sit on the edge making up stories to distract her from the goings-on next door. A sweet scent wafts off her scalp as I towel her dry and help her into pajamas. I acquiesce to her request to sleep with me in the big bed, knowing she'll sleep like a hibernating bear and I won't sleep at all. Once she drifts off, I tiptoe downstairs.

Naomi sits on the couch, absorbed in her laptop. With the warm glow of a lamp illuminating her features, she looks like her mother at fifteen. The sight of her propels me back to my adolescence, to long nights at summer camp, sharing secrets with Louise.

"What the hell is going on at my house?" Her voice wrenches me back to the present. She pulls her knees in close and glares at me.

"What have your folks told you?" I lean against the doorframe, trying to buy time to come up with an appropriate answer.

"Not much. I know that Henderson guy, the psychiatrist my mom was suing, might have been murdered." Tears fill her eyes. "Do the cops think my mom did it? Is that why they're at my house? Are they going to arrest her?"

"Whoa, there, honey." I perch beside her, curling my arm around her shoulder. "I don't have a clue what the police are looking for. It might not have anything to do with Henderson's death. It could be related to one of your mom's clients or have something to do with your dad's business." I realize as soon as the words leave my mouth that they're not reassuring.

Naomi squirms away. Her hands clench the rolled-up edge of her T-shirt. "Yeah, it could be about my dad. He's been a real jerk."

"What do you mean?" I wonder whether Mark has stopped using cocaine. Louise still hasn't told me much.

"He stays out late, then picks fights with my mom. He's been taking trips to Boston a lot too. A couple of times, his secretary called home looking for him when my mom thought he was at work. Now he's back in a twelve-step program, so who knows what he was doing?" She shrugs, but it isn't an indication of indifference.

"What do you think he's been doing?"

"Drugs." Naomi looks at her laptop and flips the cover down fast, as if she suddenly realizes I can see what she's writing. She sets it beside her on the sofa and pulls her arms tightly across her chest. "What if it is about drugs and they arrest him?" A few tears slide down her face.

I rest my hand on hers. "I don't know for sure, honey, but honestly, I don't think anyone is getting arrested tonight."

"Do you know that or are you patronizing me?" She stands up, walks across the room, and leans against a wall, directing a stony stare my way.

"You're the last person I'd try to patronize."

"This just sucks. You don't know what's going on. I don't know what's going on. And my parents sure aren't saying. Am I supposed to act like it's all just okay with me? Ignore the fights? I'm not a kid anymore. I see things. What about my life? What am I supposed to do tomorrow? Everyone's going to be staring at me. You better believe this will be all over Facebook by morning."

I groan, thinking about those speed-of-light transmissions. "It'll be challenging, for sure," I commiserate. "Why not call some of your friends tonight and ask them to buffer things for you, you know, speak up for you, that kind of thing?"

Not mollified, she mocks me. "That's a great idea."

I pause, patting the seat beside me. "Come on. I'm just trying to talk things out with you."

She sits, but with her back against the arm of the sofa. I do the same, so our feet touch.

"I don't have the answers. I think what you can do is be yourself, even in the midst of all this. You can't fix anything. Just try to focus on the normal things. Do your homework, take your dance classes, attend drama club, go shopping with your friends. If people give you shit, give it right back to them. Leave the rest to the adults."

"Yeah, you're all doing such a frickin' great job with your lives."

"Ow." I hold my hands over my heart and mime pulling out an arrow.

"Sorry," she mumbles, though she doesn't look the least bit sorry.

"Listen, Naomi. I can only imagine how frightening this is for you. It's frightening for me too. The truth is that your dad and mom and I may be bigger and older, but there are times when age doesn't make us smarter. And it's clear that some parts of your family's life stink right now." I take a breath. "I'm sorry you have to experience this so early in your own life, but at least you've got many people who love you. Sometimes that's the best we can do."

She rolls her eyes. "That's soooo reassuring."

We sit for a few moments while I stare at a colorful landscape painting over the fireplace mantel, wrestling with the desire to throttle her. My better angels win. "Since I don't have much wisdom to offer, how about some hot chocolate?"

"Alright." Her assent is a bit begrudging, but at least we've agreed on something.

When I walk back into the living room with a tray of hot cocoa, we sit beside each other, sipping in silence. As we set our cups down, Naomi leans into me, her anger deflating like a punctured balloon. "Thanks," she says. "Now I'm really, *really* tired."

"Okay, then." We carry our cups to the kitchen, set them in the sink, and I follow Naomi upstairs where I settle her in the guest room.

Tiptoeing into my bedroom, I'm relieved to see Susie sound asleep. I'm too wired to sleep, and I want to talk to Ryan, so I step into the bathroom, turn on the fan, and call, giving him the few details I have.

"I wish Louise would tell me what's really going on. I feel so in the dark, and I don't understand her hesitancy. She's become secretive and closed in a way that's so unusual."

"Maybe Kate doesn't want Louise telling you everything. If there are complicated circumstances and she shares the details, you know how that'll go—it won't remain confidentially protected by lawyer-client privilege. The best thing for you to do is to fly to New York and get out of that rat's nest for a few days."

"You're right. I'll call you in the morning and let you know what I learn."

I brush my teeth, wash my face, and step into a nightgown before slipping into bed beside Susie, but sleep doesn't come easily. I feel distant from Louise, and yet involved, and oh-so clueless. The light bars on the police cars still flash, strobe-like, flinging an eerie blue glow onto the walls of my room.

Chapter 14

Susie's face, a mere three inches from mine, is the first thing I see in the morning. Her mouth is moving so fast, I know I wouldn't understand her even if I'd had twelve hours of solid sleep, instead of two. I yawn, talk her into brushing her teeth, and reach for the phone to comply with her request that we invite her mom for breakfast. I wonder whether I'll be flying to New York this afternoon.

Louise answers on the second ring, sounding ragged.

"What time did the police leave?"

"About midnight."

"What were they looking for?"

"I'm not sure," she moans, but her voice perks up at my invitation for pancakes. By the time Susie and Naomi are dressed, Louise is at the back door. The girls race downstairs and I can hear their questions before they reach the kitchen.

"What were the cops looking for? Are you going to be arrested? Is Dad?"

"Slow down," Louise implores. "The police searched every room in the house, including both of yours." She scrunches up her face in apology. "But they spent the most time in the kitchen. I don't know what they were looking for."

Susie reluctantly detaches herself from her mother's arms when Louise asks if she and Naomi would give "the adults" a few minutes alone. Naomi's face falls, but she leads Susie from the room.

"Thanks for taking them." Louise leans against the doorframe. "It was a late night."

"I saw the lights," I say while dragging a chair out from under the kitchen table and perching on it. "Was this about you or Mark?"

She rubs her eyes and takes a minute to respond. "I don't know. They left with a bunch of bags."

"Has Mark been dealing?"

"He says no and I want to trust him, especially now that he's back in the program. It could be about me and Henderson."

"What can I do?"

"Feed me and the kids. It's still early enough to have a good breakfast and get them to school on time. I'll go upstairs and do a better job of calming them down."

Turkey bacon sizzles in the frying pan. That tempting aroma mixes with that of fresh blueberries and pancake batter on the griddle. Kate calls, looking for Louise, who comes into the kitchen to take the call.

"Yes," she says. "I don't have clients this afternoon. I can make it by three. What about Sarah? No. I want her there." She pauses. "I don't care," she says. "That's okay. Yes, today. All right. See you later." She clicks off and sits on a stool. "Food will revive me."

"This food sure will." I smile.

"Can you come to Kate's office this afternoon to review the coroner's report with us? Alex will be there too."

I hesitate, anticipating Ryan's reaction. "Can we do it any earlier? I want to support you but I have plans to fly to New York to spend the weekend with Ryan."

"The report isn't expected out until two thirty." She peers at me quizzically. "Are you ready for a weekend with Ryan in New York?" Her face changes, "Forget that I said that. It's your life. Go. Have fun. I'll fill you in when you get back."

I shake my head. "Ryan and I can reschedule. I could always fly in later."

"You sure?" It's the first smile I've seen from her that morning.

"Of course."

As the girls run in, I turn to flip the pancakes, worrying about Ryan's reaction. No matter what I do, guilt will be my shadow. At the table, I focus on food and let the girls' jabber wash over me. After they leave, I dial Ryan's cell. "Bad news."

"Hold on a minute." His voice sounds muffled. "Is this about Louise or the weekend, or both?" He doesn't sound happy.

"Both. Louise was ragged this morning. The police spent hours combing through the house."

"Looking for what?"

"I don't know," I say, relieved to hear his concern taking priority over disappointment.

"Should I call my contacts up there?"

"Not yet. Not until I'm sure if this is about Louise or Mark."

"Okay. I'm hearing something else in your voice, aren't I?"

"Louise wants me at Kate's office to look over the coroner's report on Henderson's death." I wait a moment before adding, "The meeting's at three."

"Ohh-kay," he says. "Obviously, we have to change our plans. Do you want to fly in on a later plane or would you prefer that I catch a flight to Portland?"

I sink onto a kitchen chair. "Oh, I didn't even think of asking you to do that. It's lovely of you to offer, but I don't know if Louise will want your participation at this early stage."

"I wasn't suggesting I participate. I was suggesting I come up to see you, since you obviously can't get away."

Flooding with guilt and shame, I wonder why I didn't immediately say yes.

"Look." Ryan sounds resigned. "I've got a great weekend planned in New York. Either you meet me here or I'll cancel the plans and join you there. If the answer is neither, I'll take someone else to the theatre."

"Ryan, please," I plead. "I'm sleep-deprived and confused about what's happening here. I want to be with you, but Louise asked me to come to this meeting. She's in trouble. I have to help. I can't let her down like I let Miriam down. Can't I just do that and call you afterward?"

"First, this isn't anything like what happened with Miriam, so don't even go there. And in terms of us, all I can say is it seems you want me to wait indefinitely. To hold second, or third, or fourth place in line. You can't even commit to flying down this evening or having me fly up. That means my needs don't even make the lineup. How important can our relationship be to you? Forget it." There's silence on the line. I wonder what's coming next.

"Your inability to commit has hurt me too many times, Sarah. I think I'll just stay in New York and have my own good time. Tell Louise I'm available for her if she wants my help. As for you, figure out what you want and call me when you know. It's possible I might still be available."

I listen to the empty phone line after he hangs up.

Chapter 15

Desperate longing leads me to my bed, where a nap takes me far away from my problems. The alarm awakens me at two. When the phone rings, I answer, hoping it's Ryan. It isn't.

"Can you meet me at Kate's?" Louise asks. "I'm going in early."

"No problem."

It really is a problem, though. I'm so distracted on the drive into town that I almost rear-end the car in front of me. Then, having completely forgotten to call for my parking angels, I drive around in circles looking for a space until someone pulls out of a two-hour spot on Exchange.

Alex is right there, feeding quarters into the meter in front of mine, and she fills my meter as well. When I step out of the car, she envelops me in a warm hug and we cross the street to enter Kate's building together.

"How're you doing?" Alex looks me over with deep-set eyes the color of rich chocolate. She's the only completely non-neurotic person I know and I can't quite figure her out. Intelligent, a former cop, and now a formidable private investigator—how'd she get to where she is?

"Not so hot," I say as we step into the elevator. "I'm too worried about Louise to think clearly."

"We're all worried." We arrive at Kate's floor and step into her waiting room. "At least we'll have a report that could provide some clarity." She precedes me into the glass-walled conference room where Kate's paralegal is placing documents in front of four seats.

Kate's wearing navy trousers and a light silk sweater the color of glistening snow. She takes the chair at the head of the table. Louise, looking wan and worn out, is sitting to Kate's left.

"Would anyone like coffee?" Kate's paralegal holds a steaming carafe. The aroma of fresh brew tempts me, but declining ensures a better chance of a good night's sleep. As others accept the offer, my eyes search Kate's face.

"What's happening here?" I ask.

"Henderson was murdered. Louise is a suspect." Kate holds up her left hand and raises one finger after another as she makes her points. "They had a highly antagonistic relationship. They sparred publicly at professional conferences. The tenor of their divergent testimony in the Tate case raised some eyebrows, and that scene in the ladies' room at the courthouse didn't help."

As I sit in Kate's office, I think back to all the events of that day.

Kate's voice pierces my recollections. "The DA overheard Louise's comments about Henderson's anaphylactic allergy. When we add Henderson's use of Constant Caring to harass Louise, and our lawsuit against them, it provides motive."

"Where's the evidence?" I say.

"What do you think they were searching for last night?" Kate snaps. "Let's stop talking and read the report. We'll get first impressions, take some time to think about it, and get together again tomorrow." Kate flips the first page back and we all begin to read.

> Inspection of the conjunctiva of eyes, lips, oral cavity mucosa, tongue, throat/hypo pharynx, and nasal mucosa appeared to be edematous. Gold crowns were noted.
>
> Scrapings of yellowish powder-like material were taken from the corners of the mouth and the buccal mucosal surface of the lower lip.
>
> Lungs, right and left: Both lungs were heavy, frothy fluid was expressed from their cut surfaces, indication of swelling of the lungs.

Trachea and bronchial tree: Edematous/swollen mucosa of the trachea, and both right and left main stem Bronchi.

Gastric contents were examined, and there appeared to be brownish liquid and a partially digested food, which appeared to be some sort of meat product and pieces of bread.

Cardiovascular system: Right coronary, ascending and left circumflex arteries appeared to be approximately 80% occluded with what appears to be atheromatous plaque.

Liver: somewhat cirrhotic in gross appearance with loss of sharp liver edge and firm to the touch.

"Cirrhosis?" I ask.

"And ripe for a heart attack." Kate says. "No one had to go to the trouble of murdering him. They could have simply waited for him to eat a few more high-fat meals."

"Nice thought." Alex isn't amused.

I read on.

Preliminary cause of death appears to be:

Upper respiratory tract edema, and Pulmonary edema consistent with anaphylactoid-type reaction as the immediate cause of death. Contributory cause of death: Atherosclerotic coronary artery disease.

Analysis of gastric contents and material obtained from oral mucosa to follow.

"He died from an allergic reaction?" Louise looks up quizzically.

"They found bee pollen on his mouth," Kate says.

"That's why they searched Louise's house?" I ask.

"Yup."

"What investigative process did they use?" I'm on a roll.

"Sealed off his office. Tested his coffee and what appeared to be the remains of his dinner in the trashcan. Fingerprinted everything. They identified microscopic parts of bee bodies, little legs and wings and other material on his mouth."

"That's disgusting." I turn to Louise. Her head is resting on her crossed arms. "You use bee pollen as a nutritional supplement, don't you?"

She looks up wearily. "Yes, to stimulate my immune system. I normally keep some in my pantry for just that purpose."

"Other people use bee pollen as a nutritional supplement," Alex interjects. "After Henderson's interview with the Portland paper, many people knew he was allergic to bees and that one sting could cause an anaphylactic reaction. It doesn't take a genius to assume that a nutritional supplement full of bee parts might deliver a fatal dose of venom."

"Why didn't he use an EpiPen?" I ask.

"What's that?" The paralegal looks up from her notes.

"A syringe filled with epinephrine to counteract an allergic reaction," Alex answers. "People with life-threatening allergies carry it in case they're stung or inadvertently eat something they're allergic to."

"I doubt Henderson knew he'd been exposed, so he wouldn't have thought to use it," Kate surmises.

"Is it at all possible that Henderson was taking bee pollen?" I turn to Louise. "Sort of homeopathically, to try to make himself less allergic?"

"No." Louise rolls her eyes. "No one with a violent allergy to bees would try that. Besides, a homeopathic dose would be so small that it would probably be untraceable."

"I interviewed an allergist," Alex adds. "Though it's more likely for people to have an anaphylactic reaction to venom injected through a sting or a bite, bee pollen can also cause it."

I begin nibbling on my nails.

"Don't go adding this to your list of life's perils," Louise says. She has me pegged. I change my focus, staring out the large window in Kate's conference room, where cotton candy clouds float across the blue sky.

Alex continues. "Bee pollen is widely available in natural food stores, in capsules, or a liquid solution stabilized by alcohol. Sometimes in a granular form."

"Anyone who reads the newspaper could have poisoned Henderson," I say.

"Not really," Kate counters, crossing her arms over her chest. "Most people have never heard of bee pollen as a nutritional supplement. It's generally used by people looking for cures, not poisons."

"And most folks don't know it could be fatal to someone with an allergy to bees," Louise says. "I did. And my hatred for Henderson was pretty public." Her head sinks into her hands.

"And you were in his office earlier that day," I remind her.

Kate shoots a look at me, then at Louise.

"How do the police suppose you magically inserted it into his food?" I ask.

Kate pushes her chair back, stands, and chucks the report on the table. "The fire alarm went off early that evening and the building was evacuated. The murderer could have pulled the alarm and used the ensuing chaos to get into Henderson's office and spike his food or coffee." She picks up her briefcase and tosses her copy of the report into it. "Let's give it a rest for a few hours and get back together to sort things through this weekend."

"Why don't I make dinner tomorrow night and we can talk things over at my house?"

"Thanks for offering," Kate says. "That's a great idea. Someone killed Henderson. We know it wasn't you…" she locks eyes with Louise, "but the police sure have you on their radar."

"On their radar? Come on, Kate," Louise snaps. "I'm their prime suspect. We all know why the police searched my house. And I'm sure they found plenty of what they were looking for."

Chapter 16

On the drive home, I watch people biking around the Boulevard and long to join them, to do something that pulls me out of the sticky, complicated mess of Louise's life and the challenges in my own. Biking will give me pleasure, and I happily change clothes and hop on my sturdy fifteen-speed road bike, pedaling past spring gardens bursting with flowers in the quiet Back Cove neighborhood where I live. Center-hall Colonials, mansards, and stately Victorians seem to preen behind carefully mowed lawns and brick sidewalks.

I cycle down Vannah Avenue onto Baxter Boulevard, a curving two-lane road that hugs a picturesque cove. The walking path is packed with joggers. Blue-green salt water sparkles in the cove, set off by the backdrop of the Portland peninsula. Affection for my adopted hometown fills me, along with a desire to stay put. Ryan is happy in Boston. The time has come, I think, to accept life as a single woman or find a man committed to Maine.

After ninety minutes, sweaty and calmer, I soak in my claw-foot tub, releasing the kinks from my calves, and proceed to indulge in a decadent dinner of pasta with Alfredo sauce in front of an old Hepburn and Tracy movie on the tube. Afterwards, deep sleep claims me.

Clattering in the kitchen wakes me at midnight. I traipse downstairs to find Tillie's teeth clenched around a wriggling mouse. Lola is trying to grab it. Shaking with primitive fear, I push both cats and their prey out the door. Wide awake at my least favorite hour, I begin obsessing. Have I made the wrong choices—Portland vs. Boston, Maine vs. New York, romance vs. murder, planning a future with Ryan vs. dealing with vermin?

Since Ryan always turns his cell phone off when he goes to bed, I figure this is a good time to phone him again and apologize, leaving a message and avoiding confrontation. Unfortunately, Ryan picks up after five rings and a woman's laughter trills in the background. My prepared speech dissolves and I disconnect like a true coward.

Thirty minutes of rumination keep me from sleep and when I trudge downstairs again, Tillie and Lola are patiently sitting on the back porch, sans mouse. We climb into bed together where a restless sleep awaits me, but at least it's uninterrupted.

I'm sitting at the kitchen table reading the paper when the phone rings.

"Did you call last night?" Ryan asks.

"I did."

"And?"

"I didn't want to interrupt anything."

"You have no grounds to protest."

"Excuse me? First we're going to New York for an intimate weekend to plan our future and ten seconds later you've got another woman in your hotel room?"

"You turned me down," Ryan says.

"You know the reason!"

"There's always something."

I stand up from the table and shove the chair back, fuming. "If your love for me is so tenuous that you can't keep your pants on when an emergency delays me, we have no future."

"You haven't lost that tart tongue, have you?" he says, the edge in his voice all too familiar. "I know how important Louise is, but if I'm important, you should have welcomed my offer to come to Maine."

That stops me cold. I take a few moments to reorient. "You're right. I'm sorry. That's why I called last night. To apologize."

A few moments pass before Ryan responds. "I understand your choice to stay. What I don't understand is your hesitation about having me join you. What's that about?"

"I don't know. It all feels like too much, like things are spinning out of control."

"Under the circumstances, why should I blow off expensive theatre tickets and dinner reservations at the hottest place in Manhattan?"

"You shouldn't."

"You're doing what you need to do and so am I."

"Apparently. But it doesn't seem like it's taking you very long to replace me." I rue the words the minute they leave my mouth.

"In fact, Sarah, it has taken me a very, *very* long time to even think of replacing you. I've told you where things stand. I'm trying to make decisions about my future. Let's cool off and talk in a few days."

I sink into the cream-colored, sleek recliner Ryan bought for the house when we first moved in, swing my legs onto the footstool, and think back over our marriage, knowing he's right. After Miriam's murder, I was emotionally incapable of real intimacy. Our marriage suffered, and I blamed it all on Ryan and his change from public service law to corporate law. His paychecks supported us while I returned to graduate school, began a new career, and started my psychotherapy practice. And he put up with me until, finally, he just couldn't anymore.

Though he isn't in the room to hear me, the apology he deserves trips off my tongue. "I am really sorry, Ryan. Really and truly sorry."

There's no way to avoid reality. Here we are, years later, with Ryan offering me another chance to reconcile, and I cancel out. Maybe I've already made my choice.

Chapter 17

Reporters cluster in front of Louise's house late Saturday hoping to catch a story for the evening news. They move like a herd to surround Kate and Alex as they step out of their car. I peer through my living room curtains, watching Kate make use of the opportunity for good press. Then footsteps sound behind me. Startled, I whirl around.

"Chill out, it's only me." Louise pats my shoulder.

"How'd you get here without the hordes tracking you?"

"Snuck through our backyards. The rhododendron made for good cover, and your door is unlocked." Louise squints out the living room window, keeping well out of sight.

"What's with the reporters?"

"Someone leaked the medical examiner's report, along with the fact that the police have identified me as a suspect." Louise digs an inhaler out of her pocket. The nozzle hisses as she inhales and Kate and Alex's knock comes as punctuation.

Louise plumps up a pillow and collapses into a cushy chair. Alex gives me a quick hug and settles on one end of the couch. Kate hugs me too before she lies on the sofa, resting her head on Alex's lap. I snag the recliner.

"This is my first asthma attack in years." Louise sucks again on the inhaler and slides it into her pocket.

"I'm not surprised," Alex says. "Given all this stress."

"At least the girls were spared the spectacle. My mom picked them up early today and she's keeping them overnight." Kitty still lives in a spacious ranch on the Boulevard, the same house where Louise grew up. "I wish my dad were alive." Louise sounds wistful. "Not that my mom isn't a big help. She's been a rock and, I have to say, Mark's really coming through."

"It's a relief to hear that, and honestly, you're lucky Kitty's your mom." I wish my mother could be half as supportive.

"Thanks for offering to make us dinner," Kate says. "I'm starving."

"Almost ready." I stand up and walk back through the foyer, pausing in the dining room. I've taken care to set the rectangular oak table with a willow-green tablecloth and old-fashioned china scored from a yard sale the previous summer. Yellow roses stand in a pressed-glass vase beside crystal tea light holders. A large green salad is already on the table.

Alex follows me into the kitchen. "Everything looks lovely. How can I help?"

I place slices of spinach–feta pie and roasted vegetables onto dinner plates, and Alex carries them to the table. We take our places, light the candles, say a blessing, and dig in, enjoying dinner in relative silence, except for murmurs of delight. In the break before second helpings, Alex poses the question most on my mind.

"How likely is it that Henderson was killed by a disgruntled client?"

"He was a pompous ass," I say, "but if a client killed him, confidentiality issues will make any investigation more challenging."

"We can get by those hurdles," Kate says.

"I've already identified the clients in his office the night he died," Alex adds.

"How'd you manage that?" Louise seems surprised.

"It's a small town." Alex sets down her fork and sips sparkling cider. "I know someone who knows someone. Later this week, I'll be interviewing all those evening clients to see if they noticed anything unusual. I've heard a few whispers about sexual improprieties, so the licensing-board records are on my list."

"A few of my clients alluded to inappropriate touching, but no one would say enough to let me report and none would go before the board with a complaint. Too much shame and self-blame." Louise shakes her head. "I suspect he got away with it."

"Maybe not." Alex sets her hand on Louise's. "We don't yet know who killed him."

"That would be a form of justice, wouldn't it?" I can't help smiling.

Kate shoots me a look of conspiratorial solidarity. "I've heard Constant Caring's board was debating Henderson's tenure, chafing at his consulting fees and the increasing complaints from clinicians. They weren't happy about Louise's lawsuit and were worried more might follow."

"There's an internal skirmish going on at Constant Caring," Alex adds. "I haven't nailed down any details yet."

That doesn't surprise me, after the recent sessions with Todd and Elena Owens. But I have no details, and if I do get some, client confidentiality will prevent me from sharing them—though if that happens, I know I'll be tempted, especially if they can absolve Louise.

"I'm driving to Massachusetts tomorrow to dig into Henderson's history there," Alex says. "He closed a practice in Cambridge before moving to Maine."

The oven timer buzzes. "Dessert?" I say.

"Of course," Kate answers.

"Why don't you all go on into the living room," I suggest, "and I'll bring the cookies out with tea and coffee. Who wants what?"

Alex clears the dishes while I slide the cookies from the oven onto a platter. We pour tea into a china teapot, coffee into a matching coffeepot, and set it all on two trays to carry into the living room. I step back into the kitchen for napkins, and the phone rings. In spite of everything, I hope it's Ryan.

It's not. The voice is gruff. "Don't drink the coffee, Sarah smart-ass, or you'll be next. Henderson's lonely in the morgue."

My skin prickles. "What? Who is this?" I ask, pressing the record button.

"Someone who knows just what you know, lady. Henderson knew it too. Keep your nose out of places it doesn't belong, and watch your back." *Click.*

Alex walks back into the kitchen just as I sit on the stool.

"What just happened?" she says. "You're white as a sheet."

"Someone just threatened to put me into the morgue next to Henderson." My legs shake as the kitchen disappears and I stand in

Boston's morgue looking at Miriam's body. The acrid smell of formaldehyde fills my nostrils.

"Sarah?" I'm aware of Alex's hand on my shoulder. "Kate! Louise!" I hear her voice from far away.

Louise gently takes my face in her hands. "Sarah, honey, where are you?"

I shake my head, look up. "I'm here, but everything's a little strange."

"What do you mean?" Kate asks.

I wonder how to answer that. Should I be talking about what just happened in real time, or what seems to be taking place inside my brain? I choose the former. My hand trembles as I press replay.

Louise lays her arm around my shoulders. "Do you recognize the voice?"

I shake my head.

"Another suspect could really help Louise," Kate says.

Alex shoots her a reproachful glance. "Ever heard of tact, Kate?"

"Tact or no tact, we still have to call the police," Kate retorts as she picks up the phone.

"Maybe Billy is on duty," Louise says hopefully.

After a short conversation, Kate reports that Billy is on duty, but he isn't at the station. "Because it sounds like it's related to Henderson's murder, they'll send a detective out as soon as possible."

Louise takes my hand. "Let's go sit in the living room before that tea gets cold."

As I stand up, strength floods back into my body. "That caller obviously thinks Henderson and I shared a case. It gives us something to go on. One of our clients must have a secret that could ruin someone's reputation." I look to Louise hopefully. "At least that gives us a clue about our direction. Let's comb through our cases and figure out which clients we shared."

"Maybe the same person set me up as a suspect," Louise muses.

"You set yourself up," Kate retorts, and I wonder what she's talking about, but at this moment, I don't have the wherewithal to ask.

Alex pokes Kate in the ribs before she settles in the recliner. "Think you could take a break from being so thoroughly obnoxious?"

Kate's response is a snort, but as Louise and I settle onto the couch, Kate puts one hand on Louise's shoulder and one on mine. "I'm sorry, guys. When I'm overwhelmed, I'm snippier than usual."

"You're excused," I say. "But tone it down. We've got enough to deal with already."

"I agree with you, Sarah—the caller definitely points us in the direction of shared clients," Alex says. "When you poke through your charts, see if there's a secret hot enough to incite murder."

"We listen to confidential disclosures every day." Louise nibbles on a cookie. "Secrets that could destroy reputations, careers, marriages, the entire pattern of life in a small city."

I nod. "Often it's about abuse. Physical or sexual. Disclosure can take people back decades. When that happens, the perpetrators often have a reputation as upstanding citizens, town leaders."

"We're obligated to report that abuse to the state," Louise adds. "Most perpetrators think they're free, especially if a lot of time has gone by. Now, with so many recent cases in the news, priests and coaches being outed for abuse they think they've gotten away with, I can imagine other guilty parties are worried."

"There are different kinds of secrets." I sip my tea. "Local politicians don't want a petty crime from their adolescence to come out and derail their ambitions. Medical mishaps could cost physicians their reputations, sometimes their licenses."

"And there are always those folks who were in college in the sixties and seventies who did LSD, or sifted blocks of marijuana through dormitory window screens," Louise adds.

"Now they're running corporations and have turned into models of righteousness," I say.

"Would someone kill for a reason like that?" Alex asks.

"You never know," I answer.

"How can we possibly tease out the one secret tied to Henderson?" Louise muses.

"Hard work," Kate says, standing by the fireplace. "But think of it this way: one of your clients might also be at risk and not know it."

"The risk isn't limited to clients," I say. "Louise is facing a possible murder charge. I've just been threatened. Maybe other therapists are at risk." I draw my knees up close, wishing I were anywhere but here.

Chapter 18

A car door slams. I'm opening the front door seconds later to see Billy Marshall walking up the path, wearing khakis, a white shirt, and a leather jacket. As he steps into the house, he's met by a chorus of hellos. Louise hugs him, and it seems like an awfully long time before she lets him go.

"I thought you weren't available," Kate says.

"I wasn't when the call first came in, but I am now."

"Do you need us?"

"Did any of you answer the phone?"

"No. Sarah did. We heard the message when she played it back."

"If you don't have any information to add, then I think Sarah's the only person I need to take the report from," Billy says.

"Okay. Then we might as well take off." Alex turns to me. "You and Detective Marshall have plenty to discuss."

"You don't have to go," I protest.

Kate demurs. "It's been a long day."

"I'm exhausted too. You'll be okay now, Sarah, won't you?" Louise asks as she slides her arms into a yellow cardigan.

Alex is suddenly close to me. "If you get scared, for any reason at all, call nine-one-one and go over to Louise's."

"You can sleep on the couch in the den," Louise says. "Oh, hell, you can sleep with me. Mark's still sleeping in the guest room." She blushes as she and Billy exchange glances.

I usher my friends out the door and lock it tight before returning to the living room and motioning for Billy to sit on the couch. His hair looks shaggy and kind of sexy. I sit beside him, inhaling the scent of his aftershave, something spicy and sweet. The gold flecks in his eyes sparkle beneath his long lashes.

"First," Billy says. "I want to say that most folks don't take well to being threatened. Even cops can get shaken. But we're going to talk it through. "Why don't you tell me exactly what happened? Then I'll ask you questions, and we can listen to the recording together. By the way, hitting the record button was quick thinking."

"Thanks." I smile, a short reprieve, before relaying the facts.

Billy asks questions and clarifies details. When it's time to listen to the recording, I focus on beaming in courage as I walk toward the kitchen. Then I trip over one of the cats. Billy catches me. His hands linger at my waist. We are so close, I can smell his breath. It's sweet.

We step into the kitchen and play the message. Billy hits replay twice. "So you and Henderson shared clients?"

"A few. I only know about the ones who've told me; they don't always. And some might have left my practice and entered treatment with Henderson. Unless he asked for their records, I have no way of knowing."

"What kinds of clients do you work with?"

"Normal people dealing with life transitions, some with trauma histories, some struggling with difficult medical conditions, divorces, that kind of thing. I stay away from cases that are inordinately complicated—and I try to have nothing to do with psychopaths." My mind flips back to Miriam's body in the morgue. I close my eyes, reach for the back of a chair to lean on, and try to erase the image and the smell of formaldehyde.

"Sarah? Are you all right?" Billy's voice cuts through the flashback.

I flop into a chair.

"Do you need something? Water?"

"No, I'm okay." I sigh, focusing on long, deep exhalations, eventually regaining my capacity to think. "Maybe someone has a vendetta against therapists in Portland, and Henderson was only the first one targeted."

"Maybe," Billy says, tapping his pen on the tabletop. "But this message isn't a generalized vendetta. It's clear you shared a client.

Think about who that person might be. If you come up with something, call me. In the meantime," he looks at me sternly, "please stay
clear of the investigation."

I shake my head. "I can't."

"Why not?" Billy's voice turns authoritative. "This is no game." The
muscles of his jaw ripple. He folds his arms across his chest.

Anger rises in my chest. "Don't patronize me. I'm no neophyte. I
handled felony assault cases in Boston's ghettos. A psychotic stalker
murdered my best friend when we were public defenders. His case was
originally assigned to me." I inhale and exhale, and morph into a
fire-breathing dragon. "You know what's up here. Your boss interviewed
Louise, and your colleagues just searched her house. If she's in trouble, I
have to help. Besides, if one of our clients is involved, I have no choice."

Billy's eyebrows rise. "You think you and *Louise* share this client
with Henderson?"

"I don't know, and even if I did, I couldn't tell you."

"If you know who the client is, or if you even have a suspicion, you
can and must tell me. Psychotherapeutic confidentiality stops when the
client is a risk to himself or someone else. You need to honestly assess
whether or not that's the situation. If it is, you need to tell me, and I
mean right now." His eyes lock on mine and he waits for me to talk.

I don't.

He breaks first. "This is my job. I don't care that you handled felony
assaults in Boston. This isn't Boston, you aren't a practicing attorney,
and this is not your investigation."

I still have nothing to say.

"I'm serious, Sarah. This is dangerous. I think I understand where
you're coming from, but your concerns about Louise may be misplaced.
You're the one at risk here. If you've already lost a close friend to murder,
you know what I'm talking about. That caller was warning you off. You'd
better listen. Call nine-one-one if you're threatened again, or go next
door, then call. Understand?"

I nod.

As I walk him to the front door, I can't help myself. I just have to
ask. "So you work nights?"

He stops, turns back, runs his fingers through his hair. "We work
rotating shifts. I'm working until midnight."

"This probably isn't kosher, but would you like to have breakfast? Tomorrow?"

"It definitely isn't kosher. But it's not like I just met you on this call. We already know each other from synagogue. So, yes…" He smiles. "I would like that."

"Okay. How about nine?"

"Sure. I'll pick you up."

We're standing so close, I could lean my head against his chest. I want to.

"Lock up after me. Don't take any chances."

"I won't." I smile.

He smiles back, and I swear I see him riding off into the sunset.

Chapter 19

After he leaves, I lean against the door, close my eyes, and immerse myself in the sensation of Billy—his smell, his voice, his eyes locked onto mine. That leads to a sensual recall of my recent lovemaking with Ryan, which sends me spiraling through confusion and doubt. What the heck do I want and what kind of person am I if I can go right from desire for one man to desire for another? Maybe it's the simplicity of a new relationship that's so alluring. Ryan and I have tremendous baggage. That can't compete with the lightness of a new love affair.

The cats sit in the foyer, on either side of the door, waiting patiently until I bend down and toss two catnip-filled mice into the living room. I watch them knock their prey about before I double-check the locks and climb the stairs to my bedroom.

It's a troubled sleep, hijacked by a nightmare of Henderson's murderer stalking me just the way Miriam's murderer stalked her. I awake drenched in sweat.

"Damn it, Miriam!" I shout. "Why don't you help me with this?"

The cats leap off the bed and flee from the room as a luminous form floats to the French provincial chair. Miriam is wearing the same filmy white dress.

"Who killed Henderson," I ask. "Who threatened me, and how are those things connected?" As I say that, I recognize how comforted I am by her presence, even if she's a figment of her former self.

"I'm sorry to say that even though I'm on the other side, it doesn't mean I know everything."

"I need more than that."

"I'm here, aren't I? And you're talking to me. That's kind of cool, isn't it?"

"No. That is not entirely reassuring."

"This is my first assignment. My job is to make sure you know that you're loved, and that if you ask for help, you'll get it, though maybe not always in the form you anticipate. Checking your client files makes sense. And, oh, I'm supposed to keep telling you to trust your intuition."

Miriam is there, and then she's gone. I pull the covers up to my chin, close my eyes, and eventually fall back to sleep. When the alarm rings at seven, I spread my yoga mat on the floor and do as many poses as I can until relaxation overcomes the distress in my body. Clearly, I've inherited the family clairvoyance and it has now punctured all the defenses I'd erected against it. By the time Billy arrives, I'm more composed. Thankfully, he's easy. We chat about the weather, books, and movies all the way to Bintliff's, where we jam ourselves into the entryway with four other couples for the customary wait. Billy's arm brushes mine, sending a pleasant tingling sensation along my spine. We're early enough to find seats on the upstairs deck, and stop talking about Billy's friends on the force only long enough to demolish the warm banana pancakes stacked on the plates set before us. A refreshing breeze ruffles the tablecloth.

With our appetites sated, Billy suggests a walk on Mackworth Island. I call it Magical Mackworth, the hundred-acre island adjacent to both Portland and the town of Falmouth. The former home of Governor Percival Proctor Baxter, he donated Mackworth to the state of Maine in 1946, with instructions that it be used as a "sanctuary for wild beasts and birds."

It serves multiple purposes, housing a school, a well-maintained walking trail, narrow beaches to fish, run, or swim from, and a "community village" of fairy houses, overseen by the island's maintenance crew and created by visiting children. I often drive over to take advantage of the walking paths.

Billy crosses the narrow causeway and brakes at the manned guardhouse. The guard admits us with a perfunctory wave toward the few remaining parking spots in the small lot.

We hike past an open grassy knoll just beyond the parking area. After the first turn, the view is strictly woods and water. Billy clasps my hand to pull me up a rise. Wild vines hang from trees beside the path. Chipmunks and red squirrels scamper in the underbrush. An illusory remoteness enhances the island's allure, creating the impression that I'm cocooned and safe with Billy.

"How did you decide on police work?" I ask. "Especially after practicing law?"

"I always wanted to be a cop." Billy's face lights up.

"Kind of unusual for a nice Jewish boy, huh?"

"So is moving from law to social work. Don't most folks go the other way?"

"You got me." I return his smile. "I guess we have that in common. So what made you want to be a cop?"

"Hawaii Five-O." He laughs, leading me to a spot where the pathway juts out above the ocean. A parade of boats glides by, their sails puffing out with the breeze. We stand close, gazing out at the water.

"Tell me seriously," I prompt as we resume meandering. Rugged small cliffs and views of the sea peek in and out as we negotiate the path. The scent of salty ocean, piney forest, and sweet sea roses wafts through the air.

"I knew a detective. Family friend," Billy says. "Great storyteller. He loved his work and he always made time for me. I was on the wild side as a teenager, and he didn't judge. Ironically, it was also a way to rebel. Since I was the first son in a Jewish family, my career expectations were well-defined: doctor, lawyer, rabbi, or investment advisor. Police work had a different kind of allure."

We stand aside to let runners pass. The foliage grows so thick as it arches overhead that it covers most of the sky. A cool breeze chills my shoulders. I'm grateful for the sun's warmth dappling through the leaves.

"Come." Billy leads me up a side path into a private pine grove, the final resting place for Governor Baxter's beloved dogs and horse. Sound seems muffled there. Fairy houses nestle under trees and beside narrower paths that lead to the community village dedicated to their construction.

Captivated, I kneel on the grass. Anchored twigs hold pieces of birch bark that serve as roofs for the little dwellings. Mussel shells form walkways; leaves and moss become carpets. Clamshells and acorns serve as furniture. Billy gathers bark as I create a tiny home. I reach up and tuck a wayward curl behind his ear. The obvious intensity pushes us back toward the trail, where we begin a hunt for wildflowers.

"We've missed the early bloom for wood anemone, jack-in-the-pulpit, and trout lilies, which look like dancing starfish. But the baneberry is in bloom. All native to the coast," he tells me, demonstrating his knowledge from growing up in the area.

We scramble down a slope to the beach, climb over seaweed-laden rocks, and watch a family of little green crabs crawl under rockweed. Finally, we lean back to back, relaxing on a sun-toasted boulder.

"What did you study in college?"

"I double-majored—criminal justice and religion."

"Religion, huh? Is that how you got interested in mysticism?"

"How'd you know I—?"

"Oh, women have ways of knowing," I interrupt him.

He laughs and says, "In college, I began reading Kabbalah, tried different meditation practices."

"I meditate too, but not consistently enough. I stop and start."

"It's challenging. I've been at it a long time."

"How did you end up in law school?"

"Family pressure, and my wife's preference. I figured law school couldn't hurt. I got a scholarship and did well, took a job with a Portland firm after graduation." He tosses a rock from hand to hand before flinging it into the sea. "I didn't like it enough to spend my life doing it."

"Me neither," I commiserate. "What didn't you like?"

"The rules. The stodginess. How obnoxious I became." Billy grins. "And I hated the expensive suits."

"You sound just like me." I laugh. "I left for essentially the same reasons." I think of Miriam and my smile fades. "With some added trauma."

"So you said." He looks at me expectantly, but I shake my head. He helps me up, and we navigate the tricky climb back up to the path.

"I had this idea that the legal system was about justice," he says. "But I found it too susceptible to monied influence and power. Once I paid back the student loans and had some solid investments, I trained for police work."

"Do you like it?"

"Yes. I made detective fast, but I'm still learning."

"What did your wife think?" Our hands swing back and forth as we walk.

"That I'd gone crazy. That I was throwing away a solid future. She wanted the house in Falmouth, the sailboat, the country club. It wasn't going to happen on a cop's salary."

A sudden silence hangs between us, although he doesn't let go of my hand. As we approach a bench set off to the side of the path, facing the ocean, Billy gestures for me to sit. He leans back against a birch. "Honestly, that description of my wife was unfair."

"I'm listening."

"Emily and I met in college." He picks up a stick, fiddles with the bark. "Although she knew I wanted to go into police work, when the application for the LSATs came around, she persuaded me to take the test. My scores came back high and I let myself get talked into going to law school. Truth is, I liked practicing law at first, but after a while, it just didn't fit for me. As a cop, it helps to know the law as thoroughly as I do."

"What happened to your marriage?"

"She was ready for children and I wasn't. And she was sure that she didn't want to be the wife of a cop." He squats, drawing lines in the dirt with the stick. "We separated. She met someone. Maybe she already knew him." He looks up. "She wanted the divorce. I didn't, but that's the way it goes sometimes." He stands and tosses the stick into the ocean. "You don't always get what you want at the time you think you want it."

He doesn't seem finished, so I wait.

"She's remarried. Two kids in three years."

"Ooh." I wince. "Was that hard on you?"

"Yes, and no. I think I've gotten over Emily. She's doing exactly what she wants and so am I." Billy reaches for my hand, pulls me upright. As we resume our walk, he says, "Your turn."

"Wait. I have one more question. Well, maybe two. I've also studied Jewish mysticism. I try to hold the awareness that spirituality can infuse everything we do, but how do you bring a mystical orientation to police work?"

He stops, turns, and dazzles me with a sparkling smile. "You know the Kabbalistic creation story is all about shatterings, right?"

"Yes."

"I love the idea that God emanated light into darkness and holiness into vessels, creating the Tree of Life. And how they shattered, causing shards and sparks of holiness to fall throughout the universes."

I nod.

"And the idea that the second time, the re-emanated vessels were connected closely enough to contain all that holiness. You know how clear Judaism is about our job—to partner with God—to collect those shards and repair the world. You see it in your work, and I see it in mine. Light comes through everywhere, including the broken places. There's plenty of shattering in police work."

"I love the foundational belief that holiness is imbued in everything," I say. "But while it's an easy enough concept to embrace sitting in synagogue or celebrating a wedding, the rubber meets the road in the difficult things in life, in the dark places."

"Exactly." Billy smiles. "It's challenging to hold a spiritual orientation when dealing with crime, but I do my best. Just holding that awareness keeps me compassionate and grounded."

"I try to do the same in my practice, where I'm a witness to stories of the worst kinds of abuse. It can be challenging, but I focus on the holiness inherent in each person's capacity to heal. That makes all the difference."

We walk the paths in silence for a while, before I turn to Billy and stop to ask another question. "How do you deal with the possibility of having to kill someone?"

"So far, in eight years, I've only had to draw my weapon. But I think of it this way—if it comes to saving someone's life by taking another, that's my job." He resumes our walk. "Those were good questions. Now, it's your turn."

I tell him about leaving law and the dissolution of my marriage. "Ryan and I intermittently reconnect, and the whole thing is up in the air right now," I say. "We were together in Boston recently and made plans to meet in New York, but I backed out and things collapsed—as they usually do. It looks as though we're both moving on."

A chilly onshore breeze blows in, with a thickening fog in its wake. As we reach the car and settle into the front seats, he draws me close, bending his head until his lips meet mine. A powerful heat surges between our bodies and the windows get steamy. When we come up for air, a line of cars idle in wait for our spot in the small lot. I would have ignored them, but Billy starts the motor and drives me home. We indulge in a few more minutes of lip-lock in my driveway. He promises to call. I walk into my house, sprawl on the couch, and replay the sensation of his mouth on mine.

Chapter 20

"What's going on up there?" my mother asks during our Sunday evening phone call. "Something tells me you're in trouble."

"I'm okay, and I already told you what's going on with Louise."

"I don't believe the only person in trouble is Louise. I see it spilling out over you as well. My intuition never lies. Please take a self-defense class, or let Louise teach you some moves. Remember the demonstration Louise did for me on my last visit?"

"Yes."

"Did I tell you that when I came back to New York, I got my book group interested? We all signed up for an introductory self-defense class." She laughs her deep, mirthful laugh—a laugh I love. "You should see us, this group of old biddies! We like it so much, we're continuing. You're all alone up there, honey. I think you should learn some moves."

I picture my mother having a blast knocking her friends down and getting knocked down by them. She's surely no old biddy. In fact, she's beautiful, with her silver hair always perfectly coiffed and her trim body attired more stylishly than I could ever manage. She looks years younger than her chronological age of seventy-two.

"I'll look into a self-defense course. Thanks for suggesting that. It'll make me feel more able to take care of myself. Have you seen Aunt Zelda recently?"

"Off on another trip. She told me she spoke with you. Do you need her advice, honey? She's going to be out of town for two weeks."

"No. I'm okay. She already gave me some advice."

"I'm glad. Your aunt is a fount of wisdom. A bit kooky, but definitely tuned in."

Through the kitchen window, I notice Louise en route to my door. "Gotta go, Mom."

"Take those classes. You never know when you might need to defend yourself."

I wonder what my mother is picking up on. I have to find a way to add self-defense into my busy schedule. "Okay, Mom. Give my love to Dad." I'm happy to hang up and turn my attention to Louise.

"So, how are you?" She pulls out a chair, sits across from me at the kitchen table, and bats her eyelashes. "Any sex?"

I laugh. It's nice to have something other than murder to discuss. "Breakfast, a hike, a little smooching. You were right. He's hot."

Louise blushes. "Ah, what I'd do for a little romance." She closes her eyes for a moment. When she opens them, her brow is creased. "Moving to the darker side, Alex wants to review our client cases for connections between you, me, and Henderson. Do you have time tomorrow night?"

"Yes. A few of my clients are on vacation, so my day is ending early enough for me to see Janice at four thirty. Where do you want to meet?"

"Alex's office."

"I'll walk over after my session. I can get there by five forty-five."

"Good. Thanks. Gotta take Susie to a party." She stands up, hugs me, and steps out the door.

I inwardly groan at the idea of sorting my client list, but I decide to start by flipping through old appointment books, which are stored in a locked file cabinet in my basement.

As the sky turns inky black, I sit at the dining room table with a cup of tea and a notepad, listing every client who'd mentioned being in treatment with Henderson. Some of my clients might not have disclosed it, even though I always ask about experiences with prior therapists as part of information-gathering during intake sessions. I've got to be careful to stay ethical when asking those questions now, since my motivation is more focused on finding Henderson's killer.

While replenishing my tea, I veer off into regret over my recent reconnection with Ryan. We've been a merry-go-round ever since we divorced, both of us struggling to move on. We each have had other relationships, but they haven't lasted, and in the interim, we circle around each other and get re-involved, only to separate again. I decide not to think about that, and return to my client list.

Checking off one woman after another, I realize again, to my amazement, just how many clients were sexually abused as children. Some are plagued with terrifying replays. Others suppress the entire experience until they give birth or their memories return in full force when their own child reaches the age they were when the abuse occurred. Painful memories can blindside them, the same way flashbacks of Miriam's murder keep blindsiding me.

Past sexual abuse seems as possible a motive for Henderson's murder as anything else. Disclosure to a therapist requires a report to state authorities, but we can only report the abusers our clients identify. Some they don't remember, others they won't disclose. The possibility of a report is a threat to the present life of perpetrators, no matter how many years have passed. I find myself wondering about George Tate. His ex, Brooke, might have spilled compromising information about George to Henderson when she was in treatment with him. I wonder what Todd and Elena have seen, especially since Todd admitted that George has been acting strangely.

Miriam suggested that checking the client lists was important, and I feel that now, even more so, myself.

As I get ready for bed, it occurs to me that my mentor, psychiatrist Jim Barr, might be able to help sort through all of this. We collaborate on cases, and I consult with him about perplexing issues with clients. Yes, I need to talk to Jim. I'm calmer just picturing his smile. I phone and leave a message.

Jim starts his day very early. At 7:15 the next morning, his secretary, Carolyn, calls.

"Hi Sarah. Jim's eight o'clock just cancelled, can you get here by then?"

I do a quick calculation. My clients sessions start at nine-thirty. "It'll be a little tight, but I'll be there."

Jim's office is tucked away in a low-roofed brick building just off Route One in Scarborough. It takes me twenty minutes to get there, with a stop at Lois's Natural Foods for chai tea and muffins.

Carolyn, Jim's sixty-five-year-old secretary, white-haired, blue-eyed, and motherly, welcomes me. "It's been a few months, hasn't it?"

"Yes. I haven't felt the need for supervision until now." I smile.

"Go right in." She points toward Jim's door, and he welcomes me with a hug. Black-haired, gray-eyed, and freckled, Jim stands a foot taller than me, with broad shoulders and a ready smile. His capacity to put people at ease and treat them with both respect and kindness keeps his schedule packed and his waiting list brimming, even after Constant Caring downgraded his status to a non-participating provider.

"Good to see you, Sarah," he says. "What's doing?"

"So much that I intend to talk as fast as I can."

"Go for it." He waves me to the brown leather sofa and takes his regular seat in a large club chair.

"Okay with you if I munch on the muffin while we talk? I brought you a blueberry."

"I can always count on you for that," he says, reaching for the bag I'm holding out.

"First, how's Judith?" Jim's wife and I sit on synagogue committees together.

"She's great. Enjoying some time off. Taking Ralph for more walks on the beach than he'd like." He laughs. Ralph is his old black lab, who sometimes accompanies Jim to the office to act as co-therapist.

I kick my shoes off onto the worn Persian rug and tuck my feet beneath me as I tear apart the muffin, pop some in my mouth, and swallow before speaking.

"So," I begin. "It looks like Henderson was murdered." I watch Jim's eyebrows rise. "And Louise is a suspect."

"Because of that to-do in the courtroom I heard about?"

"Yes, along with something the district attorney overheard her saying." I take another bite of my blueberry muffin. "As if that weren't enough, someone phoned me and said I should mind my own business unless I want to keep Henderson company at the morgue."

"How frightening," he says. "Are you okay?"

"Yes and no," I answer. "I think we've got a situation here where a client's secrets are threatening some psychopath. So, Louise, Kate, Alex, and I have met to talk about it, and we're trying to figure it out. And now I'm here to ask for your help sorting it through."

Jim crosses his arms behind his head and stretches his long legs out in front of him. "Hmm, that *is* rather disconcerting. Are you thinking that Harriet Connors might be the link?"

"I'm wondering. After all, how many women who were sexually abused as children try to sue their perpetrator decades later? And she left for Europe rather suddenly. Does anyone else come to mind?"

"Why? Do you think I might be involved too?"

"Maybe. I've talked about many of my cases with you, and we've shared a number of clients."

"Well, now that you mention it—I received an odd call a week or two ago. It sounded vaguely threatening. But it was too incoherent to decipher. Hmm…on second thought, I think that's too much of a leap." He sips his coffee, and we sit in silence for a few moments. "Let's talk about your cases," he says. "You and Louise shared a physician, I think, who was using cocaine and made a fatal mistake in the operating room. Wasn't Henderson involved in that one?"

I nod. "Yes. The widower sued the doctor, and the case was settled for millions. The doc went to an inpatient drug-treatment program, but he lost his license, went bankrupt, and eventually relocated to another state. I don't even know if he's practicing medicine any longer, though that wouldn't make him less likely to murder Henderson. But why would he threaten to kill me?"

"I thought you and Henderson collaborated on getting him into the treatment program. It was rather pricey, also an unusual program for Constant Caring to support."

"True. Probably the one and only time Henderson and I worked together on anything, but Constant Caring wasn't footing the bill. The doc had a disability policy that covered his treatment. So it wouldn't have taken anything off the bottom line at Constant Caring."

"The doc might have relapsed and blamed Henderson, then you, for the loss of his license to practice medicine. That could be motive." Jim takes a big bite of his muffin.

"Okay, that's another possibility," I say, watching him chow down on the muffin before sipping from a steaming cup of coffee. "Anyone else?"

"You had a woman who was so narcissistic that she fit almost every category for the disorder listed in the diagnostic manual. Remember, you sent her to me for consultation when you felt out of your league in treating her? I agreed with you—not because you lacked skill—she was just not treatable."

"Sylvia," I moan. "I was so glad to refer her on, but Henderson insisted on evaluating her and interfering with the referral."

"Yup." Jim smiles. "She looked so good, so professional, so well-credentialed, but she was a shark who'd just as soon swallow you whole as chew you up into chunks."

I laugh. "Boy, was I afraid of her."

"And well you should have been. Even a slight insult to her sense of self would have sent her into a black rage aimed at eviscerating you. I was relieved you referred her."

"Well, what do you suspect? She had a bad interaction with Henderson that so offended her she nursed her resentment for a year before figuring out how to kill him—and now she wants to do the same to me?"

He shrugs. "You never know. By nature, narcissists take everything personally. They can nurture grudges, waiting for a chance to get retribution. If Henderson inadvertently injured her, then or later, I could imagine her rage provoking murder."

"I'm surprised at you, Jim. It seems so easy for you to come up with suspects."

"I'm an avid reader of mysteries." He grins, popping the last bit of muffin into his mouth. "My final suspect would be that businessman you and Louise both treated. He'd embezzled hundreds of thousands from his bank, and no plea deal was going to cut much from his sentence. Remember how enraged he was—and he directed that at you, Louise, *and* Henderson. I never understood how he came to have any interactions with Henderson, but—" Jim shrugs again—"sometimes Henderson got involved in cases for reasons I never figured out. He was peculiar and secretive himself."

"Those are good possibilities. Thanks, Jim. Now can I tell you what else is happening, personally?"

"Of course."

I tell him about Miriam and her recent appearances, along with my own therapy to banish guilt and flashbacks.

"I have so much respect for you, Sarah. And I trust that you'll soon embrace your psychic abilities, or your intuition, whatever you want to call it, and make it another wonderful skill you wield in the world. Trust yourself."

"That's what Miriam says."

"She's right." He smiles and stands. "I hate to say it, but our time is up. Call if you need me. You don't have to come into the office for this—it's not really supervision and I'm not charging you for my time. Call me at home if you need to talk about any other aspects of this investigation. Or come by. Judith will make you tea, Ralph will sit at your feet, and we'll brainstorm, okay?" He reaches down to hug me and I smile all the way back to my office, thinking about how my life has changed since I moved to Maine.

In a small state, boundaries can get muddled. Jim, as my mentor, taught me hypnosis and gave me supervision. We also attend the same synagogue and share friends. When I'm seeking formal consultation, I see him at his office and pay for his time, but we also have a friendship, share holiday observances, and get together for pleasure.

I'm glad I got to see him this morning, but with my own therapy late that afternoon and the meeting at Alex's that evening, the day feels packed. My first client is a man struggling to come to terms with a divorce his wife initiated. That's followed by a couple whose adolescent son was caught with a huge stash of pot. I break for a half-hour lunch and see three clients in quick succession before making calls and ensuring I've written all my case notes carefully. Then I stop home, feed the cats, and drive into town for my own therapy. The time and temperature sign blinks from the top of a downtown high-rise: 4:20 p.m. and sixty-five degrees.

I'm humming along with a song on the oldies station, until my reverie is interrupted by an advertisement: "Constant Caring—not just a name, but a philosophy. Constantly caring for you and your family's health." I wonder how caring Henderson had been as the company's psychiatric consultant and whether George Tate, as CEO, cares anything for his subscribers. My client and Constant Caring director, Todd Owens, doesn't seem to care much about anything, at least not from what I can tell in therapy. I shut off the radio to focus on finding a parking spot.

It's a relief to sink into my chosen couch in Janice's office.

"How are you?" she asks.

"A budding romance, I think. A new nightmare, and a real-life threat."

"Where do you want to start?" She leans forward, a look of concern on her face. I fill her in on the details.

"EMDR won't change appropriate fear," Janice says. "And even if we can change it, we don't want to, do we?"

"No. I need the fear right now. It keeps me alert. The more thoroughly I can resolve this trauma, the more ably I'll be able to handle whatever comes my way."

I focus on the images in my head associated with identifying Miriam's body in the morgue. What becomes clear to me is the love and support Ryan provided, even through his own grief. I talk about that, and the memories keep coming. Miriam's funeral. The sobbing—mine, Ryan's, and Miriam's parents', our colleagues and boss from the Public Defenders Office, friends. Images and sensations flood through me as I relive the aftermath, when all I could do was curl up in bed in my Brookline apartment.

"I was unwilling to even go outside," I say. "Ryan couldn't reach me. I can see now how much I shut down. It was just grief. Grief and guilt. I couldn't handle it. I couldn't believe Miriam was really dead." I reach for the tissues, dab at my tears, look up at Janice. "I see how incapable I was of appreciating Ryan's loyalty, his caring and concern."

"It was all those things, Sarah, *and* trauma. The trauma complicated your grief, and it's important not to minimize that." Janice and I talk about Ryan, then Billy, about the choices I face in going back to the familiar or moving on to new challenges. We end with a visualization practice, where I imagine myself swinging in a rope hammock strung between palm trees on a warm sunny beach.

When we finish, I walk through the Old Port, my feet hitting the uneven brick sidewalks. Gulls swoop overhead before heading towards the bay and the fishing boats. I think about Miriam, how she died and I survived. I experience a new sense of life's preciousness, and commit to filling my life with pleasure, for myself and for Miriam.

Louise is waiting for me at the entrance to Alex's office, and we climb the stairs together. The walls of Alex's office are exposed brick, like Kate's, punctuated by wide windows looking onto Middle Street. Green plants of every size and shape fill the room. I settle into an old upholstered armchair. Louise takes the weathered leather couch. Alex hands us a crisply organized list: the names we've sent to her, a compilation of known mutual clients, and a list of ones we suspect we might have shared with Henderson.

We review the clients, paying particular attention to cases where disclosures might be threatening to someone. I share Jim's thoughts, and we toss possibilities around. We end up with twelve clients. Five cases involve spouses who are physically and emotionally abusive enough to face criminal charges if reported. Two clients quit religious sects and described sexually inappropriate conduct by their pastors. Three clients left our practices to enter therapy with Henderson. Two of Louise's clients who also had connections to Henderson are seriously dissociative. Their childhood abuse was so severe they've developed separate personalities to cope, and some of those personalities do not know about the abuse. Louise told me about one of them, Teresa, but neither she nor the other client has any known connection to me. I wonder aloud whether a dissociative client could have killed Henderson.

"Anything is possible," Louise says. "But those clients are at the bottom of my list."

"Why?" I ask. "Don't they have amnesia between personalities?"

"Often, each personality has a separate history, name, and physical characteristics. Some even have different genders, but being dissociative doesn't equate with violence. They're unlikely suspects."

"What are the connections between these clients and Henderson?" Alex asks.

"Henderson approved the sessions. There aren't hordes of clients with this disorder."

"What about Teresa, the client who called you recently in crisis?"

"She's on the list, but she's extremely fragile," Louise says. "I don't think she's capable of aggression."

"What about one of her alters?"

"It's possible, Sarah. I haven't met all of them, but I just don't see it."

"Have you considered any other clients, Louise? Someone who might be particularly protective of you?" Alex asks. "Someone who may have seen coverage of the Tate trial and known that you and Henderson were adversaries?"

"Seems farfetched. Especially since we suspect the same person may have threatened Sarah."

"Investigations often hinge on what at first seems farfetched," Alex replies.

We finish at 7:45 with a better sense of the cases that involved Henderson, Louise, and me—but we can't get far without a clear motive. More important at the moment, we're all famished. It's late, so we vote for Japanese food and head to Benkay on the India Street side of the waterfront. The waitresses, dressed in kimonos, welcome us warmly and lead us to a corner table that at any other time would have felt cozy. Right now, nothing feels cozy. The hot towels and green tea are meager compensation for the chill in my gut. There's too much at stake and too little to go on.

Halfway through the meal, our conversation is interrupted by a loud dispute at the bar. Alex peers over the railing separating our section from the entry aisle and the bar. "George Tate," she whispers. "Looks like he's had a bit too much to drink. He's being escorted out."

"Whew." Louise rolls her eyes. "That guy is self-destructing faster than a plane in free fall. He needs a good therapist."

We crack up. So it isn't empathetic—we all have our limits.

Chapter 21

Tuesday morning I get a call from Detective Pomerleau, the officer in charge of the Henderson investigation, requesting my presence at the station. I speed-dial Kate, who arranges for the interview to take place at four that Thursday. Wednesday night, I take a long hot bath and meditate before bed, but my sleep is interrupted by a dream.

Jim is standing on the red Persian rug in the middle of his office, his kind eyes troubled by something or someone I can't see. Staring at the half-open door, he's mesmerized by a bell sleeve on a white chiffon blouse as it floats back and forth. Ribbons of rainbow-colored light stream from the glass prisms of the doorknob. As the door closes, he glimpses a stiletto heel.

Jim glides across the room to slip a file into place and lock up his patients' secrets before drifting out of the building. Late-afternoon sunlight glints off the polished chrome of his red Corvette. He settles into the cushy leather seat, turns the key in the ignition, swings out of the lot onto the Black Point Road, and shoots through the busy intersection on the tail end of a yellow light. He gradually presses his foot to the gas pedal, ramping up speed on the initial straightaway. As the road begins to wind through the marsh, sloping downward and curving to the left, Jim presses lightly on the brake. But the car picks up speed, hurtling toward the first curve.

He jams the brake pedal to the floor. Nothing. The car speeds faster, flying through the bend in the road. He rams in the clutch and downshifts into third. The engine screams. A car merges from the right. Jim jerks the wheel to the left.

There is no time. There is no control. The Corvette fishtails. Trees whir by, blurring into a mass of color as the car spins round and round.

His head flings backwards and snaps forward. The car smashes into the guardrail and takes flight. The last thing Jim sees is color—the blood red of the Corvette and the gray-blue hues of the sky reflected in the cold gray water of the marsh.

I jolt awake as someone screams my name, my heart beating a breathless hole through my chest. It's Miriam's voice, but she isn't there, she isn't anywhere. The clock reads three a.m. Is this my apprehension about the police interview? Why is Jim careening out of control? Shouldn't I be behind the wheel?

Resigned, I grope for the diary on my bedside table, calming my breathing before wearily jotting down details and trying to find myself in the dream. Nothing makes sense. I wonder if I should call Jim. Is this a psychic event? Precognition, like my dreams about Miriam?

I fall back asleep for a few hours and awake with time to clean the house, shower, and dress in a tailored skirt and blouse—an outfit left over from my legal days. I tell myself to forget the nightmare and focus on the interview with Pomerleau, but I can't yet. I have to call Jim. Luckily, he's in between clients and his secretary puts me right through.

"I had a nightmare last night that involved you," I say. "It was terrible. I woke up screaming. Your car flipped into the Scarborough marsh. The brakes didn't work."

"That sounds terrifying," Jim says.

"It was, Jim. And confusing. You were driving a red corvette, not your truck. And I felt as if I were you, drowning in the swamp." While pacing through my living room, I recount all the details, the way the office looked, the client's high heels, the chiffon blouse. "I'm not sure what the dream means," I say. "I know I'm anxious and all sorts of stuff is going on, but I can't take the same risk I took with Miriam. I didn't tell her about that awful dream I had about seeing her in the morgue. I don't want to worry you, but if this is a precognitive dream, consider yourself forewarned. Maybe you can do something. Get your brakes checked."

"I had the truck in for service last month, but I'll bring it in again as soon as possible. Let's find time to talk about this further. I know you've got an interview at the police station, so don't add me to your list of worries. I won't take any chances."

I check the stove three times before I can make it out the door, something I haven't done in a long time, not since the bad old days after Miriam's murder. Checking and rechecking is a behavior that started then. Now it's my response to intense distress. I feel slightly off all day in my sessions with clients, but no one seems to notice. I offer my four o'clock client a spot on my free Friday, but she says she's doing well and prefers to wait for her appointment the following week. I don't have a five o'clock that day, so it's easy for me to finish up at 3:30 and drive downtown. With the next day a Friday, I know I can do any extra paperwork or note-taking at home while I toss in a few loads of laundry and clean the house.

A metered spot is waiting for me right across from the Portland Police Department, a brick and glass building imbued with all the charm of 1960s' architecture. The building anchors one corner of Franklin and Middle streets. The FBI and a prestigious law firm stand across from it, looking quite a bit more stately than the police station, where the brick facade juts out over the sidewalk. Kate approaches as I dawdle by the glass display case filled with police patches.

"Look, Kate, the Biloxi, Mississippi, patch has a lighthouse. And Roswell, New Mexico, has an oil well and a haystack."

"That's very nice. Now stop procrastinating." Pointing me toward a low, blue-cushioned bench in the reception area, she announces our arrival to a burly cop behind a glass partition before she sits beside me.

"Why are you so nervous? You spent plenty of time in police stations when you practiced criminal law."

"I wasn't the person being interviewed."

"You aren't a suspect. All they want to know is what time you saw Louise in Henderson's office. Tell them the truth." She pats my shoulder.

The cop behind the window calls my name and buzzes us through a set of double doors. Another officer leads us down a narrow corridor and into a small blue elevator. We step off at the fourth floor, where the Bureau of Investigation is housed. Computers, phones, and blotters sit on an assortment of tan metal desks strewn with paperwork. At least a dozen detectives fill the room. Some sit at desks, making notes and talking on telephones. A few brawny guys stand before a white message board engrossed in discussion. Others occupy a table in a glass-walled conference room.

A few of them wave to Kate, and she steps over to talk with them, while the officer accompanying us leads me to a small room just off the main one—a tiny windowless space. It can't be more than eight by ten feet. As I stare suspiciously at metal-framed chairs with tweedy blue seats, Billy walks in. "You're not being interviewed in here," he says. "I talked to Pomerleau, and he agreed to meet you in Chief Downey's office."

"With the chief?"

"No. He's out of town." Billy ushers Kate and me down another hall to a spacious office. "I'll come back to get you when the interview is over," he says, punctuating that notification with a nod to Pomerleau, who settles us into no-nonsense armchairs.

Pomerleau's rumpled gray suit seems color-coordinated to match his thick gray hair. His white button-down shirt has clearly seen better days. He looks like a guy whose love of beer and pretzels has overcome a meager desire to exercise. One of the buttons has popped off under the pressure of his protruding belly, and a white undershirt peeks out.

Kate discusses parameters while I scan the room. Large windows provide an expansive view of the harbor. Commendations and plaques cover the walls. When the negotiations finish, Kate drags her chair right beside mine. Pomerleau rolls the desk chair he's sitting on to face me and turns on a recorder.

In response to Pomerleau's questions, I give my name, age, profession, and other personal information.

"I understand you saw Louise Gold in Harold Henderson's office the day he died."

"Yes."

"What time was that?"

"It was just about noon."

"Are you sure?"

"Yes."

"How do you remember so specifically?"

"Louise and I were in court that morning. We finished right at eleven. I wanted her to come into town with me to go shopping and grab some lunch, but she said she had to go home. It took us ten minutes to get home, and then I drove to Exchange Street, found a parking space across from the Exchange, and did a little shopping. I just happened to look up above the shops and noticed Henderson standing in his office window, with a woman who looked like Louise standing behind him. Later, I asked her if she'd been there and she said yes."

"So she lied to you about having to go home."

I frown and my lawyer training kicks in. "That wouldn't necessarily be accurate. She did go home. Maybe she changed her mind about staying home."

"When you asked her later about being in Henderson's office, did you try to find out why she was there?"

"Yes."

"What did she tell you?"

I pause, remembering that she told me she didn't assault him and had no intention to. "She wouldn't say."

"She refused to tell you?"

"I wouldn't characterize our conversation that way. We were interrupted and never really got back to it."

"Why do you think she was there?"

I have to bite my tongue to keep from blurting out any number of sarcastic responses. "I have absolutely no idea."

Pomerleau stares at me appraisingly. The silence is oppressive. "What was your connection to Dr. Henderson?"

"We were colleagues. As Constant Caring's psychiatric consultant, he sometimes also approved and oversaw referrals to me."

Pomerleau asks whether I think a client could be responsible for the murder, and about my thoughts on the threatening call I received. I mention what Jim said, that he might have had an odd call about Henderson too. I also say that I do think a client might have murdered Henderson, or someone who had a secret they didn't want disclosed. Pomerleau asks a few more questions that call for suppositions on my part. I tell him what I know, which isn't much. He walks to the window and picks up the phone.

"Marshall? She's done." He turns back to me. "Detective Marshall will see you out. Kate and I have more to discuss."

Billy is there before I stand up. He leads me through the corridors, stopping briefly in his office. Memories of my interviews at the Boston precinct after Miriam's murder begin rolling through my head. The detective on her case was really kind to me, and he went after Miriam's murderer like a bulldog. As his face comes into focus, my legs begin to shake. My face is hot, my hands are suddenly clammy.

"You don't look so good. Do you need to sit down?"

"Probably, but I'd prefer to just get out of here."

"I'll walk you to your car." He glances at his watch. "I'm off duty now."

My nod is grateful. We navigate through the narrow corridors to the station exit. We cross the street to my car.

"Are you okay to drive?" he asks.

"I think so."

"Why don't I just follow you home? If you feel unable to navigate, pull over and I'll drive you the rest of the way."

He does follow me, and when I pull into my driveway, he parks behind my Subaru, opens my door and helps me out.

"How about if I make you some tea? Then I'll order a pizza. We can sit for a while and see whether you can talk about what's going on. Okay?"

My head moves up and down and my feet do a slow-motion walk to the front door. Billy does just what he said he was going to do: puts up tea and orders pizza. I tell him I'm going upstairs to get into pajamas. When I come down, I find that he's located my collection of rhythm and blues, tossed together a salad, and fed my cats. The pizza comes hot and crisp-crusted. We eat in the living room, sitting companionably on the sofa. The cats lie on either side of me, purring.

Eventually, I'm capable of speech. "I'm being flooded by bad memories of Miriam's murder. It's like a time warp."

He's listening, as if he has nowhere else to be. Of course, he's a cop who used to be a lawyer, both listening professions.

"It's like a bad movie in my head. When one scene loses its intensity, another takes its place."

"Is that like progress?"

"I don't know."

"What are you remembering right now?"

"The house Ryan and I owned was in Brookline, not far from Harvard Street. You know the area?"

"I do. Had family in Brookline. Visited them often."

"Ryan and I bought a sweet brick two-family. We had one apartment and rented the other. It was on a side street, off Harvard, between Commonwealth and Beacon. You know where I mean?"

"Kinda."

"Ryan was home when I got there that afternoon." I nibble on a hangnail. "His face was gray. People say that, and you don't think it's for real, but it is. His face was literally gray."

Billy moves closer, slings his arm across the back of the couch behind my shoulders. "This okay?"

"It's good," I say and return to the story I'm compelled to tell. "The police called before I got home."

"Uh-huh."

"We had to go to the morgue to identify her. Afterward, we were at the police station frequently, talking to detectives." I blow out a long breath. "Today reminded me of that, except, of course, today wasn't at all like that. But the images came back, and the emotions, and it's as if I'm immersed in it all again. Sometimes I can't make it stop."

Billy reaches toward me and settles my back against his chest. He stretches his legs out on the couch, bracketing mine. I lean into him and he holds me while I cry, my head against his chest, his arms wrapping around mine, like he's my parentheses.

"I still miss her so much," I say between sobs. "And now something is happening to Louise, and I don't understand it, but it scares me. And she still hasn't told me why she was in Henderson's office the day he died." Billy's body tightens, but then he softens and he stays with me as my tears ebb and I continue to talk.

"I think I let her down—Louise, that is—somehow. I'm not sure. And Miriam. I should have insisted Miriam come home with me. Well, I did, but she wouldn't listen. Still, it was my mistake."

He doesn't try to tell me I'm wrong. He simply says, "You didn't pull the trigger." Otherwise, he listens as I talk about the police station, the investigation, the trial. I talk so long and cry so hard that the next thing I know I'm waking up two hours later, with Billy's arms still around me. He must have fallen asleep too, and I nudge him awake. "Will you stay?"

"If you want me to."

"I do."

As we walk upstairs, he presses his hand to my back like a physical support. In my bedroom, he strips to his shorts. We climb into bed and spoon. He rubs my back, lifts my hair, and kisses my neck. We sleep.

I feel washed clean when I wake up at six the next morning. "Billy?" I say, nudging him. "I think I'll be okay." Then I fall back to sleep.

When I wake again, it's to the aroma of brewing coffee. Tossing on a plum-colored vintage robe, I meet him in the kitchen.

"Good morning," he says, like it's a normal everyday kind of experience we've shared. As if I'm a normal person, as if he's spent the night many a time.

"I don't know if I could've gotten through that, through the night, without you. Thanks."

"You would've. And you're welcome. How about you let me make you dinner tomorrow night?"

"I'd like that, but I think I owe you."

"You don't owe me. And I like to cook."

"You're on then."

"I've got to get going. You going to be okay?"

"Yes. I'll call my therapist and try to get in there today. But I'll be okay now, even if I can't see her. I don't know if I can explain it, but for some reason, I'm more grounded. It's as if my feet are planted in the present. And I'm not so scared anymore. Something has shifted."

We walk to the door. He opens it, turns back, and draws me close. His kisses are tender. I immerse myself in pleasure, all too aware that life is short, and way too unpredictable.

Chapter 22

A warm June rain splatters against my windshield on the drive to Billy's Friday night. The Rosemont Corner neighborhood, a treasure trove of old-fashioned bungalows and hip-roof colonials, is a five-minute drive from my house, but I've never visited the street where he lives. The wooden clapboards of his small 1920s' home are painted sea green and the shutters a crisp white. The garden brims with perennials. Rugosa roses hug the front porch, imbuing the air with their sweet scent.

He meets me at the door and settles me into a cozy living room furnished with a pair of green velvet couches, Victorian lamps, and a tapestry chair. The warmth from the freestanding gas-fired stove dispels the dampness.

"What a lovely home." Its vintage charm stands in stark contrast to the modern chic of Ryan's condo. I wonder how the night will go, whether the relationship will deepen.

"Thanks. Hungry yet?" He points to a tray of appetizers arrayed on a marble-topped coffee table. The corners of Billy's mouth turn up as he watches me fiddle with my hair.

Butterflies in my belly flap their wings at warp speed. "I feel a little nervous. Like I have—*schpilkas*. You know Yiddish?"

"Well, I know some words. *Schpilkas* is one of them." He sits beside me. A seductive scent wafts from his neck. I smile, blush.

"I'm fine taking this as slow as you like," he says. "I suspect you're not interested in rushing into anything, especially so soon after the recent, uh, Ryan thing."

I murmur agreement, sampling a cracker, sniffing appreciatively at the aroma of basil and garlic drifting into the room.

"Lasagna, Caesar salad, and cannoli for dessert. It's not quite ready, so...would you like a tour?"

"Yes, please."

"I love older homes," he says, "and this is a classic Montgomery Ward." We pass through French doors into the dining room. A mission-style stained glass chandelier hangs over a square oak pedestal table that could have come directly from my grandmother's house—a place I adored.

After appreciative oohs and aahs, Billy directs me into another room, extending his arm toward a wall of floor-to-ceiling built-in bookshelves. "My library."

Many of the authors on his shelves populate my own.

"And," he points to another section, "my collection of Jewish mysticism."

"Those dire warnings from the rabbis about the dangers of delving into their secrets almost put me off, though luckily not completely. Have you read everything in here?"

"Most of it. Some of it more than once."

I slide a book off the shelf, replace it, take another. "I've read many of these books, but there are quite a few I haven't read. I could happily spend a lifetime reading them."

"It's tempting, isn't it? But there comes a time when you have to focus more on how you live your life, integrating what you've learned."

"Doing your part to repair the world?"

The sound of a buzzer echoes from the next room. Billy leads the way as we move into the kitchen. He opens the oven to check the lasagna, and the sight of bubbling sauce sets my mouth watering.

"Ten more minutes." He resets the timer. "While we're waiting, I'll show you the rest of the house."

The stairs to the second floor are carpeted with an aged oriental runner. "This was a three bedroom, one bath. I added a bath downstairs, combined two bedrooms up here, and enlarged the bathroom to make a suite."

It looks luscious, but my *schpilkas* return. Determined to dissolve them, I lean against the wall, draw Billy toward me, and twine my arms around his neck. He rests his palms on the walls beside me and leans in, letting his lips meander down my cheek, over the front of my neck, and into the hollows of my shoulders. He roams up the other side of my neck and stops at my lips. My stomach dips as his tongue explores my mouth. The stubble on his chin tickles. His lips are tender.

We separate when the buzzer rings again. "What a delicious aperitif," I comment.

"You'll like the main course too," he says.

"Good, 'cause I'm so hungry." It's pretty clear he understands that my hunger is not simply for food.

The dining room table is set with white linen and old-fashioned china. We light Shabbat candles and chant the blessings together, sipping wine from etched glasses and tearing off pieces of challah before Billy carries out a huge salad and steaming lasagna. The wine dissolves the knots in my stomach, while Billy keeps me entertained throughout the meal with stories about his family.

After dinner, he insists on cleaning up himself, settling me back on the velvet sofa. Candles bathe the living room in a soft glow. I curl up, slightly tipsy, listening to Van Morrison, and close my eyes. When Billy joins me, the warmth of his body is irresistible, and I tuck my head into the curve of his neck. He tips his face to meet my mouth. I've always considered kissing an art form, and Billy's kisses are deep and luscious. His hands cup my face, then caress my back and shoulders. My fingers stroke his curly hair until I slide them under his shirt and run them up and down his back. Waves of pleasure ripple through my body, and I think about how lust, once lit, has its own momentum.

An image of the last man I dated arises. The relationship didn't last long. A surgeon, he was a few years older than me. The sex was great, our backgrounds compatible, but he was a bit too self-involved, and I knew the relationship couldn't go as deep as I wanted. My focus returns to Billy and nothing distracts me. A clock chimes eleven and we separate slightly.

"I want to stay," I murmur, "but I think I should go...maybe in... umm...half an hour?"

Our eyes meet, and I smile sweetly while pressing my body closer to his.

Chapter 23

Lucky for me, hardly anyone is on the road as I drive home in a state of reverie. Sleep comes easily, and I awaken early to pick up bagels. Billy knocks on my door at ten, and we indulge in a leisurely breakfast on my back porch before driving to Mackworth Island for another long walk. We talk and laugh, swinging our linked hands back and forth. Every so often, we stop for an embrace and some mouth-to-mouth. When our explorations teeter toward indecent, we drive back to my house and spend a few more hours in heated embraces. He leaves at six, saying he won't be available for a few days as he's covering for another detective, but he'll call as soon as he's free.

That's fine with me. I need time to myself. Jim had left me a message saying he'd had the truck checked out and all was fine, I shouldn't worry about him, but we should find a time to get together to talk about my dream.

I drive to the supermarket and wander through the aisles, trying to shake myself back to Earth for the drive home. When I get there, Louise is standing at the end of the driveway. She doesn't look good.

"What's wrong?" My heart thuds in my chest.

"Let's go inside," she says, lifting one of my grocery bags from my arms. I can see she's barely holding back tears.

"Just sit." She points to the table. I slide out a chair for her and one for me. She pours water into the kettle and turns on a burner. "Let's wait till the tea is ready."

"No. Tell me now."

"It's Jim."

"No!" I yell, pushing back from the table, jumping to my feet. "No! Don't tell me this! Don't!" Chills snake up and down my spine and I feel electric, as if I'm a live wire. "Don't tell me his truck flipped over a guardrail and into the marsh. Don't tell me he's dead!"

"Sarah." Louise is on her feet reaching for me. "How do you know?"

"Don't tell me!" I sob.

Louise puts her arms around me, and we cry together. Eventually, I push away and sink back into the chair, resting my chin on my hands. "I dreamt it the other night. I can't believe it really happened."

"You dreamt about this?"

"Yes. I wondered if it was a precognitive dream, or just a consequence of my foreboding about going to the police station." I examine her face. It's ashen, her eyes widened in shock.

"I wasn't taking any chances. I called Jim and told him all about it. He listened and said he'd get the brakes on the truck checked out. And he left a message saying that he'd done just that. How can he be dead?" my voice breaks.

"I can't believe it either." Louise sobs.

The electric kettle clicks off. I rise in a daze. Jim, dead? I just saw him a few days ago. I warned him.

"The funeral is Monday," Louise says.

Tears slide down my cheeks.

"Do you want to sleep in my guest room tonight?" Louise asks.

"No," I answer woodenly, wondering how I can go from the pleasure of the time with Billy to the death of my beloved friend and mentor? How can I stand this continuously unpredictable life where the only things that can be counted on are loss, pain and suffering, and death? I lay my head on the table and cry until I'm all cried out, barely aware of Louise's departure. The phone rings, and I let it go to voicemail, checking it only before dragging myself up the steps to my bedroom. It's Judith, asking me to read a poem at the funeral. I know exactly which poem Jim would choose.

Finally, I flop into bed, not bothering to wash or brush my teeth. The phone rings, and I answer this time, still sniffling.

"You've heard." Even Billy's voice offers no comfort.

"Yeah. Louise told me. The weird thing is that I had a precognitive dream. I called Jim and told him all about it and he had the brakes checked. He knew. I warned him. How helpful can this psychic stuff be if you warn people and even that doesn't change things?"

Silence at the other end. I realize Billy must be trying to put together the pieces. Then he says, "I don't know, Sarah. It sounds as though you had information, and you gave it to Jim, and he did everything he could do."

"I need a way to think about this, Billy. I'm feeling so bereft. What spiritual wisdom helps you cope?"

"I don't know how helpful this is going to be for you right now, but when I'm struggling, I go back to the basic tenet of Judaism. We trust that God is always present, right here and now, in everything, in every moment, even in the hardest moments, the darkest of times, even in death and loss and grief, even when nothing makes any sense."

"That's it, isn't it?" I sigh.

"Yes," he says gently. "That's *always* it. I know you and Jim were close. I'm so sorry I can't be there with you tonight or tomorrow. I have to work, but let me pick you up Monday. I'll drive you to the funeral."

"That would be good," I say, knowing nothing about the day will be the least bit good. I call my aunt. She answers on the second ring, and I tell her what happened.

"How strange that you would warn him, and nevertheless he died." She pauses. "This does happen though, darling. We cannot always change what is fated. Sometimes we can, but not always. It must have been Jim's time." Zelda is silent for a few moments. "There is something much larger going on here. Jim's death is a part of that. I will do my best to clarify this over the next few days. Please be very careful. Very, very, careful. I love you, honey."

That phone conversation leaves me anxious. The cats seem to sense my distress. They snuggle in close, and it takes another hour, but eventually I fall asleep listening to the sound of their purring.

Monday morning a hot shower washes away some of my fatigue, and I slip on a black dress, adding silver earrings and a long silver necklace with a turquoise hamsa. If I ever needed a hamsa to ward off the evil eye, that time is now.

I see Billy's car as it turns the corner, and I'm out the front door before he's cut the engine. He jumps out, comes around the back of the car, and wraps me in his arms. I lay my head on his shoulder, and we stand there together before stepping back to look at each other. He doesn't look like he's gotten any sleep. He opens the passenger door and settles me in before closing my door and slipping into the driver's seat. We barely speak en route to the synagogue, and he follows me in, his hand resting lightly on my back as we enter the sanctuary, my sanctuary, to say goodbye to a dear, dear friend.

Friday night worship services in this room normally keep me centered and connected to something larger than my petty struggles in life, but today, there's no solace. My heart is shattered.

Louise is standing in the second row of seats, tendrils of her long red hair framing her freckled face as she waves a long arm to catch our attention. I manage, finally, to suck in a deep breath. Louise sometimes does that for me—acts like an anchor, a steadying force. Once I reach the second aisle, Mark wraps his arms around me and holds me tight. Louise takes the seat beside him, and I sit between her and Billy, who takes the aisle seat.

"Are you up for this?" Louise says as she sinks into her seat. "I can read the poem if you can't."

I force a smile. "Thanks, but I need to do this—for Jim and for me. He loved Mary Oliver's poetry. And I love it too." Jim meant so much to me that honoring his memory in this way is important to me.

"Oh, there's Kate." Louise pops up and waves. She needn't have bothered. Kate is like a heat-seeking missile. Alex is a few steps behind her. The crowd seems to part. Louise, Mark, Billy, and I stand to let them by. Kate stops to give each of us a kiss on the cheek before sliding around us to take her seat. Alex grabs me in a tight hug. "You doing okay?" she asks.

"Hanging in." Their presence comforts me.

The rabbi approaches the bimah, and the crowd settles down. Judith sits in the front row, and Ralph, Jim and Judith's dog, lies on the floor beside her. No service for Jim would be complete without Ralph. I long to sit on the floor with Ralph's head in my lap, but I'm in a seat between Louise and Billy. Billy's arm is around my shoulders. The large room falls silent, and the service begins. Beautiful psalms, lovely melodies, tributes to Jim from many friends, and then it's my turn. I stand up, slightly shaky, and step past Billy, making my way to the front of the room.

"I'm Sarah Green," I say, pausing to clear my throat. "Jim was a dear friend and mentor. He taught me the power of poetry." I read a poem Judith has selected for me from Jim's favorite book of poetry, and a hush falls over the room. I make it through the reading, but my voice cracks as I conclude my remarks. "I know Jim is here today, suffusing us with his shining spirit before he departs for other realms."

Tears stream down my face, but it doesn't matter. The one thing I know for certain is that a rich life depends on friendship, love, and trust. Ryan might have been here, but he isn't. Billy is. Eventually, whether it's Ryan, Billy, or someone I haven't met, even with love will come death and the need, in the end, to let go. Jim's death will inevitably precipitate another reckoning with these struggles. This day of his funeral is excruciating, but I have a suspicion that before this pain eases, my life is going to become much more difficult.

Jews sit shiva after a death. For a week straight, services are held at the home of the deceased, where friends and family bring food, reminisce, and come together for the recitation of Kaddish. Louise and Mark drive us to Judith and Jim's house Monday night for shiva, while Billy goes home to catch up on sleep. En route, we pass the spot where Jim's car went over the guardrail and I can't help staring, but by the time we reach the house, I've repressed, at least temporarily, the gruesome images. Mark parks on the side of the road, and Louise takes my hand as we walk under a canopy of pine trees to the front porch. We hug Judith, set our casseroles on the dining room table, and settle into the sofas in their den, where we've spent many an evening watching movies, playing cards, and discussing the nature of life.

Kate and Alex show up shortly afterward. When Ralph pads in, I slide onto the floor and coo to him. He lays his head in my lap and I stroke his fur. He lifts his face, staring soulfully into my eyes, and plants a big wet kiss on my nose, which provokes my first laugh in days. My next breath involves a deep inhalation of his doggy smell, which comforts me enough that I can key into the conversation. Alex is in the midst of suppositions.

"Judith said Jim brought the truck in to his service station right after you told him about your dream, Sarah. His accident doesn't make sense to me. How could he have lost control?" Alex says. "Especially since he took that road home every night."

"Most accidents happen close to home," Kate says in a clipped voice. "Stop trying to make this more than it was."

Alex looks at me. "Maybe there's something more in your dream. We should talk about it in more detail later this week." She turns to Kate and her tone turns angry. "Don't tell me what to do. I've got a feeling about this and it isn't a good one."

"Well, of course it isn't a good one, we just lost a friend," Kate retorts. "But there isn't a sinister motive behind every damn car accident."

"Sarah dreamt about it, Kate. There is something else going on here, and we need to figure it out." She rises abruptly and leaves the room.

"What's going on with the two of you?" Concern threads through Louise's voice.

"I'm angry about Jim's death," Kate says, "and tired. My cases are tough, there are still too damn many of them, and Alex is insisting I take more time off." She looks up with chagrin. "I'm taking my frustrations out on Alex. Excuse me. I think I have an apology to make."

We watch her maneuver through the bodies in the living room. Ralph starts to snore and Louise looks over at me. "Want something to eat, honey? I'm going to make myself a plate."

"Sure, whatever." I watch Louise extricate herself from the cushy sofa and head off to the dining room before I take her place on the sofa next to Mark. He slides his arm around me. I lean against him and close my eyes, wishing I were anywhere but here, dealing once again with death.

Chapter 24

I'm in the kitchen filling the cats' dinner bowls when there's a knock on the back door. When I open it, Susie's standing there.

"Can you come for dinner? Mom's making spaghetti with turkey meatballs, and Grandma brought dessert."

"Sure, honey. I just have to make a call first."

"Okay, come soon," she commands.

"Yes ma'am." I watch as she disappears into the bushes separating our houses and dial Aunt Zelda, who picks up on the second ring. "I'm so glad you called. I've been trying to get some information for you." She fills me in, and I'm still thinking about her comments when I lock my door and walk across our lawns. Mark steps out his back door, dressed casually in jeans and a white shirt. The worry lines seem slightly less deeply etched on the sides of his mouth, and a warm smile spreads across his face as he looks at me.

"Sorry to have to skip dinner. It smells great. Just want you to know that I miss spending time with you."

"Thanks," I say, grateful for the hug he offers.

"I'm off to a meeting."

"Hope it's a good one."

Louise's kitchen is steamy, courtesy of multiple pots boiling on the stovetop, and filled with the smells of garlic, basil, and tomato sauce. "Want any help?"

"Just plunk yourself down at the counter and start on the appetizer."

Louise wipes her hands on a red dishtowel. "Dinner's almost ready."

"Sarah, dear, how nice to see you." Kitty tenders a warm embrace and a sweet smile. Her salt-and-pepper hair is so perfectly coiffed, she looks like an advertisement for elegant aging. "Are you okay in here, Louise?"

"Fine, Mom. Things will be ready soon. Can you keep the girls occupied?"

Kitty departs, and I turn back to Louise, watching her reading glasses slide to the tip of her nose. She peers at me over the rims and points at a garlicky carrot appetizer on the counter. "Want some?"

The grated carrots tumble off the cracker en route to my mouth.

Louise carries a strainer to the sink.

"Mom," Naomi whines. "When are we eating? I'm starving. I have homework, and Jimmy's calling me at eight."

"We'll eat soon," Louise replies. "And we'll be done in plenty of time for you to talk with Jimmy. If you're starving, have some carrot dip."

Naomi stuffs a cracker piled high with dip into her mouth and barely finishes by the time she begins speaking. "Hey, how're things going, Sarah?"

"Okay, sweetie. Thanks for asking. What about you? How are things between you and Jimmy?" I raise a suggestive eyebrow.

"Amazing! He asked me to the junior prom." Naomi's face lights up as she talks about her boyfriend and the upcoming dance.

"Want help shopping for a dress?" Louise and I are polar opposites in that realm. I love to shop. She hates it. When her kids need clothes, I take them. We all benefit.

Naomi grins. "Yeah! How about next Saturday? I saw some things I really like at Tavecchia."

"Those are a bit sophisticated for someone your age, don't you think?" Louise groans, either due to the weight of the spaghetti pot she's carrying to the sink or because a dress from a high-end boutique means a big chunk of change.

I love the prospect of spending someone else's money at one of my favorite stores. "Saturday's fine." I grin back at Naomi. "We'll check out a bunch of shops."

She turns to her mom. "Want some help? I can cut the garlic bread."

Louise shoots me an appreciative glance as Naomi slices the bread, tosses it in a basket, and departs for the dining room with the end piece stuffed in her mouth.

"I can't wait to fill you in on my conversation with Aunt Zelda, and developments with Billy, and…I need your advice."

"Sure." Louise glances up briefly, pauses from ladling sauce onto the pasta. "We can talk after dinner. Mark's at a twelve-step meeting and has a one-on-one with his sponsor after that. He'll be home late."

"How's that going? He looks so much better, and he gave me a hug."

Louise's smile is pained. "It's okay, considering everything. He's finally invested in recovery and is reconnecting with the girls and me."

During dinner, first Susie, then Naomi talks a blue streak, with Kitty hanging on every word, or at least pretending to. As soon as their plates are cleaned, she takes Susie upstairs to get ready for bed, while Naomi disappears to talk with her boyfriend. Louise and I clean up before settling on the sofa with cups of tea.

"So, what's up?" Louise asks.

"I'm continuing to have that nightmare about Jim's accident."

"The one that ends in the slimy marsh?"

"Yes. And now I hear Miriam's voice calling my name. That's what wakes me up."

"Hmm," she murmurs, like the good therapist she is. "What did your aunt say?"

"We spoke just before I walked over here. I asked her one question, and I swear, there must have been five minutes of dead air time before she responded."

"Maybe there were a lot of folks on the other side scrambling for her attention." Louise laughs. "So—what did she say?"

"That Jim is insistent I understand something." I brush my hair back from my face. "As if the psychic stuff weren't already a bit daunting before this, you know? Now I'm recognizing that precognitive dreams are part of the package—but it's frustrating to know that even warning people might not be enough to save their lives. Aunt Zelda said there was no question that I've got to accept the information coming to me from unusual channels and start figuring out what to do with it. She also said there is significant danger all around me and my friends. That includes you, honey."

"Ooh, that's spooky."

"Tell me about it. Zelda doesn't believe Jim's death was an accident. She said we need to look carefully at everyone we're in touch with, even our clients."

"Do you think we should just keep our focus on clients in looking for Henderson's murderer? But how could that be connected to Jim's death?"

"It could involve a client we all saw," I say. "If Jim's death was not an accident, like Aunt Zelda assures me, then it's beyond coincidental that two local psychiatrists would be murdered one right after the other."

"I don't think the police are treating Jim's accident as anything other than an accident."

"We'll have to convince them otherwise. And, Louise, in all this time you've never come clean about what you were doing in Henderson's office. How can I help you—or even sort through all the clues—if you aren't being completely honest?"

"I don't think it's related." Louise avoids eye contact before adding, "Why don't you tell me about your deepening relationship with Billy?"

"Well," I say. "I'm excited about dating him and it feels right...easy... natural to be with him, but...." I hesitate.

Louise shifts position. "But what?"

"Too much is coming at me, and I don't totally trust my judgment. I mean, it wasn't so long ago that Ryan and I had that passionate reconnection, and I was all fired up about reconciling with him. Now I'm all fired up about Billy."

"So?"

"So, I'm a bit worried."

"About what?"

"Losing myself. Not trusting my judgment. The possibility that I'll fall apart if I invest my heart and it doesn't work out." The words fly out of my mouth in a rush. "Miriam said I shouldn't be afraid, but I don't want to lose it like I did in Boston."

Louise locks her eyes on mine. "You never lost it. You were traumatized by Miriam's murder. You had PTSD and complicated grief. You experienced a profound shock, and then you recovered. You worked hard at that, and you're a strong person. Stop doubting yourself."

She walks to the sink, pours herself a glass of water, and drinks it down while looking out the back window. "Sarah, you have more courage than anyone else I know, and a deep capacity to face up to the worst parts of life—and to heal."

"That sounds nice, Louise, but really, think about what's going on right now."

"What?"

"I have a dead friend sitting in my bedroom chatting with me at night. I've been struggling with flashbacks. I had a precognitive dream predicting Jim's death, and now I'm having recurring nightmares that seem to be a recapitulation of his accident and drowning. I fell apart after my interview at the police station." I hold both hands out, palms up. "These are not the characteristics of a very stable person, are they?" I smile in the midst of recounting all this drama. "What if I'm really nuts?"

She laughs. "Nuts? Good clinical diagnosis you've got going there, honey."

"It's not funny."

"Stop it." Impatience tinges her voice. "There's nothing wrong with you."

"My dreams aren't normal. Seeing and chatting with Miriam isn't normal. Dreaming about Jim's car accident and death before it happened, that wasn't normal." I pause, suck in a deep breath. "That was so totally not normal!"

Louise slaps the countertop. "Damn it, Sarah, what the hell is normal? You adore your Aunt Zelda and she sure isn't normal, but you *know* she's tuned into folks on the other side. So you're like her—it's a friggin' gift. What, you think the rest of us are normal? We're all nuts in our own way. I mean, really. Who are you comparing yourself to? Me? If you only knew!"

The air in the room has changed. I can sense something else emerging, something Louise has been hiding. I hold her gaze like a magnet. "What? If I only knew what?"

She looks away, out the window again. I hear evasiveness in her voice. I've never heard Louise sound evasive, not to me, not ever. "Nothing," she says. "I'm sorry, but listening to you insist on your craziness is making me crazy."

"No. Not good enough. What's really going on here? What aren't you telling me? Is this about Mark? Or are you finally going to come clean about why you were in Henderson's office?

Louise seems to be holding her breath, then she holds my eyes and says, "I can't. I can't tell you. It involves another person. I can't break his—or her—confidence."

"Who are you covering up for?"

Louise doesn't answer.

"Do you know who killed Henderson?"

"Of course not!"

"There is no 'of course' or 'of course not' that's going to work between us right now. The way I see this, I'm standing here telling you that I don't trust myself, and you're standing there telling me that you don't trust me either. When have I ever broken a confidence? When have I told a secret or spoken out of turn? I took the kids while the police searched your house. I gave up a weekend with Ryan in Manhattan to come to a meeting with you and Kate and Alex going over the coroner's report. I made dinner the next night for all of you so we could discuss why you're a suspect and who should be on the list instead of you. I've gone over cases with you and Alex. I did my best to protect you with Pomerleau." I stop to take a breath.

"When have I not told you something you needed to know, like seeing Mark in Boston? All this time you're keeping secrets, and I haven't known the first thing about what's going on with you! Why can't you tell me what the hell you were doing in Henderson's office that afternoon. I feel like you've been lying to me."

Louise, white-faced, looks as if she is being held upright by the kitchen counter. "All of that is true, but what I'm keeping secret isn't related to Henderson's death."

"You were in his office the day he died. Of course it's related." I'm already on my feet, heading toward the back door. As I reach for the doorknob, Louise snaps, "Don't make this bigger than it needs to be."

I yank open the door. "I love you, Louise. But right now, you're really pissing me off. I hope this is all worth it, lying to me about needing to be home after court when you were actually going back into town to see Henderson, keeping this big secret, and whatever else you're doing. I hope whoever you're doing this for is worth it. I hope risking our friendship is worth it."

Chapter 25

A thick fog must have crept across the peninsula while Louise and I were arguing. The spotlights shining out from both our back porches create spooky stripes on the ground, transforming our backyards into an eerie landscape. I run home, scrambling to unlock my back door, hurtling through it, slamming it shut, and clicking the deadbolt into place.

The house seems dark—very dark—so I switch lights on and off in every room, checking to assure myself all is as it should be. Once upstairs, I fill the tub with bubbles and soak until my fingers pucker. Then, exhausted by ruminations and lingering grief, embarrassed by the rage and recriminations I directed at Louise, and confused by her behavior, I snuggle into bed beside the cats and somehow fall off into a sleep as deep as the dead.

A loud crash shocks me awake, propelling me upright in bewilderment. The cats perch, wide-eyed, beside me, their tails bushy. Heart thumping, I listen to more noises from downstairs; someone's in my house. I pick up the portable phone and slip out from under the comforter, praying the old wooden floorboards won't creak as I slide the raspy bolt across the bedroom door. Though I know it won't offer much protection, it's something between me and the intruder as my fingers dial 911 and my voice whispers into the phone. "Someone's broken into my house at Eighty-eight Mackworth Street. I'm upstairs in the bedroom, and I can hear whoever it is smashing things downstairs."

"Your name?"

"Sarah Green."

"Okay, Ms. Green," a calm male voice says. "I'm notifying our officers right now. There, it's in the computer. Do you have any guns in the house?"

"No," I whisper, wishing I had one in my hand and knew how to use it.

"Okay. You're in the Back Cove, yes? Hold tight. Three cars are right near you at Woodfords Corner. If you count to thirty, they'll be at your door. I'll stay on the phone with you until they arrive."

Sirens sound before he finishes the sentence. Lola and Tillie leap off the bed and onto the back windowsills. I pad over to the front windows and watch two squad cars pull up, stick out my head, and wave. An armed uniformed officer nods acknowledgment. Two others disappear down the driveway.

"What do I do now?" I ask my dispatch angel. "Stay in my room? Go downstairs?" I tiptoe to the back window and peek out. The door beneath me slams. More footsteps sound inside the house.

"Just stay put. An officer has entered through the back door and is clearing the downstairs. The others are checking things out and will tell you when it's secure."

This guy's voice is so reassuring, I think I could marry him, sight unseen, if he'd only ask.

"Everything's okay now, Ms. Green. Your house is full of Portland's finest. Detective Marshall is on his way up your stairs. You can hang up the phone now, okay?"

"Yes, thank you so, so much."

"Sarah." Billy's voice sounds from right outside my bedroom door. I unlatch it and throw myself into his arms. He holds me tight.

"Whenever you're ready, Ms. Green," a voice floats up the stairs. "There's broken glass down here, so wear shoes."

I extricate myself from Billy's embrace, quickly throw on some sweats, slide my feet into shoes, close the door to keep the cats safe in the bedroom, and head downstairs to meet the police and prepare to clean up whatever mess awaits.

Every light in the house is lit. A silver-haired detective with a craggy kindly face and a rumpled beige suit introduces himself as Joe Sullivan. He waves me into my own living room and onto the couch.

The phone rings. Sullivan picks it up and says, "Uh huh, uh huh, uh huh," then hands it to me.

"What in God's name is going on? Are you okay?" Louise sounds frantic.

"Someone broke in."

"I'm coming right over."

"Don't, please."

"Shut *up*! Of course I'm coming over—just as soon as I call Kate and Alex. Tell the police, so they don't shoot me," she demands.

Sullivan sits across from me. His partner, a tall lean guy who looks like he starches and presses his jeans and his face into submission, leans against the mantel. "I'm Detective Boudreau," he says. "We missed our intruder, but we've got cops out there with a police dog trying to track him."

Sullivan interjects. "There's a mess all over your kitchen and dining room, and unfortunately our evidence technicians are making it worse dusting for fingerprints."

"That's the least of my worries, Detective. I'm just happy he's gone and you all got here so fast. How'd he get in?"

"He?" Boudreau interjects. "What makes you think it's a he?"

"You said so just now. You said you're trying to track *him*." I look around for Billy, but apparently, he's letting his colleagues handle this. "I also kind of assume it's a guy. How many women commit burglaries?"

"Enough."

"The point of entry was your dining room window," Sullivan says. "There also seems to be a connection with Henderson's murder—"

"What? What kind of connection?"

The detectives exchange glances and Louise chooses that moment to march through the front door. "What happened here? Oh, hello, Joe." Louise knows some of the cops on the force from her domestic-violence work. Sullivan tips his head. "Someone broke in?" Louise asks. Heads nod.

"The connection is part of a message he or she or they left you."

"What message?"

Sullivan points me toward the dining room, where a piece of construction paper sits on the table with bloody-looking scribbles amid the upended remains of a plant.

Nosy, nosy
posy, posies
grow on graves
Henderson knew
you do too.
Shut up! Shut up!
Or you're next.

I lower myself into one of the dining room chairs and rest my head in my hands. "What is going on? Why would someone target Henderson and then me?"

"We can't answer that, but our evidence technician will take this in," Sullivan says kindly. "We'll try to get something from it, but I'm not hopeful. Where's your office?"

"Why?"

"If this guy is worried enough to break in here, he might have also burgled your office."

"It's only a few blocks away," Louise says.

"Suppose you follow us over with Detective Marshall?"

Louise and I follow Billy to his unmarked cruiser and he drives us to the office. As predicted, the place is trashed. The file cabinets have been broken into and our folders are scattered across the floors of both our offices. Billy has to leave, but assures us he'll be back when we're finished. It takes two hours to put things to rights and when the office is secured again, I call Billy and he drives Louise and me home.

"Sorry to tell you this, Sarah," Billy says after I unlock the front door, "but I'm still on duty. Are you staying, Louise?"

Her face flushes and she stares at him for a moment before answering. "Yes."

"Good." He turns to me. "I'll call you later to check in." He wraps his arms around me and kisses the top of my head.

My eyes are glued to his back as he walks to his cruiser. Kate and Alex drive up as Billy drives off. Louise, looking more exhausted than ever, begins sweeping the kitchen floor. I turn to her before our friends come into earshot.

"Don't stay. Kate and Alex are here now. But before you go, tell me why you've been acting so weird around Billy. Did you lie about your relationship with him, too?"

"I don't have the faintest idea what you mean. There's no weirdness between Billy and me."

"I shouldn't have even bothered to ask," I sputter. "All of a sudden I can't trust you to tell me the truth." Alex walks in during my accusation and Louise walks out without even attempting to respond.

"What was that about?" Alex asks.

"Louise and I are not getting along at the moment. Thanks for coming out in the middle of the night."

"Of course. Looks like there's plenty of cleaning up to do here. We're at your service. I made baklava tonight, so you're in luck. I brought the leftovers. After we clean up, we'll be all set for a bout of emotional eating."

"What a mess!" Kate strides past me into the living room and scans the debris.

I fill them in on the break-in at the office and the note the intruder left. Fortified with their presence, I walk into the kitchen. Plates lay smashed across the counters. Slivers of glass shine between the coffee grounds.

"Aren't these your grandmother's canisters?" Kate asks. Yellow shards of porcelain litter the floorboards. The black "C" of the coffee canister sits upright against the wall.

"Yes, the poor things. They traveled all the way from England to New York. Stayed intact throughout her life, and traveled up to Maine, just so some schmuck could trash them. Damn it! Who is this guy? What does he want?"

Alex lays her arm around my shoulder. "Let's think of this another way, shall we? Let's ask what we want." She narrows her eyes and smiles nastily. "We want to find this bastard and make his crummy little life even crummier."

"That's right," Kate agrees. "This lowlife has no idea who he's tangled with. He's doomed."

"He's going to plead for mercy and get none." Alex grins wickedly. "And then he's gonna wish he never heard your name."

I smile. Revenge sounds sweet. I've had enough.

Chapter 26

Kate and Alex do the bulk of the kitchen cleanup, while I work the dining room. Mark stops by, toolkit in hand, a bit bleary-eyed. He hugs me, nails a sheet of plywood over the broken dining room window without much comment, and leaves. Kate, Alex, and I collapse in the living room after finishing, tossing around revenge fantasies and passing the baklava until Kate notices the time and returns home to tend to the animals. Alex stays for the night.

"We'll get a security system installed as soon as possible, and I'll stay here until we do," Alex offers as we make our way upstairs.

"How much will that cost?"

"Don't worry about that for now. The important thing is that you're safe."

"The reason I ask is I'm wondering if Louise and I should get one for the office too."

"We'll figure it out tomorrow," she says.

It doesn't take long to settle her into the guest room and get myself ready for bed. Despite how tired I am, sleep doesn't come easily. I stare out the back window, where my flowers float, ghost-like, under a full moon.

Bright sunlight and the scent of strong coffee await me as I awaken, leading me to keep my shower hot and short. A freshly baked scone is disappearing into Alex's mouth as I enter the kitchen, grateful to accept the full plate she offers me. After demolishing breakfast,

I'm ready to check my voicemail. I square my shoulders, put the phone on speaker, and hit "play."

"Did you enjoy my visit, girlie?" The high-pitched male voice is tinged with a Maine inflection. "If you want to stay alive to pet your little kitties, you'd better back off."

The knot in my belly tightens, but so does my resolve. "Let's figure out who this guy is so we can torture him."

Alex grins. "Glad to hear you're sticking with that attitude," she pauses. "I've been thinking. Suppose you had a client in this kind of situation. Someone trying to sort through her history to figure out who was harassing her. What would you suggest she do?"

"Hypnosis. It's an effective way to access buried or blurry memories, or to connect pieces of memory that belong together." I smile. "I've got a therapy session this afternoon. How timely."

Sitting across from me, Janice exudes a tantalizing sense of wholeness. I want that. I don't want to be frightened by a stalker. I don't want a devious best friend. Most of all, I don't want to be hamstrung by neuroses. I understand, more clearly than ever, that the only person capable of changing my life is me. Toward that end, I fill Janice in on Louise's evasions, the break-ins, and my intentions for the session.

When I entered the field of psychotherapy, I was skeptical of hypnosis. I pictured gold watches in nightclub acts, out-of-control people squawking like chickens. I was surprised to discover that trance states induced by therapists are remarkably like the tranquility that flows through me at the end of a good yoga class. I now know that clinical hypnosis simply engenders states of deep relaxation that open doors to things below our normal consciousness, to dreams and memories underneath the surface.

"You know how this goes," Janice says. "Settle into a comfortable position and follow the rhythm of your breath, remembering that all hypnosis is self-hypnosis." Her voice softens. "You might imagine breathing in comfort and breathing out discomfort." I follow her suggestions, moving from my breath to my tranquil place—a hammock, sand, swaying palms, the murmur of surf rolling in. Her voice is so soothing that despite my earlier agitation, I can even smell the salty air.

"You might float back in time, to when certain information that might be useful to you now was completely available to your conscious mind." Her voice softens further, her cadence slowing. "Information about one of your clients who might have also worked with Louise, Jim Barr, and Harold Henderson."

My mind's eye takes me to my office where I see a slightly fuzzy image of me, sitting in an armchair. A woman sits across from me on the sofa. Everything is dreamlike—the interaction between us, the conversation, the colors. Before long, Janice is calling me back, and we begin to discuss my experience.

"Details might come to you over the course of time," Janice says, seeding a post-hypnotic suggestion.

We finish up. I'm oriented and awake, but images and sensations cling to me. Alex arrives home just as I do, pulling into the driveway behind me. She carries a small suitcase and a bag from the supermarket. "How'd it go?" she asks.

We unpack groceries and talk about the session.

"Sounds fruitful. Now, might you enlighten me about the fight you're having with Louise?"

I take a deep breath, gather my thoughts, and launch into it. "Essentially, Alex, Louise lied to me. After court the day she and Henderson testified, I asked her to come to town with me and she insisted she had to go home. Thirty minutes later, I saw her in Henderson's office. She admitted to being there, but she's been completely unwilling to tell me what she was doing there. We're all knocking ourselves out on her behalf, and it pisses me off that she can't level with me."

"Does Kate know?" Alex asks, reaching for her cell phone.

"Yes, I talked with her about it before my interview at the police station. As Alex punches a number into her phone, I head to my bedroom for a nap. Within minutes, I'm in dreamland.

The mahogany leather of the sofa is comfortably worn. A woman sits at one end of it, her long shapely legs crossed at the ankle; red-leather high heels fade into the red of the Persian rug on the floor of the office. An obviously expensive red-leather purse rests on the floor. Long delicate fingers topped with red nail polish reach for the straps. A sizable diamond set between deep red rubies flashes in the light. The purse snaps open, a pen scratches on paper. She looks at the tall man behind the desk. A check is passed from hand to hand. The legs straighten and the red shoes move toward the door.

The sweet purr of the motor reverberates through his body as he pulls out onto the road. He strokes his palm over the soft leather stick shift, gradually increasing the pressure of his foot on the gas pedal, breaking slightly in anticipation of the curve at the marsh. No response—none at all. He jams the brake all the way to the floor, but the car speeds faster, spins wildly at the curve. It slams into the guardrail and flips up and over into the marsh.

Someone shakes me, and I awake breathless and disoriented. My mouth is dry, and I'm cold, very cold. Alex's brown eyes come into focus beside me. "Nightmare?"

"Yes, but…" I sit up, shivering, and try to collect my thoughts. "The hypnosis jogged something loose. I know the client, and she was also one of Jim's. In the dreams, I think he's been trying to show me that his brakes were intentionally tampered with." I stare at Alex. Alex stares back, waiting for more.

"I'm not sure why he was driving a red sports car in my dream. That has to be a clue from my unconscious. It's such a far cry from his truck that it has to mean something, but I can't get the connection. When I think about cars like that I associate things like flashy, show-offy, rich, fast—but I'm not sure where that takes me."

"Do you have or did you have any clients that fit that description?"

"None that I can come up with at the moment, but there must be someone." I pause. "You know how much I resist accepting the psychic skills that run in my family? But this time there's no other explanation. My aunt is sure Jim was murdered, and now, so am I."

"I've had a funny feeling about Jim's death too," Alex says, "even more so once you told me that Jim had a garbled message on his phone referencing Henderson. Kate minimized my concerns, but now that you and I are in agreement, I'm going to pursue it. Tomorrow, I'll call some friends in the police department and see what's happened to Jim's truck. They can still evaluate it, as long as it hasn't been demolished." Alex removes a pencil from behind her ear and reaches for the pad atop my bedside table. "Who's the client?"

"Harriet Connors. Louise was also involved in her treatment."

"I'm going to ask Louise to come over so we can sort this through together."

"We have to, don't we? Why don't you call her while I pull myself together? I'll meet you downstairs."

Louise is sitting beside Alex on the sofa as I walk into my living room and settle into the recliner across from the two of them. Is Louise contrite? I can't tell, and at this moment, I'm not sure I even care. What's important is talking about my dream and conclusions.

Louise listens carefully and agrees with my interpretation. "The high heels, the purse, the nail polish. You even nailed her diamond ring." She rises and begins to pace. "I can't believe I didn't put this together myself, since I made all the referrals to you and Jim, then tussled with Henderson about Constant Caring picking up the tab."

Lola lies beside me, flipping her tail. Tillie is batting around a toy. I can almost see the charged molecules in the air.

"Can you back up and fill me in?" Alex says.

"We mentioned this case early on," Louise responds. "Harriet was suing the man who sexually abused her when she was a child. She was also trying to sue the state. I asked Sarah to see Harriet for hypnosis."

"Why?"

"It's not my specialty and Harriet needed to reduce her level of stress."

"She also wanted hypnosis to retrieve memories," I say, "and that was beyond my skill set, especially considering the lawsuit. I didn't want to testify, not with something as controversial as sexual-abuse memories. Louise and I talked it over and referred her to Jim. He was much more experienced in clinical hypnosis. In fact, he trained me."

"Jim was happy to work with Harriet," Louise continues. "And I was thrilled to have his collaboration. Harriet is a complex patient and we needed a psychiatrist on board. When her eating disorder flared up, along with serious depression, Jim and I jointly recommended inpatient treatment."

"I assume Constant Caring denied coverage?"

"Exactly. Jim appealed the denial, Henderson got involved, and it got convoluted fast," Louise says.

"How so?"

"Jim had no use for Henderson. He questioned Henderson's expertise in second-guessing our treatment recommendations. That's when Henderson made sure Jim lost his preferred-provider status with the insurance company, which meant Jim's clients were no longer reimbursed for their sessions with him. Jim complained to the Insurance Commission, alleging ethical violations by Constant Caring. He followed up by filing a lawsuit against them."

The hair on my arms prickles. "Then Jim's brakes failed."

"I'm with you on this now, Sarah," Alex says. "My doubts that Jim's death was an accident were well placed." She turns to Louise. "How soon can you get Harriet Connors into your office?"

"Not very soon. I have no idea where she is. Sarah saw her last, when Harriet dropped off a check on her way to a new assignment. She said she was going to the Adriatic coast, right?"

I nod.

"I wasn't expecting her to leave town at that point in her treatment," Louise says, "but she's a sought-after fashion model, the jobs pay well, and she can be called away suddenly."

"Didn't you say you were going to call her?" I ask.

"I did say that, and I tried. Her cell phone had been disconnected."

"What's the status of her civil suit?" Alex asks.

"I don't know," Louise says. "I was deposed by her attorney. I'll pull her file in the morning and call her attorney. Sarah, can you dig out your notes?" She turns to Alex. "I think we should meet again tomorrow night, with Kate."

"Okay." Alex looks to me for confirmation. "After work, here?"

I nod. Louise gets up to leave, and we don't hug before she walks out the front door.

"That was kind of frosty," Alex says.

"I'll get over it," I say. "I might be making too big a deal out of this. Louise is a steadfast friend, and..." I pause. "I guess we're all entitled to our secrets."

"That we are," Alex concurs.

"Meanwhile," I say as I walk towards the television set, "Why don't we pop in a DVD of my old favorite, *Compromising Positions*. "Maybe we'll get some inspiration from Susan Sarandon and Raul Julia. And if not, we can simply enjoy the sizzle between them."

I figure we've worked hard enough for one day. It's time for a little relaxation. Harriet and Henderson can wait.

Chapter 27

The next morning, the glass company replaces my dining room window, at a cost of $500, and the security company installs my system, with special pet-friendly motion sensors. My hand shakes as I write that check. I'm sorry Henderson was murdered, because at this moment, I want to kill him myself. Alex departs with her suitcase as I leave for work.

Mid-afternoon, Louise walks into my office, waving a manila folder. "I found it, but before we get into Harriet's case, I need to say a few things."

"I'm listening."

"First and most importantly, I'm sorry." Louise eases onto the sofa across from me, propping her chin on her hands. "I am *really* sorry. I haven't been able to sleep since you walked out of the house. I wish I hadn't added deception to the list of things we're both dealing with."

"Me too." I stare at her face, searching for my next-door neighbor, my best friend, the woman I've trusted since the first day of summer camp so many years ago. I want to forgive her. "It's impossible to explain it all to you right now—"

"Why? Why can't you tell me what's going on?"

"The night Henderson died and I called you, it wasn't just because of shock and fear. I wanted to tell you everything."

"You could have."

"I know." She opens her hands. "And I'd just begun when Mark interrupted us."

"Sure." I'm not interested in cutting her any slack. "But then he left."

Louise stands up, pours a glass of water from the pitcher on the sideboard, and holds it up. "Want some?"

"No."

She paces. "I should have told you before that, but I was scared, it was such a can of worms, and I needed time to absorb it all myself. I...I still do."

"In the past, that's exactly the kind of thing you would have shared with me. The fact that you haven't is making me aware of a weird distance between us. And for the first time ever, I feel distrustful of you. I don't like that at all."

"I wanted to tell you, honestly. I've wanted to talk with you for a while. I started to tell you. I would have told you, and I should have told you, but we got interrupted. And then Kate called and told me not to talk about it."

"So Kate knows why you were there?"

"She does, and once she told me not to discuss it with anyone, I couldn't tell you. As my attorney, she didn't want you to know things that might get you into trouble or vitiate attorney-client privilege because I'd shared them elsewhere." Louise sighs. "You're an attorney, you must get that."

"Of course I do, now. It would have helped if you'd told me that up front." As I speak, something shifts in my consciousness, the way it did at Jim's funeral. My anger isn't all about Louise, regardless of what secrets she's keeping. It's really about me. I shouldn't need Louise to trust me with everything in order to trust myself. I lost some of that when Miriam was murdered, and it's only now that I can see how it's hampered my life. If I can't trust myself, whom can I trust? Not Ryan, who no longer knows me. Not Billy, who doesn't know me well enough yet. Not Louise, who knows me perfectly, but is mired in some complication that, so far, is none of my business. It's time to get a grip—and move on. "Okay," I say. "Maybe I overreacted. Let's leave the issue of secrets alone right now and start talking about the case."

Louise perches on the sofa, laying the folder on the coffee table, and says, "It might be good to review what we know."

"Sure."

"Jim lost his preferred-provider status with Constant Caring when he and Henderson disagreed over Harriet's case, and you think your nightmares are Jim's way of telling you that his death wasn't an accident. Maybe the person who murdered Henderson also tampered with Jim's brakes. If so, then maybe the same person threatened you?"

"Exactly."

"Why?"

"Maybe it has something to do with Harriet's civil suit against the perpetrator."

"Who was the perpetrator again?" It seems like we're really close to something here.

"It was...someone...who lived near her when she was child, if I recall correctly. The complication in Harriet's recovery of damages had to do with a trust fund shared by other recipients."

The downstairs door opens and closes. We both jump.

"Probably my next client." I force a smile.

"We need Jim's notes on Harriet's hypnosis sessions." Louise closes the folder and tucks it under her arm. "Do you think we can get them?"

"I don't know, but I can dig out my own. What we need most are the details of Harriet's lawsuit against her abuser. I can find his name in my notes, and we could always look up the complaint. Why don't you call Kate and ask her to get in touch with Harriet's attorney? Maybe he has Jim's notes, that's not something we can get from the public file." I sit back, tapping the tops of my fingers together, pondering the connections.

Louise stares out the window again. "I should track down Harriet. Maybe she didn't leave town so suddenly just because she was offered a modeling job. What if she was being threatened too?"

A dead stillness permeates the room. I wrap my arms around myself to counter a sudden chill. "This is really creepy."

"I'll call Kate now," Louise says. Her face has turned pale. "When's your last session? I'm done at five."

"I finish at five thirty."

"I'll wait for you. We can lock up together and follow each other home. I'll call Mark and my mom. She can be home in time for the kids. Mark can wait outside for us. We'd better be extra careful with new referrals. We don't want the murderer in our office."

"What if he's already here?" A shiver of fear snakes up my spine.

Louise straightens her skirt. "We'll have to rely on your highly tuned antenna."

I pick up the phone to call Alex, who quickly promises to follow up on Harriet's perpetrator—is he in prison or out? I dedicate a few minutes to yoga breathing, so I can shift my focus from my own fear and be fully present for my next client, a woman with her own serious fears—the potential success or failure of chemotherapy for breast cancer.

Chapter 28

Elena and Todd seem subdued as they enter the office. Elena takes the armchair. Todd sits on the sofa. He speaks first: "I've resigned from the board at Constant Caring."

My eyebrows arch up in surprise, but I quickly channel some self-possession and consider an appropriate response. "You've been thinking about resigning for some time now. Are you relieved now that you've actually done it?"

"Well, I'm relieved!" Elena interjects. "I just can't wait for Todd to be completely out of there. The company is such bad news. They force their clients to fight for health insurance benefits they've already paid for, while the company gives their executives enormous salaries and eye-popping bonuses."

"Elena, we agreed not to go there." Todd adjusts his tie. "Don't push it." Ice cubes could crack under the coldness of his stare.

"Okay, okay." She raises a placating hand and tucks her legs underneath her as if she's feeling a chill.

"I told you I'd do it and I did." Todd says, licking his lips. "The letter is written. I submitted it today. I won't be going back." Todd appears to be looking for an expression of support from Elena, maybe appreciation, but she's fidgeting.

"I've also asked Todd to cut contact with George." She hesitates as she swings her eyes back and forth between me and her husband. "George scares me. He's really changed."

"How so?"

"When he first took the job as CEO, he was happy. He and Brooke and the kids, well, they seemed like they were all good together. Then George began working harder, and he seemed to close off, and, well, I don't know—he just changed."

Todd's face hardens. Elena pauses as if looking for something from him. It doesn't appear to me that he's offering what she wants, but she continues. "The board had concerns about some of Henderson's consultation fees, and George couldn't explain those fees to the board's satisfaction. They brought in an auditor and George got jumpy."

"Stop it, Elena." Todd gets up and walks to the sideboard, pouring himself a glass of water. "The board at Constant Caring is on top of that. This isn't the business of our couples therapist."

I struggle to formulate an appropriate inquiry, all too aware that my curiosity is less about this couple and more about Henderson's murder. I've learned that sometimes it's better for me to remain silent than to say the wrong thing.

"Todd, could you pour me a glass of water?" Elena asks.

He complies and returns to his seat.

"I'm very proud of you for resigning. I know it's been a struggle." Elena speaks in a conciliatory tone, but my curiosity aside, I can't help wondering why the session is so focused on Constant Caring and George Tate instead of the irritations and aggravations in the marriage.

"This has been difficult for me in a different way." Elena turns to me and then back to Todd. "I'm worried that George will be furious at you for resigning, for bringing those ethical issues to the attention of the board. He was so vindictive with Brooke."

Todd shifts uneasily. "That's why I talked with the auditor—to get some clarity. And that's why I resigned. I agree it's important to limit contact with George, at least for a while."

"I think we should call the police," Elena adds.

I sit up straighter.

"Not that I don't trust you, honey," she says. "I don't trust George."

Todd stiffens. "No police. We agreed. Don't push it or I'm out of here."

"Why the police? Are either of you in danger or do you have reason to believe that anyone else is in danger? Because if that's the case, the police have to be contacted."

"No! No one is in danger!" Todd's vehement denial sets off alarm bells in my brain.

"That's not completely true!" Elena bristles. "You said yourself that George has gone over the edge."

"Elena, stop this ridiculous catastrophizing. Next you'll be worrying about George sneaking into our house and murdering us in our beds."

"I don't know what he's capable of anymore. What if George murdered Henderson?"

"Do you really suspect him of murder?" I ask.

Todd barks, "No! Not at all. I've known George for more than forty years, and he is completely incapable of murder."

"Do you suspect that George could do you or anyone else harm?"

"Even if Elena's wildest fantasies about him have any connection to reality, it wouldn't affect us. I'm not threatening him. I simply did my duty as a board member to bring certain issues to light. George will know I'm resigning to avoid participating in any board evaluation of his performance. As his first cousin, it's a conflict of interest. Until now, his paranoia hasn't been directed at me, and I don't think that will change. We go back too far."

"Paranoia?" I ask.

Todd's sigh takes up all the air in the room. "Wrong word. Henderson made him nervous. George didn't trust him. That's what I'm referring to."

"If that's all it is," Elena says, "then why did you have such an elaborate security system installed at home?"

Todd sucks in a long slow breath. "I told you why. After three local robberies, we'd be fools not to protect our art and your jewelry."

Elena's nostrils flare. "I think you're afraid of George, of what he might do when he gets your letter of resignation. Maybe he'll be suspicious. His drinking is out of control. Brooke says she thinks he's mixing alcohol with his sleeping pills, and that's not a good thing. I know," Elena says, turning to me, "because George and I both occasionally take Seconal for anxiety and sleep. We have to. We are both allergic to benzos, and don't do well on other sleep medications. That's about the only thing we have in common." She looks at Todd. "Honey, you promised me you'd talk about George in these therapy sessions."

"Okay, okay," Todd says. "Next week."

Elena smoothes her skirt and looks at me. "Sarah, you'll understand everything after our next session. Then you can really help."

After they leave, I sit in the silence, concerned about my ability to help them with their marriage. Todd's minimization of Elena's fears poses a conundrum. I'm stunned by Elena's suspicion that George Tate killed Harold Henderson, but until I have a sense of how possible that is, I can't know if she's exaggerating the risks to their safety. Tate's an expert on automobiles, with his fancy collection of antique cars. I wonder if he tampered with Jim's truck. I can't imagine George Tate breaking into my house, smashing my china, and leaving messages on my machine, but someone did, and I still don't have a clue who.

Chapter 29

Louise follows me home from the office. Mark is standing guard outside our houses. He meets us, and walks me into my house. I turn off the new alarm, then reset it for stay mode with a sigh of relief. Tillie flops in front of me, rolling over to expose her belly, offering me the opportunity to squat and indulge in a soothing connection.

I heat the kettle and pour a cup of tea. Billy calls. "I'm going to have a late night here. I just wanted to let you know."

"Thanks. I appreciate that."

As the phone clicks off, the blinking message light catches my attention, but I ignore it. The desire to soak in my tub takes precedence, as does the possibility of learning to use a gun. I'll have to call Alex and set up a training session. Maybe I'll buy my own gun. At the moment, the image of myself with a weapon feels empowering.

I soak in my claw foot tub, wondering about my post-hypnosis dream. Could all this craziness be centered around Harriet Connors and the lawsuit against her abuser? Why would he target me, Jim, and Henderson? Could he have also set up Louise for Henderson's murder? Murder would be a bit of an overreaction to our roles as Harriet's therapists. On the other hand, maybe Harriet is just a symbol of something or someone else. Maybe George Tate killed Henderson, as Elena supposes, in some misguided attempt to shore up the finances at Constant Caring. Maybe the red Corvette in my dreams is a symbolic reference to George and his collection of fancy cars.

I startle as the bathroom door pushes open, but it's Tillie. She leaps onto the marble-topped vanity and stares at the stenciled wisteria winding across the yellow walls. Lola pads in and rolls around the floor, licking her paws. We relax together until the doorbell rings.

I hop out of the tub, grab a towel, poke my head out the window, and call down, "I'll be just a minute."

"Mind if I leave the flowers on the front steps?" the deliveryman calls up.

"No problem." I pull on jeans and a T-shirt and walk downstairs. When I lift the top of the white box, the scent of roses perfumes the air. Two dozen red, long-stemmed, with a note from Ryan.

"I was a complete jerk. Please forgive me. I'm flying to New York in two weeks. How about a do-over?"

My face flushes. Ryan? Now? What am I going to tell him—because he said he was moving on, so have I?

Wrestling with ambivalence, embarrassment, and pleasure, I sniff the fragrant blossoms, clip the stems, and arrange them in a tall crystal vase, a wedding present from my aunt. My past lies before me, offering another chance. There's no question about my affection or passion for Ryan, nor his for me. But Ryan and I have had innumerable chances, and we've always screwed them up. I've always screwed them up.

If things were different, a chat with Louise would sort me out, but that isn't about to happen, so I stow the flowers in my bedroom to avoid questions I don't want to answer, whip up a quick dinner, and watch the news until Kate and Alex arrive. They're smooching on the front steps when I open the door. "Nice example you set." I grin.

"Exactly." Kate grins back.

Louise arrives a few minutes later, and I arrange the tea and cookies on the coffee table in the living room. Kate and Alex sit on the sofa. Louise and I flank them in chairs. While Louise catches them up on the day's deliberations and our suspicions, I chew on my fingernails, wishing for an alternate reality.

Louise props a pillow behind her back and settles in before speaking. "Harriet was my client for a few months. We'd been working with a trauma-treatment technique, EMDR, and in that process, Harriet recalled explicit memories of sexual abuse that occurred when she was in elementary school. Her recall involved a neighbor." Louise clears her throat. "I've mentioned that she travels for work, so she'd be in the office and out again, although I insisted that we have at least four months of consistent appointments to start the trauma treatment. I didn't want her jetting off when she was in the middle of tough memories."

"I've heard that this isn't uncommon—people remembering abuse many years after the fact," Alex says.

"That's right, and this technique can trigger memories. A number of things can trigger recall, but in this case it was EMDR. Because of the complexity of the issues and Harriet's stress level, I referred her to Sarah for hypnosis."

"We began with simple techniques focused on relaxation," I say, picking up the story. "Then Harriet wanted to use hypnosis for memory retrieval. That technique sometimes helps people recall more details, although memory is mutable."

"What does that mean?" Alex asks.

"Memories return in different ways—through images, emotions, sensations, smells. Sometimes the recall, though seemingly true, might not be totally accurate. There's controversy over the hypnotic techniques used, as well as how exact the facts are that emerge from that kind of recall. Some specialists think these memories are unreliable. They've accused therapists of using suggestive questioning techniques, as well as 'implanting memories.' Quite a bit of research is focused right now on the construction of memories."

"Other clinicians," Louise interrupts, "believe that in certain cases, specialists in these techniques are hired guns for perpetrators trying to escape responsibility for the trauma they've caused."

"I didn't doubt Harriet's memories," I say, "but this is tricky work. I wasn't comfortable with my level of skill and I didn't want to go to court. Louise and I agreed Jim would be the best hypnotherapist. Also, Harriet needed a psychiatrist. So having Jim on board helped in multiple ways. Of course, it didn't help Jim. Henderson shut him down fast."

"After a few months of memory retrieval, Harriet's eating disorder worsened," Louise says. "Jim and I both felt she needed inpatient treatment, but Constant Caring disagreed. We filed appeals. They denied inpatient care. Harriet left on a fashion shoot. Somewhere in the midst of that, completely unbeknownst to me, Harriet hired an attorney and filed suit against the Department of Human Services, the Department of Corrections, and her abuser."

"Can you give us the details?" Alex asks.

"Here's where it gets involved," Louise replies. "Harriet learned that her abuser had a prior conviction for sexual abuse before the Department of Human Services dumped him in town. This was way before notification laws, so no one in Standish could've known a convicted sex offender was moving in."

"Harriet's lawsuit claimed the state was negligent and failed to provide adequate treatment and oversight when they knew the guy was a danger," I add.

Kate balances her teacup on her knee. "Interesting, because you can't sue the state of Maine without permission from the legislature. There's a rule about the statute of limitations in such cases."

"That's right." Louise chomps on a cookie before turning back to Kate. "The time limits for the statute hadn't run, because the victim has to recognize there was a crime, and this was Harriet's first recall of the abuse."

Kate holds up a cautionary hand. "Were both of you deposed?"

"I was," Louise says.

"We were both scheduled, along with Jim and Henderson," I say. "Everyone was deposed except me. They didn't get to me before the suit was put on hold."

Alex refills my teacup as I search my mind for something from that afternoon's therapy session with Todd and Elena. Something connected to Harriet, but I can't remember what.

"Henderson was deposed?" Kate peers at Louise. "Why?"

"He evaluated Harriet when Jim and I appealed the denial of inpatient treatment," Louise replies.

"So you all had a connection to this client." Kate sits straighter, looking excited.

"We did," I say.

"Why was Harriet's suit put on hold?"

"There was something odd about it, a trust that Harriet was attempting to access. It had to do with other beneficiaries, but I don't remember all the details." I look to Louise. "Do you?"

"Yes, the last I heard, the court was making a determination about whether the trust could be accessed."

"Maybe someone wanted to shut down that litigation and to do so, he killed Henderson—and maybe also killed Jim," I say.

"We don't know that Jim's death was murder," Kate replies.

"Judith said Jim just had that truck in for servicing," Alex replies. "It doesn't make sense that he'd lose control of it so close to home. He took that road every morning and every night."

You keep trying to make Jim's accident more than it was," Kate says.

"Why are you so averse to the possibility that it might not have been an accident? We don't know enough to shut down this line of inquiry," Alex says with a snip in her voice. "I've contacted the police and am waiting to hear back."

"Well, I still think the connection you're trying to make with Henderson is far-fetched." Kate sits back, clasping her hands behind her head and staring at me. "It certainly wouldn't stand up in court."

"On the contrary," I say. "It's entirely plausible. This case connects Henderson, Jim, Louise, and me. Maybe we don't know exactly what prompted the murders, but we have a number of strong motivations for murder here: greed, the protection of reputation, and the avoidance of prison."

"Kate." Alex glares at her partner. "We're brainstorming. Cut the attitude."

How Alex puts up with Kate sometimes confounds me, because Kate can be a tank. She'll roll back and forth over your body and not understand why you might feel flattened. She's smart, beautiful, loyal, and a generous friend, but she doesn't know a darned thing about tact. Kate relents. "Let's check into the status of that suit. Alex, can you do that tomorrow?"

"Top of my list."

"Anyone else you all shared?" Alex asks.

"Brooke Tate. She saw Henderson, Louise, and me," I say.

Louise shakes her head. "Brooke has no connection to Jim."

"Then the link has to be Harriet. I dreamt about her after hypnosis, and my gut says these are important leads."

"Sure they are," Kate says, licking chocolate off her fingertips. "We just aren't sure where they're leading to, and we have a long way to go."

Chapter 30

It's a new day, and I dredge up the courage to phone Ryan and thank him for the flowers. He's all sweetness and light, detailing his intentions for a rendezvous. "How about heading to Nantucket for the Fourth of July?"

"I don't think that's going to happen."

"Why not?"

"Perhaps that little detail about the woman you're seeing?"

"That's not a problem for me. What about you? Are you seeing someone?"

"I've started to."

"You're kidding."

"Why do you find that surprising?"

"It isn't surprising," he murmurs. "It's disappointing."

"Our timing seems to be off."

"You could say that. Why don't we talk again in a month or so, or…" He hesitates. "You can call if you change your mind."

Before I can muster up an appropriate response, Ryan hangs up. I figure he has more ground to cover in therapy.

I know Billy won't be thrilled that my friends and I have created our own investigative team to catch the murderer. And it isn't as though I'm completely sure about my relationship with him anyway. The intensity between us kicks up my sense of vulnerability. When we're apart, I worry about my capacity to commit, and his, but when we're together, I settle down like a dog with a tasty bone.

Billy arrives for dinner, and worry isn't on the menu. As I stand at the sink, humming and spinning the salad, Billy's arms snake around my waist as he croons along with Sinatra.

After we've eaten, Louise walks in the back door, unannounced, while Billy and I are slow dancing. He steps away from me. She seems flustered. His hands slide into the pockets of his pants.

Louise fidgets. "Sorry to interrupt. I just wanted to ask if you could watch the house next weekend. Mark and I are going up to Rangeley. A friend offered us their summer camp for the Fourth of July weekend."

"Sure," I say. "I'll even water your plants."

"Thanks. I'll see you later," she says, pivoting to make an uncharacteristically abrupt exit.

"What was that about?" I ask Billy.

"I don't know." He shrugs, and we leave it there.

It doesn't take long for Billy to lead me into the living room and onto the couch, where he tucks my curves into his lanky frame. He doesn't depart until midnight.

I'm sitting in my office, finishing up notes on clients after a long day, when Alex phones.

"Can you meet me at Kate's in half an hour?"

"I could manage forty-five minutes. Do you want me to see if Louise is still in the office so we can drive over together?"

"No. Keep this meeting to yourself, please."

Traffic in Portland is congested at the end of the day, at least as congested as it gets here, though it's nothing in comparison to Boston or New York. I note that disparity with pleasure on my drive to Kate's office, and then score a parking spot right outside the front door. From the waiting room, I can see Alex pacing the glass-doored conference room, rolling up the sleeves of a blue-and-white-striped shirt while speaking on her cell. Kate waves me into her office, where I sink into the couch. A few moments later, Alex joins us, leaning against the door.

"What's up?" I ask.

"Major roadblock." Alex combs her hair back from her face, looking more stressed than I've ever seen her.

"You okay?"

"Not really." She drops into a chair. "This investigation is chock full of closemouthed witnesses. Even in Massachusetts, where people know me and my brothers, I still can't get anyone to talk."

"Your brothers haven't been able to help?" Two of them practice law in Boston, one owns and manages a restaurant, and one is a detective on the Boston force.

"Adrian and Cosmo gave me an office, a phone, and supplies, along with an intern to help with research. Giorgio checked Henderson's police record, but only found an OUI. Dimitri fed me, all of which was great, but it didn't get me very far with the investigation."

"So, what now?"

She leans forward. "We need cash."

I uncross my legs and sit up straight. "For what?"

"Information."

"Since when do you pay for information, especially when you aren't planning to use it in court?"

"I pay when I need to, Sarah. Not often, but it happens. Louise and Mark are broke. Kate and I have been footing some of the bills."

Kate comes out from behind her desk and plants herself in front of me, feet spread, hands on her hips—a classic power stance. "You know how it is when you're working a case. You do what you have to. You practiced law. I doubt your hands were always clean."

"Whoa." I stiffen and stand up. No one looms over me in an argument. "Don't make this personal. My legal days were eons ago, and right now they're irrelevant, except for the fact that we never paid anyone for information. It was the Public Defender's Office. We didn't have a nickel to spare."

"Alexandra and I have already put in four thousand," Kate says testily.

Alex breaks in. "Kate, take it easy."

We all take a collective breath. Kate retreats to her desk. I sit back down after she does.

"It doesn't matter if we can use the information in court." Kate's tone is more urgent than hostile. "At least we'd have something to go on, and it might direct us to other things." There's a hint of pleading in her voice, along with fear. "The police believe Louise is their best suspect. She had motive, method, and opportunity."

"I've been wondering about that myself." The doubts swirling around my mind settle heavily on my shoulders.

"What do you mean?" Alex asks.

"She's hiding something, maybe a few things, and she's protecting someone."

"She's not protecting a murderer, and she did *not* off the guy herself," Kate says. "I'm not about to spill attorney-client confidences, but I'm one hundred percent sure Louise doesn't know who killed Henderson. We'd better figure out who did, before she ends up being charged."

"It's really that bad?"

Kate nods.

"We need two thousand," Alex says.

"Wow. I just took a few thousand from savings to cover the costs of replacing my window and installing the alarm system." I have more in savings and know I'm resisting because I'm feeling frustrated, but this is neither the time nor place.

"I suppose we could dig deeper into our own savings," Alex says.

"No, that wouldn't be fair. I'll have to cash in a CD, but I can have two thousand to you tomorrow."

"Thank God that's over." Kate opens her top drawer, reaches in, and lifts out three chocolate bars, tossing one to Alex and one to me while tearing the wrapper from her own.

"If you'd started this conversation by offering me chocolate," I say, "I'd have handed over the money without a complaint."

Chapter 31

Alex has been in Massachusetts for a week. Louise and Mark are up at Rangeley. My sleep is fitful. I know it's influenced by discomfort about the empty house next door. This morning, though, the sunshine is brilliant, a gentle breeze is blowing, and the scent of honeysuckle wafts through the windows. I pour iced tea into a tall glass and take up a chair on the patio while phoning my aunt.

"Sarah, darling, what a wonderful surprise," she purrs, although I figure she knew who was on the other end of the line before she picked it up. "How are you? Any more interesting experiences with the other side?"

"Not really, but I'd love to tell you about hypnosis and my dreams."

She listens intently and asks good questions before commenting. "I'm proud of you, darling. You're paying attention to your sensations, and the dreams are becoming clearer. It will get easier as you go along, I promise." She pauses. "Miriam is right beside you, and your other friend Jim floats in and out. They're both telling me you must pay very close attention now, staying alert to information, however it might come, which is different for all of us." She pauses again, but the deep breath she takes is audible. "You might even see another luminous form. When you were little, it happened quite often."

"It did?"

"You talked about it quite a bit, and then shut it all down. Now you're getting back in touch." She inhales and exhales, long and slow.

"Are you smoking again, Aunt Zelda?"

"Yes, I am, and don't you dare tell your mother! I'm seventy-six years old, and I'm going to die from old age in a comfortable bed surrounded by loved ones, not psychopaths."

"Are you saying I'm surrounded by psychopaths?"

"Well, let's just say there's more than one psychopath interfacing with your energy field at the moment. I'm sorry for blurting that out. I'm sensitive about the smoking, and worried about you. Did you get that gun?"

"Not yet." I have to smile. I haven't mentioned my intention to arm myself to anyone, not even Alex.

"Well, don't dilly-dally, dear. Call that handsome detective you're seeing and get in some practice."

"How do you know he's so handsome?" I laugh, already knowing the answer.

A moment passes and her tone turns serious. "Oh, don't worry. I never pry into things that are none of my business. You'll be okay in the end, but you must be very careful right now. Remember that Miriam can help."

I'm not reassured.

"You have other guardians. Trust that, even though life can be perilous." She tsks. "I have to go now. I'm meeting your mother for lunch. I love you."

I retreat indoors, checking all the window locks on the first floor. When the phone rings, I wonder what Aunt Zelda wants to add, but it's Alex.

"I'm headed home from Massachusetts with news. Can you come for dinner?"

"Sure. What's on the menu?"

"My mom loaded me up with spanakopita and moussaka. You'll get a Hellenic feast along with a tour of the gardens and all the dirt."

"That sounds wonderful." I don't add, especially because Louise's house is empty and the entire street eerily deserted. It's a hot Fourth of July weekend, and most of my neighbors must be at the beach. My novel engrosses me for the afternoon. I feed the cats dinner and get ready to go to Kate and Alex's.

A stiff onshore breeze has blown in, and while rummaging in my back seat to make sure I have an extra sweater, I notice an unfamiliar car parked across the street. The driver's face is obscured by a newspaper, and his passenger slouches under a baseball cap in the shotgun seat.

Unnerved by their presence and my aunt's warning, I lock the car, race-walk into the house, and dial Billy.

"Stay in the house until the squad car arrives. Then grab that can of pepper spray I gave you, set the code, and drive out to Kate and Alex's."

The moment the cops show up, I'm out the door, keeping my foot planted heavily on the gas pedal until the city limits appear in the rearview mirror. After a few more miles, the charms of the countryside dilute my jitters. Route 114 takes me past the tangy scent of manure at Smiling Hill Farm and eventually out to the Broadturn Road, where modern reproductions of southern Civil War estates vie with oversized country homes, displacing the dairy farms that once dotted the landscape. Manicured lawns flourish where pigs, cows, and working horses used to graze.

When Holmes Road finally appears, I'm flooded with relief and turn onto Watson Mill Road with a smile. The ancient farmhouse Kate and Alex have renovated shines in the sun. It sits back from the road, the wide expanse of lawn newly mowed. Bright white clapboards set off forest-green shutters cut with moons and stars. I know the barn is filled with hay and horses. Hostas line the front walk, geraniums bloom in big planters on the front steps, and window boxes overflow with a jumble of ivy and pink rose begonias.

The wide drive sits beside a long, narrow, side porch. Alex saunters out of the barn and over to my car, her olive skin deeply tanned and her skin smelling of horses. Her Labrador mutt, Niko, meets me with a swishing tail and a few licks. When he's taken all the salt from my palms, Niko looks into my eyes, plops down, and rolls around in the dirt.

"Nice welcome."

"He only does that for his favorite humans." Alex grins. "I need a shower, but Kate will be right out." She gestures to the porch, where green-painted rockers with padded chintz cushions beckon. A white wicker coffee table holds a glass pitcher and pink Depression-era glasses. Alex and Kate have a good division of chores, one that makes the most of their divergent talents. While Alex digs, plants, and weeds, Kate drags home one vintage piece after another from yard sales and auctions to which I often happily accompany her. She must have snagged the glassware on a solo jaunt.

The screen door slaps shut behind Alex, but Kate comes out only a minute or two later, cool and calm in cream-colored linen shorts and a matching tank top. Her blonde hair looks even lighter, probably bleached by the sun.

"Hi, honey." She gives me a hug that is significantly cleaner than Alex's. The tense posturing of the prior week has disappeared. "We're feasting on spanakopita, moussaka, sugar snap peas, and a salad loaded with feta—all the veggies straight from our garden."

"Yum. What a treat."

Alex returns in cut-off jeans and a yellow T-shirt, carrying out a tray laden with cheese, crackers, and red grapes. While snacking, I fill them in on the strangers parked in front of my house, and they invite me to spend the night.

"Thanks, but Billy's going to stay over." Their eyebrows rise in unison, and I blush. "Tell me what you discovered in Massachusetts."

"Sit back," Alex says. "This is no short story. You often said you couldn't figure out why or how Henderson ended up in a helping profession, right?"

"Yes. He didn't seem the type."

"What he liked about it," Alex says, "was helping himself to his clients' money."

"Psychotherapy doesn't pay that well. Especially since the advent of managed care."

"He had a lucrative side business."

"I'm all ears."

She smiles. "Blackmail."

"Come again?"

Alex runs her hands through wet hair. "He was into extortion. Must have kept a detailed account of his clients' confidences, then used them to increase his income courtesy of the vulnerable people they spoke about in therapy sessions. He may have even recorded some of those sessions just for that purpose."

"I bet those payments were significantly higher than his fees from Constant Caring," I say with a smirk. "How'd you find that out?"

Alex rocks back and forth on her chair as she speaks. "I connected with another investigator, Matt Hewitt, who trained with me years ago. Turned out he worked a few cases that involved Henderson. In one of them, Matt set up an elaborate sting using a phony physician's office. His associate booked a therapy appointment with Henderson, ostensibly to deal with her distress over sexual advances made by her orthopedic surgeon. Matt posed as the surgeon."

"Nice."

"After Matt's associate spilled her supposed secret to Henderson, he contacted 'Dr. Matt' to set up a consultation for an alleged knee problem. Matt donned a white coat and sat behind his desk as Henderson pulled out a small tape recorder, saying he wanted to play back his prior orthopedic consultation." Alex smiles. "Henderson wasn't playing back an orthopedic consultation. He was playing back his recording of Matt's associate's disclosure of the doctor's impropriety."

"That's what we call *chutzpah*!"

"That's not all," Alex adds. "Henderson proceeded to suggest monthly installments of four thousand dollars."

"Cheap, compared to the possibility of losing one's medical license."

"True enough," Kate adds. "God only knows how many such clients were in Henderson's stable, each paying close to forty-eight thousand dollars a year."

"What then?" I ask.

"Reverse blackmail. Matt recorded a DVD of Henderson's pitch. In the face of that, the good doctor agreed to repay Matt's clients, discontinue his other blackmail contracts, and leave the state. Maine inherited him."

"You'd think he'd have learned something," I say, spreading goat cheese on a cracker. "On the other hand, I suppose if you're used to the lifestyle, it would be hard to do without. Who was he blackmailing here?"

"I'll know more once a colleague accesses Henderson's banking records. I'm also looking for a ledger. Want to help me pore through paperwork later this week?"

"I'll be more than happy to do that. No wonder someone killed him. With his access to healthcare records at Constant Caring, he'd have enough secrets to retire to Tahiti."

"You betcha. That Constant Caring connection must have put him in hog heaven."

The kitchen timer begins buzzing, and Kate stands. "Dinner's ready," she announces, sliding her arm through Alex's. I follow them in, noting some additional flea-market finds. A white-painted dresser stands in the hallway topped by an Asian lamp with a fringed shade.

"That is gorgeous," I say. "And the house looks just lovely."

"Thanks." Kate smiles. Her taste in high fashion when it comes to clothing seems contradictory to her affection for old furniture and knickknacks, but when she pairs her finds with handcrafted high-end furniture, it creates a home Martha Stewart could love.

We sit on benches at a weathered farm table decorated with French-style placemats and glass dishes. The room turns cozier right before my eyes, as the evening sky changes color and candlelight casts a soft glow on the lavender walls. We dig into dinner without speaking. As the darkness deepens, the chirping of crickets fills the air, sending me into blissful relaxation. Watching my hostesses, I notice a few odd facial exchanges between them.

"What aren't you two telling me?"

"Stop reading into things," Kate admonishes.

"Tell me I'm wrong."

"I can't." She grins. "You're picking up on things before I'm ready to share them."

"That's life with an intuitive."

"Ah, you're finally in acceptance mode. That will make life easier for all of us."

"You're not going to get away with deflecting my attention," I say.

"Okay." Kate grimaces as she sets down her fork. "There is actually something Louise should have told you by now. Something that is not protected by attorney-client privilege."

My stomach twists.

Kate adds. "Some things were not appropriate for Louise to confide, and I told her so. Some things were because of attorney-client privilege. Others, well, I thought she shouldn't share the information—not just to protect someone else, but to protect you, in a way. But things have changed. She wishes she could have been the one to tell you, but we discussed it earlier and I have her permission to fill you in."

I've had my fill with waiting, but when the information comes out, it's a doozy.

"Henderson was blackmailing Mark."

My fork clatters to the plate. When I can catch my breath, I ask, "The cocaine?"

"Yes. And with Henderson's access to Mark's psychotherapy records, he also knew about Mark's affair with his secretary during Louise's pregnancy with Naomi."

"That's ancient history."

"Not if you're hoping to run for mayor after you retire," Kate interjects. "Henderson knew all about Mark's past drinking problems and his participation in AA."

"Maine's vast recovering community sticks together. Disclosing Mark's AA membership would only ensure he'd win an election, not lose one."

"That's not what Mark thought. He kept paying Henderson and didn't tell Louise. The pressure drew a straight line to relapse, and once Henderson found out about Mark's use of cocaine, he upped the ante."

"How did Louise find out?"

"She knew about the cocaine because she walked in on Mark snorting it. She didn't know about the blackmail until Henderson laid it on her that afternoon, after the Tate hearing."

"Okay, but why did she go to his office?"

"To confront him. She wanted to know if he'd illegally gone through Mark's psychotherapy records, which of course he had. Henderson told her to get lost. He wasn't worried about Louise turning him in, given a spouse snorting coke and paying blackmail."

"No wonder she wanted to kill him. I thought she'd gone over the edge, but after hearing this, I'd say she was exercising remarkable restraint."

"That's the problem," Alex says. "Henderson's dead and Louise has motive."

"So does Mark," Kate says. "He burnt through their equity line paying Henderson and buying cocaine."

"What a double life."

"Whose? Mark's or Henderson's?" Alex asks.

"Both." My appetite has disappeared. Kate waves Alex and me onto the screened porch, where we sit watching fireflies light up the darkness. Kate returns with hot tea and settles into the settee with Alex's head in her lap. I'm too tired to sort through any more details, and part of me doesn't want to know anything else.

"As much as we trust Billy," Kate says, "please don't talk to him about this. The more the cops know about the blackmail, the more interesting Louise and Mark will look as suspects, even though it's likely Henderson's history of blackmail was being replicated with many others here in Maine."

"Do you think Mark could have poisoned Henderson?" I'm overcome with guilt even asking.

Kate shakes her head. "I doubt it, but he did have access to bee pollen."

The room tilts as the entire scenario hits me. "But…but…if Mark killed Henderson, that means he knowingly set Louise up as a suspect!"

"You've known Mark a long time. Do you think he could have done that?" Kate asks.

I think about the wonderful friend Mark has been over the years, the good dad who loves his kids, the husband who loves his wife, the upstanding contractor who wants to someday be a city councilor. Then I consider his addictions and everything they can lead to. Kate and Alex wait, tense, for the verdict.

"No. I don't think so. Mark could never do something like that."

Kate disagrees. "We all know Mark is a loving, decent guy, but cocaine is powerfully addictive. It messes up the brain. People will do almost anything to ensure they have it, and Henderson was sucking up all of Mark's capital."

"At this point," Alex says, "I don't think we can rule anyone out."

Chapter 32

Clouds obscure the moon, making the sky seem incredibly dark on my drive home. At the city limits, my heart begins to pound. Anxiety's tricky, and mine has a combination of precipitants—the parked car, its strange occupants, the situation with Louise and Mark, and the likelihood that Billy and I are about to dive deeper into our relationship.

When I cruise into the driveway, he's waiting, extending his hand to help me out of the car. His warm smile and even warmer embrace comfort me. We walk into the house with our hands linked, and he leads me to the couch, where he settles on an ottoman in front of me, looks into my eyes, and launches into police business.

"We ran the plates. They belong to an ex-con with a long history of burglary and assault. Ever heard of Tony Grazio?"

I close my eyes, search my memory, and come up with nothing. "Don't think so. At least the name's not familiar."

"Could he be an ex-client or the spouse of an ex-client?"

"I'd remember an ex-client, but there's no way to know the husbands, or ex-husbands, of every married client, especially since they might have different last names." I pause. "Could he have been sitting out there waiting for Louise?"

"Maybe. Either way, I don't like it."

"Me neither. What do you suggest?"

"Spend the night at my place. I don't think you're safe alone here right now, even with the security system."

Aunt Zelda's predictions about psychopaths interfering in my life seem accurate. Despite my conflict over not disclosing to Billy the secrets Kate and Alex shared, it doesn't take me long to stuff a small suitcase with the few things I think I need. After feeding the cats and setting the alarm, I get back in my car and follow Billy to his house.

He carries my suitcase and unlocks the front door. I enter the house in front of him and something stops me before I take my second step inside.

"Are you all right?" he asks.

"Just hesitating for a moment."

"Is it about Grazio casing your house or uncertainty about staying here? As I've said, we don't have to push anything."

"Push anything?" I laugh. "I have no interest in holding back. I don't care how we got here—a car with an ex-con casing my house, Henderson's murder, my home invaded, threatening messages on my machine, whatever. All I know is how right this feels."

We carry my things to his second-floor master bedroom and take full advantage of his king-size four poster. It doesn't take long to learn just how skilled Billy is at cherishing a body.

I awake alone. Detailed images of the night's passion flood my field of vision and reignite intensely pleasurable sensations. The only thing to do is snuggle back under the covers and relive the experience. I don't open my eyes until the floorboards creak. Billy is dressed in jeans and a T-shirt, holding out a steaming cup of tea. "How are you this morning?"

I sit up and smile. "Umm, sensually sated, and greedy for more. Happy. And I'm…" I pause, searching for the right word. "A little nervous."

He sets the cup on the side table and lowers his body onto the bed beside me. "I've noticed there's a thin line between the thrill of pleasure and the excitement accompanying danger. Why don't we concentrate on the pleasure?"

Two hours later, I'm practically purring. Billy extricates himself to get dressed again. "Enjoy the tub—or the shower if you prefer. Towels are on the rack. Take your time. I'll start breakfast."

"The service here is superb. I don't know if I'll ever leave."

After my bath, I wander into the kitchen and find Billy elbow-deep in pots and pans. I press up against him, winding my arms around his waist and resting my head on his back.

"Did I tell you I have the day off?" Billy turns and points me toward a round oak kitchen table where breakfast is set out. We spend the next hour savoring sticky buns and demolishing an entire quiche. As he licks a finger and collects the last few crumbs from his plate, I struggle to muster up the capacity for speech.

"I'm free too, once we stop at the house to feed the cats."

The cats are peeved by my disappearance, but recover quickly once food and affection are dispensed. Billy can't keep his hands off me. Mouth to mouth, tongue to tongue—the heat of his body steams right through his clothes. We part, take a few deep breaths, and race each other to my bedroom. I open the windows, and a sultry breeze wafts in as Billy's mouth glides down my neck, creating a trail of delicious sensation. Clothing falls to the floor. We catch fire. Eventually, we nap. When I awake again, I trace the outline of his lips with my finger. Every cell in my body is humming with pleasure.

When night falls, we take a break to talk business and decide he should move in with me, at least until we know more about Tony Grazio. Billy does his best to reassure me.

"While there is some danger, you've got protection. I'll be here, you have a security system, the patrols will be increased, and Mark and Louise are next door."

I smile, thinking that Louise and Mark's presence doesn't inspire confidence, though I can't yet share those thoughts with Billy.

"What do I do about seeing my clients?" I say. "There's no way to keep the office secure. I seem to be struggling to figure out what the real threat is in the here and now, because some of it's getting braided into past trauma. It makes it hard to know whether I'm overreacting or fearful for good reason."

"I get that," Billy says. "I think as long as you and Louise are both in the office at the same time, you can keep working. Put both nine-one-one and my phone number on speed dial, just in case. And if our relationship is adding any angst, I want you to know that you face no danger from me. My days of casual sex were over a long time ago. I've waited years for someone like you to come along, and for me there's nothing even slightly casual about our relationship."

I study his eyes. Although his statement is reassuring, my heart is in free fall, and there's no safety net for that.

Chapter 33

With a plan to keep the home alarm set during the day and sleep next to Billy at night, things seem safe enough.

As soon as Billy leaves to pack his clothing for an extended stay, I phone Louise to tell her the blackmail is no longer a secret, at least not from me. Knowing about it helps me understand why Louise wasn't honest with me, though if I were in that situation, confiding in Louise would have been my first priority. But it's easier for me to access compassion and forgiveness now that Billy's love is filling my heart.

Louise isn't answering her phone at home, so I leave a message on her confidential office voicemail and turn my attention to the delightful advances in my relationship. Floating through the house, I hum while cleaning out dresser drawers for Billy.

I don't hear from Louise, and Billy keeps me occupied when he returns to the house. Billy and I leave for work at the same time the next morning. Louise's office door is open when I get to work, so I walk in.

"Where have you been?" I ask. "Did you get my message?"

"Yes. But I'm stretched, strained, and not having nearly as much pleasure as you. I'm sorry, but I can't talk right now. I've got to prepare for my next session, and my day is packed. Let's find time to talk tomorrow."

It isn't the tête-à-tête I've been hoping for, but at least I have a date to connect with her.

My day is packed with clients as well, and they seem to be as stressed as I am. It's difficult to be so immersed in my own tension while delving into their trauma, but it's also easier for me to see a way out of their situations than to see a way out of mine.

Alex phones, inviting me to sift through newly acquired records. I figure her office will be safe enough, but check it out with Billy. Though the week has been intense with clients, I've done all my paperwork and billing by the end of the day Thursday, and can give Alex and the records my attention on Friday.

My parking angels assist in locating a spot in front of a Middle Street gallery. Alex's office is upstairs, so she regularly strolls into the gallery to enhance her collection of paintings by talented local artists. Today my view is focused on manila folders, stacked evenly on Alex's enormous old oak desk. Some also occupy the large coffee table in front of the couch. "What the heck is all this?"

"We've hit the mother lode."

"Constant Caring documents?" I crow. "How'd you get your hands on these?"

"Can't tell you, but you can see why I need your help."

We spend an hour determining which folders hold what information before spreading the documents relevant to our investigation out on a long rectangular table and cherry-picking the ones to read first. Alex slides an ottoman up to one side of the coffee table, while I sit across from her on the couch.

We divide the stack in two. Half are redacted letters to subscribers and their therapists explaining the company's denial-of-benefit statements, while others look to be private notes from Henderson to George Tate detailing his rationales for the denials.

The explanations aren't new to me, as many of them accompany insurance remittance statements I receive on my clients. The denials run the gamut: not medically necessary; eligibility not confirmed prior to treatment; treatment not authorized; ineligible benefit for the diagnosis given; maximum benefit paid; services not covered; provider not eligible; benefits for this claim have been adjusted; and my personal favorite, the medical information we requested from you has not been received—this claim will be reprocessed upon receipt of the requested information.

Most healthcare providers believe the last rationale is purely an avoidance tactic to enable insurers to hold onto cash and drive providers and subscribers so crazy they forego the pursuit of reimbursement.

"This email from Henderson to George Tate proves I'm not paranoid. Listen to this!"

"'We can delay payment, obfuscate the benefit package, and confuse both providers and subscribers with the following clause: this contract does not cover charges for treatment, services, or supplies that do not meet our criteria for medical necessity or are not normally provided for the treatment of this condition as determined by our medical staff and/or an independent health care professional reviewer.

"'We can also deny a claim for psychotherapeutic treatment by labeling it an unproven therapy. It will enable us not only to meet the company's bottom line, but to exceed expectations.'"

"I bet the insurance regulators would be interested in seeing that," Alex says.

"This might sound morbid, but if you think of what happened to Henderson, he got exactly what he dished out."

"What do you mean?" Alex looks puzzled.

"A termination of benefits."

"Oh!" Alex snorts. "You…are…*wicked*."

I focus on separating Henderson's routine paychecks from his consults and correlate them with his records of bank deposits—another of Alex's mysterious acquisitions.

After two hours, we figure out the pattern to his weekly deposits: Some are from private-practice clients and some are routine insurance reimbursements for client sessions. Henderson utilized different banks for the disparate incomes. One bank received the large consult checks and other hefty sums not accounted for by our documents, another the biweekly paychecks from Constant Caring and client checks. As Alex looks through Henderson's ledger, she finds initials appended to deposit notations.

"How did you get these records?" I ask.

"Friends in low places."

"So much for client confidentiality."

"Many of these notations are just initials attached to client numbers, and we can't correlate those with names."

"If someone wanted to figure out folk's identities, they could do it with this. We have plenty of names here. Aren't you worried about that?"

"No. I'm focused on murder, not the violation of patient confidentiality. That issue is not our problem, so let's not borrow trouble."

I put together client names or initials and the numbers Henderson's attached to his clients, separating out the deposits that might be blackmail. That takes another two hours, and I finally stand up to stretch while Alex swings her legs onto her desk and asks, "What have you got?"

"Unfortunately, Mark's initials, all over the place, going back a ways."

"Surprised?"

"No. Well, yes. I'd been hoping there wouldn't be this many. It might or might not have been a ton of money to Henderson's other clients, but to Mark and Louise, it was a fortune." I sigh. "I think these are George Tate's initials all over the place. I can't begin to imagine what the CEO of the insurance company himself was paying Henderson directly for. His checks could have been reimbursement for Henderson's expert testimony at the trial, his so-called therapy sessions, or blackmail. How do we know?"

"Until we have more information, we have to guess."

I smack my fist on the table. "This guy was truly despicable. He not only used his clients and abused their confidences, he besmirched the field of psychotherapy. That makes me really mad."

"I get that," Alex says. "On the other hand, we are in possession of a long list that expands the number of suspects beyond Mark and Louise. Why don't you focus on that?"

"Focus on the positive, right?"

"You've got it."

When my eyes start to cross, we call it quits.

"I want to tell Billy about Mark and Louise as soon as it's feasible," I say.

"Not yet," Alex warns.

I set down a pile of papers and stand up. "It better be soon. I'm sick of having secrets in my close relationships. I hear enough secrets in my practice to fill the Pentagon, and at least one of those secrets led someone to commit murder."

Chapter 34

My drive home is filled with delicious anticipation, and I walk through the back door to find Billy preparing a marinade for a fine looking steak. He wraps his arms around me and holds me close.

"How was your day?" he asks when we separate.

"Very interesting."

"How so?"

"Sleuthing was the order of the day, although I'm not at liberty to disclose everything. It did, however, make me hungry." My eyes wander to the smoking grill and back to Billy. "For many things," I smile. "And how was your day?"

"I did some sleuthing of my own," he replies. "Tony Grazio was picked up last night for a parole violation. He's back in jail. His last cellmate was a guy named John Cass. Do you know him?"

My mouth opens to speak, but nothing emerges, not even a croak.

"That's one way to answer. You okay?"

I nod, try to swallow over the lump in my throat.

"Tell me."

"I…I…uh, need a moment or two to figure out what I can tell you."

His eyes narrow. "You're in danger, sweetheart, so you'd best tell me everything."

My mind races through various considerations. "There's no conflict," I finally say, with a sense of relief. "Once Harriet Connors sued John Cass in civil court, all the details became public record. So yes, I can tell you everything. I've never met the man, but I know about him. He's a sex offender."

Billy's expression is more cop than lover, though he's listening intently and observing closely.

"One of his victims, Harriet Connors, is Louise's client. She saw me, too, for hypnosis, for a short while. The issues were too complex for me. She needed a psychiatrist, so we referred her to Jim. Harriet was suing Cass for sexually abusing her when she was a child, and she was seeking damages from a trust fund Cass shares with relatives."

"Was Jim Barr deposed for that lawsuit?"

"Yes, along with both Louise and Henderson. My deposition hasn't been scheduled. I've felt that Harriet is the connection among us all, but Kate thought it was a stretch. I bet she'll change her mind once she knows Grazio was casing my house and Cass and Grazio were cellmates. That's no coincidence. Especially if Grazio has a record for burglary."

"A rather impressive one," Billy says. "Tell me more about Henderson and Jim and the lawsuit."

I fill him in on all the connections. Though I don't like keeping things from Billy, I do stop short of revealing Henderson's blackmail business. I'd promised Kate.

"Let's take one thing at a time," Billy suggests. "Grazio's prints are on file. I'll have them checked against the prints taken from your house the night of the break-in."

"If Grazio is in jail, I'm safe for now, right?"

"Grazio is in jail, but Cass isn't."

"You mean he's been released?"

"Yes, a few weeks ago. He maxed out and walked."

"You can check the prints, though, right? If Cass was here, he'll be arrested."

"If we can find him."

I take an inventory. Billy's clothes are hanging in my closet. His toothbrush and shaving stuff sit beside my makeup in the bathroom. The bed is big enough for us both. Even the tub fits two. Though I might be the target of a murderer, it isn't like what happened to Miriam. I have forewarning. My lover is a detective. A security system protects my home. The police are involved. A solid group of my friends, including a top-notch private detective, are checking all possible leads. If I'm not safe with all of that, it's my time to go.

If I die now, at least I'll die happy.

Chapter 35

Immersed in another week of intense client sessions, I keep my cell phone charged and both Billy and the Portland P.D.'s phone numbers programmed into speed dial. On Monday, Louise waves me into her office during my lunch break.

"We haven't seen much of each other lately," she says apologetically. "Even though we've both been working, I could see you've been as packed with clients as I've been. I haven't even had time to tell you that Mark went into inpatient treatment. The girls have been off at camp, and now the three of us are going to take some time together before Mark's return." Louise looks out the window for a minute and we share a short silence. "At least he's doing well in the program."

"I'm glad to hear that. Is it covered by insurance?"

"Yep. Thank God."

"Are the girls okay?"

"Camp was good for them." She straightens some papers on her desk. "The girls and I are going to take some time off and go the beach, go hiking, maybe take a few nights in Acadia."

"Do you want me to cover your clients while you're away?"

"If you can."

Her avoidance of eye contact makes me uncomfortable, yet the dark circles under her eyes indicate she's under serious strain. "How are you, really?"

She rubs her hands across her face. "Tired. My marriage is hanging by a thread, and although I wish I could muster up some enthusiasm for your romance, my life is disintegrating, while yours seems incredibly passionate. I'm jealous."

I balance on the arm of her sofa. "I used to fantasize about a high-school boyfriend whenever my marriage with Ryan hit a rough spot. Were you doing that with Billy? Imagining that if things flopped with Mark, you could take up where you left off?"

She flushes, turns away. "No, not really. Well, maybe, sometimes. Especially after you told me you'd seen Mark in Boston with another woman." She meets my gaze, finally. "Mark swears he's not having an affair. The woman is his dealer's wife. She was in a tough position, trying to get out of that marriage, and Mark insists he was just being supportive, connecting her with a good lawyer. I'm trying to trust him, but it's not easy." She checks her watch. "I've got to go. The kids will be home soon, and I need to relieve my mom. She's waiting for them."

Things feel really off between us—even Louise's hug is a limp one. "See you later."

"Probably," she says listlessly, picking up her purse and walking out the door.

I finish my last two sessions, one with a couple who seem more invested in being right than being in relationship, and one with a nurse struggling to keep up with a shrinking staff and an increasing caseload on her hospital floor. After finishing my notes, I check messages.

It's almost six by the time I lock up, happily anticipating a cozy evening with Billy, who promised to pick up dinner from Benkay after he gets off duty. My plans are disrupted when I turn onto my street and find it occupied by a slew of police cars and news vans.

Damn! What now?

I'm forced to park at the top of the street, and run the rest of the way, reaching home just in time to see Louise being led out of her house in handcuffs. TV cameras are rolling as reporters shout questions.

"Louise!" I call. She turns her head to acknowledge me, resignation and shame filling her face. A beefy-looking cop puts his hand on her head and pushes her into the back seat.

My cell phone slides so quickly into my hand, it's like an appendage. "Kate, I'm in front of my house watching a horror show. Louise is in handcuffs in the back of a cruiser. Can you do something?"

"I'm at the station now. The DA gave me a courtesy call."

"Obviously, she also called out the press for a perp walk."

"Damn. I was afraid of that. Alex is headed to your house and I'll be there with Louise as soon as I can get her out. Tell Billy everything, and I mean *everything*. We need his help now. I've gotta go."

The press disperses after the squad car pulls away with Louise. I run up the driveway and knock on Louise's back door. Kitty answers in seconds, throws her arms around me, and begins to cry. We hold each other until her sobs subside.

"What the heck is happening?" I ask.

Susie must have heard my voice, because she runs into the room and tugs at my skirt.

"Auntie Sarah, why did the police take Mommy away? Daddy's away and it's only us and Grandma, and I'm scared!"

I scoop her up, pink bunny in tow. "It's going to be okay, honey. Mommy will be home soon. Aunt Kate's seeing to that. Meanwhile, your grandma will take care of you and so will I."

She, too, cries herself out in my arms. As she begins to fall to sleep, Kitty takes her from me and carries her upstairs to bed. I walk into the living room and sit beside Naomi, whose tear-stained face displays a mixture of anger and fear. She lets me pull her into my arms. A few minutes pass before she extricates herself.

"My friggin' family is falling apart. Do you think they arrested my mother for that doctor guy's murder? Is she going to go to prison?"

"I'm sure this arrest is a mistake, honey. Kate will have her out, probably in an hour or two. Things will get cleared up. You can count on Kate."

"I'll never be able to show my face at school again."

The stress she's going to face with her peers lands on me with a thud. I try to come up with something mildly helpful. "It'll probably be big news for a few days, and for sure that will stink. But like the last time, some other news will take its place and everyone will forget about it."

"I doubt that. People will put this on their Facebook page and laugh about it for months." She shakes her head. "And what about my parents? Do you think they'll get divorced?" She tilts her head and looks at me with a cynicism I haven't seen before—but considering the circumstances, it seems an appropriate response.

"I certainly hope not. You have to remember that their marriage is strong. Everyone makes mistakes, but mistakes can be forgiven."

"I hate them both. They're total losers."

A long pause and a few deep breaths are in order. I take them before resuming our conversation. "I understand that's how you feel right now, but please remember that feelings change." I reach for her hand. "I'm so sorry you're going through this. Adults can make really stupid decisions sometimes."

"My parents are models for stupidity. My father relapsed, my mother's a suspect in a murder. How much worse can this get?"

There is no rejoinder for that, so we sit beside each other for a few moments without speaking.

"I'm going upstairs. Thanks for coming to check on us." She leans in and kisses me on the cheek. As she goes up the stairs, Kitty comes down. "Thanks so much, Sarah. I needed help and you arrived."

"Call me anytime, Kitty. Anytime at all." We hug, taking mutual sustenance from the connection.

Walking into my own home has never felt so good. Especially since it looks like Billy just arrived. He's unpacking warm takeout from Benkay. I suck in the tangy aroma of yakitori, with overtones of scallops and scallions. It makes my mouth water. Tillie is sprawled across the dining room table. Lola rolls around on the floor.

"You missed all the excitement."

"On purpose," he says. "I heard about it on the scanner and didn't want Louise to see me as she was brought out in cuffs."

"I'm sure she'd appreciate that, if she knew."

Billy scoops our dinner into Japanese blue and white bowls as I set the dining room table.

"We need to talk," I say, as we sit down and begin to eat. Between bites of the delicious dinner, Billy learns everything Kate and Alex recently confided.

"Remind me why you couldn't have told me this as soon as you learned about it?" Billy is clearly not pleased.

"Kate insisted it was part of their defense. How could I disclose it when you'd have to tell your superiors?"

He has on his cop face, which is giving me a long silent appraisal. Thankfully, it's interrupted by the doorbell. Alex stands on the stoop.

As she steps into the foyer, I ask, "What happened to provoke Louise's arrest?"

"One of Henderson's clients returned from a long trip to South America and called the police the minute she found out about his murder."

"And?" Billy prompts.

Alex takes a seat at the dining room table, as I resume my place and finish the last of my dinner.

"She said she bumped into Louise on the back stairwell that leads to Henderson's office."

"It's no secret she'd been there," I say.

"The first time. But none of us knew, until now, that she went back later—the evening Henderson was poisoned."

"She went back to Henderson's office that evening?" I'm incredulous. "How would that be possible? Louise called me that night. She woke me up and insisted I come over to watch the news. She and Mark had been arguing and she was totally thrown by Henderson's death. She never said a word about being there."

"She didn't tell Kate or me either."

"We were in synagogue that night," Billy reminds me. "You made those fabulous desserts for the *oneg*, remember?"

"So while we were at synagogue, Louise was back in Henderson's office? What was she doing there, confronting Henderson about blackmailing Mark? Refusing to pay him anymore hush money?" I feel unable to take all this in. "And then she called and asked me to come over when the news reported Henderson died that evening during his group. She never once mentioned being at his office that night. How much more duplicitous could she be?"

"Did anyone else see Louise in the building?" Billy asks as he rises to clear the table.

"I don't think so," Alex says. "They were on a private staircase, used only for clients who didn't want to be seen coming or going. I suppose that also included his blackmail victims." Alex stares out the front windows of my living room, sticking her hands in the back pockets of her jeans. She turns to Billy, who now stands behind his dining room chair. "What's the official play-by-play of the night Henderson was murdered?"

"The story I'm privy to says the group members didn't see anyone coming in or going out that evening, although other occupants of the

building have said that the fire alarm went off and everyone was evacuated." Billy pauses and looks thoughtful. "According to the group's
accounts, Henderson opened his office door for his group, poured coffee for himself from his personal carafe, offered the group members tea,
took a few sips of his coffee, and began the group. Within a few minutes, his face turned blotchy, he grabbed his throat, and he keeled over.
One of the women called nine-one-one while another did CPR, but he
was dead when the ambulance arrived."

I look up. "Between Louise's appearance in Henderson's office
and the details of his death, even I'd arrest her. What the hell has she
been thinking?"

"She clearly hasn't been thinking at all," Alex says.

"I hate to say this," Billy murmurs, "but maybe she did poison him."

His willingness to voice such doubt surprises me, though I'm more
shocked by my own reply. "Maybe she did."

Chapter 36

Alex's cell buzzes. It's Kate, saying she needs her at the police station. Billy and I alternate between pacing and flipping through magazines. He finally settles on *Mother Jones* and I rifle through my well-worn stack of *Cottage Living*, doing my best to compartmentalize and soothe myself. For me, cottages bring up images of a bucolic lifestyle, relaxed and easy times in climates where porches and hammocks do year-round duty.

When car doors slam out front, Billy yanks open the front door. News vans are pulling up just as Kate and Alex arrive; together, they guide Louise into my house. Dark circles ring Louise's eyes, and her rayon skirt is wrinkled and askew. I point toward the sofa and head into the kitchen, returning with a tray of coffee and tea. Louise sits beside Billy on the couch. The tension is palpable. Though Louise looks up gratefully as I set the tray in front of her, I don't smile.

"I'm so sorry. I feel like such an idiot."

"And well you should," I say, settling on the sofa with Billy as the buffer between us.

"I know what you all must be thinking, but I didn't kill him. Yes, I was there that night, but not to poison his food. I should have told you—all of you." She turns to Billy. "Especially once the police searched my house and we all knew bee pollen was the murder weapon, but honestly, at that point, I didn't think anyone would believe me."

"You think we're more likely to believe you now?" Exasperation fills my voice. I turn to Kate. "How'd you get her out of jail?"

Kate is staring at me appraisingly. "I turned the information about Henderson's blackmail activities over to the P.D. Alex also found sur-veillance tapes from the jewelers downstairs from Henderson's office. The shop has a separate set of security cameras. My research assistant has spent the last two days reviewing them."

"Looking for what?" I ask.

"The jewelry store keeps their tapes for months before reusing them, and their cameras cover both the front and back entrances to the build-ing. The police only had tapes covering the front. The day Henderson was murdered must have been payday for his blackmail business. A lot of people came in and out of the back entrance. Louise was one of them, but now they have a lot more suspects, including Mark."

Louise looks beseechingly at Billy. For some reason, everything is suddenly magnified a thousandfold: facial expressions, movements, words, and my sensations around them all. They spin through the room, taking shape and form in geometric patterns, pinging off the walls. Now I wonder if Mark killed Henderson, whether he really could be sitting silently while Louise is the prime suspect. Betrayal feels as close and oppressive as the humidity.

Kate and Alex stand up to leave. Louise, too. She again locks eyes with Billy, avoids eye contact with me, and murmurs a soft goodnight.

When the door closes behind them, I get up from the sofa, walk to the far wall, and lean against the fireplace mantle. Cradling my elbows in my hands and taking a deep breath, I reach for courage. "What is up with you and Louise?"

"What do you mean?" Billy's body language broadcasts a change from languid to alert.

"You know exactly what I mean. There's something between you, and it isn't just friendship after a long-ago romance."

"It is just friendship. We go back a long way."

"I'm aware of that," I say, attempting an icy stare. "You dated in high school. That's not what I'm referring to. I sense something between the two of you, something unresolved, something more than friendship. What is it?"

He doesn't respond.

"Billy," I say. "Louise is visibly uncomfortable around the two of us, especially when we're affectionate. I passed that off to—I don't know what—maybe surprise or jealousy, but there's something else going on."

He rests his arms on his knees, looks at the floor, then back at me. "This isn't really my story to tell."

"You want a relationship with me, buddy, you'd better be honest, or you can just get up and get out right now." Anger is taking over. Chill out, I try to tell myself. You're overreacting. But I feel what I feel, and I can't change that.

Billy doesn't take well to my tone. He straightens his shoulders and crosses his arms in front of his chest. "Louise should have discussed this with you. It's on her, not me, to tell you."

Somehow, I manage to measure my response. "Given the circumstances, how little she's explained to me about anything, it's way past time that *someone* told me. And if it's not you," I start walking toward the front door, "it'll be her—and I don't care that there's a murder charge hanging over her head or if Mark hears it or anything!" I fling open the front door and start out when Billy voice stops me and I turn around, watching his face as he speaks.

"It happened months ago." He speaks matter-of-factly, but both his palms are facing the ceiling, in a "Who me?" gesture. That pisses me off even more. I'm on the front steps.

"Louise was having trouble with Mark," he calls after me. "She suspected he might have relapsed. She needed a friend."

I turn and talk through the open door, "I was her friend. She could've talked to me."

"Sure, but she called *me*. Are you going to blame me for that?"

"No." I take a tentative step or two back.

"I suggested we meet for coffee. She said Starbucks wasn't private enough."

"Uh-huh." My voice sounds icy, even to me, as I walk back into the house.

"So I offered to make her dinner. She accepted. We had a few drinks. She talked about the marriage, the kids, all of it." He runs his hand through his hair. "She misread my signals."

My heart hardens. "And?"

Billy's eyes lock on mine. "She's a beautiful woman. It'd been a long time for me. I can't say I wasn't tempted." He shrugs. "It got"—he hesitates, spreads out his hands—"intense, fast. But Sarah, just as fast, I knew it wasn't where I wanted to go, so I stopped it. I got up and said I was sorry for taking advantage of her in a weak moment." Billy's eyes scan my face. "She said she was sorry for putting me in that position."

"That's it? That's the extent of it? I don't think so. What aren't you telling me *now*?"

"Really, that's about all."

I wait. I can see Billy's aware that I know there's more.

"She said she wanted to move things in that direction with me, but she understood that it wasn't the right time. Now hold on—let me finish. Then I said I didn't think there was ever going to be a right time for us, though we'd probably always have some attraction to each other because of our history. She left. Things went back to how they'd always been, and that was that."

"It doesn't look like that was that. It doesn't sound like it and it doesn't feel like it."

"What are you suggesting?"

"There's an energy between the two of you." I'm thinking he probably really wants Louise, but he's settling for me.

"If your intuition is broadcasting something else, all I can say is, it's probably because we never talked about that night. There's some awkwardness and embarrassment now. Nothing else is going on between us. Nothing. Not for me."

"I really appreciate your telling me the truth, finally," I say, aware of how splintered I feel inside. Part of me wants to run into his arms, but another part of me wants to scream at him. I compromise with myself. "I want you to go."

"Sarah. This all happened before you and I really knew each other. It was a momentary exchange of affection that couldn't go and didn't go any further. We recognized it and moved on."

Anger churns in my gut. "You and Louise look at each other," I begin, "in this certain kind of way. There's intensity and excitement. You haven't moved on. She certainly hasn't. Maybe you'd better figure out who it is you'd rather be sleeping with."

Billy's eyes narrow and he snaps back. "Haven't I shown you in every way that I'm interested in you? Just you? What more do you want?"

Why can't I trust that? I want to kiss him and kill him and throw up—all at the same time. "In all the obvious ways, yes, you have shown me that." I'm barely holding back tears and my voice cracks. "But neither you nor Louise came clean even when I asked you. Now I don't know who I can trust, so I have to trust myself, what I notice, what I sense. Most of my life, I haven't trusted myself enough." I ache to reach out and touch him. "I trusted Louise. That was a mistake. I trusted you." Tears well up and trail down my face. "I've had all I can take of half-truths from the people I love. Right now I need to be alone. I need for you to go."

"Fine." He gets up and heads for the door, where I'm still standing.

"Not just for tonight," I say. "I want you to pack all your things and go *away*."

I watch his face closely for a reaction. Maybe it's his cop training or his legal practice. Or maybe he really doesn't care. Because there is no discernible reaction. Not a raise of his eyebrows. Not a furrow in his forehead. Not a twitch of his lips. He simply looks at me, almost curiously, then turns and walks upstairs.

While collecting dishes and second-guessing myself, I listen for his footsteps on the stairs and meet him in the foyer. Half of me wants to take back my words, enfold myself in his embrace. Half of me wants to clobber him with a baseball bat for his failure to tell me the truth about Louise.

"You sure this is what you want, Sarah?"

"For right now, yes, this is what I want." I bite down on my lower lip. "I really care for you, Billy. In fact, I think I love you. That's why I took things so slowly. That's why I waited to sleep with you. You should have told me about this thing with Louise before we slept together. You owed me that, at least. I feel betrayed. I feel as if sleeping with you may have been the biggest mistake of my life."

We stare at each other while my traitorous cats wind themselves around his legs. He reaches down to pet them, then stands upright. "Actually, Sarah, that's where you're wrong." He hoists his bag and opens the front door. "I'd say *this* may be the biggest mistake of your life."

Chapter 37

The next few days are agonizing. I'm at war with myself. Part of me wants to call Billy and apologize, beg his forgiveness, do everything possible to reconcile. The other part of me wants to stay tightly coiled and cut off from any emotions.

Nothing else is going well either. The police haven't found a match between Grazio's or Cass's fingerprints and the evidence taken from my home and office. Tony Grazio is back in jail. John Cass is a free man. The police don't know where he is; he doesn't appear on the surveillance tape, and he hasn't registered anywhere as a sex offender.

Kate downgrades my Harriet Connor theory from promising to tenuous, while Alex, Louise, and I disagree with her evaluation. We haven't identified any other clients with connections to Jim, Louise, Henderson, and me.

My personal therapy focuses on Louise's and Billy's betrayal. Twisted in knots, I wish Billy would call, but he doesn't. If he did, I'm not sure what I'd say.

Things at the office are tense too. My anger at and disappointment with Louise are barely containable. Avoidance is my main tactic. Our few conversations are brief and strained.

After a few days, she confronts me, insisting we talk. I refuse. I don't want to hear her version of the events of the night with Billy. If they turn out to be different, I don't know what I'll do.

Later, worn down by her persistence, I reluctantly agree to an evening walk on the Boulevard. Our sessions end at the same time, so we lock up together, follow each other home, change, and meet in front of our houses. Though our walk begins in silence, we don't stay silent for long.

While navigating the steep stone steps on the slope from Hersey Street to the Boulevard, Louise speaks first. "I am truly sorry for misleading you. Our friendship is incredibly important and precious to me, and I can't believe how badly I've screwed it up." She stops at the bottom of the steps and waits, but I don't respond, so she continues. "I know you don't trust me now, and it will probably be a long time before you're willing to trust me again."

"You've got that right," I snarl, sprinting across the Boulevard. Louise follows, both of us dodging cars. We jog. I stop to catch my breath, scan the scenery, and avoid Louise's gaze. More limber runners jog by. A delicious fragrance wafts from the linden trees, planted as a memorial to World War I veterans. I think about time, and loss, and endings.

We begin to walk the path.

"What exactly are you apologizing for?" I ask. "Lying about Henderson, not telling me about your sexual come-on to Billy, or not telling me about Henderson's blackmail racket?"

Louise stiffens, and her freckles darken against her face. From the glare in her eyes, I know that she's seething. She stops in the middle of the path and sets her hands on her hips. "The price of admission to a friendship is not a blanket relinquishment of privacy. I didn't *owe* you any disclosures. The fact that my husband relapsed or was being blackmailed was none of your fucking business unless I decided to make it so." She straightens her shoulders, raises her chin, and glowers at me. "And I never slept with Billy, so don't even go there."

The path teems with people out for a stroll, and those within hearing turn their heads for a closer look as they pass. My gaze strays to the couples; my throat chokes with sadness. Ryan and I walked this path many evenings as Portland's skyline shimmered, mirrored in the cove. Every Fourth of July, we carted folding chairs down the steps to watch fireworks burst into the sky. Now I've lost Ryan, chased Billy away, and my friendship with Louise is in tatters.

Even so, I do have issues to raise. "How could you come on to Billy and then not tell me, especially when you kept trying to set us up?" I look at her through narrowed eyes. "You know, that was really kind of creepy. Were you trying to have an affair by proxy?"

Louise blanches, as if I've slapped her, but she doesn't respond immediately. She sinks onto a bench beside the path, and I sit beside her, wordless for a few minutes. Then she begins to speak, very softly. "The whole thing with Billy was completely my mistake. I don't remember exactly what was going on with you at the time, but you weren't doing so well. Maybe it was after another failed reconciliation with Ryan. I didn't think you had the capacity to listen."

I hate hearing that, but I know it's entirely possible that was the case.

"I'd just found out about Mark and the cocaine. It was too much to handle, you know?"

I nod. "That must have been overwhelming for you. I'm so sorry that was going on, and that you didn't feel you could talk to me about it. I'm shocked that you didn't talk to me about it. I've always tried to be there for you, even when I was in the midst of my own *tsuris*."

"I know that. I think this was just a combination of the most embarrassing things that ever happened to me. And the thing with Billy... well, he and I go way back, almost as far back as you and I. He's still so sexy, and I drank too much. It was stupid of me to come on to him, but you can't tell me you've never done something like that." Her face fills with chagrin. "He responded. That felt great, but it didn't last long. He pulled back. He was kind, but very clear and firm." Her face flushes. "It was humiliating. I wanted to talk to you, but then I didn't want to think about it. Billy and I never talked about it. I see now that we need to."

I'm flooded with relief to hear that Louise's story agrees with Billy's, but I'm not finished. "You should have told me once Billy and I got serious. It was an awful position for him to be in. His old-fashioned gallantry added to the problem—but he shouldn't have been in that position where he felt the need to keep your secret from me, your best friend. He wouldn't have been, if you'd been the kind of friend you used to be."

"You're right. All I can do now is say I'm sorry and try to clean things up."

I kick a stone into the cove. "And," I keep my voice low and even, "you've been my best friend for decades. What you do has always been my fucking business. Especially now. Not only have I been working my butt off trying to build a defense for you, helping Kate and Alex investigate Henderson, I also kicked in two thousand dollars from my savings account, so Alex could pay for information in Massachusetts."

"What? Why?" Louise fumbles for a tissue in the pocket of her gray sweatshirt, then wipes her eyes.

"Because they asked! Why else?"

"Geez, what an ass I've been." Some people passing by stare with undisguised curiosity, but Louise ignores them. "Over the years," she says, "clients have spoken about behaving in ways that don't comport with how they know themselves, as if they can't believe what they're doing and saying, but can't help it either. That's how I feel." She props her elbows on her knees and lays her forehead in the cupped palms of her hands.

"I get that, but why did you keep trying to set me up with Billy if you wanted him yourself?"

"Why aren't you hearing me? I didn't want him! Except in my fantasy life where I'm fifteen, not married, and don't have children." She smiles. "And I knew you and Billy would be good together. I've known that for a long time." She looks at me. "I haven't known how to manage the awkwardness with him, especially since I don't want to give up the warmth of the friendship we've had, but I'll figure it out." Then she laughs. "Don't I have plenty of work to do in therapy? I'd better find someone and schedule an appointment."

"Let's walk." I stand up and reach out a hand to pry her off the bench. We make our way down the path and around the cove, dodging the traffic to cross the Boulevard, hike the steps, and walk down Clifton Street. When we reach our street, I lean my butt up against a tree trunk and catch my breath.

"So about Billy," I say.

"Yeah, about Billy. I watched him fall in love with you in a flash. It's obvious he's crazy about you."

I flush with pleasure, then grimace, unsure if his love has survived my rigid and unforgiving cutoff. "That might all be past tense given that I've kicked him out—and might have lost the chance to commit to the most promising romance I've had in a long, long time."

"I don't think so," Louise says. "I'm going to call him to clear things up between us, and I'll explain what's been going on with you."

"I'd appreciate that." Though I'm exhausted, I know we aren't finished, so I dredge up the courage to say what I need to say. "I'm really sorry that you felt I couldn't help you when you needed help, and I'm hurt that you didn't give me the chance to try. And I'm mad about your dishonesty and how it affected me. It made me doubt myself. That was the last thing I needed."

Louise meets my eyes. "I know. I made many, many mistakes. I thought if I just sat tight, the police would find the murderer and everything would be okay. I missed you terribly, and what made it worse was that I was the one shoving obstacles between us."

"Okay." I hold up my hands in a gesture of surrender. "Thanks for your apology. I accept it and still love you, but let's not delude ourselves. Repairing our friendship will take time."

She nods, extends her arms, drops them, holds them out again. "Can I hug you?"

"Yes."

We hug. It isn't the same, but it's a start.

Chapter 38

First thing the next morning, Louise phones. "I spoke with Billy. It's definitely not over between the two of you, at least not for him. He's just waiting for you to call."

I obsess about whether to call or drive to his house and apologize in person. Too chicken for the latter, I phone. He isn't there. I hang up on his answering service and call again Saturday, and Sunday night. Same deal. My sleep is fitful, and it makes for a bad day at the office on Monday with multiple trauma clients, one after the other. I feel stretched and strained, barely able to hold things together during the sessions.

Todd and Elena are my last clients, and they're late. My fifteen minutes with yoga postures turns out be a prescient choice, because when they finally arrive, it's clear we're going to have a doozy of a session.

"Todd didn't want to come to this session today," Elena begins. "He's reluctant to discuss family history, but we've agreed, finally, that it's crucial."

"Okay." I watch them for a moment. "Where would you like to begin?"

"I suppose you'll want the lineup?" Todd pinches the bridge of his nose and briefly closes his eyes.

"That might be a good starting point."

"My mother was one of three kids—two sisters, one brother. Their father was a nutcase."

"How so?"

"A pervert. My mother didn't speak much about her childhood."

"Why not?" Elena leans forward from her place on the sofa. Todd sits to her left, on a chair.

"She was relieved to escape." Todd's Adam's apple bobs up and down as he swallows. "There was some weird thing between my grandfather and my mom's sister, who was never quite right either. She married a loser and had a kid, then completely fell apart after her own mother died."

"You have another cousin?" Elena asks in astonishment.

"Believe me, you wouldn't want to know him, Elena, which is why you don't. Like I said, his mother, my aunt, was strange. Beautiful, but strange." Todd gazes at me. "Hair like yours. So dark it was almost black, long and curly too. She was about your height, at least as I remember it. Curvy like you," he adds, appraising me as if he's never seen me before.

His whole performance is incredibly creepy, but I force myself to think clinically. I wonder if he's dissociating—one part of him separating from the other, moving into a more childlike part of himself, disconnected from the rest of his personality.

Todd closes his eyes for a moment, then turns to Elena. "This aunt and her husband were drunks. After my grandmother died, my aunt moved back to the farm to take care of my grandfather. She left her son, my cousin John, with his father."

Todd's face seems to waver before me. It blurs, then morphs into a child's, then an adolescent's. I close my eyes. When I open them again, the condescending attorney I've come to know is examining me.

"Are you back with us now?"

"I never left you. I closed my eyes for a moment to capture a thought more clearly."

"Good to know." He moistens his lips. "At some point, my aunt took off and no one ever saw her again. A few postcards came every so often, from different parts of the country, but no personal contact. Who knows what happened to her?"

"You never told me any of this." Elena appears befuddled and I share that befuddlement. Something is odd—off. I wonder if it's the slow pace of Todd's disclosure or his emotional detachment.

"This isn't the kind of thing one speaks about. My mother didn't discuss it. I didn't know my grandfather very well. I was at the farm only once for a weekend sleepover with my cousin John before my grandmother died. John and I shared a room. Once was enough." Todd smirks. "It was what those in your trade might call traumatizing."

"How?" Elena asks, reaching her hand out to touch Todd.

"George's father had closed a big deal and wanted to treat his sisters and their spouses to a weekend in the Big Apple. George went skiing with friends, but John and I got stuck at the farm." Todd pops his knuckles. I wince.

"Honey," Elena says anxiously.

"I woke in the middle of the night. John was crying. My grandfather was getting out of John's bed. As soon as the old goat left the room, I slid my pocketknife out of my knapsack and stuffed it under the pillow. Good thing, because I woke up the next night to find him in bed with me. When I reached under the pillow and popped the blade, he hopped out of the bed like it was on fire."

"How awful!" Elena exclaims.

"Must have been a regular occurrence for my poor cousin, and then John's mother left him with his father, who wasn't much better."

Elena is wide-eyed.

"No. John's father wasn't a pedophile," Todd says. "Just a drunk. After John's mother disappeared, my mother and George's father invited John to join us for vacations, and he did for a while, but when my mother and John's father had a falling out over something, we lost touch."

"Then what?"

"One weekend when George and I left prep school to see the Sox at Fenway, we bumped into John."

"I'm so surprised you never spoke about this," Elena says.

"I had good reasons. John wound up in foster care for a few years, but by the time we met up with him, he was living on his own. George and I felt awfully guilty. There we were, having a blast at a prep school, and John hadn't even gotten through high school. He was weird, and kind of a loser, working as a car mechanic."

I control my negative response to Todd's contempt and return my focus to his story.

"After that, we stayed in touch intermittently, sent him money when we could." Todd hesitates. "You can see why I never talk about that side of the family."

"How do you think you were affected?" I try to sort through the charged atmosphere, aware that Todd's defenses may be the reason for his condescension, but I'm wondering, yet again, whether his personality is fractured somehow. Is his behavior a personality disorder, or is it a consequence of more trauma than he's admitting?

Todd pinches the bridge of his nose again and takes his time before answering. "I wonder if I was affected. I know some people like to dig through the past, but that's never interested me. I'm fairly sure my grandfather didn't touch me, but what if I wanted to make sure? Is there something therapists can do to help me remember?"

I sit back, think about his request, and wonder why he's asking if he doesn't have much interest in digging through the past. "A hypnotic technique called memory retrieval might help, although it's a bit controversial. A trauma treatment called EMDR helps people recover from experiences of trauma, and sometimes in that process, buried memories come to consciousness. Although I use those techniques, you and Elena are my clients for couples work. Since this kind of work would be your own individual therapy, I'd refer you to a colleague."

"Would it give me the details? Make the memories clearer?"

"It might. It might not. These things depend on the person and the situation."

"Perhaps we can discuss that further another time," Todd says.

Elena gestures for Todd to sit beside her on the sofa. When he does, she holds his hand between both of hers. "Do you think," she asks, "that George might have a problem like your grandfather or aunt?"

"Mental illness?" Todd shakes his head dismissively. "No, but George drinks too much and so did they." He falters. "Well, I'm no specialist. I don't really know the answer to that question, do I?"

"I'm confused, honey," Elena says. "I thought it was your mother's father who left you the inheritance."

"Yes," Todd snorts. "He was a creep who lived like a pauper on that crummy farm, but he had money."

"What happened to your cousin John? Brooke never mentioned him."

"I doubt George ever discussed John with Brooke. John married a woman as peculiar as he is, and we aren't often in touch. Sometimes he calls us for money. George helps them out more than I do."

"George takes care of your cousin?" Elena's voice is filled with disbelief. "I can't see George being intentionally kind to anyone."

Todd runs his hand over his face, as if checking for beard growth in the past hour. "In the past, George was kind to you and Brooke and the children." He turns to me. "George's father was wealthy. My family had money, but not nearly as much, and my uncle's generosity allowed us to live a much nicer life. We spent summers in their guest cottage on Swan's Island, where George and I sailed, played tennis, did all sorts of things together." He smiles. "George and I were always close. We went to prep school together, then we both went on to Yale, and we've spent a good deal of time together as adults, with our families, until his marriage fell apart."

"And he became an angry alcoholic," Elena sputters.

"I see the conflicting loyalties," I say.

"Yes," Todd agrees. "Elena has an attitude." He rises, paces the office, then returns to the rocking chair. "Some of our inheritance is invested in Constant Caring. It makes things challenging for all of us when the company isn't doing well. George's drinking is affecting his judgment." Todd watches Elena. "Maybe he's taking too many sleeping pills. Didn't your doctor say a person could become dependent?"

"Yes," Elena answers. "I read that someone could get confused, or have emotional ups and downs, and even have hallucinations. And you're definitely not supposed to take them and drink alcohol." Elena's eyes hold mine. "I'm extremely careful about medications. I read the labels and all the warnings."

She returns her attention to Todd. "What about the trouble George was having with Henderson? I got the idea that you thought he might have been involved somehow with Henderson's murder."

"I never implied anything of the kind!" Todd snorts. "You're the one who's pushing that nonsense. You'd love to see him go to prison, wouldn't you? If George were going to kill anyone, it would be Brooke." He stops, stares out the window. Elena sits still, chastised.

The clock indicates we've gone over time and I'm drained. "We need to wrap up."

"No, not yet," Elena says. "There's something else I need to ask before we leave. Todd, since you submitted your letter of resignation from the board, has George threatened you?"

Todd stares at her defiantly.

Despite the tension in the room, that question has to be answered, although I'm not sure how to facilitate that without alienating Todd. "If there's any possibility your cousin could have been involved in Henderson's death, or that something at Constant Caring might have precipitated the murder, you should talk with the police."

"I don't need you to give me directions on my legal obligations," Todd says angrily. "The police have interviewed the entire board of directors, and that includes me. They've interviewed George and any-one else at Constant Caring who might have a shred of information about Henderson."

"Okay," I say, backing off as gracefully as possible.

They write out a substantial check for the two-hour session, and I lock up for the night, wondering about Todd's family. I speculate about what happened to his aunt and wonder whether his cousin John ever received treatment for his childhood trauma. But I have my own issue to attend to that evening—delivering an apology to Billy.

I soak in the tub, rehearsing many versions of my apology until I'm ready to leave a message. Clad in my pajamas, I sit on my bed making notes before picking up the phone. Billy answers on the second ring.

"Hi." My belly falls ten stories. I'm completely unprepared for a real live conversation.

"Hi yourself."

"I…um…I think you were right," I stammer.

"About what?"

"You said that telling you to pack up and go might be the biggest mistake of my life."

"Hmm. Where does that leave you?" His voice is soft and encouraging.

"It leaves me needing to apologize." I smile. "Right now, so here goes: I'm truly, truly sorry for not listening to you with an open mind. I'm sorry for not trusting you and for being so rigid."

Billy doesn't let me hang out there in the wind, waiting. "Thanks for acknowledging that. I owe you an apology too, for letting discretion morph into dishonesty."

My heart fills. "How about I make you a luscious dinner and we talk things through in person?"

"That works for me. I've got a full week, so it'll need to be Saturday."

"Saturday. Seven o'clock? My house."

"See you then."

I hang up and slide under the covers. For the first time since Billy left, I fall right to sleep.

Chapter 39

Elena Owen's voice is barely recognizable when the phone jolts me awake at four in the morning. "Todd's in the emergency room. They think he tried to kill himself. He's full of alcohol and pills. Can you meet me at the hospital?"

"I'll be there." My face burns with shame as I wonder if I missed something during the session, some sign that should have led me to assess Todd for suicidality. Reviewing every moment of the session while I stumble into jeans and a T-shirt, I'm finally able to reassure myself that Todd hadn't appeared the least bit likely to kill himself. After spooning food into the cats' bowls and grabbing a shawl in case the air conditioning is on full blast, I head for the hospital.

The roads are empty, adding to the eeriness of the errand.

Elena paces the waiting room of the ICU, her face looking as if she's aged a decade overnight. Brooke Tate sits in a nearby chair, knitting.

Elena reaches out for my hands and holds them in hers. "I don't know what happened. I can't imagine Todd doing anything to hurt himself, not with the kids, you know? Maybe he felt ashamed after the session? I thought we got to a good place, didn't you? Did he sound to you like he was despondent or suicidal?"

"No. Not at all." I lead her toward a private alcove with three chairs where we can speak more freely. "Sometimes people do feel vulnerable after disclosing a long-held secret," I say. "Though nothing about Todd's behavior even remotely suggested this. Why don't you tell me everything that happened after you left my office?"

Elena waves Brooke over and she settles beside her cousin-in-law.

"When we left you, we collected the kids from their friends' homes, picked up pizza, and watched a movie before putting them to bed. Todd and I talked a little—though not about anything we discussed in the session, just normal stuff about schedules and kids. It was fine. He seemed fine." She rubs a hand across her eyes. "I was exhausted and so was Todd, but after dinner, he checked his messages and said he had to meet George." She swallows. "I said it had been a long and intense day and he should just wait until tomorrow…um…today, to deal with George, but he said he couldn't. He kissed me and said it had felt good to talk about things. He said he felt closer to me than he had in a long time."

I nod and Elena continues. "I wanted him to stay home, but he wasn't going to and I'd already taken my sleeping pill, so I didn't have the energy to argue about it. He said I shouldn't wait up, and I couldn't have anyway."

"I'm not surprised by any of this," Brooke interjects. "George eviscerates people. If I didn't have the kids and hadn't been lucky enough to get into Louise's office, I might have killed myself."

"Todd seemed fine when he left," Elena repeats.

"What happened after that?"

"At about two in the morning, our alarm system began to shriek. When I reached over to wake Todd, he wasn't there. I got the girls out the front door and handed them over to our neighbors just as the police drove up."

Elena wraps her arms tightly around her chest, as if they can hold her together. "The police found Todd slumped in the back entryway between the garage and the house. He must have pulled the sports car into the garage, unlocked the door, and passed out before he could enter the code." Tears flow down her face and Brooke reaches out to put her arm around Elena's shoulder.

I walk to the nurses' station to locate tissues, grateful for the break. By the time I return, Elena has composed herself. "They brought him here."

"He's in good hands." Brooke pats Elena's hand.

"We were on the brink of really changing things. What could have happened?" Elena's gaze is fixed on me as she dabs a tissue at her eyes.

"I don't know," I say, pulling on my shawl, seeking warmth and comfort myself. "Todd wasn't despondent when he left the office. Is it possible he's in some other kind of trouble?"

"I've been worried sick that George would get back at him in some way because of Todd's resignation from the board. Maybe there was more trouble at Constant Caring than he told me about. I don't know," she says. "I can't think straight. I need coffee."

"I'll get it," Brooke offers. "Sarah?"

"Hot tea with honey, thanks."

As Brooke walks down the hall, I pursue Elena's last conjecture. "Is there anything you've heard about George or the board at Constant Caring that might in any way link to Henderson's murder?"

"Nothing specific. George and Henderson were fighting about money. Even though Henderson testified for George during the divorce and custody hearings, their relationship was very shaky. Ask Brooke. She knows more about that than I."

When Brooke returns, I sip my tea gratefully and ask her the same questions.

"George had a love-hate relationship with Henderson," Brooke says. "He loved that Henderson was so stingy with the company's money and so creative and fierce in his denials of benefits. But personally, nothing was ever enough for Henderson. He always wanted more money, more power, more influence, but would George murder Henderson? I don't think so." She gazes out the window and apparently reconsiders. "You know," she says, "given the degree to which George has deteriorated, maybe I can't be so sure of that."

I look at both Elena and Brooke. "I'm helping Louise's lawyer and investigator look into Henderson's murder. It's possible that these things are all connected. Would you give me permission to share some of this information with them, and maybe..." I hesitate, looking at Elena, and then just come out with it, "some of the things we discussed in our sessions?"

Elena's permission isn't valid for Todd's disclosures. However, I've now heard it from Brooke, outside of a therapy session. If Todd did try to kill himself, then he's a danger to himself, and that waives confidentiality. I still have to deal with the fact that the waiver allows a disclosure only to the police, a hospital, or those at risk, and not lawyers and private investigators. Elena offers me just what I want.

"Do whatever you think might help," she says.

"If it can help Louise, you can repeat everything I've said," Brooke adds. "Absolutely everything."

The sun is shining and the morning air refreshingly cool as I drive home. Mister Bagel is on my route, and my Subaru turns in of its own accord. While ordering, I bow to a family idiosyncrasy and ask the young woman waiting on me to dig out the bread dough from the center of my super bagel before loading it up with cream cheese, lox, and tomato. My mother is under the delusion that digging out the dough cuts the calories in half. I know better: If you don't dig out the dough, you can't stuff it with as much cream cheese. Whatever the calorie count, eating soothes me and gives me time to think about everything that's transpired.

When I call, Kate, Alex, and Louise tell me they're all willing to meet this morning, though Louise insists on driving. We talk nonstop all the way downtown to Kate's office, trying to get back to normal, though a slight edge of discomfort still simmers beneath the surface.

Alex is waiting by the bookshelves in the conference room, pouring coffee. Kate is sitting at the head of the table. Alex holds out a cup in silent offering, and Louise grabs it as I plunge in, sparing no details.

"If you lose your license for violating confidentiality," Alex says, "I'll hire you."

"Thanks." My tone is tart. "That's ever so reassuring."

My cell phone rings just as I finish giving them the story. The toxicologist has just delivered his report to Elena. "Todd was full of alcohol and sleeping pills. The same sleeping pills George and I take, Seconal. That's why they think he tried to kill himself." Her voice trembles. "But Sarah, none of my pills are missing! I count them, every day. Besides, Todd hates pills. He won't even take an aspirin when he has a headache. He was with George, and George takes Seconal. I think George tried to kill Todd."

"Is anyone listening to your suspicions?"

"No."

I suggest the only thing I can think of. "Call the police. Ask for Detective Marshall. Tell him everything. He'll listen."

Chapter 40

On Thursday afternoon, Elena calls to say Todd is much improved. He has no memory of attempting suicide and thinks he'd been out drinking with George, but doesn't remember where. I'm not familiar with the effects of an overdose and know little about Seconal, other than how dangerous it can be in the wrong hands, but I've worked with clients who've had retrograde amnesia after a shock and wonder if that could factor into Todd's lack of awareness.

I speak with Alex that evening, and she suggests we take our confusion out to Mackworth Island the following afternoon to sort through things together.

The next day dawns hot, but an ocean breeze springs up by midmorning. I focus on cleaning house and preparing for Shabbat. Louise's mom is coming for dinner and accompanying me to synagogue afterwards.

With preparations complete, I drive to Falmouth, slowing at the entrance to the island. After my perfunctory wave to the uniformed guard, he lifts the gate. Alex and her dog Niko are waiting at the farthest end of the lot, exactly where the last parking spot is located.

"How are you?" Her concern is evident.

"Todd's doing better, so that's a relief. On the other hand, I'm seeing Billy tomorrow night for the first time since our fight, and I'm edgy about it." I squat to pat Niko.

"I'm primed to be a listener on any subject," Alex offers, "although I'm on a timetable. Kate and I have early reservations for dinner and a show."

"That's okay. Kitty's coming for Shabbat dinner, and I have to be home by four." I wipe sweat from my forehead. "Let's head for some shade. Can I take Niko's leash?"

Niko wags his tail and licks my hands as I hook him up. We hike through the clearing and into the woods, with stops so he can sniff everything within reach. It's early August and raspberry brambles proliferate on one side of the path. We pick some and pop them into our mouths, puckering up and keeping our eyes peeled for wild blueberries. The ocean shimmers through the trees, and puffy white clouds dance across the blue sky. Seagulls wheel on the air currents, and boats sail by on the bay.

"You and Billy are great together. I'm sure this was just a hiccup, and you'll patch things up."

"I'm certainly going to try. And if he wasn't interested in doing the same thing, he wouldn't have said yes to dinner tomorrow night." I scan the area before continuing. "What has me spooked is Todd's toxicology report and the question of whether George Tate should be the prime suspect. But I wanted to talk this through with you before going to Pomerleau."

"Tell me more."

"Elena said Todd and George were together the night Todd supposedly tried to kill himself, which Todd claims he doesn't remember. The toxicology report indicates sleeping pills in Todd's blood—the same ones Elena and George take. Elena counted her pills. None were missing."

Alex whistles, and Niko turns. "Sorry, boy," she says. "I wasn't whistling for you."

"And don't forget, George's initials were all over Henderson's ledger."

"I remember that. It says motive to me."

"Elena is afraid of George. She's said many times that she's worried George might hurt Todd. Todd also had a top-notch security system installed in the house. Since George used to collect antique cars and work on them, I'm stuck on the idea that he might have tinkered with Jim Barr's brakes and murdered him to end the lawsuit Jim filed against Constant Caring."

"I'm with you on that one. I just wonder, was Jim's lawsuit a sufficient motive for murder?"

"George could have lost a great deal of money if the company took a hit."

"I guess it's a good thing I've been pulling every record I could find on George Tate." Alex smiles.

As I smile back at her, I stop and look, peering down the trail.

"What's up?"

"I thought I saw someone familiar, but never mind. Let's take Niko down to the beach."

We follow the dog down a steep trail and watch him race ahead, chasing seagulls across the narrow strip of beach.

"I think we're very close to solving this mystery," Alex says.

"I hope so." I run behind Niko, tossing sticks for him to retrieve until the ocean breezes turn the air chilly, and we return to the parking lot. I rub the goose bumps from my arms. Alex plucks a towel from her trunk and dries the dog as we make plans to check in with each other on Sunday. She waves and drives out of the lot. I jog to my car, not realizing someone is trying to get my attention until a hand reaches for my shoulder. Startled, I jump.

A short-haired, thirty-something woman in frayed jeans, navy sneakers, and a baseball cap is beside me. Her face is thin and slightly scarred by acne, and she looks vaguely familiar. She says, "Could you give me directions?"

"Sure," I say agreeably, "although the guard at the gatehouse probably has a map. Just give me a minute to grab my jacket." As I slip my arms into the sleeves, something cold and hard presses into my neck.

"Don't turn around." The voice is a man's. "Get in the driver's seat and keep your mouth shut. Got it?"

I slide behind the steering wheel with my mind a frantic jumble—what's happening here?

The back passenger door opens and I start to turn my head to see who's there.

"Start the car!" the man says, leaning forward from the back seat to hold the gun to my neck. "Look straight ahead and drive out of the lot to the left, past the guardhouse. Nod to the guard and head over the bridge."

Just then someone pounds on the rear window. I jump.

My captor slides down the window to talk to whoever's out there. I glance in the driver's side-view mirror and though my view is distorted, a skull-and-crossbones tattoo decorating a skinny man's neck is visible enough.

"T, no," he says. "This isn't the plan we agreed on. You move her car, and I take her in. Give me the gun."

"No!" The person behind me now sounds sulky and feminine. "I want to take her."

My mind cramps in confusion. Who's in the car with me? A man or a woman?

"My wallet is right here," I say. "Take whatever you want. Just please let me go."

"Shut up!" the guy outside yells through the window. I see him whip his head around to survey the lot. He opens the back door. "We have to stick to the plan, T. Gimme the gun!"

In the mirror, I now see the woman who'd asked for directions stepping out. She hands him the gun and he presses it to my head through the open window while they argue.

The side-view mirror gives me a good look. The man shrugs and hands the gun back to the slight woman before stuffing his hands in the pockets of his jeans, walking to the car beside mine, and driving out of the lot.

"Leave the keys on the seat," the woman orders, "and get out."

I do, hoping she won't pay close attention. I'd slipped the ignition key off the ring and into my pocket while they were arguing. As I slide out of the car, I wish I hadn't left my pepper spray at home. The island closes at sundown. Only three cars remain in the lot. No people are in view. The guardhouse is far away. If I scream, no one will hear me, and I have no idea of the woman's intentions.

Standing next to her, I see her shiver and stare at the gun in her hand as if she's never seen it before. When she speaks again, a little girl's voice comes out of her mouth. "Can we walk in the woods?"

"Sure." I've now heard three voices coming out of her mouth: a man's, a woman's, and a little girl's. I finally get it. Her personality is totally fragmented. I figure it should be possible to wrest the gun out of the hands of a little girl—if she stays that way. She shivers again. "Ooh, what's this?" A little boy speaks. "Cops and robbers!" He holds the gun out to me. "Your turn?"

I reach out a hopeful hand, but he jerks back with a giggle. "No! I keep it." He shoves it into his belt and says, "Let's go."

We walk past the outhouse. A car door slams, startling us both, but the driver is inside the car, starting the ignition; he won't hear or see me.

I watch my companion shake and switch back into a little girl. She clasps my hand and drags me toward the path as if I'm her reluctant mother. Things are moving too fast, and curiosity, numbness, and terror shift places inside me. Numbness usually indicates dissociation, so I wonder if in this way the woman and I have something in common. It could offer a path to connection.

At the tree-lined path that hugs the shoreline, the bamboo has grown so tall that it towers over us. Bittersweet vines hang off tree limbs, so thick at points they choke the life out of the huge birches and basswoods. The edge of the path is shady, and I hope she steers clear of the steep paths heading down the cliffs. Just two months earlier, Billy and I were peering into pools full of periwinkles. I wonder, will I ever get to apologize to him in person?

My assailant hums and swings my hand, and I can't think of a thing to do to escape her. Even if I could, I'm afraid that if I do, she'll turn into the man who held the gun on me. None of her personalities seem to have any connection to the others, which indicates she's pretty far gone.

We approach a pair of granite blocks, constructed during the Civil War when the island was a Union facility. The little girl pulls me up onto the pier and outward, toward the edge. My heart races. Is she going to push me off? Can I push her off? While she's acting like a child? I don't know! Shock has turned off my brain's executive function.

Four teenage boys are standing at the end of the pier, but there's no way to get their help without putting them in danger. She still has the gun within easy reach.

Is this Louise's client? What was her name? Something with a "T." It hardly matters, since her identity begins to switch again. It's palpable—as if the energy is shifting around her. A hardness settles in and her face changes. Her eyes narrow and her shoulders broaden. It would be a fascinating transition to my therapist's eye, if the hostile male voice didn't utter the next sentence.

"Get your ass back on the path, lady. We're going into the woods." He pats the butt of the pistol. "I've got a nice piece here."

My hands shake as I scan my brain for any information that might help me get through to this person, but there are too many identities and they shift too fast. I wish I hadn't been so squeamish about taking on clients whose bodies held different personalities. When I trip on a tree root in the path, he grabs my arm roughly and drags me along.

I've got to make some kind of connection. But with whom? Him? Her? Whoever's in there must have had horrible childhood trauma. Maybe this brutish guy is her protector personality. "What's your name?"

"What do ya want to know for, girlie?"

I freeze. The voice on the phone!

"Move it," he growls.

"Tell me. Who are you?"

"Buddy. I'm Buddy. But my name ain't gonna matter to you for very long."

Shaking with fear and fury, I wonder how much time we have before his accomplice finds us. The ignition key is tucked into my pocket, and he'll be pissed that I've thwarted his plan. Maybe the island will close before he returns and the guard won't let him back on, or maybe the guard will search for me when he notices my car in the lot. I try to remember if the guard is armed; but no, I don't think he has a weapon.

The skies have darkened. I'm not sure if the sun is setting or the sky is clouding over until I hear a low distant rumble. Buddy leads me to the left, off the path, toward the little pine grove. We enter a clearing in the midst of the woods, one of my favorite parts of the island, the pet cemetery.

Buddy hustles me through a small gate into a circular graveyard bounded by a wall of stacked stones. The circle encloses a large boulder, a few tall trees, and the gravestones of the former Governor Percival Baxter's animals. Buddy shoves me up against a tree. I force myself to focus, which means staring at a bronze plaque on the boulder in the circle's center.

It reads, "The State of Maine accepted the gift of Mackworth Island and covenanted to maintain forever this burial place of my dogs. Percival P. Baxter."

Shivering at the thought of Buddy burying me under the leaves here where worms could feast on my body, I focus on the plaques dedicated to the governor's dearest friends.

Jerry Roan
A noble horse and a kind friend
Died Mar. 1, 1904 at 35 years
Gov Baxter's
Dogs
For
40 Years
his constant
companions

1887–1926

Buddy mumbles and paces, then prods me with the handgun's muzzle as I stumble across the dogs' graves. He pushes me up against another tree until I face the woods.

"What did I do? Why are you so angry with me?"

Buddy's face is so close I can smell his breath. I think he needs a better mouthwash. He apparently thinks I need the gun jammed up under my chin, pressed hard against my throat. "Shut! Up!" he demands.

The longer I remain in Buddy's orbit, the more I lose my resolve. I try to hang on, but I'm overcome by numbness and as I start to let go, I remember something clinical, that denial and dissociation are unconscious defenses to intolerable reality. I lose track of time.

Buddy is on his knees, rummaging around in the knapsack. I'm shocked back to reality when he pulls out a rope and stands up. The sight of it scares me more than the gun. The last thing I want is to be tied to a tree in a dark woodsy cemetery during a thunderstorm, easy prey for bugs and little animals. Mice, maybe even rats, could chew on my body. "Please, Buddy, tell me what I did wrong. Maybe I can fix it."

"Too late, girlie. Too nosy. Should've minded your own business."

"What was I so nosy about?"

As he approaches me with the rope, all I can do is pray. Dear God, give me courage. Give me a miracle, and if you can't do that, give me acceptance and peace.

The thin veil between worlds evaporates. I sense Miriam's presence and hear her voice. "I'm right beside you." I reach out my hand and she holds it, showing me images that offer a path out of this dilemma.

"Buddy," I say, "you're trying to protect the others, aren't you? You take care of the little girl, and the little boy, and others, right? It's an important job."

He stops and looks at me, like he's seeing me for the first time.

"They're not at risk from me, no matter what you've been told. I would never hurt them. Truth is, my job is to help—just like Louise helps—and I think if you hurt me, it will also hurt them. They've seen more than enough violence. You don't need to add to that."

Buddy stares vacantly, cluing me in to the possibility that all the child personalities might now be hearing me.

"Look around," I say gently. "Children have been building houses for the island's fairies, pixies, and nature spirits. More and more keep coming. They're here now. If we're very quiet, we might even see them."

A shake of the head and the little girl alter is back. She leans her head sideways and her eyes widen in surprise at the rope and the gun in her hands.

My voice takes on the soothing tone I use for distraught clients. "Why don't we look around? We can explore the fairy houses."

She smiles.

"Why don't you put those toys down? Right here," I pat the ground beside me.

She drops the rope, gun, and knapsack at my feet and begins wandering toward the closest fairy house. She sinks to her knees in front of it. My hand closes on the handle of the gun. I won't shoot the little girl, but I will shoot her accomplice, if I can figure out how. Why didn't I listen to Aunt Zelda and have Billy or Alex show me how to use a handgun?

She gazes back at me shyly. "Can we make our own fairy house?"

"Sure. Why don't you look for bark and acorns and some pretty leaves?"

While she does that, I sneak away, toward the path. She doesn't seem to notice. A crackling clap of thunder shakes the earth. Afterwards, I hear another voice. Loud.

"Damn you, Teresa! Can't you do anything right? Where's the damn car key?"

Teresa! The name of Louise's severely dissociative client.

As her skinny companion with the neck tattoos approaches, I hide behind a large oak. Entranced by a fairy house tucked in the trees, she's oblivious to him until he grabs her by the shoulders and begins to shake her. "Where is she? Where are the keys to the car? Damn you! You blew it!" His slap echoes across the forest floor.

Tightening my grasp on the gun, I race around the corner and yell, "Protect them from him, Buddy! Protect them from him!" Then I run.

Under a darkened sky, the woods fill with ominous shapes. A bolt of lightning splits the sky; another crack of thunder follows. I keep running, the gun tight in my hand. Footsteps sound on the trail behind me.

"When I catch you, bitch, you're dead!" a man yells. It isn't Buddy.

The little girl calls out, "Wait for me! Wait for me! Don't leave me here!"

I trip on a tree limb in the path, recover my balance, keep running. The air is thick with electricity.

More lightning, more thunder. The storm arrives in full force. Rain pelts my skin. The ground quickly turns muddy. I slip again, skin my shin, drag myself up, and run onward, refusing to look back. I can't hear anything over the pounding rain.

The parking lot appears ahead. My breath is ragged, my sides hurt, my calves cramp, but I continue to run. Blue lights flash.

Just as I reach the outhouse, he catches up with me. I jump as his hand grasps my T-shirt, yanking it tight across my throat. I slip. My ankle snaps. Excruciating pain propels me down.

He has me pinned to the ground, one hand on my wrist, the other trying to rip the gun from my grasp.

A loud crack splits the air.

Light flashes in the darkness.

The pain in my ankle merges with a roaring in my ears. Something heavy falls on top of me.

Someone screams—maybe me.

Everything goes black.

Chapter 41

I flail helplessly in thick darkness, incessant buzzing filling my ears. My eyes are sticky. Fear shatters the stupor and I catapult up. White-speckled linoleum, blue walls, unfamiliar bed, Louise sitting in a chair beside me.

"Well, hello already." She smiles, pats my hand, and stands up to press a buzzer next to the bed.

"Sarah." Billy's voice. I turn and his face comes into focus. He brushes the hair from my forehead. "Welcome back to the land of the living."

I struggle to separate my tongue from the roof of my mouth. "What happened?"

"What do you remember?" he asks.

A white coat enters the room. A tall self-assured woman with cropped black hair interrupts. "Let me ask the questions first, okay? I'm your surgeon, Dr. Schwartz. How are you feeling?"

"Drugged. My chest hurts, my ankle is encased in lead, and there's two feet of air between my forehead and my brain."

"That's the anesthesia. You fractured a rib and broke your ankle. I pinned it in surgery. The medication should wear off soon, and then you'll want more. Your recovery will take some time."

"How long?"

"Hard to say. We'll know more tomorrow."

Too much, too fast. The room tilts.

"Get some rest. I'll check in later. A resident or two may stop by, but I'm the doctor in charge."

The next thing I'm aware of is waking up to find Billy sitting in Louise's chair. I try to sit up and stabbing pain shoots through my chest.

"What can I do, honey?" Billy asks.

"Honey?" I slur. "Does that mean I can skip the groveling?"

He grins. "I forgave you the minute I heard your voice on the phone."

I clasp his outstretched hand. He leans over and kisses me.

I take in that pleasure and think of something else I want. "I need water. My mouth is doubling as the Sahara Desert."

He reaches for a plastic cup and hands it to me. After I drink my fill, I ask him, "Any food around this place? I'm famished."

"Louise stowed Kitty's stuffed cabbage in the nurse's refrigerator," he says. "I'll have to nuke it."

"I'm happy to take that stuffed cabbage, even with a side of radiation." A shooting pain through my ribs accompanies my laugh.

Daylight, nighttime, it all blurs. I wake briefly to find Janice sitting in Billy's chair.

"You look pretty good, all things considered," my therapist says. "You made the front page of the paper. I figured you could use a hypnotic healing audio. I didn't know what you had here, so I brought my ancient technology—a trusty little cassette player." She tucks it in beside me. "You can rewind this easily if necessary, and as you know, the more often you listen, the faster you'll heal. Be careful not to hit record, or you'll tape over it." A soft touch, a sweet smile, and she's gone. I only remember she's been there when my hand brushes the slim tape recorder beside me in bed.

"What time is it?" I look up. Kate is sitting beside me. Alex is leaning against the wall flipping through magazines. "And what day is it?"

"Early afternoon, Sunday."

The last thing I remember is my intention to cook a nice dinner for Kitty and go to Friday night services. So it must be two full days later. "Can someone please tell me what happened? Why am I here?"

"Well," Alex says, "that's a question for your guru, not your lawyer."

"Don't make me laugh!" I cry. "It feels like there's a knife in my chest."

"We don't know what happened. We only know the beginning and the end," Kate says. "Maybe you can fill us in on the middle?"

"She'll have to be awake for more than twenty minutes to do that,"

Louise says, holding a glass vase chock-full of pink and yellow roses. "A gift from the girls."

"Aw. Isn't that the sweetest thing?" I start to tear up, wondering why I'm so emotional over a bouquet.

"It's all right, Sarah," Louise sets it on the bedside table and drags over another chair, which she promptly occupies. "You're still a little loopy from the drugs. More important," she adds, "I successfully way-laid your mother, who was planning to fly up tonight."

I groan from another kind of pain.

"No worries. You have a short reprieve. I convinced her to wait a week."

"Thank you very, very much," I murmur.

Alex lays her hand on mine. "I'm so sorry I left you. I should've waited until you were in your car."

"Don't. Please. It's not your fault. Who'd have thought anyone could be kidnapped on Mackworth Island, with a guard a few yards away?"

"Hard to imagine," Kate says. She's standing on the other side of my bed.

"I want to wake up, and to do that I need caffeine. Could someone get me regular tea with milk and honey?" I manage to ask before my eyes close on their own.

It's just a catnap. When my eyes open, the bed is cranked up and a tray beside me is loaded with steaming tea and buttered toast. I start eating and drinking and the next thing I know, it's all gone. Finally, I'm ready to say one word. I turn to Louise "Teresa."

"Yes. Louise's head bobs up and down. "I know. Teresa Mosher."

Billy walks in, sits beside me, takes my hand.

"Yes," I say. "Teresa Mosher and I had a little, uh, session, on the island."

"Apparently so, along with her husband, John Cass."

"John Cass?" I look at Billy. He nods and gestures to Louise.

"It turns out that John Cass is married to Teresa. And there's something else. Are you ready to hear it?"

"I don't know. Only one way to find out."

"John Cass is the first cousin of George Tate and Todd Owens."

"*That* John? You're kidding!"

"If we'd known that connection," Louise says with a sigh, "a lot of things would have made sense a long time ago."

"Wow, that's for sure."

"Can you tell us what happened to you?"

"On the island? With Teresa? I had an intense tutorial on multiple personalities." Shivering, I draw the thin hospital blanket up over the hospital gown and run my hand through the tangle of my curls.

"Wait. Let me help you," Louise murmurs. She rummages through her purse and a minute later sweeps my hair atop my head and pins it into place. "Are you sure you're up to this?"

"No, but at least I think I can stay awake for it. It might be good to get it out." I scan their faces. For a moment, they all blur. So much for clarity. But then everyone comes back into focus, and I begin. "I'd just opened my car door when this woman came over and asked for directions. She turned into a guy named Buddy, who stuck a gun in my neck."

"I've never met Buddy," Louise says.

"I didn't really understand the depth of this kind of fracture in someone's personality, but I caught on pretty fast, believe me." As I adjust the blanket, a stabbing pain rips through my side.

Alex takes a pillow from the closet and lays it on my belly. "Try this. It helped me when I broke a rib in a fall from a horse. Pillows—and drugs."

"Thanks," I say. "Now where was I?" I tell them all about my experience on Mackworth. "I definitely spent way too much time with Teresa, and a bunch of her frightened alters competing for air time."

"Teresa never fractured so badly in my office."

"I doubt she brings her gun to therapy. Something, or someone, pushed her to shatter like that. And guess what, Louise? While it was happening, while Buddy was waving that gun at me—I dissociated too. Makes me think Teresa and I aren't all that different."

"No, honey, that's not true. You're very different. Dissociation is a long continuum. You know that from inducing trance in clinical hypnosis."

"I'm not so sure about anything anymore," I say.

"Well, I'll clarify. We all have parts—you know that. I'm not talking pathological parts. One part wants the chocolate, another part wants to lose ten pounds, but they interact. There's nothing pathological about that."

"Right," I say.

"On the other hand, Teresa's parts don't know each other, not at all. She was so severely abused as a child, she fractured completely, and recently she's been under enormous strain."

"Her creepy husband must be part of that. Where is she now?"

"On the psychiatric floor," Louise says briskly. "I hope she can recover."

"I'm not thrilled about being in the same building."

"It's a locked ward."

"As long as it stays locked," I add, before continuing my story.

"Focusing on the fairy houses was brilliant," Louise says.

"The thought of worms feasting on my corpse was great incentive. And Miriam helped me. How did you know to look for me?"

"Kitty said you'd never stand her up for a Shabbos dinner," Louise replies. "She remembered you'd said you were meeting Alex for a walk on Mackworth that afternoon, so we got ahold of Alex. When she told us she'd left you there an hour earlier, we called the police."

Billy takes up the narrative. "The patrol cars got to the island just a few minutes before you ran into the clearing."

"I remember the blue lights. And then falling."

"John grabbed you and you both went down in the mud."

"We were wrestling for the gun."

"He was winning," Billy says.

"Thank God he didn't shoot me."

"He didn't have the chance," Alex interjects. "One of Falmouth's finest shot him first."

All I can say is, "Wow." No wonder I made the front page. Then I think to ask, "So, uh, how is he?"

"In critical condition. ICU. Might make it, might not," Billy says.

"What made these people want to kill me or leave me threatening messages or break into my house?"

"We're in the process of figuring that out," Billy says.

"I'm sure Teresa broke into the house and left the phone messages when she was in her Buddy personality, because Buddy called me 'girlie' on the island. Now that I know Teresa's husband was John Cass, I bet he was the driver." I'm getting excited, piecing things together. "And I'm sure they're the two folks in the car parked outside my house on the weekend of the Fourth of July, when I called you, Billy, then drove out to Kate and Alex's house for dinner."

"Yes," Kate says. "You were right all along, Sarah. Sorry for doubting you. The connection appears to be Harriet Connors's lawsuit against Cass, just as you thought."

"The department is piecing it all together," Billy adds. "Todd Owens has been a big help."

"So Todd recovered, good." I'm getting tired again, and my chest and ankle are aching, but I want to hear this. I need to. "How has Todd been helpful?"

Alex answers. "He told us the family history, starting with the connections—that John Cass, George Tate, and Todd Owens are first cousins. Apparently, John and Teresa met in a foster home and kept in touch after John was moved elsewhere. When Teresa was old enough, they got hitched."

"And they were together when John sexually abused Harriet Connors," Louise adds.

"Nice marriage."

"You can see why Teresa is the way she is. A horrible childhood, then a disturbed husband abusing young girls. It replicated her own abuse."

"Then, all these years later," Alex says, "when Harriet filed the lawsuit, she targeted a trust fund that was shared by the three cousins. That threatened the only financial security John and Teresa had."

Light dawns in my brain.

"Todd told the police that George and John were enraged about the lawsuit's potential to drain the trust," Billy says. "We suspect the two of them colluded in murdering Henderson."

"Really? Why?"

"This is where it gets, uh, interesting," Alex responds. "John usually asked George for help when he needed money. Once he learned that George was the CEO of Constant Caring, he tapped their relationship further to get Teresa the best therapy possible. George was willing to help out in that way, arranging for Teresa's treatment, but he must have had to make a special point of talking with Henderson about her, to make sure that Constant Caring would pay Teresa's therapists' claims without restriction."

"Ah," I say.

"If so, it would've piqued the curiosity of a guy like Harold Henderson."

"Then," Kate says, "it wouldn't have taken Henderson too long to figure out that Teresa was married to George's cousin. Hell, George might have even told him. When Henderson was deposed for Harriet Connors's lawsuit and discovered John Cass was the abuser, he put two and two together. That gave him a juicy bit of information to use to blackmail George." Kate sighs. "After all, a close relationship with a pedophile wouldn't look too good for someone who touts a blue-blood heritage and runs a managed care company."

"Wait, wait. You think George Tate killed Henderson to protect his inheritance and reputation?"

Billy takes over. "That's our working hypothesis. George had help from John Cass. John may have killed Henderson. We've got George Tate in custody."

"What's he charged with?"

"Attempted murder of his cousin Todd. It's clear he laced Todd's drink with Seconal, hoping to kill Todd and make his death look like a suicide. But Todd made it home and to the back door. The alarm saved his life."

"What a sociopath George Tate must be," I say, shocked.

"That's not all," Billy adds. "We're fairly sure he murdered Jim Barr, by disabling his brakes."

"So you and I were right about that," Alex says.

"Poor Jim," I say, as grief washes over me. Louise hands me a tissue and we sit in silence for a few minutes.

"Todd Owens believes all of this?" I ask.

"He's still in a bit of shock," Billy says. "But yes, he suspects that's the scenario."

"I tracked Harriet down in Europe," Louise says. "She left precipitously, because she was threatened."

"Why did they target me?" I ask.

"We suspect George believed both you and Jim Barr had elicited more detailed information through hypnosis with Harriet, and George was afraid other damaging secrets would come out during the lawsuit."

"My head's spinning," I say. "What, was George another perp?"

"Maybe," Louise answers. "Kate's about to retrieve Jim's records of the therapy sessions from Harriet's attorney. Hopefully, we'll get more details from Jim's notes."

"Wow," I mutter. "George Tate, the CEO of a managed-care organization, is also a sexual abuser?"

"It's no surprise to us that they come in all sizes and shapes and careers," Louise says. "I think George Tate was so scared that he talked John Cass into getting Teresa to break into your house and leave those threatening messages. Probably didn't take too much talking into, with the threat of the trust drying up."

"Where does Tony Grazio fit into all this?" I ask.

"Not sure," Billy says. "But he's not going anywhere. We can question him when we have a clearer sense of what to ask him."

By now, I can hardly speak, and the rest of my senses are quickly shutting down. "I think I've...had enough...for now."

Billy fluffs the pillows behind my head. "All you need to focus on right now is healing. And we're going to help you do that."

My friends gather around the bed and rest their hands on me as Billy chants the Priestly Benediction:

Yevarechecha Adonai veyishmcrecha;

Yaer Adonai panav elecha vichunecha

Yisa Adonai panav elecha veyasem lecha shalom.

May God bless you and keep you.

May God's face shine upon you.

May God grant you the most precious gift of all, peace.

Immersed in gratitude for the many blessings surrounding me, I fall into a long, deep, dreamless sleep.

Chapter 42

The room is dark. I awake frightened and disoriented. Todd Owens sits in the chair beside my bed. "How are you, Sarah?"

"Todd?"

"Yes. This isn't a dream." He grins. His face looks younger.

"I heard what happened," I murmur. "Are you okay? What are you doing here?"

He uncrosses his legs and stretches. "I wanted to see how you were. I'm a lot better. They released me from the hospital a few days ago."

I shake myself awake and try to think. The police might believe George Tate is responsible for Todd's overdose, but they don't know what I know. "So. The Seconal."

"I didn't try to kill myself."

"What happened?"

"Long story."

"I'm not going anywhere."

He laughs. "Well, I won't be writing you a check for this session."

"It's on the house." It seems as if his ordeal has brought out a lighter part of Todd's personality.

I try to rearrange myself in bed and grimace in pain. Todd rises and rearranges the pillows behind my head, then returns to the chair and begins to talk.

"I told you that while my family was well-off, the Tates were loaded. My father was envious, although my mother never coveted anything belonging to someone else. She called my father greedy, and later said I'd inherited that from him."

"Not many people acknowledge that."

Todd smiles. "It's true about me. My cousin John, on the other hand, was angry. Abandoned by his mother, neglected by his father, abused by his grandfather, he couldn't understand why our rich families didn't come to his rescue. Still can't. And maybe he's right, maybe we should have. But it turned out that the foster home was the best thing that ever happened to him. It gave him stability, and he met Teresa. She's been good for him. Most of the time, anyway."

I notice Todd is no longer making eye contact, and wonder if he's overwhelmed with shame.

"Ol' Grandpa had been doing it for years, to John's mother. That wasn't a secret in George's family. They talked about it openly and made sure to keep George away from his grandfather. My family never discussed it, so you can imagine my surprise—shock, really—that weekend I spent at the farm."

"Of course."

"Did I tell you I pulled a knife on my grandfather that night?"

"Yes, you did say that in our session." I keep my voice modulated, but a sensation I've become all too familiar with—fear snaking up my spine—is making me squirm.

"I did it one other time, too," Todd says. "Many years later. The only other time I was ever alone with him. I was already in law school."

"What happened?"

"Nothing happened. I mean, nothing he did. He was old by then, weak. I was young and strong. I wanted his money. He owed it to me. He owed it to John, too, and I figured George should share. I made sure we got what we were entitled to."

"How?"

"I went to visit him, bringing along a document that created a trust fund. George, John, and I were the beneficiaries. The bastard signed it. Right then and there."

My body gets it first. Chills, hair standing on end. Then my brain kicks in with an aha! My own trauma, plus the long absence from the criminal courts, seems to have blunted my radar. Despite my suspicions that Todd might have a personality disorder, he had snowed me—and everyone else. I lie there, barely able to move, trying to figure out what to do.

As I fidget, my hand brushes up against the tape recorder Janice left for me. I shift again slightly, just enough to surreptitiously lift my sheets and find the record button. I press it.

"How did you have that trust witnessed?" I ask, trying to buy time, thinking that eventually, a nurse is bound to check on me.

"I paid a classmate to sign the trust document before I drove down to the farm. I knew how to cover the bases." He looks at me, smiling in a self-satisfied way.

A psychopath. Definitely. "Did you kill Henderson?"

"Yes." He smiles again, as if reliving a fond memory. Perhaps he's pleased to take credit for that murder.

"Why Henderson?" I ask, more with curiosity than accusation.

"He was threatening my future."

"You weren't alone in that," I say gently. "He was blackmailing many people."

"I know."

"What was he using to blackmail you?"

"The family relationship, and another thing."

"Another thing?"

Todd looks up, makes eye contact briefly. "Harriet Connors."

"What about her?"

"Henderson got his hands on the file and nosed out my participation."

I shift, wincing from two kinds of pain. "Participation? In the sexual abuse?"

"You're obviously uncomfortable. Take these." Todd removes a vial of pills from the pocket of his blazer, shakes out a handful.

"No, thanks. I'll wait for my nurse. She should be here soon."

"I'm not offering. Believe me, it'll be painless and quiet. I just went through it myself." Todd's voice is calm as he flicks open a switchblade. "Blood would complicate my plans, but I'll go that way if I have to."

I look at the pills he's placed in my hand. "What are they?"

"Seconal. They'll put you to sleep."

They sure will. A long sleep, one from which I might never awaken. I wonder how fast they'll work. Todd hands me water and stands close while I swallow. Then he insists I open my mouth, where he finds the pills I've shoved under my tongue. He holds the knife to my throat. "Swallow them."

I do, but as he turns to sit down, I make a move for the call button.

He notices. "Go ahead, Sarah. Press all you want. No one will hear you. I disconnected it."

"You're good at what you do, aren't you?"

He smiles. "Very."

"I suppose there's a little time left," I say, wondering what perverted kind of justice would allow me to survive Teresa Mosher and John Cass, just to be murdered in my hospital bed by my own client. I silently call for Miriam's help. Within seconds, I see her appear in my room. Then she floats down the hall.

"Since I probably won't be waking up to share any information," I say to Todd, "would you mind telling me a bit more about Henderson?"

"I don't mind at all," Todd replies.

His composure is as amazing as his capacity to con me and everyone else.

"That's George's fault." Todd stands and ambles around the room. "John called George to get help for Teresa. They needed insurance, so she could get therapy. She was coming apart. John threatened to go public with all the sordid family background if George wouldn't help them. He panicked. He told Henderson not to limit Teresa's therapy. That set Henderson on alert, and he insisted on evaluating Teresa himself."

"So what if he got the family connection? That wouldn't necessitate his death." I notice how detached I feel, kind of floaty.

"Hey, it could've been a problem if, in her therapy sessions, Harriet Connors remembered more details of her childhood. Especially since Henderson referred Teresa to your friend Louise, who was also Harriet's therapist." Todd acts as if my lack of comprehension is a personal insult.

I know now what's behind his whole devious setup. But I want him to lay it all out, for the tape recorder. "Sorry. I'm missing the point," I reply.

"How did you ever practice law?" he asks scornfully.

Speech is becoming a problem. My tongue is thick and heavy. " I never sh-sh-shed I was good at it." I hope the nurses will get back in time to pump my stomach. Then I wonder how they'll know it needs to be pumped.

Todd's next disdain-filled comment catches my wavering attention. "The family trust was at risk from Harriet Connor's lawsuit."

"Oh yeah," I reply, my eyelids heavy. "That's the only part I had a clue about."

"That's all?" His tone is incredulous.

"Yeah. There's more?" I mumble, holding tenuously onto consciousness.

"Harriet's memories could have proven problematic."

"For whom?" I'm fading fast.

"Why do you think I was your client?" he asks contemptuously. "You think I needed therapy?" He snorts. "I had to know whether you knew Teresa and I were there."

I yawn, not able to tell what I'm saying and what I'm simply thinking. "Where?"

"John's apartment." He shakes his head as if I'm a complete idiot. "Harriet was a pretty little girl who lived in an adjacent apartment. A pretty little girl whose parents were never home. Things happened to that pretty little girl in that apartment, and I was there for some of those things. They were pleasurable things, pleasurable for John, and pleasurable for me, and perhaps a little pleasurable for that pretty little girl, though now she says not."

My skin crawls as he speaks. Psychopath, sociopath, pedophile. I wonder who else he's sexually abused over the years. His own daughters? Todd, oblivious to my disgust, continues to talk.

"I told Teresa and John that accomplices go to jail. They flipped out. John had just gotten out after serving a long stretch, and Teresa was falling apart. They made the threatening calls, broke into your house. Why do you think Harriet Connors left the country so suddenly—and Jim Barr had to die?"

Todd looks at his watch, stands up, and paces. "Tired enough to sleep now?"

"Yes."

"Good. My lovely wife and cousin George are rather attached to these sleeping pills. It was very easy for me to get my own prescription and make it look like George tried to kill me. George is in police custody right now and a search of his home will find bee pollen. For that, the poor guy will spend a long time in a cell. John and Teresa too." He pauses. "If John lives. He took a bullet, you know. Ah, but our time's up. Or yours is. Me, I'm bound for Brazil. Most beautiful young girls in the world. No extradition treaty." Todd's voice sounds very far away. "You're going to have sleep apnea—a fatal episode, unfortunately." He yanks a pillow from behind my head.

My eyes jerk open.

Voices sound in the hall.

Todd turns.

I reach my hand out from under the covers and fumble for something on the bedside table. My hand locates the vase of roses from Louise. I will myself to pick it up and maintain my grip.

As Todd turns back to me, I use my last ounce of energy to smash it into his head. Blood spurts onto his hands. He staggers, slips on the floor, wet from the flowers, and grabs the bed for balance.

The last thing I see is his face, red with blood and fury as he jams the pillow over my nose and mouth. My head sinks back into the mattress from the force of it. Unable to slip my hands between my face and the pillow, I try to kick, but one leg is encased in the cast and the other beneath bedcovers, both feeling as if they weigh a hundred pounds. I stop struggling, and float off.

Maybe death is this simple, I think, until I hear a familiar voice.

No, no—it…can't…be.

A crash.

The pressure of the pillow eases as it falls from my face. Gasping for breath, prying open my eyes, I see Todd falling backwards—his body parts superimposed on something familiar. I want to care, but I don't. A warm wave of velvet is enveloping me. Submerging me.

I care only about staying there, under it, floating further and further away into the deep soft darkness.

Chapter 43

"Thank God, you're finally awake. I don't want to spend my entire visit to Portland in this hospital."

No. Not possible. Oh. Yes, it is. Her face comes into focus. "Mom? Hi there, Mom."

She fluffs my pillow. "Sit up a little, darling. I'll get you a glass of water and call for the nurse." She strides to the door. "Could a nurse please come check on my daughter!" No call button for Shirley Green when a loud voice will do.

In less than a minute, a nurse scurries into the door. "Oh, Mrs. Green, don't forget the call button." She smiles and puts her arm around my mother's shoulder.

"Now, dear, I told you girls to call me Shirley, and I promise, I'm going to bake more for you before I go back to New York. You'll swoon over my brownies."

The nurse laughs as she takes my pulse, then pops a thermometer in my mouth. "You've slept a long time," she says. "We had to do a gastric lavage."

I raise my eyebrows questioningly.

"They pumped your stomach," my mother says.

"You're a real lucky lady," the nurse adds. "And with such a mother, my goodness." She smiles again at Shirley. "We're all in awe."

I close my eyes and count to ten. My prayers are answered when Louise slips into the room.

"Hi, honey, how're you doing?" She steps between my mother and me.

Dilution is a wonderful strategy and this time I don't even have to arrange it. Within minutes, the room is full of my friends: Kate, Alex, Louise, even Billy, who thankfully, must have made my mother's acquaintance while I was unconscious. I'm sure by now she's interviewed him thoroughly and assessed his qualifications to join the family. Apparently, he passed muster.

"Billy, one more chair, dear," Shirley says sweetly. I look up to meet Billy's eyes, which are full of good humor.

"I'm dying from suspense. Could someone please fill me in? The last thing I remember is being suffocated by a sociopath."

"Shirley, you're the heroine," Kate says. "You do the honors."

My mother inhales deeply, straightens the jacket of her plum-colored suit, crosses her shapely legs, and launches in. "Well, you remember I told you that my book group took a self-defense class?" She tilts her head, as if waiting for praise.

"I vaguely remember that."

"You never listen to a thing I tell you," she chides. "I told you that we all enjoyed it so much, we decided to continue. I've taken classes for a year and a half." She looks at the assembled crowd and preens. "Even though Louise," she says, pausing momentarily to pat Louise's knee, "thought I should wait a few days to fly up here, something did *not* feel right. What kind of mother would leave her daughter alone in a hospital after such a horrible experience? So, I discussed it with your father and he drove me to JFK. When I got to Portland, I took a cab right to the hospital, even though it was rather late."

"And we're so thankful you did!" Kate chimes in. I guess she's already snagged some of my mother's chocolate-chip Mandelbrot and is angling for a permanent slot on the list of care-package recipients.

"Go on, Mom, I'm really curious. Are you saying you tangled with Todd?"

She pins me with a look I've come to know all too well. "That's exactly what I did. I took the elevator to this floor and there were no nurses to be found anywhere. Such a thing. I had to shout until someone finally came to the nurses' station. What a little bitty thing she was, and how she could lift a patient, I don't know." She tsks. "She walked me to your room and a man was standing over you, wearing a very expensive suit. I know. I shop for your father. I always have. What good wife doesn't? At first I thought he was a doctor, of course—because of the suit—but then I saw the mess on the floor, that vase and the flowers, and I realized he was pushing a pillow onto your face!" Her eyes widen in emphasis. "I told the little bitty nurse to run for help."

Closing my eyes, a clear image comes to mind. A little bitty nurse left my seventy-two-year-old mother in the room with a murderer and me? Great medical care.

"I know what you're thinking," she says. "I told her I know self-defense. Then I shouted, 'Get your hands off my daughter!'" My mother looks around, waiting for applause. For once, she surely deserves it. "The man turned around and I saw blood all over his face. Disgusting. Did you hit him with that vase?"

"I did. Cracked it right on his patrician nose."

"Good job. We make a fine pair, you and I." My defenses melt: praise from my mother. My mother, she gave me life, and now she saved my life. Who would have thought?

"The stupid fool ignored me," my mother continues. "I guess he didn't expect any problems from an old lady in high heels. Hah! Little did he know. I grabbed him and twisted his arm and flipped him over with such force, it knocked the wind right out of him. While he was struggling to breathe, I took my left foot with these lovely high heels and I dug it in, right where our teacher showed us, and went to town. By the time the other nurses arrived with the security guard, that man was in serious pain." She smiles. "I hope he already has all the children he wants, because, believe you me, he will never again produce sperm."

I press the pillow to my belly and, despite the pain, I laugh until I cry.

Chapter 44

"You tell us," Alex says.

I've finally been released from the hospital and have slept in my own comfortable bed. My living room is filled with my friends and my mother, and all of them are chowing down on pizza.

"Give me another piece before I tell this story, please."

"Do you need anything else? Napkins, soda, water?" My mother, chic and slim in jeans and a cream-colored silk shirt, has taken charge.

"We're all set, Shirley," Billy answers. "Why don't you sit down and relax?" He pats the seat beside him. She smiles broadly and complies.

"The bottom line is this: Henderson picked the wrong family to blackmail," I mumble between bites.

"That Todd Owens is one sick, you'll forgive the expression, eunuch," my mother replies. "Even if he does have exquisite taste in clothing. He sure won't be needing those suits in the slammer."

Louise, sitting beside Mark on the loveseat, bends over with laughter.

"Todd Owens was terrified that Harriet had remembered his participation in her sexual abuse," I continue.

"Todd was another perpetrator?" Alex seems completely taken aback by that revelation.

"So he said. And if Harriet had remembered that, Todd's law career and life as he knew it would have combusted."

"John Cass recovered sufficiently to answer some questions," Billy adds. "Once he understood what was going on, he realized that Todd had set them all up. He's through with keeping secrets for that family."

"About time," Louise says.

"Yep. John's furious. Todd had them convinced that Sarah and Jim had learned all the details during Harriet's hypnosis sessions. Todd told John that Teresa could be jailed as an accomplice, simply because she was living with John at the time of the abuse. Teresa became terrified, and fractured further with the added pressure of threatening Sarah."

"How sordid," my mother says. "I may be seventy-two, but I still know a thing or two. You shouldn't work with people like that, dear. You should go back to practicing law. Not that criminal law." She makes a face. "Maybe real estate. You'd have a solid and stable income. You'd meet nice people, and you could have a lovely office in a downtown building with a doorman."

I smile and look as if I'm willing to consider that, just to cut her off, but Alex interrupts to continue the story. "Todd set George up too. The supposed suicide was his way of making it look as if George tried to kill him."

"Right. Todd seems to know a lot about Seconal," I say.

"You're yawning again," Kate observes. "We're leaving. Get some rest."

Billy is the last to go. My mother absents herself in the kitchen, saying we should have some private time.

Billy takes me in his arms and holds me, brushes his hand gently down my cheek, and kisses me. "Take a nap," he says. "I'll be back later. Your mother invited me to join you for dinner. Your father's plane should be arriving in two hours." Billy smiles. "I'm obviously getting the formal review."

"You've already passed or you wouldn't be invited to dinner."

As Billy opens the front door, my mother scurries out of the kitchen, kisses his cheek, then returns to the living room.

"He's very handsome," she says, tucking a blanket around me. "He's Jewish and he's smart, and I like him. But are you sure you're completely over Ryan?"

Under normal circumstances, my mother's comment would have sparked a fierce rejoinder or an intense argument. But all I want to do is sleep. So I do.

Chapter 45

"What the hell has been going on around here?" Ryan gently shakes me awake. My mom stands beside him, smiling conspiratorially.

"Louise is driving me to the grocery store, dear. Ryan will stay with you until we return." She kisses Ryan before walking out the door, purse in hand.

Ryan looks terribly handsome in jeans and a blue-and-white-striped button-down shirt.

"I can't leave you alone for a minute, can I?" He sits beside me and takes my face in his hands. "God, I've been so worried about you." He leans over and kisses my cheek.

I try to sit up, wincing from pain. "This damned rib!" I mutter. "Now what the heck are you doing here?"

"Your mother called. I rearranged meetings to drive up." He walks to the front door and locks it. "I want at least thirty minutes of time alone with you. Say you're happy to see me."

"I am. I'm happy to see you. I'm somewhat overwhelmed at the moment, given that my mother is here. Oh, and a few people recently tried to kill me. You know it would be…challenging…anytime you showed up, but right now, well, it means a lot to me that you care enough to drop everything and come here, of course, but—"

"But…I'm being a self-absorbed ass as usual, right?" He smiles, but his smile seems a bit sad to me. "I drive up here because I'm worried about you, and I can't stand not knowing how you are, and then I get here and it's all about me." He holds up his hand to stop me from objecting. "Don't be so surprised. I'm working hard in counseling, honest. A lot of my work has been focused on us."

I bite my tongue.

"You're shocked, right? Plus, you're seeing a lawyer-turned-cop. Your mother tells me everything."

I laugh. "She's such a traitor."

"I hear she saved your life."

"Amazing, isn't it?" I smirk. "Leave it to Shirley to become proficient at self-defense."

"Well, let's leave your mother out of it for the moment," Ryan says. "I came here to see how you are. Will you tell me what happened?" His eyes caress my face as he holds my hand, and I give him the gory details.

"Thank God you got yourself out of that mess," he says. "This is what happens when you leave a potentially lucrative legal career to tend to the mentally ill." He rises abruptly and throws his hands in the air. "Are you ready to rethink your career choice?"

"Not at all. You sound just like my mother."

He chuckles, sitting back down beside me. "Listen, ex-wife of mine, you're something else. I just had to know you were okay. I had to see for myself."

"I am. I've learned a lot about myself, and about other people."

"Like what?"

I touch his chest, rub my hand up and down the soft material of his shirt. "Ever since Miriam's murder, I've been held captive by fear. Now I know I'm a lot stronger than I thought. I'm not saying I have no fear—I'll always have fear. Hopefully, though, fear won't take up so much space in my life anymore."

"You know, I was thinking on the drive up here that we're always focused on solving other people's problems—I mean us, you and me, and most lawyers and therapists. That's what we do. We spend our time helping people get out of the messes they find themselves in. What's interesting me right now is that *we* find ourselves in similar messes too, and when we recognize that, we grow the most ourselves."

I smile at him, and consider what he's saying. "I think that's true. In fact, for the first time since Miriam's death, I think I might be okay." I smile. "Then again, it could just be the drugs."

"It's not the drugs. You've always been much stronger and braver than you ever gave yourself credit for."

I push away far enough to stare into his familiar, loving face. "You're right. It's not the drugs. I can stand up to challenges. I don't think I'm crazy. I've seen what it looks like to fragment, to crack wide open, and I know that isn't what happened to me after Miriam's murder and that it won't *ever* happen to me."

"I'm glad to hear you say that. Any possibility you'll change your mind and move back to Boston to marry me?" He pauses, but soon fills the silence. "You wouldn't have to work if you didn't want to. You could take art classes, volunteer somewhere, do whatever you want. I make more than enough for both of us."

I don't answer right away. When I do, what I say is tinged with a remnant of regret. "That's a truly lovely proposal, Ryan, but I can't accept. It's not that the invitation doesn't tempt me, or that I don't still love you. I'll always love you, but I'm involved with someone else now. It's serious."

"I know. But I had to ask, one more time."

"Even if I weren't involved with Billy," I say softly, "I like my life here, despite what's happened. And you know, you and I, we've taken different paths. It would be hard, probably even harder than before."

"Okay. I can accept defeat for the moment, but you aren't getting rid of me. You got that?"

I smile. "I never want to be rid of you. I'll always want you in my life."

We turn at the sound of a car pulling into the driveway. "Your mother will probably kill me for not staying," he comments. "She invited me to dinner."

I laugh at the thought of Ryan and Billy together at dinner with my parents and me. Leave it to Shirley.

"But it seems," Ryan says, "that things are under control here. I'll drive up the coast and play a round at the Samoset. I've got clients up there. No reason to waste the trip."

"Waste the trip? Excuse me?"

"Oh, that's not what I meant," he says defensively, and there we are. Ryan recovers quickly. "One could say that if my intention was to take you back to Boston with me, I have failed."

"Ryan…"

"It's okay, Sarah. This isn't the last chapter. Just try to stay out of trouble for a while," he admonishes.

"Yes, dear."

"My fifty minutes are obviously up," he says, and I see that therapy has definitely made a difference. He gives me a sweet quick kiss before standing up and unlocking the door. As he opens it, he comes face to face with Billy.

I suck in my breath.

Billy holds out his hand. Ryan shakes it. I figure that handshake communicates a lot.

"Take care of her," Ryan says.

Billy looks at me, and back to Ryan. "She takes pretty good care of herself. But if she ever needs backup, I'll be right behind her."

Chapter 46

Maine in late September. The leaves begin their transformation from green to gold, orange, and red. Mornings are crisp and cool, afternoons warm, and the evenings snap with a pleasurable chill.

The whole Constant Caring affair has finally begun to fade from my mind, now that the people who plagued me are no longer threats. Todd Owens has been indicted for Henderson's murder, Jim Barr's murder, and my attempted murder. George Tate has been indicted for fraud, though there's talk of a plea. Teresa Mosher is in a specialized facility for trauma survivors in Arizona, and John Cass is back in prison.

To mark the summer's end, Billy rents a vacation cottage for us on Peaks Island in Casco Bay. We kayak and swim in the cold ocean, nap in a striped hammock on the front porch, stroll the beach, scavenge for sea glass and shells, and eat. Having nixed a place with television and Internet access, some nights we listen to a radio, read poetry aloud, and discuss Jewish mysticism and other forms of spirituality. At night, I lie cocooned in Billy's arms as we make love in the moonlight. At sunrise, pink hues suffuse the sky and bathe the bedroom in unearthly light.

While Billy is out biking one afternoon, I doze on the hammock, floating up to consciousness when I sense another person's presence. A wiry old woman is standing on the porch, briskly swinging her broom. Her gray hair is pinned up in a haphazard bun. Wrinkles line her deeply tanned face. When she finally looks at me, she deliberately pushes her eyeglasses to the bridge of her thin nose, leans the broom against the wooden screen door, and tightens the strings of her apron.

"It's fine for you to use my house," she says. "I don't mind visitors, as long as you're respectful. But," she adds, pointing a long bony finger in my direction, "I like things kept nice and tidy."

Transfixed, I manage to say, "Yes, ma'am," then stare at her until she disappears—transformed into dust motes that float away on the soft breeze.

Later that evening as Billy tends the grill, I choose an ancient cut-glass vase from the back corner of the built-in china cabinet and spend a few moments washing and drying it. Then I fill it with white daisies, yellow asters, and pink cosmos fresh from the front garden. "Thank you," I whisper, "for allowing us to share your home."

Shimmering light suffuses a corner of the room and though it disappears almost as quickly as it appeared, I don't doubt what I've seen. I don't doubt it at all.

The End

Acknowledgments

It took a village to get this book written and edited, and edited again, and again. If I listed every one of my readers, members of various writing groups, teachers, friends, and classmates—the acknowledgments would comprise a book.

Thanks to my many writing teachers, particularly Maggie Butler, Susan Conley, Meredith Hall, and Mary Carroll Moore. Thanks to David Kutcha at the University of New England's Maine Women Writers Collection, who led the classes where I wrote to my first prompts and mustered the courage to read my work aloud. Thanks to the talented members of my various writing groups—Brenda Buchanan, James Hayman, and Richard Bilodeau; Joanne Turnbull and Mihku Paul Anderson; Maggie Butler and Cindy Butler; and Michelle Cacho-Negrete. Thanks to Dr. Nosrat Hillman for her medical expertise in Pathology. Thanks to the Maine Writers and Publishers Alliance, a wonderful resource and home for Maine writers, and to Jim and Donna Brosnan, who mentor so many writers over five days during Maine's glorious summers at the Ocean Park Writers Conference.

Thanks to Deke Castleman, my indispensable, talented editor, whose encouragement took me over the finish line. Thanks to Michael Castleman, a fine writer and friend, who read my first draft (and many successive ones) and responded with editorial wisdom laced with humor—and who did not tell me to bury that first draft and find another way to spend my time. Thanks to Mark Chimsky, who read an early draft and offered editorial commentary and encouragement. Thanks to the Simmons family, Leslie, Miles, Liza, and Sophia, my cheering chorus, who read many drafts and responded with feedback laced with love and encouragement. Thanks to Leah Wohl Pollack of Invisible Ink, who caught innumerable punctuation errors over the years.

Thanks to my colleagues and friends: Celia Grand, LCSW, Deborah Grant, LCSW, and Molly Stanley, LCSW, who advised me on clinical aspects of the book, and to John Goodman, attorney and former police officer, who gave me a tour of the Portland police station, read the manuscript, and offered feedback. Thanks to Joan Kidman, who hired me when I was a rookie attorney, mentored me, and many years later read the manuscript and offered feedback. Thanks to Shelley Cohen-Konrad, who tossed around the original ideas for *Termination of Benefits* before heading off to Simmons College for her PhD in Social Work. Finally thanks to my former neighbor Constance Tidd, my first enthusiastic reader, who offered both encouragement and insight.

Most of all, thanks to my husband, Joe, who listened to innumerable drafts, offered important suggestions, provided the title, and was willing to include my characters on many dinner dates.

Thanks to other friends and readers not mentioned here, who helped along the way. It took so long to finish this book and get it to publication that memory fails.

Any and all mistakes are mine alone.

About the Author

Jane Sloven is a psychotherapist and retired attorney who lives in Portland, Maine, with her husband, Joe, and pooch, Benji. She graduated from American University with a BA in Literature, New England School of Law with a JD, and the University of Connecticut with an MSW. In addition to clinical articles, Jane's short stories and essays have been published in *River Poets Journal: 2013 Special Edition, Tales From the Matriarchal Zone; River Poets Journal: 2016 Special Edition, Signature Poems; Chicago Now; Write to Woof*, 2014 Grey Wolfe Publishing, LLC; and Grey Wolfe Publishing, LLC's *Literary Journal Legends: Paranormal Pursuits* 2016. Jane has co-authored an anthology, *Compassionate Journey: Honoring Our Mothers' Stories*. She is working on a sequel to *Termination of Benefits*.